My defeated adversary, on his knees, raised his eyes to mine. He was older than I expected; there were long strands of gray in the hair which had been covered by his helmet. His eyes already had the dullness that says death is not far away.

"Make it clean, young one. Make it clean."

My sides were still heaving from my efforts, and I barely managed to answer in a dry cracking voice, "It will be. Go to your gods in honor, barbarian."

I struck. The blow was good; his head separated properly. I had hit him just between the vertebrae. If I had missed the right spot, it would have probably taken two or more blows to cut through the thick corded muscle of his neck.

As it was, the strike was perfect. The crowd roared their appreciation.

BARRY SADLER

A TOM DOHERTY ASSOCIATES BOOK

This is a work of fiction. All the characters and events portrayed in this book are fictional, and any resemblance to real people or incidents is purely coincidental.

MORITURI

A Tor Book
Published by Tom Doherty Associates
8-10 W. 36th St.
New York City, N.Y. 10018

First printing, September, 1982

ISBN: 0-532-48045-8

Printed in the United States of America

Distributed by Pinnacle Books, 1430 Broadway, New York, New York 10018

MORITURI

BOOK ONE

CHILD OF THE SANDS

1

Ave, greetings, and may the gods find you well, my unknown reader. If, indeed, anyone ever reads these words which are written down by a former slave and now freedman, Albinus the Greek.

I am called Lucanus, named for the wolf, and the name suits me well enough, for the arenas of the Empire have been my hunting ground for over thirty years. I cannot recall how many times I have responded to mobs chanting my name when they wished me to finish off a downed adversary. Aye, it pleased them well when I would answer their cry and slit the throat of another fighter.

I will not be offended if you are saying, "From where does this common gladiator derive such vanity as to record his memoirs?"

To that I say, "Why not?" True, I do not have the thin, delicate bloodlines of the noble houses of Rome, and my fingers are better suited for the grip of a sword or spear than for a stylus with which to write poetry. Even so, I am a man as others are, and perhaps more than most, for there are few that could have survived for as many years as I in the arenas of the Empire.

Death comes to all, some late in life and to others before they can draw their first breath. I have lived with death at my side for thirty years but always before I knew there was a chance to live if I was clever or fought hard enough. But now there is no chance. Next month I will die. There is no escape for me and I am not sure I would run even if I thought I could get away and my door were not watched. But I promise you this, my distant reader, my death will be the one I have merited. The irony of it is in some ways laughable. I will die on the blade of a gladiator, but it will be a woman's hand who controls it. A woman whose delicate neck I could snap between the fingers of one hand as you would a dried twig. *Bitch!*

In many ways it is my own fault that this state has come to pass. I refused to listen to the warnings from Claudius to keep out of Livia's way. The mother of the Emperor Tiberius was not to be interfered with. I had heard rumors about her, but in my pride and ignorance I would not listen. I was too sure of my own strength to know fear of her. To my loss, I have learned that the enmity of a woman like Livia is more deadly than the vaunted legions of Caesar. But I am what I am.

I am a child of the sands whose first memories are of blood and torn bodies. The sands were my childhood playgrounds, and instruments of death were my toys. Death has always been my companion and it is death that has given me this house and my wealth. From death I received the accolades of the crowd and was brought into the noble houses of Rome where many of the noble ladies found their pleasure under my hard body. Which was certainly a pleasure for them after the weak, flabby frames of their husbands, whose weapons were only those of words or documents they would not have to inforce themselves. You probably think I am vain and proud. Perhaps so. I know that the power of words has come to me too late to do any good. I know those thin-faced, balding men in their togas of state have more real power than I could ever achieve with a bared sword. But, still, I have always felt contempt for those who dealt with death at a distance rather than facing their enemies. I don't suppose it really matters how the end of a life comes unless you're the one whose existence is being terminated.

Perhaps it is because I know the fates are sharpening their scissors to the threads of my life that I wish my story told. Emperors can have themselves made into gods, but for me, if there is to be any eternity, it will have to come from these scrolls.

But I digress. Forgive me if from time to time I seem to wander a bit. Old wounds and wine fumes in my head nag at me as a fishwife does her husband. Seldom do they give me any peace. There, I did it again. Where was I? Ahhh! Yes, now I remember. Albinus has said that to tell a story one should always begin at the beginning. Greeks are so logical, aren't they? So be it, you sodomite. (Albinus didn't want to write that down, but I made him do it anyway. He does follow the Greek manner in ways of love.) I wonder why they call it the Greek way? I have surely seen enough of other races that practiced the same affection for men. For all that, he has been a faithful servant and teacher. Albinus has tried for some years now to make me lose the gutter speech of my youth. So the words I use here are mostly his and still do not come easily to me. All right, all right, Albinus, I'll get on with it. Albinus doesn't think I should be writing this either, but he goes along with me because he knows he is in my will and I still have time to change it. Don't bother protesting, Albinus, it doesn't matter to me as long as you live up to your end of the bargain. Now, from the beginning, you said. From the beginning . . . .

I was born in the lower regions of the Circus Maximus where the beasts are kept before being let loose in the arena. There my mother gave whelp in a cage that was not being used at the moment, and I was born red and squalling midst the grunts and screams of hungry beasts. Who my father was, there is no way to tell. Possibly he was a Gaul or from one of the tribes of Germania, for though I have the coloring of the Latin, my eyes are blue and my bones thick and large. But that is just a guess, for my mother's job was not only to feed the men but service their other needs as well.

The only reason that I didn't end up on the trash heap outside the city walls was that she was a slave, and only the children of freedmen may be thrown away. Slaves always belong to somebody as does the fruit of their bodies. Also there would be little expense for my owner in raising a boy child that could be fed from the leftovers of the gladiators and the beasts. My master could have always made a small profit from my resale or even my death if he decided to use me in one of the spectacles that provided amusements for the pleasure of the populace. Even a small child could be used in the dramas where the sacking of a city is reenacted and the population put to the sword by the victorious legions of Rome. For that small death my owner would receive a couple of small silver coins in compensation.

Obviously I survived, even though my mother died before I was yet a year old. It was told to me sometime later that instead of giving me to the beasts or the mob, the circus master kept me alive because the gladiators considered me to be lucky for them and would rub my black-maned head for luck before going into a fight. Maybe the ones who lost didn't rub hard enough. The gladiators said I had the will to live.

Porcius Verrus, the lanista whose school of the secutors I later attended, told me that after my mother's death (her neck was broken by the too amorous attentions of a Scythian retiarius) I had already found another source of food. I was found nursing alongside a couple of kids, butting my way in to get to one of the she goat's fat nipples. When the gladiators saw this, they made the joke that even though I was not Romulus or Remus being suckled by the bitch wolf, Rome, it was still close enough. They named me Lucanus at that moment. The veterans among the fighters insisted when they saw this that I be allowed to live. For surely Father Janus had smiled upon me, and it would bring bad luck to the circus to let me die.

It was also told to me by Verrus that the gladiators themselves had taken care of the Scythian net-and-trident man by fixing his next contest. Mother, it seems, was well thought of.

I was given into the care of various slaves until I was old enough to fend for myself, which was not long in coming. All things considered, I was fed well enough even when the fighters weren't around, for animals were always being brought in for upcoming events. Their handlers and the bestiarii would often give me scraps of meat they saved from their animals. It was said that what they gave me was not always the flesh of animals; to that I can only respond, "What difference?" Whatever it was, it kept me alive and I grew in strength every day.

By the time I had reached my seventh year, the circus master, old tightfisted Crator, had thought of a way in which I might help pay for my keep and provide a little amusement for the crowds.

When an event is over and before the next is to take place, it is the custom to send out slaves in costumes dressed as Charon, the boatman who ferries the dead over the River Styx, to drag out the bodies from the arena. They carried with them a long pole with a sharp hook and a mallet and spike. With the spike they would strike and drive it into the braincase of any who weren't quite dead or who were too badly crippled to be saved for later shows. Of course, this was only done to slaves that had no real value. Gladiators were usually spared if they weren't too badly injured, as they could always be resold as bodyguards or used to train tyros, the beginners of the schools. The slaves would beg and cry not to kill them, but the gladiators were different. I have heard them tell us, "Hurry up and get it over with," and curse us for taking too long to get to them, especially those with gut wounds. They knew the longer we took the more pain they would have.

I can recall, even now, how pleased I was at the crowd's applause and laughter when I came out to the sands my first time. Dressed in my gray hooded costume of death and prancing and gyrating from one downed man or woman to the next, I could hear the crowd roar with laughter as I leaped and rolled, then struck with my mallet and spike. They were so pleased that I actually had a few coins thrown to me, which old Crator let me keep. That was the first of the rewards I was to receive from an admiring public. Naturally, I was still too small to haul a grown man from the arena with the hooked poles, so Crator had them leave me the small women and dwarfs. These I could handle with little difficulty, though I do remember being scared witless once, when I stuck the hook into the collarbone of a woman who was pretending she was already dead. She jumped up screaming and took off running around the arena with three attendants in pursuit, and me. The silly bitch was finally cornered by the wall. The stands shook with laughter at the sight, and then she tried to climb the walls, only to fall back to the sand, to face our mallets and spikes. She was frothing at the mouth, eyes rolling wildly. Then she just dropped over dead. She had been so excited that she wouldn't even listen to us when we tried to tell her the crowd had given her the thumbs-up sign and she was not to die.

From that time on, I was a regular attraction at the games, developed a few fans and had several offers from women to visit them. But Crator, for all that he was a cheap old reprobate, refused their offers, saying it was not time for me to get involved with that sort of thing. It would spoil me for the future. Crator then mumbled something filthy about women and men who used children. I think that was the point where I first realized the old wastrel actually liked me, in his own manner, and that I actually had a future. A future! A staggering thought for a boy slave.

I made myself useful in a dozen ways, not only to Crator but to the fighters and beast handlers. I knew them all and for the most part they were kind to me. I would help staunch the flow of wounds with hot tar and irons, or tie the lacing of the animals to be cleaned. My playmates, until I was old enough to go into the streets, were cubs of lions, leopards and other cats.

Every day I learned a little more about my world from those who came here to die. The Circus Maximus drew the best men the world had to offer. The laquedarii fought with lariats of braided leather: bestiarii took on the animals. I usually preferred the lighter-armored thraces with their longer curved swords over the retiarii with their nets and tridents. The premier fighters were the heavyweights. The secutors with chest and calf armor usually carried a version of the short sword and wore a broad-brimmed helmet with a perforated face mask. The heaviest of all, the postulati, were slow in their movements, but nearly impossible to dispatch with a single blow as they were covered in armor from crown to heel. Like Hercules they would pick their spot and take on all comers using heavy two-handed swords capable of slicing a man in two at the waist. These were the men I admired and envied for their skill and courage.

When the games were over I had a certain amount of freedom after I had finished my duties of sweeping and cleaning or doing whatever needed to be done. It was, "Get Lucanus for this or that," constantly, but I didn't mind. I had seen the faces of too many starving freed children not to know how good I really had it. And if old Crator got drunk now and then, and chose to break a stave over my shoulders when he thought I was getting too lazy, then that was certainly his right.

For me the circus was the best world in existence and a playground like no other. During the munera I would watch everything, then play out the scene when the games were over. Putting on a helmet and using one of the smaller round shields and a dagger instead of a sword, I would imitate the fighters. Faking a crippling blow to make my imaginary opponent overconfident, I would strike him with my shield under his guard, then thrust my sword to his heart through the opening that I had made by my cleverness.

The contests in my imaginings were always the best the populace had ever seen, and time and again they would demand that I be given the rudis, the wooden sword. It meant freedom if you were a slave, or the purse of the Emperor if you were an auctoratus, a free fighter . . . . Such an ambition—for a child to dream of receiving the rudis from the hand of Imperial Augustus himself.

For a time I considered becoming a bestiarius. The way they handled the large cats especially fascinated me, and what I learned from them concerning the ways of animals served me in good stead through the years. The beast men taught me that many of the lions and leopards sent to them had to be taught to kill humans. Many times their treatment had been so bad at the hands of whoever caught them, that their confidence had to be rebuilt by slow and careful training.

My favorite among the beast men was a large black man from Carthage. He had a way with animals I have never seen since. He knew them as they did themselves, and better. In some way he always knew the right thing to do. Bosra would smile at me with strong yellow teeth and enter one of the cages with only a rod for protection. He would play with the cats, slowly taking the fear of man away from those whose fierce spirits had been beaten or starved from them. Bosra had infinite patience. He would take his rod and touch the flank of a cowering beast, then jump back, away from them, rolling his eyes and making the body sign that meant fear when the animal looked at him. This he would repeat over and over again. He let the animal win every time. Even a timid wave of the beast's paw was enough to make Bosra cower and back away until the animal he was working with began to believe that he was the stronger and that all it took was a look to drive this two-legged animal into a state of fear. Once this was achieved, and the beast's confidence partially restored, it was time to move on to the next phase, and teach them to kill humans, for man was not the cat's natural prey.

To do this, I often assisted Bosra in preparing crippled or old slaves of no value, by tying them up. Bosra made it a practice to break the arms of all the slaves. Once he had not done this, and when the leopard he had been working with for weeks was ready to make a tentative strike, the slave had bounded up and, in his panic, struck the leopard straight on its nose. This violent act on the part of the slave destroyed weeks of Bosra's patient work. From that time on all slaves had their arms broken and feet tied, even the women. Bosra was given what he wanted. He would give his charges pieces of human flesh from those slain in the arena to get them used to the taste, so they would more readily accept the slaves as prey.

I still believe that Bosra also helped himself occasionally to a helping of the same, especially when it was from a fallen gladiator of proven courage. He had told me that the people of his tribe believed that eating the heart and liver of a brave man would give them some of his courage. It was a sign of respect to do this and an honor. It was even done by members of the same family so the good spirits of the dead would not be lost.

Still, I always felt a sense of revulsion at feeding people to the animals, and still do to this day. Even Bosra's explanation that the victims felt no real pain didn't help. According to him, the power in the animal's jaws and paws is so strong that the first bite or strike numbs their prey so they don't really feel much pain, it is mostly panic that sets them screaming. Even so, there is always a difference between men fighting each other, and feeding tied-up slaves to the cats and wild dogs.

But, as I have said, I learned many things that I used in later years. Bosra would show me how to spot the exact moment an attack was going to come from one of the cats, and how to read the signs that meant both danger and fear. He pointed out the way a cat would move before charging; its muscles would ripple down its shoulders and flanks, its tail would begin twitching at the tip, then the rear haunches would gather as the cat lowered itself, belly down, to the ground. These and a thousand things more I learned in my childhood. For I knew that one day I too would take my place on the sands and face death from both man and beast. This was my school, and to fail a subject would bring death in the future.

I had no need for fine manners or cultured speech. It was required that I do as I was told, quickly, to obey without question. Everything else I learned had to do with the giving and taking of death. There was much to learn, and Crator assisted me. Indeed, he encouraged me and even ordered the others to give all the help they could to further my strange education in the fine art of slaughter.

Crator himself had fought in the arena long ago and had won the rudis and had been given his freedom. He had also been a lanista and had trained many of the legendary gladiators of our time. I think that Crator saw me as a fighter he could experiment with.

I knew he was going to use me in other amusements soon. He had told me, while in his cups, that I was growing tall and strong enough to be put to other uses. Then he had pinched the stringy muscle of my arm and mumbled something about putting some meat on me.

2

From that time on, I was fed from the same kettles as the regular staff at the circus. The steady diet along with what Bosra gave me soon put more meat on my bones. Not the bulging kind, but long stringy sinew. It seemed I could never get enough to eat to equal what my growth and body demanded.

Crator made it clear with a good beating that I was not to venture far from the circus, nor was I to go near the street children who could only bring me trouble. The few times I did get to go to the market or deliver a message to one of Crator's sponsors and ran into some other children of my age, I understood why he had ordered me to keep my distance from them. They were all thieves and had no future other than one day being crucified for their crimes or being sold as slaves, only to find themselves food for one of the cats at the circus.

Twice I had fights with the street urchins. Both times the boys were larger than myself, but they had not had the benefit of regular food nor had they attended my school. It took little effort to convince them to leave me alone, especially when I cracked the skulls of two of them. I picked up a stick and used it as I had seen the gladiators use their weapons. I began striking and slashing at them, screaming battle cries. They figured out that it was useless to attack me as they would receive more than they could give.

My first official fight came about when I was ten. For the previous six months I had been in the care of an old friend of Crator's, a former retarius who earned his keep as an instructor at one of the schools outside the city. In his time, before a slash from a curve-bladed sica cut his hamstring, he had been a major contender with over forty kills to his credit. According to Crator, he was one of the best net-and-trident fighters he had ever seen and had made his owners a fortune. When he was crippled, they gave him his freedom and a good-sized purse in appreciation. Now he worked as an advisor and instructor, and was constantly in demand. I think he took Crator's job out of friendship and curiosity, for I was by far the youngest one he had ever been asked to instruct.

Cammilus then was my first lanista and he worked me as he would a grown man—constantly. Taking me into the arena when it wasn't in use, he made me run lap after lap around it, jumping over hurdles. He was a tyrant and I came close to loving him. Crator would sit in the stands and watch, his ever-present bowl of wine beside him. He would say nothing, only watch, leaving Cammilus to do his job. Cammilus talked to me as he exercised me, telling me of his years in the arena. It wasn't enough to just show me the moves: how to use the lead weights on the edge of the net to snap at the eyes, how to switch toss in mid-move from high to low, tangle the legs of my opponent in the net and close it before he could rise, and, above all else, how to move so as to present as small a target as possible.

We spent many hours on the sands sweating under the sun, going over a move so many times that I thought my arms would drop from their sockets. This crippled old fighter and I did our macabre dance, twisting and leaping, and whirling the spiderweb net, trying to snare each other. He even made me fight against him using the sword, saying the best way to understand your opponent is to know how he fights and how he sees you. I have never forgotten those words and they are as true today as they were then.

The happiest day of my life was when Crator gave me a present. He had gone to the expense of having a miniature costume of the retiarii made for me. When I made my premier appearance I would be perfect in every detail, down to the leg greaves and the cunningly worked right arm sleeve made of joined rings of steel. For my left arm I had a wrist guard of leather with squares of iron sewn to it. A small cone-shaped helmet of steel finished off my rig.

When I first tried the costume on, I strutted up and down in front of a polished bronze mirror making fierce faces. I was sure I would drive anyone I faced into a fit of absolute terror. I pretended I was the finest fighter in the history of the world. The veterans poked a little fun at me but I didn't take it too much to heart, they were always teasing me about one thing or another. I think it was because so many of them had lost their families when they were sold into slavery that they treated me as they would their own sons. If any of them got too rough, it was at the risk of their own skin. I had many friends among the scarred old fighters and they had ways of taking care of anyone who gave them trouble, both inside and out of the arena. There were things that could be done to insure that the object of their wrath would find his days reduced in number; even the rudis, the wooden sword of freedom, could not protect him.

My first fight took place in celebration of the victory of Augustus over Brutus and Crassus, by which he became sole ruler of Rome and the Triumvirate was dissolved forever.

The games held for three days to celebrate the event went on nonstop, throughout the night, the arenas were lit up by the glow from thousands of torches. Four thousand men died in those three days, and I tasted my first real blood.

True, in my role as Charon's helper, my mallet and spike had already winked out the life force of a couple of hundred or so. But this was to be different. I was to fight as a gladiator.

When we entered the arena I was at the head of our contingent. I wore nothing but my armor and helmet and was naked from the waist down. Before going on, Crator had called in a hairdresser and masseuse. My hair was oiled and curled, the dark locks shining from under my steel helmet, my body rich with the sheen of expensive oils. I was well tanned and had not an ounce of excess tissue on my frame. Being naked didn't particularly bother me. Nudity is common in Rome, but the excitement caused my immature organs to shrivel up even smaller until they were scarcely larger than chick peas.

Crator knew the effect that my young unscarred body would have on the audience, and he played it up to the hilt. When the crowd finally became aware of me, you could hear at first a hushed murmur, then a laugh, as one, then another, cried out, "It's young Charon. But where are his jewels? Some of his comrades must have stolen them from him!"

I ignored their insults and marched proudly to the stand where the Emperor's seats were under massive gilded golden eagles, flanked by his Pretorians in their red cloaks. I was the first in the column. The stands grew silent and I looked up into the face of the Master of Rome. It was a good face, strong and intelligent. Beside him I saw for the first time the patrician features of the Empress Livia. Even now, I can recall her cold uninterested look, as if I were no more than an insignificant piece of offal. But she was beautiful, in a cold, distant manner, and when she looked directly at me my already diminished organs grew even smaller. Swallowing a lump of fear, I raised my trident in salute and spoke for the first time in unison with the other fighters the ancient words of the gladiators. "Ave, Caesar, Te morituri Salutamus. We who are about to die salute you." Augustus smiled at me, and I thought I caught a look of interest then from Livia. At the signal of the trumpets we turned and marched in ranks back to the center of the arena where we paired off with our opponents. To my chagrin, I found out that my foe was a Dacian dwarf.

The dwarf was dressed in the old-style armor of the Myrmillones with a wide-brimmed helmet bearing the fish symbol of Gaul, a rectangular shield and a small version of the Gladius Iberius, the famed shortsword of the legion. He came up to my eyes, so I still had the reach on him, especially with the trident. But I didn't like the look in his eyes. As with many of his kind, his face was set at odd angles and his body was slightly twisted, but what there was of him was all muscle, and I had seen too many of them in the arena as acrobats and clowns as well as fighters not to have a great respect for their agility and capabilities.

There were four sets of us paired off for this event, and Crator had made sure I would be near the Imperial box. The Games Master gave the signal for the games to begin and we squared off.

I was still a little disappointed that I didn't have a regular-sized opponent, but that soon passed when the little bastard came in with a shield smash, then did a swift low circling turn that whipped him in close, and nearly laid my gut open on the first slash of his blade. It did leave a thin red streak across the rigid muscles of my stomach and that was enough to take my mind off anything but him. What the rest of my team was doing was not of any concern at the moment.

The dwarf laughed and teased me, saying he would not only open up my gut, but would show the crowd he had organs the size of a regular man when he used me like a woman. Because, he said, I wasn't too different from a girl with my thin arms and unblemished skin.

I knew what he was trying to do, to make me lose my temper, but it didn't make taking his insults much easier. So I just concentrated on what Cammilus had taught me. I tried not really thinking, just letting my body move by itself; letting my moves come by instinct rather than design.

Cammilus had told me often enough, "Let your body do the thinking and it will do what is needed when it's needed."

The crowd laughed at the first cut on my gut and that stung more than the dwarf's words. He backed off and began a slow circle, taking his time, trying to get me so the sun was in my eyes. With his wide-brimmed helmet he had the advantage where that was concerned, for his eyes were shaded even if he was directly facing the sun. So I moved slower than I should, letting him take the advantage, giving him the impression that I was unsure and hesitant about what to do. My lunges with the trident were half-hearted and he easily parried them. The crowd mocked me and told the dwarf to make it quick, that I had already bored them. The miniature Dacian took to the crowd's demands like a born entertainer, and merely toyed with me, blocking my feeble tosses and strikes half-heartedly.

Then he made the mistake of looking up to the stands to see if Augustus was watching. I whipped my net forward, giving the twist of the wrist that snapped the lead-tipped ends out. They struck him across the face, laying open one eye and cutting his cheek to the bone. The mob roared with glee; perhaps there would be a fight after all. I almost nailed him right then with a straight thrust to his groin that forced him to back off rapidly, swinging his sword wildly to cover himself as he tried to regain his balance. The dwarf began to move oddly, shaking his head from side to side. But I didn't have time to worry about it much. I made a long lunge that went over his shoulder, and managed to hook one of the prongs of my trident into his shoulder, and using all my strength jerked him forward. He fell on his stomach, which surprised me. I didn't think I'd pulled him that hard. The little man rolled and came back up on his feet, still shaking his head, in time for my trident to slip under the lip of his helmet and catch him in the throat. He went down, and I stood on top of his body, one foot on his chest, working my trident out of his windpipe. He made ghastly gurgling and wheezing sounds as his final breath escaped, and his spirit departed for whatever after-life he believed in.

I was truly a hero and the mob loved me. Money rained down from the stands and was quickly collected by arena attendants, who brought it to me later. They would, of course, receive a percentage for their services, but this money was mine. I had earned it as a gladiator, a killer of men. Even if he was a little small.

It was some time later that I found out the reason for the dwarf's strange behavior. Crator had doped his pre-fight drink of posca. That hurt my feelings terribly, for I was sure that I was ready to take on anyone. Crator's action to protect me drove me into a sulk for weeks. I had been certain of my prowess and my victory. But such is the vanity of children. Crator knew better and was taking no chances.

He had, as he said, other plans for me . . . .

3

One day Crator granted permission for me to accompany Cammilus into the city. The old limping veteran and the youngest of the arena fighters—we must have made an odd pair in the streets.

Cammilus carried the haft of a trident to use as a staff, aiding his crippled leg, and woe to the pederast who paid too much attention to my youthful body.

It was good to be out, walking in the warm sun of Rome. Rome! The mother of the earth, where all roads lead, and I believed it. In the markets all the races of the world were to be found. Proud, hawk-nosed princes from Arabia, mingling with shaggy-looking, giant-sized barbarians from the frozen lands across the Rhine. There were even small yellowish men with slanted eyes who said they'd traveled "the silk road," bringing their precious cargo of fine cloth to Rome, all the way from the distant land they called Han. To my young ears they seemed great storytellers. They even asked us to believe that the cloths they'd carried for such a distance were made by worms. Cammilus and I laughed at them. Did they really think us such fools to believe a story so ridiculous? They didn't seem to mind if we laughed. Many a wife drove her husband to the money-lenders with her nagging, just to get the coins to purchase a handkerchief or shawl made of the shining cloth.

There was a particular place in the city that Cammilus liked to visit, and I considered it a privilege when he allowed me to accompany him there. It was a tavern that catered to gladiators, and many old retired fighters were to be found there. It was a hostel called The Rudis, named after the wooden sword of freedom. The innkeeper had won it in the arena not once, but twice.

Here Cammilus would rest in the courtyard when the days were warm, letting the sun sink into his old feeble bones. He gossiped freely with his old cronies, the retired fighters and others who were still earning their keep in the arena. They all had one thing in common that bound them together and made them a very exclusive club. They had survived.

I was content to sit in a corner, out of their way, and listen to their tales of great contests of the past and their interesting lives. Cammilus would sometimes allow me to have a small bowl of thin, watered-down wine, if I was a good lad and did not interrupt them too much with my questions.

A favorite of Cammilus' and mine was an old silver-haired fighter of gentle features and manners. Turnus, once the premier thraces of all Rome, had had over thirty kills and thrice that amount of overall victories in single combats. Never once had he been forced to cry out for thumbs up. Now he looked more like a grandfatherly teacher of philosophy than what he'd once been. But his spine was still straight; even the ravages of time had not bent his back.

He and Cammilus would lean over their table, filling their clay bowls with a mixture of the Greek Lesbius wine and just the right touch of pure spring water. They both considered themselves men of taste and would never drink uncut wine as the younger fools did.

The two of them would argue for hours over which was the best, the retiarius or the thraces. The argument was one that would never be settled. They had fought each other before. They'd struck and beaten each other, laying open wounds with their weapons; the fight had lasted over two hours. In the end, with darkness falling, the games master had called the battle to a halt. They had both been so exhausted they could barely raise their arms in salute, but the audience knew that the fight had not been a set-up. It was a true contest between two masters who had freely given their all.

Old Turnus would sometimes pinch my arm, telling Cammilus that he should be ashamed, that I had no business with the trident and he should be training me with the sword. Cammilus would deny this suggestion from Turnus, but I think he knew the old man was right. He started showing me a few techniques with the blade after that.

Turnus would often take me aside, running his blue-veined fingers through my hair, and sigh over the tragedy of one so young being initiated into such an evil business. Then he would whisper to me, thinking Cammilus couldn't hear, of tactics with the sword that had served him well in the past. Of course Cammilus did hear, but he pretended he hadn't.

Times were good for me. I felt as if I were one of them. Though they made me the butt of many of their jokes, I knew they held a true fondness for me.

On this particular day, a secutor, from the school of Evander, tried to get too familiar with me, sliding his hand under my loincloth and attempting to fondle me. He found himself flat on his back, bleeding at the mouth, his jaw nearly broken by a butt stroke from Cammilus' trident staff. The angry and embarrassed secutor grabbed a knife from one of the tables and charged Cammilus, only to find old Turnus barring his way. He growled, "Get out of my way, old man!"

Cammilus started to protest at Turnus' interference, but Turnus spoke, tight-lipped, not taking his eyes from the secutor in front of him.

"Cammilus, old friend, I've never asked you for much before. But I would ask this of you. Let me handle this for you. I too am fond of the child, and you have the honor of protecting him every day. Allow me this one time to show him my affection."

Cammilus grunted his agreement and stepped back out of the way. I was afraid for old Turnus. He looked so fragile and weak standing there before the secutor.

A knife that I never knew he carried suddenly appeared in old Turnus' hand, from somewhere beneath his robes. He placed himself only steps away from the big fighter and spoke with a smile, through clenched teeth. "You seem to hold a fondness for those who are not your age, secutor. Maybe you should try one with more experience. Come now, and let me kiss you with my blade."

The secutor laughed and mocked him. "Kiss me, old man? I'll give you a kiss with my own blade, one that will end your life. It should have been terminated years ago."

Turnus slipped out of his robes. His body was bare except for a loincloth. The sight of him made the younger fighter cease his laughter. There were a few wrinkles and some grey hair, but Turnus' body held no trace of flab or loose skin. He was thin and heavily scarred, but every muscle in his body looked as if it had been carved by a master sculptor.

Turnus called the attention of those seated about him. Speaking in his same gentle voice, he asked that they all witness that before him stood a child molester, a coward who lacked the courage to face one thrice his age. He mocked and slandered the secutor until his words drove the blood from the man's face.

With a cry of rage, the secutor lunged, his knife held low for the gut stab, only to find himself facing a blank wall and Turnus standing behind him, still mocking him in that same gentle scholarly voice. "What's the matter, secutor? A child lover must be faster than that, even to take on an old man."

The secutor charged at him again, lunging and slicing. He tried to close with Turnus as he sliced, but found his blade being turned so easily that it seemed to glide by with no effort on Turnus' part. But Turnus had laid a long thin opening along the secutor's rib cage.

Never had I seen anything like this. The old man was doing as he wished with the younger and stronger fighter. Turnus never wasted a move, or used any strength, it was all done with a series of graceful motions. He used deflection, smooth lunges, gliding and slanted movements that required a minimum of effort. Turnus soon had the secutor bleeding profusely from a dozen or more cuts. He could have killed him any time he'd wanted to, and everyone knew it.

When the old man had finally wearied of his game, he sliced the secutor's wrist open on the underside, severing the tendons and the great artery. The man's hand hung by a thin strand of meat at the bone. The secutor grabbed his wrist to slow the flow of blood and ran out of the inn, screaming. Turnus wiped his dagger on a table rag and replaced it in his loincloth. Picking up his robe, he donned it, carefully adjusting the ties.

I was so proud of him that I thought my heart would surely burst from its cage, and so was Cammilus, though he merely grumbled something at Turnus as to how his age was slowing him down. We all knew that he didn't mean it. It was just their way, one fighter to another.

I wished old Turnus could have lived long enough to teach me some of his techniques, but not long after that day, he was found in the alley outside The Rudis, dead. A fishknife lay beside him and his hand had been lopped off at the wrist.

Whatever happened to the secutor I don't know, for he was never seen or heard of again. Though, some time after Turnus' death, I noticed that Cammilus was smiling to himself occasionally and humming melodies a lot, where, just shortly before, he'd been constantly sad and depressed over the loss of his old friend. I think to this day that he somehow managed to avenge Turnus' death.

We rarely visited the inn after Turnus had died. Somehow, Cammilus could find no pleasure in it. He would sit alone a lot, and I knew he was thinking of the good days and good times they'd enjoyed in the ring and out. Whenever I tried to cheer him up, he'd shush me quickly.

Crator had me continue my training under Cammilus. I had urged him for some time to have someone give me instruction with the sword, and he'd finally relented. I was permitted to fence and spar with some of the swordsmen now and then. But he mostly kept me hard on the net and trident.

Three years after he became my trainer, Cammilus died peacefully, crossing the river of death in his sleep. Now I had only Bosra, the African, for company and instruction. Bosra was growing old. The wool of his hair was all grey, and his skin was getting an ashen look to it. Time was weighing heavy on the old man's shoulders and he knew it. He began to speak more often about returning to Africa, where he could spend his last days in the life he had known as a child and a young man.

I missed Cammilus a lot, but the memory of youth is short, and there were other things to occupy my attention. I had progressed in the arena, and Crator had been careful to see that I was never overmatched. He selected those I fought, not by their age but by their size. There was a period of about two years when I didn't fight at all. I was either too small for some or too large for others. I was still growing and gaining weight rapidly, and the weight was all muscle. At the time Cammilus died I'd already reached the height of a full-grown man, though my strength was not as great and my legs sometimes got in my way, in the clumsiness of youth.

Crator was careful not to enter me in many death matches. I received a number of wounds in my fifteenth year, but none very serious. To my humiliation, I lost several matches, mostly due to overconfidence and carelessness. I learned a lot, though, in particular not to trust an opponent to be what he appeared. I was tricked twice by men who pretended to be wounded worse than they actually were, and had turned my back on them. If those had been matches to the death I would have joined Cammilus beyond the river, condemned to listen to his cursing and nagging forever, telling me what a fool I'd been for not paying attention to his lessons.

Crator was always there when I needed him. Though he was not a man given to demonstrations of affection, I knew there was a bond between us that went beyond that of master and slave. Once, while sleeping in my cubicle, I felt a hand's touch and awoke. It was Crator, standing over me, pulling my blanket closer to my throat. When he saw that I was awake, he cleared his throat awkwardly and said gruffly that he didn't want me to catch a chill. After all, he had an investment to protect, didn't he? But I knew otherwise, and from that moment on I would have done anything for him, as I knew he would do for me.

I trained even harder, with a series of instructors of different styles and techniques. I noticed there was always a slight reluctance on their parts to show me too much. I understood; one day we might have to face each other in combat on the sands. Still, I couldn't help but learn a lot from them. The art of sword-use and shield-play became instilled in my brain. I knew that I was fast becoming more than just a good luck piece for the veterans. I was getting big, leaving my childhood way behind.

After the hard training sessions each day, and a light but nutritious meal, Crator would sit with me into the wee hours, going over the fine points of the day, toning my knowledge and senses. I think I learned more about the wily ways of the arena from these sessions at night than I did on the training field.

As I grew, so did my reputation. One of the results which came out of this was the fact that the street urchins began to give me a wide berth when they found out who I was. There was a large sense of satisfaction in having my own fans and knowing I could inflict fear on the would-be toughs with a mere glance in their direction. I'm afraid that for a time there I had a touch of bully in me. But Crator put a stop to my growing arrogance soon enough. He brought me into his office and gave me a cursing that still gives me a twinge to this day.

As the years increased, so did my size and strength. I believe that Crator was experimenting with me to see just how much I could learn and how strong I could become. He kept me in constant exercise or training. It was a rare day when I had nothing to do and was allowed to go my own way.

I really didn't mind the hard work; it felt good. And when I did take a day off, I sometimes felt guilty about it. I knew that all the exercise and training would serve me well one day. Most of my time was spent with the net and trident, though Crator did see that I was familiar with other weapons.

I knew in my sixteenth year that my days as a net-and-trident man were numbered. My body was becoming too thick with knotted muscle. A retiarius has to be very light on his feet, and a retiarius who possessed a thick body like mine usually had his career brought to a quick and brutal end with someone standing over him with a sword to his throat.

It was about this time that I noticed a heavily scarred, bull-necked old fighter who often came and sat with Crator in the shade while I trained and exercised. His head was as bare of hair as was Crator's and the two would often sit, one skin head close to the other, and talk in low voices. They would look in my direction and nod their heads as if coming to some sort of an agreement. It gave me an uneasy feeling, I must confess.

This went on for some time. The old fighter would not be seen for a while; then he would return and the two would commence their plotting again. Twice I saw the stranger in the stands during contests I was participating in.

Crator called me to him one day after I'd finished a sparring session with Cammilius. The stranger was with him. Crator, his ever-present bowl of wine in his hand, introduced me.

"Lucanus, this is Celer the lanista. You will be going with him."

I said nothing; a slave does not question his owner. Even though it was perfectly within his rights to do so, I still felt somewhat hurt that Crator was willing to sell me.

Celer the lanista stood and came to me. I was taller than he by a couple of inches. He walked around me, poking here and pinching there. He looked close at my eyes and bade me open my mouth to inspect my teeth. He made a comment in a low rasping voice that if a man's teeth were sick then so must his body be.

Though I was taller than the lanista, he still outweighed me by a good fifty pounds, none of it fat, just one band of muscle overlaid by another that reached all the way to his skull. His head seemed to rest on his shoulders; there was no neck. He was an ox of a man who moved smoothly, with surprising grace for one so thick in body. The rasping of his voice came again.

"Do you know who I am?"

"No, master," I replied dutifully.

"I am Celer the lanista, of the school of Vannius Messala. My old and good friend Crator here has given you into my charge. He says you are to be a swordsman and after watching you, I agree with him. During the time you are in my custody you will obey without question."

He raised his ham-like fist to my face.

"Do you understand me?"

I responded quickly. "Yes, master!" There was no doubt in my mind that, though he was much older than I, he could pound me into jelly.

I knew then that a major change was about to occur in my life. I looked questioningly at Crator, but he merely continued sipping from his bowl and smiled at me before he spoke.

"Do not get yourself worked up, little wolf. As Celer has said, he is an old friend and the lanista of the best school for the thraces in Italia. You are to attend his school at Antium. It is time for you to advance, and I do not have the necessary facilities nor the proper instructors here for you." He paused for another sip of his wine. "Celer shall either make you or break you. Obey him as you do me."

Crator handed Celer a document which he quickly scanned and signed. I found out later that it was the lease agreement assigning me to Celer for a period of two years.

Celer stuck the paper in his tunic and waited. Crator

rose from his chair, his belly swaying. For a second I thought he was going to embrace me, but he did not. He just spoke a little gruffly and told me to get the hades out of his arena. I liked the old bastard, and though I hated to leave him, I knew he was doing what he thought was best for me. I bowed my head.

"As you wish, master."

With the playful dismissal of his foot to my buttocks I went to my cubicle to gather my few personal belongings which, when they were all put together, made a bundle I could easily carry under one arm.

I cleaned myself as well as I could, without taking the time to wash properly. Celer had the look of a man who was not long on patience.

He was waiting for me outside the fighters' entrance, sitting in a two-wheeled cart that was harnessed to a mule. I knew now that at least I would not have to walk the forty-odd miles south to Antium, nestled in the hills among rows of vineyards and olive groves.

I said nothing as I climbed into the cart, and neither did Celer. I moved directly to the rear of the wagon, because a slave did not sit beside his master unless ordered to do so.

And thus I left Rome for the first time.

4

About midday, Celer told me to move up and sit beside him. I had a feeling that Celer was cruel at times merely for the sport of being cruel. He was simply a tough man and seemed to demand the same from anyone he worked with.

As we continued on our jogging course, he pointed out different and interesting things to me. I soon found myself enjoying this new venture immensely. It was a good feeling to be sitting high in the cart while passing slaves and freedmen and their women working in the fields. Serveral times we passed the estates of the great and the rich and Celer would give me their names, none of which I recognized. I had to confess, I was absolutely ignorant of anything and everything that had naught to do with the arena.

The sun felt warm and friendly and there was a fair breeze coming in from the sea some thirty miles away. All in all it was a fine day for me.

It was very near dark when Celer decided to call our journey to a halt for the day. Even though the countryside looked peaceful enough, he informed me, there were still bands of escaped slaves turned robbers who preyed on unwary late travelers. It happened seldom during daylight hours, he said, for the routes were patrolled by mounted Legionnaires on a regular basis. But the dark of night gave the thieves their chance.

Celer halted the mule at a small walled inn. They let us in; the gates were closed behind us. He took a room for himself and I was ordered, as were all slaves, to sleep in the stable with the mule. He had food sent out to me shortly after our arrival. A thick slice of still warm dark bread, a generous hunk of cheese and a handful of olives. I obtained water from the courtyard well for my drink.

The inn kept two watchmen on duty through the hours of darkness, a couple of retired Legionnaires I learned, who supplemented their meager pensions in this way. I was free to walk the interior of the small compound as long as I stayed out of the main room. I could enter there only if summoned. There were two other slaves sharing the stable with me that night. One was an old man with no teeth who had a talent for numbers and kept the accounts for his master. The other was a well-fleshed, dark-haired brute of about thirty. He was a Dacian, captured during the wars and sold on the block. He hadn't accepted his new status in life very well and already wore the scars of punishment.

A brand on his face signified that he had tried to run away from his owner at least once. The next time he tried would probably be his last. Crucifixion was not uncommon for a repeater.

There were five or six other guests beside Celer staying at the inn that night. One of them, the owner of the foul-tempered Dacian slave, was a traveling merchant who had several pack animals inside the shed with us. His wares had been removed from the animal's backs and taken inside with him for, I suppose, obvious reasons.

I came very close to having trouble with the Dacian within minutes after our arrival. I'd moved a couple of his master's animals over a bit to make room for Celer's mule, and he'd shouted loudly for me to keep my damned ugly animal away from his own. I suppose my mild and courteous manner encouraged his bravado. I tried to explain very politely that I had not intended to crowd him. He approached me and shook his large fist in my face, telling me to watch my step around him this night or he would rearrange my pretty face. I said nothing to him in retaliation. I knew that Celer would have short patience with me if I got into trouble and caused him embarrassment, and in addition I did not relish having my back stripped by his lash.

I located a place to retire outside the shed. I figured it would be best if I kept my distance from the Dacian. I made a fair bed with my cloak thrown over a pile of hay and nestled down in the soft, sweet-smelling, dry grass to rest. It was a fair night, with a gentle wind that rustled the leaves of the trees and made the evening most pleasant. It was the first time I had spent a night outside, and it was an enjoyable sensation. I lay there for some time, watching the night birds swoop low, give their short high-pitched cry and dart off too quickly for the eye to follow.

From where I lay, the sounds from inside the inn were muted, as if from a much farther distance. On the walls, the two guards stood their watch, talking in low voices, relaxed. There probably hadn't been any trouble in these parts for a good long time.

I had just drifted off, or so it seemed, when I heard a soft clicking sound that brought me to full awareness instantly. It came again. I stood, wrapping my cloak about me, so as to see what was happening. I moved through the dark, staying to the shadows by the shed and merging as one with the black of the night, reaching a spot nearer the wall and the sounds. The two guards were at the other end of the compound, talking in whispers.

A shadow detached itself from the dark near the wall then, and as it moved, another slid deftly over the top of the wall and ropped to the yard. Then another . . . and another. A voice muttered something. It came from the first form I had seen move on the ground. It was the voice of the Dacian.

As the men moved I saw weapons in their hands, knives and swords it appeared in the dark. Oho! I thought, there's foul play afoot this night. I knew without being told that the Dacian had made some sort of deal with the men coming over the wall—a deal to steal whatever was in his master's packs inside and probably anything else they could lay their hands on. Four men they totaled, counting the Dacian. Not a great number, but they probably didn't expect much difficulty with either the two guards or the rich travelers inside. The guests, including the innkeeper, were not fighters and they knew it. But they knew not about Celer and myself.

I wasn't particularly worried about the bandits killing us; I was more concerned to make the most out of the situation. If I cried alarm too soon, I would probably receive little credit. No, it was best if I let them take their plan a little ways further. Therefore I stayed undetected in the shadows, searching the area slowly for something to use as a weapon. I would need one when the time arrived for me to play hero.

The four of them crept slowly around to where the guards, still unaware that they had unwelcome visitors, stood casually chatting. The three wall jumpers remained behind a small outbuilding while the Dacian, whistling nonchalantly so as not to startle the sentries, walked out into the open, a wineskin in his outstretched hand. The guards noticed his presence, as was intended, and one of them called down to him.

''Who is it there?''

The Dacian responded in a slightly slurred voice, as if he'd had too much from the skin of wine, and extended his hand up to their position. ''It is only I, Masters. The slave of the merchant, Hasdro. The shed was a bit stuffy and I came out for a breath of fresh air to clear my head.'' He waved the skin.

One of the guards called back to him: ''What's that you have in your hand, lowly one? Have you been stealing some of your master's goods?''

The Dacian laughed softly and spoke drunkenly. ''Goods? Goods is it that you say, Masters? That is true enough; this is the best item that my master has with him on this journey. Never have I tasted or drunk anything so fine as this rare vintage.''

He now had the guard's attention. His maneuver was a clever one, for all Romans consider themselves connoisseurs where wine is concerned.

''What is it that you have in that skin, comrade?'' one called down to him. Aha! Now it was comrade instead of slave. The Dacian had them squarely fooled now for sure. He shook the skin, letting it gurgle loudly.

''It's a half-full skin of fine Lesbius wine of Greece, the nectar of the gods. Those of Holy Olympus themselves would find this vintage to their liking.''

One of the guards told the other he'd heard of the wine and that it cost a full denarius a skin to purchase. The other whistled through his teeth and added that it must surely be deliciously sating. He spoke to the Dacian.

"Would there possibly be enough there for us to each have a sip, friend? You know we are good fellows and more than likely would forget to tell your master that you have dipped into his wares." The other guard chuckled.

The Dacian laughed most pleasantly and good-naturedly.

"Certainly, there is enough here for the three of us. Give me a hand up and we will all test my master's ware to make sure it hasn't gone sour and that it is fit to sell."

The guards laughed and lowered their ladder for him to ascend. Why, after all, should they be worried? They were both armed, and he seemed like a nice harmless fellow. The Dacian climbed up and leaned against the wall, handing them the wineskin. They both drank, and agreed that another sip was called for before they could pass judgment on whether it was fit for market. While their attention was on the wineskin, the Dacian moved silently up behind them. It was so easy. He gave them each a gentle push with his hands, both at the same time, and they tumbled silently from the wall. Their bodies had barely touched the ground below when the Dacian's bandit friends were on them, smothering the weak cries with their bodies while their knives searched for vital organs. The struggle was quickly over, the two wine-tasting sentries dead, their own precious red vintage pouring from a dozen openings made by the blades of the bandits.

I moved back slowly, still out of their sight, and finally found what I'd been looking for, a makeshift weapon. Near the spot where I'd been sleeping lay a wooden pitchfork, not the trident type, but a regular four-pronged fork with sharply honed points. It would serve my needs.

I knew their next move would be to enter the inn. There was nothing of any value outside except the animals; they would be last on their list. I had heard no sounds from inside, so I figured that all must be asleep by now. If the Dacian and his cohorts had their way this night, I knew that none of those inside would ever awaken. They probably planned on taking them out one at a time, knifing them in their sleep. I couldn't find anything wrong with their plan, except my presence.

I moved closer to the doorway of the inn, keeping to the shadows. I remember now how my pulse began to advance, the blood pounding in my ears in anticipation of what was to come. It was somewhat like the arena.

They moved to either side of the door and waited a moment. I chose this time to let loose with my howl of warning.

"Murder!" I cried loudly. "Wake up or die!"

At my yell, they were startled for a second. The three men who had come over the wall broke through the door. The Dacian saw me then and turned to me, sword in hand. He cursed me for a meddler.

"I told you to keep out of my way, pup. Now I'm going to split you open."

When he started forward, I moved out, holding my pitchfork in the short lunge position, my left hand gripping near the head and my right holding the haft near my waist. I think I must have been grinning as I moved into position for he suddenly got a puzzled expression on his face when I didn't appear to be backing down. Then, from inside, I heard the sounds of fighting. From a great roaring bellow, I could tell that Celer was in the thick of it and I almost felt sorry for the would-be killers inside.

The Dacian probably thought that all the noise was from his friends doing the slaughter on men who did not know the first thing about combat. He would have been correct except for the presence of the lanista, Celer. The door came open as one of the three men tried desperately to get out of the inn. I saw Celer grab him by the hair and pull him back inside while ramming fourteen inches of sword blade into the man's returning back.

I had taken long enough; it was time to get on with it. I had wanted to stall the action long enough so that Celer could see me do in the Dacian. I had kept the fool at bay until Celer could finish off the three inside; now I moved. I thrust first at his face and then shifted in midstroke to the gut. He sliced at my poor weapon with an awkward downstroke of his sword. It was a futile gesture.

Celer stepped out just then, and I moved fast. I hooked the sword at the crossguard, holding it between the prongs of my fork, and with a quick twist of my wrist the sword flew from his hand and across the yard of the compound. I moved him up against the wall, then, barring any route of escape, held him there. Celer moved up behind me and slapped me on the back with his hamlike hand, hard enough to stun a full-grown hog.

"Well done, Little Wolf. You saved us from those amateurs."

I grinned at him. "Thank you, Master. What do you wish me to do with this one? Should I kill him?"

He told me not to do him in for the moment; to tie him up. In the morning he would be turned over to the Legionnaires that patrolled this particular section of the road.

The Dacian's master was overcome with gratitude. As with many who are merchants, violence to their person is the greatest fear they possess, other than the loss of their money. He offered Celer a gift of silver, which naturally Celer accepted with great style. They placed the Dacian in my safekeeping until morning, which was still a few hours away. I moved back into the shed, along with the old man and the bound Dacian, spending the remainder of the night with the smelly animals. But even they smelled better than the Dacian and the old man. The Dacian prisoner gave me looks throughout the night that would have shriveled the heart of a Greek statue. It never bothered me in the least. I wasn't sure I really had a heart anyway at that age, and after all, he had done me a favor by putting me in the good graces of my new master. One up again, I was. My prisoner was in a foul mood and made dire threats to my person. Then, making a full turn about, he offered me bribes. How he could offer bribes I knew not, for he had nothing but his life remaining, and tomorrow he would lose that.

It was without reluctance that I released him to the tender mercies of the Vigeles the next morning. We had to delay our departure for a couple of hours until the innkeeper's servant had fetched the soldiers from their barracks to the inn. I personally, was in no rush. It gave me a little time to catch some sleep while Celer kept watch over the Dacian. Before we hit the road, the Vigeles had the Dacian well on his way back to the magistrate. There, it was a sure bet, he would hang upside down on a stake before sunset. That suited me fine. I hadn't liked the bastard much to start with anyway. He'd called my mule ugly.

This was only a minor incident and I mention it only to emphasize the fact, that, without formal education, I was forced to use wit and wile to survive with my owners, just as one must do the same to survive in the arena. My shrewdness and quick wit saved me more than once, at the same time bettering my position in life.

Celer loosened up a bit on the rest of the trip. He even gave me two of the twenty silver denarii that the merchant had rewarded him with. All in all, I came out quite well on the entire deal. It was only fair that Celer got most of the money; after all, he'd done the only killing of the evening.

When I say that Celer loosened up a bit, I don't mean to imply that we became friends, only that he trusted me a little more. At best, he was a bull-headed taciturn individual who never said much, but when he did have your ear he did not like to repeat himself, as I was to find out later.

I had heard of the school of thraces, owned by Vannius

Messalla, from some of his gladiators. They fought from time to time in muneras and festivals at the circus. They all had good reputations and from this short trip with their lanista I understood why. The man had a quality in him that said power. He was a completely professional fighter and trainer of fighters. I found out sometime later that he had even won the rudis from the hands of Augustus Caesar for a performance where he'd killed seven opponents in one match.

The school first came into sight as we crested a small hill and left the stones of the Appian Way, exchanging them for a dirt sideroad.

5

The school was situated atop a low hill, surrounded by vineyards and olive groves. The walls were about three meters high and of plastered stone. The academy covered an area of about five acres. Off to one side sat a separate and more expensive-looking estate, which I found out later was the home of Vannius Messalla.

We went directly to the home of the master. Celer handed the wagon over to a house slave and ushered me inside. I caught my breath. I'd never entered such a palace before. There were paintings on the walls, depicting gladiatorial events, and colorful murals of strange lands and peoples. I thought to myself that surely even the Imperial Augustus himself did not live in such splendor. I was very self-conscious about my poor appearance, and I found myself trying to walk without letting my sandals touch the highly polished marble floors. It was impossible, I soon found.

Celer spoke to an elderly servant who asked us to wait in the hall for a moment. He disappeared behind a door of black wood, trimmed with gold leaf. A short time passed before he returned and nodded for us to go in. He closed the door behind us when we entered.

I had thought the hall was rich, but this room made it seem pale. There were vessels of silver and gold on carved stands, statues of men whose faces showed great strength and courage. There were also a few statues of gods, some of which I recognized. There was one of a silver Mars, standing over the body of a downed opponent, his sword raised above his head in victory.

But it was the man behind the desk who made the room what it was. It was not his dress; though rich in material, it was plain in design. It was his bearing. He'd said nothing to either of us as yet, but I knew somehow that there was a mind behind that unsmiling face that missed nothing. Messalla was neither tall nor short. He was not thin, nor was he fat. It was a total concentration of his being that gave him this aura of power, not the physical kind but the greater strength of a man who knows what he wants and is used to having his way. I can tell you that I was more than a little frightened of him.

He looked me over closely, eyeing me up and down, then turned his attention to Celer. I felt that in his one short look at me he knew everything there was to know, including my innermost secret thoughts.

Celer bowed to him, moved closer to the desk and handed over my papers to him. He read them over carefully and nodded in acceptance. When he spoke, it was with precise and measured words. He wasted nothing, not even a breath.

I didn't catch much of what was said, though my name was mentioned several times in the conversation. I was too busy gaping at the furnishings in the room. Celer snapped his fingers to bring me from my state of shock. I stumbled forward like the bumpkin I was and bowed to Messalla.

He eyed me through sharp dark eyes and spoke to me for the first time, and, I might add, for the last. His voice never changed expression, the tones never rose or fell, but the sincerity of his words was not to be doubted.

"I accept you. Remember what I tell you because you will not be told again. In the School of Messalla, two people hold the power of life and death over you, the lanista and myself. Celer has told me of your actions in the events of last evening. You did well. Keep that attitude and you will be treated fairly. But if you do not obey, or should you try to escape, there will be no second chances. I have but one law here. Total and instant obedience. Anything to the contrary is punished by death, administered on the spot. If you survive our training, you will have the privilege of knowing that you have made it through the finest school of the thraces in all the Empire. With the training you receive here you will have the opportunity to achieve great things in life. Your past history certainly speaks well of you. Train hard and obey while you are here. Disobey and die! Those are your only options. Welcome to our school!"

With that he dismissed us. Celer took me from the house and walked me the short distance to the walled school. I had not expected such strictness; but somehow I knew that Messalla meant every word he'd said.

Celer called for the guards to open the gates and allow us to enter. Inside, I found myself staring at a miniature arena, a small Flavian. The training compound held stands for private shows, stands that could only be filled by the invited elite. There were about twenty men sparring and a few singles going through exercises. They never stopped what they were doing, even though Celer and I passed close to them. I found out later that one only ceased his exercises if he was ordered to do so. I did notice that the pace of their activities picked up as we passed by.

We entered the barracks. Inside it was cool. Celer showed me to a wooden bunk with two blankets neatly folded at the foot. There was no mattress, only smooth bare boards. On the floor at the end of the cot sat a small square box that Celer quickly informed me was to be used for my personal issue. Everything in the barracks was identical, even the boxes.

A man came in then, carrying the curved sword of the thraces and wearing half armor. He was powerfully built, though not heavy. He saluted Celer with his sword.

Celer spoke to him: "Are you ready, Pyrantis?" Celer told me to put my things on the bunk and come with them. I did as ordered, following them to the opposite end of the barracks and out into a smaller compound that was surrounded by the same wall that enclosed the rest of the school.

Celer walked to a rack that contained many weapons of various sorts and sizes. He selected a sica, similar to the one that Pyrantis was carrying. He handed it to me with only one word: "Fight!"

I stood there stupidly, staring at him for a moment, then accepted the sword. In the time it took him to release the weapon to me, I damned near lost my head from its position at my shoulders. Pyrantis had anticipated the order and made a giant swoop with his own weapon. I somehow, though awkwardly, managed to block the blow, recovering quickly. Though young, I still had a lot of ring savvy, and I wanted Pyrantis and my lanista to know it. Automatically I went into the on-guard position, just in time to ward off the next series of thrusts and slashes. One of them nicked me on the shoulder, just enough to bring blood and settle me down. I moved everything from my mind except the man in front of me.

I counterattacked them, wildly throwing a series of strikes and thrusts of my own. They accomplished nothing. Pyrantis managed to block everything I threw at him, and with little effort. He pricked me again, this time on the cheek. I fought back, him keeping the pressure on me, aborting my countermoves. He rained one blow after another on me, hard ringing strikes that left my sword arm numb and tingling with needles. He thrust and pounded at me until my back was against the wall, the point of his sword against my throat. My chest was heaving from the exertion, yet he was breathing normally, giving no sign at all of having been sapped by our frantic sparring. He looked me closely in the eye and stepped back, lowering his sword point to the ground.

I stood where I was. It was over and I was glad. He turned his back to me and I was tempted to run him through, a thought that rapidly disappeared. I knew that I had just experienced my first lesson. He spoke to Celer.

''He will do. The boy is strong, and quick. I thought he would fold much faster than he did, and I can tell that he likes to fight. He had the spark in his eyes when I cut him, and I could see the desire to kill me. That's good! His wrist is strong and he has good body motion. He will learn, if he lives.''

Celer grunted in agreement and turned to me.

''Pyrantis is our senior instructor. You will obey him at all times, without question.''

I bowed my head in agreement as Celer walked away, leaving me there with Pyrantis. My body and face were still flushed, not from the heat of the fight, but from embarrassment and humiliation. Pyrantis walked over to me, laughing.

''Do not feel bad, young one. You did much better than I expected you to. Now, forget your anger and come with me, there are things you must know.''

He walked me back to the barracks, returning my sword to the rack before entering. He ordered me to sit on the bunk, and he sat on the one opposite, wiping his forehead with the back of one hairy hand.

''Ease yourself, young one! Pyrantis will not eat you.'' He relaxed and smiled openly. I returned his smile a little shyly, still unsure of what was happening.

"Now, pay attention to what I say. You have met your master Messalla, and have already learned that there are no second chances here. But understand this! I am not your enemy. If I am hard on you during your training, it is only to better your chances for survival. The harder I work you, the higher your odds for living.

"You are the youngest that I have ever worked with, but your age does not matter to me. You will receive no special favors or attentions until you earn them. I have but one mission and that is to turn you into a thraces that this school can one day be proud of. Another piece of advice, make no friends while you are here. Keep to yourself and tend to your own business. You will not be harassed or bothered by the others, and your private possessions will be safe from theft. You will turn over to me all that you own for my safekeeping. You will be issued exactly the same items that the others here have. Your personal belongings will be returned to you when you leave. Or should I say, *if* you leave." He smiled knowingly at his remark; I assumed he had seen a lot of trainees die. I shivered a little.

He told me to open my box. Inside were a set of sandals, two tunics of white linen and a heavy cloak of blue wool. This was the standard dress, I was to find out. There was a large spoon for eating, but no knife, and a cup and bowl of baked clay. That was it. I could see that this was to be a Spartan existence.

After I'd turned over my few possessions to him, including what little money I had, he took them to his room at the end of the barracks and returned. We went outside, where he showed me around the compound. He waited while I ran to get my eating utensils and, when I joined him once more, he took me to the kitchen where we ate. Meals, I soon learned, were served twice each day. At dawn and shortly before dusk. There were no lamps, either in the kitchen or in the barracks. Expensive oil would not be wasted and besides, there was nothing for us to do after dark anyway. We were all so exhausted at the day's end that we could only sleep from supper, straight through until the cock's crow, when we would rise and begin again.

There were twenty-eight others at the school. We were broken down into different categories, based on individual degrees of proficiency. Pyrantis informed me that less than one out of four would make it successfully through the complete training program. Those who were injured beyond repair or those that proved unfit were returned to their masters, or, if they happened to be owned by Messalla, were sold to lesser schools.

He stayed on the field with me for some time, pointing out one man and then another, explaining what they were doing and moving on to something else.

It was on my second day, about an hour before dusk, that Pyrantis called out for all those training to cease their activity. The students formed into two neat ranks, marched at his command to the rack and placed their swords one by one inside. The rack was locked and carried inside by four of the men. It was orderly, and I began to enjoy the discipline they so displayed.

Once again, they formed in two ranks. Pyrantis and I stood before them. He spoke one sentence to them all.

"This man is called Lucanus!"

With that he instructed me to join the men in the second rank, placing me next to a Sarmatian, who had fair eyes and hair. He then called us to attention and dismissed us for cleanup before supper.

I was lost. Not knowing what to do, I followed the movements of the others. We cleansed ourselves from jars of water, neatly placed on waist-high racks. We then retrieved our eating equipment, and lined up to go to the kitchen.

I didn't have much of an appetite. Everything was moving much too fast. I don't even remember what the menu was that night. I merely accepted what was placed in my bowl, filled my cup with water, and sat down. I chewed and swallowed automatically until both were empty. Like the others, I washed my bowl and cup and walked back to the barracks and replaced them in my box. Not a word was spoken to me during the meal or on the return to our quarters. I caught several wondering looks, which I assumed were due to my youth, but no words.

They prepared their bunks for the night with two blankets, one atop the other. I did likewise, imitating their every movement. A few of them broke off into small groups, discussing the day's training. I was not invited to join their discussions. With the fall of darkness, all of them moved to their individual bunks and the doors of the barracks were locked. Pyrantis entered his own room at the end without a word to anyone.

The man in the bunk beside me happened to be the Sarmatian who stood with me in ranks. Now he spoke to me.

"If you feel like you have to take a leak during the night, don't attempt to unbar the doors and go outside. The guards are instructed to kill on sight. There is a spot at the end of the barracks. Use it!"

With that, he rolled over, beginning to snore almost the moment his head touched the boards of his bunk. I was certain I would lie there awake most of the night, but it was not to be. My eyes closed without my being aware of it and the next thing I knew there was a sharp rap on the sole of one foot which brought me out of the dark.

My eyes jerked open. It was near dawn and my first day of actual training.

6

That day began a period in my life that I thought would never end. Even the auctoratii, of which there were several, had to endure the same pain as the rest of us. Celer and Pyrantis together enforced a discipline that I was certain was far more strict than any of Rome's Legions had to endure.

From my first day, they never let up for a moment. It was a constant revolving routine of swordplay, supervised by Celer, or the lifting of weights and logs, looked after by Pyrantis. Bracelets of lead were placed on our wrists, and more weight was added at regular intervals. I spent enough time at the chopping posts to have reduced several large oaks into kindling. Celer had us fight each other with wooden or dulled swords, standing on beams that were about two feet in width and approximately four feet off the ground, to develop our sense of balance. Retiarii and secutors were brought in to spar against us, providing us with all possible combinations of instructions, enabling us to face any opponent, fighting any style.

The only times we were allowed to leave the school were when we went on crosscountry jogs of ten to twenty miles. Even then we were under the watchful eye of our lanista and mounted guards.

The auctoratii were treated no different than the others. Though they were free men when they signed up for the school, they had relinquished their rights of decision in doing so. There was no way out except for the ones I have previously mentioned.

Sometimes advanced students would leave us, moving on to one of the two permanent teams owned by Messalla. One team fought in the eastern provinces of the Empire and the other throughout Italia and Gaul.

For the first few weeks, every muscle and joint in my

body ached; then suddenly the pain disappeared. In spite of the intensive physical torture that awaited me each morning after breakfast, I gradually began to look forward to each day's training schedule. I could actually feel my strength and stamina increasing, and my body was filling out from the good diet of plain but plentiful food. I gained nearly twenty pounds in three months, all of it muscle.

We learned how and where to strike for an opponent's vital areas, as well as the areas that only looked vital and bled a lot so as to excite the arena crowd. Show business, Pyrantis called it. Part of the game. We were taught the art of watching a man's eyes and the movements of his body for tell-tale signs of weakness or faults.

We weaved through swinging balls of iron, with spikes an inch long that could crush your skull if they touched you, or rip you to pieces. This was to teach us rhythm and how to watch from the corner of the eyes for the unexpected. These and a thousand more training techniques were inflicted upon us daily, but I flourished under the regimen and was promoted into the advanced classes. The time I'd spent in the arena earlier had given me an edge over the others and the advice from old Bosra concerning men and animals aided me greatly. I was yet smaller than the others, but I was gaining on them rapidly.

Celer and Pyrantis were absolutely devoted to their craft and drove us mercilessly, cursing and swearing when we erred and patiently going over a specific movement a hundred times until we'd mastered it.

They taught us how to breathe in order to conserve our energy, to pace ourselves and our movements, and to work as a team, one serving the other.

Shield work was nearly as important as the sword. If a man could use the shield properly, he had an extra weapon at his disposal. Its edge could smash a throat or break an arm. It could be used to attack as well as defend. The sica, we learned, with its longer blade and curved style, was not as good as the shortsword for thrust purposes, but it had its own advantages. It provided one with a longer reach, and the curve of the blade helped in deflecting an enemy blow with the minimum of effort on a fighter's part.

Several times Messalla came to inspect our progress, but never did he speak one word to any of the students. He conferred only with Celer, then left. I learned that he had other properties, from Rome to Africa, and he would sometimes be away for months on end. His absence didn't matter to us. Celer and Pyrantis were more than most of us could contend with anyway. They held our complete attention and enforced the same discipline whether the master was in or out.

Up to this point they had only executed one man. He had tried to escape. His punishment was swift and without mercy. I found out that he was a slave like myself and had been enrolled by his master. It made a believer out of me, even though I personally had no desire to leave the school. He had tried to sneak over the walls, only to be apprehended by the guards. The following morning we were called into ranks before breakfast. The poor devil was tied to a chopping post, and a half-dozen guards were lined up before him. Without ceremony, Celer waved his hand and the man was turned into a human pincushion, quivering and bleeding as six spears nailed him to the post. Not one of them missed its target. I wasn't surprised to find that the guards were former fighters, Legionnaires and gladiators. They were experts with their weapons.

Celer stood in front of us, his hands lightly on his hips, nodding at the still-quivering corpse.

"That man was a fool! He chose his fate. If he'd continued his training and fought in the arena, he would have at least had a chance to survive. This way he had none. All of you think it over. Fight and have a chance to live. Try to escape and you die. Be certain of that: there is no other choice for any of you."

The body was dragged away, and we marched to the kitchen to eat breakfast. None of the students said a word.

If a man committed a minor infraction, such as moving too slow, he was loaded with weights on his back and made to run until he dropped. This was, at least to Celer's mind, better than a flogging, for it not only taught the man to respond faster to commands but also served to strengthen him at the same time. It was not considered punishment, only advanced training. Ha!

After a few months, we were sent out to participate in local contests. None of these were death fights, though three men had died from wounds that had become infected. I performed with the rest of the students in team matches and a few single combats. I was never overmatched.

Celer and Pyrantis were always there watching over everything. After the contests, back at the school, we were brought in and criticized individually. Either Celer or Pyrantis would reenact certain parts of the fights to show where we had erred in technique and to emphasize what we'd done correctly. After the solo counseling the entire team was assembled, and all participated in analyzing the events. I learned much from this novel approach and rapidly grew to appreciate why Crator had sent me to the School of Messalla.

It was nearly a year into my training before I was entered in a death match. By this time I knew I was ready. I knew, too, that soon I would be ready for Rome. I was looking forward to seeing old Crator again. Celer had told us that a team of the most advanced students would soon be sent to represent the school in the arena of Rome and had told me on the side that I was to be one of them. At the same time, he added, I would also be returned to the charge of Crator, though I would still have to fight for Messalla a number of times each year to pay off my training debt. A portion of my winnings from each fight would go to him as payment for this training. That didn't bother me, for Crator seldom allowed me to keep much for myself anyway. I wouldn't miss it at all. The thing I wanted most right now, was a woman!

During the next days, faces came and faces went. Some were lost in the death matches locally, others went to join the teams of Messalla elsewhere, and those who didn't measure up to his standards were sold.

It was spring when the team bound for Rome was selected. We walked the distance back to Rome, escorted by guards. I didn't see the reason for such tight security, for all the men that were chosen were reliable. I suppose it was simply standard procedure. Celer accompanied us, leaving Pyrantis behind to run things while he was away. I bade farewell to Pyrantis before we left and thanked him for his teaching. I was now nearly eighteen, ready for anything, and had never felt better in my life. I could accept anything the world had to offer me.

I was at the head of the line when we reached the outskirts of Rome. A compound had been set up outside the walls to house the five teams of gladiators that had come to visit the city and join in the games. I was probably the only one of the group that would stay after the fights.

It was with a pleasant and relaxed feeling that I wrapped myself inside my blue cloak and fell into a good restful slumber, eager for the events that were to take place in two more days. I was impatient to show Crator what I'd learned and how much I'd grown. It would please him, I hoped. Yes! In two days, I would fight in the Circus Maximus!

BOOK TWO

THRACES

1

We left the confines of the walled training center to walk the few miles to the arena. Crator had been in to see me the day before and asked after my welfare. You know the kind of questions. Was I getting enough to eat? And had the lanista obeyed his orders about keeping the whores away from me? The rest of the students, if they did well enough, could have one of the women visit them in their cubicles for a couple of hours. But Crator, the old bastard, told the lanista to keep his poxy harlots away from me. He would not have me weakened by disease. Sometimes I wished he would mind his own business. I think it was harder on me to hear the sounds of rutting going on all about me than it would have been to deal with a slight touch of the pox. After all, I was a full seventeen then and still had not been initiated into the pleasures of Venus. To be sure, I had no shortage of offers from some of the other gladiators who preferred the Greek way. But that was not to my liking, though I must confess that sometimes in the dark all that grunting and gasping going on about me made me think about it for a moment or two.

It was the hour before dawn when we formed up to march to the gates of the city. We went by way of the Milvan Bridge, wrapped in our cloaks to keep the chill of the morning air from our bones. To our right we passed the field of Mars and the monuments of Agrippa. From the road they appeared ghostly in the wavering wisps of mist rising from the damp ground. It had rained lightly the night before. The only sounds were those of our sandaled feet slapping on the close-fit stones of the road. The rest of Rome was still in their beds or just rising. It would be another hour before they took to the streets in any number.

We followed the Flaminian Way until it reached the prison near the Quirinal Hill, then took a side street to the Circus Maximus.

The memory of those gray silent columns and the statues of Emperors long dead stayed with me. What intrigues could they tell of? I could see the ever-burning flames of the sacred fire of Jupiter glowing hazy red in the mist surrounding its site, knowing that shifts of priests were constantly in attendance, keeping the flame alive. To them it was the life force of Rome. When the flames died, so would the Empire.

Though I was only a slave of Rome, I always felt myself to be Roman and promised myself that one day I would be a citizen with the rights of citizenship. I never thought about doing anything other than what I was trained for, but the idea of owning myself was a separate goal. I wondered how I would deal with it.

A chill ran up my spine and I wrapped my cloak closer about me. We entered the rear gate of the Circus, the one where the animals were usually brought into their cages. Once inside, the chains were removed from the ankles of the tiros in our troupe. It was the practice to keep them chained on their way to their fights, not that they would have had any real chance to escape. We were escorted by a squad of old veterans who were fully armed with spears and swords. We knew that we would have little chance against them if we chose to resist. As for myself, the thought never entered my mind. Even at seventeen I considered myself a veteran and professional. I knew there were worse lives than the one I had.

We went into the rooms assigned to us and found spots to wait. We each had our own way of killing the hours until we were called on. Some, especially the oldtimers, managed to lose themselves by going to sleep, as if they hadn't a care in the world. Others hummed to themselves or paced restlessly back and forth, until not knowing what else to do they just sat down on the straw and waited too. It was the tiros I watched the most—the pale faces and greasy pallor of their skin, hands that trembled until they had to clasp them together to stop the shaking. I knew as did the other old fighters that most of them would die this day. They were not a good lot. Most were from farms and had never held a weapon in their hands until they had been sent to the barracks. It was unlucky for them that this munera came too soon for them to be properly trained. None of them had even been in a non-kill event before. They were sheep going to meet their butcher and they knew it.

Celer came and squatted down beside me, grunting a bit as he did so, grumbling something about getting too old. His shaved head glowed from the light of the torches in their brackets set on the stone walls. It was still dark here, though dawn was well advanced outside. He scratched his groin and grumbled again as was his habit:

"Well now, young Lucanus, this is a big day for you. Your first major event. True, you have had some wins in the provinces last year. But this is different. This is the Maximus and here the game is for keeps. The mob loves to give the sign to kill. If you will live through this day, remember what you have been taught. I think you have the makings of a winner and you could survive a long time if you use your head instead of your muscle. The one that can think lives the longest. Play to the crowd, and even if you do fall they may give thumbs up if you have amused them enough. Remember, nothing is too bizarre or strange. In fact, the more outrageous you can be the better. Either astonish them by your kills or make them laugh. Each of those can serve to prolong the beat of your heart. How many have you taken out now, my young Hercules?''

I asked him, ''Do you mean how many have I killed since I came to your troupe, or do you count those I terminated when I played the child's role of Charon?''

Celer spat a gob of phlegm into the straw. ''I know how many you've killed since you've worked for me, stupid. Four. I want to know altogether.''

I replied, ''I never was very good at numbers. Probably something over a hundred. But I really don't know. I fought in specials as a retiarius for two years before Crator sent me to your school. But most of those were not to the death, unless a fighter was so badly wounded he wasn't worth saving. I only killed two in all that time, and Crator beat me severely for both of them, raising hades with me about how stupid I was to have wounded my opponents so badly they had to be put out. I guess I cost him a pretty coin in the payment he had to make in compensation to the owners.''

Celer spat again and scratched his head with a dirty nail. ''Well, you won't have to worry about pulling any blows today. The only thing I can tell you is to watch out. You never know what underhanded trick will be played on you. I know we're only set for one fight, and if we win that's supposed to be it. But you can never tell for sure. The Games Master might just decide that things need to be livened up a bit and turn a dozen lions loose on you when you least expect. I have seen it happen before. And just because Crator owns you, don't think he won't do it if the games are going badly. He knows where his bread is buttered, and he must please the mob if he's to keep his job.

So keep on your toes and watch everything, especially your back.''

Celer was a wily old devil who knew the value of showmanship himself. Though I wasn't his best fighter, I was the youngest, and he counted on my youth and appearance to draw the crowd's attention. In fact, I was a pretty good-looking young man then. My body had no major scars, only a few thin slice marks that served to accent the otherwise smooth skin and muscles that hid a reserve of power that even Celer wasn't sure of. So far, I had never fought to the point of exhaustion. Perhaps it was because I was so young that I had greater powers of recuperation and could catch my wind faster than the older men. He knew that I would give a good performance, and if I attracted the attention of the women, it would bring a demand for me to appear in more of the big money contests. I also knew that his deal with Crator was that he and Messalla would get forty percent of my winnings.

We still had about two hours to wait, and Celer had each of us eat a bowl of boiled millet and barley. It is well known that barley thickens the blood and helps staunch the flow of blood. That and a swallow of posca to rinse our mouth with would be all we would have until after we returned. Those of us that would return . . . .

Our team was all thraces. We would be going against a like number of ten fighters of the Myrmillones from the School of Rubrius Trogas. They were heavier men than we were, and wore the old-style costume with the wide-brimmed helmet, a mesh-iron shoulder guard, leg greaves and wide leather belts. We of the thraces wore lighter armor and a small iron buckler rather than the larger rectangular shield of the Myrmillones, which resembled closely that of some of the Legions. Also, while the Myrmillones used a sword identical to the Gladius Iberius, we carried our slightly longer weapon, with a curved edge and wider girth, the sica.

Celer told me earlier that while the rest of our team would wear loincloths, I was to fight naked with only shoulder guard, helmet and leg greaves, not even the leather belt to give my gut some protection. I protested, but he wouldn't give in. He wanted me to stand out from the rest of the men and attract the attention of the mob.

The games began. As usual there were warm-ups with clowns and jugglers; then came the andabatae, slaves who fought blind with knives, groping for each other, helped along by the arena attendants who prodded them in the right direction with red-hot irons. They shared the stage with old men fighting with filled pig bladders and other clowns. This usually didn't last long before the crowd grew bored and wanted something more to keep them amused.

The next event was the bestiarii; a few dozen lions, leopards, and wolves were let loose in the arena all at once, then hunted down and killed by the beast men. We had, of course, heard the grunts and coughing roars of the great cats earlier as they were being prepared. Now we could hear the laughs of the crowd as one of the beasts went down and a half-starved leopard started to feed on it while it was still alive. The cat started at the face. I suppose that is what the mob found so amusing. It took a bit of time for the dead animals to be cleared away and fresh sand spread and raked. From our cubicle I could see several of the bestiarii limping back, two of them carrying a comrade whose stomach had been laid open. He was trying to keep the large intestine from bulging out and dropping on the ground. He was a dead man, it would just take a little while.

I would have liked to be one of them. I always enjoyed seeing them work the animals. They had style, though most of the gladiators and even the mob didn't consider them to be as entertaining as the gladiators. I admired them for their coolness and grace. From my time with Bosra I knew the thought and care that went into their craft.

It was time to get ready. We helped each other tie up the shoulder harnesses and as usual grumbled over the fit. Something was always wrong. The greaves weren't right, or the helmet didn't fit properly. Mostly it was a case of pre-fight jitters. It would pass.

I stood in front of a polished copper mirror and checked myself out. I did make a pretty picture. Tan, smooth-muscled, my hair oiled and curled to the nape of my neck, the helmet only covering me to just below the ear. Bronze leg greaves set off the picture nicely. And I thought, "Maybe Celer knows what he is doing after all sending me in this way." I felt no sense of shame about my nakedness. I was pretty well put together, and the days when my testicles would draw back as far as they could were long past.

We moved to the gates leading to the arena proper where Celer stood ready to hand us swords as we went out. When we came back the swords would be handed back at the same spot. It paid to be cautious. Fear of going out to fight could make a new, or even an old fighter, go mad sometimes, and again when we came back a killing lust was still on us. One never knew for sure, so it was best to take no chances.

It was our turn. We stepped out into the brighter light of the circus. The contrast after the dark took me a few moments to adjust to.

We formed up in two ranks and marched to face the Imperial Box. The other team of the Myrmillones did the same from the other end of the arena. I was surprised to see the standard of the Emperor flying over his seats. I didn't think he was going to be here this early. As we marched, the sun beat heavy on my bare shoulders. I put away from my mind and body the cold chill that always rushed over me at these times and looked at the stands. They were over-flowing, with nearly six thousand people. One section had been reserved for members of the Pretorian Guard who were not on duty, and they were dressed to the hilt with their plumed helmets, gilded armor and blood-red cloaks draped over their shoulders, leaving the sword arm bare. I knew that few of them could have lasted more than a minute or two with the worst of the veterans of our troupe, and probably would fare not much better with the tiros. Near them, the box reserved for the Priestesses of Vesta was empty. As usual, the noble's virgins showed little interest in the public pleasures of the masses and thought these displays were beneath their dignity. The only times they made an appearance was when something important was about to happen, and then they stayed only long enough to establish their presence. Then they would silently file out and return to their inviolable sanctuary.

The Vestals had tremendous power and influence. All came from noble families; they were trusted with the secrets of the Empire. They were, or so the people believed, the only ones in Rome that could not be bought or corrupted. This gave them a control over the mob that even Caesar had to respect. But they were all women, and I wondered about them sometimes, how they could lead a manless existence forever. Surely it must drive them to some kind of madness.

My reflections on the merits of the Vestal virgins was brought to a stop. Our troupe reached the mark in front of the Emperor's box at the same moment as did the Myrmillones. In one voice we gave the obligatory salute, Hail Caesar and so forth. This was the second time I had appeared before him. From the short look I caught, he looked tired and heavier; his color was not good.

We turned at the command of the arena master and waited for the signal to begin.

The musicians played a fanfare, which ended in a drum roll and clash of cymbals. The fight was on. Warily we squared off, each to one of the others. As with most fights, we began slowly at first, feeling out those in the wide-brimmed helmets, testing their reach and speed with a few tentative strikes and slashes, but nothing serious. It was a kind of unspoken agreement to start this way to make the game last longer. When the crowd gave signs of becoming restless, the pace would again, by unspoken consent, speed up.

The man I faced was heavier than the others on his team. There were rolls of fat around his waist and his responses were slow. Easy kill I thought, this one has been too long from the arena, he's fat and sloppy. I was concerned about how long I could carry him to make it look good, when the pace picked up. I made a combination strike with shield and sword, and repeated the strike three times, each time a little quicker. I thought that it would look good if I just nicked him a bit to start some blood flowing. But each time he just barely managed to counter me. The ox just stood with his feet more or less planted in one spot, waiting. A little angry at myself for not scoring, I picked up the pace of my attack, not paying any attention to what the rest of the team was doing. They had their own problems, and I knew that no one had gone down because the crowd had not called for a throat to be cut or cheered loud enough.

Again I moved in, starting slow, my buckler held out far to the front, right leg trailing, my sica held low to the right side. I lunged forward, bringing my right leg out to the front as far as it could reach, then following up with a short movement of the left leg. This kind of movement put me right up into his face. It is a deceptively fast way to close and hard to counter. My sword was in the right position, a slightly angled upward slice that would change midways into a gut cut with a twist of the wrist. It should have scored, but again, somehow he just managed to deflect the cut, and even countered clumsily and made a touch on my chest with his shortsword. Nothing serious, just a long red line that burned more from the sweat that was beginning to flow freely on me. It was frustrating. I knew I should have had him again, and the cod had actually scored first blood. I was getting a little irritated.

The crowd screamed. Someone had gone down. I took a quick glimpse to see if it was one of ours, but it wasn't. One of the Myrmillones had lost his sword arm at the wrist and was holding the stump with his good hand, resting on one knee waiting for the judgment of the crowd and Caesar. It came. The audience was bored. My teammate, I think it was Graptus, a Gaul, followed the dictates from the royal box and slit the man's throat with a long slice of the sica. The crowd roared with pleasure as the heavy-weight's jugular opened up to spout. A scarlet fountain sprayed all over Graptus, giving him a truly fearful aspect which the crowd loved.

The fight was spread out all over the arena. My man was still like a log, just holding his spot as I pounded at him, trying to get through. I was mad now and just wanted to get in a killing blow and get it over with. Never had I been so infuriated by anything. The man had no style at all; he was fat and slow. I knew I was the better swordsman. Yet I couldn't break through to him. By great Jupiter's brass balls, I have not to this day ever experienced anything like trying to kill that great lumbering cow of a man.

Graptus had gone to help one of our nearer comrades who was getting in trouble. He called out to me, "Lucanus, you better get on with it, or old Frigern there will turn you into a eunuch before finishing you off."

Frigern! I backed away a space. Now I knew why I had had no success with him. I knew most of the gladiators that fought in Rome. But Frigern was a Goth who fought mostly in the provinces and, from what I had heard of him, he never lost. His clumsiness and slow moves were all a deception. He was just letting me wear myself out. Gulping, I caught my breath and tried to control the heaving of my chest and pounding in my temples.

He spoke. I wished I could see his face behind its perforated covering. "Come to me, little one, old Frigern won't hurt you too much. You're young, and maybe they'll let you live if you just put on a good show. So come ahead and pound at me a bit more, then I'll cut you just enough to make it look good."

Look good my ass. From what I had heard, the son-of-a-bitch didn't know how to make anything but a killing blow. I saved my breath instead of answering him. Some of the audience had heard Graptus call his name, and it drew their attention to us. From the corner of my eye I saw even the great Augustus lean forward in his seat a bit for a better look.

I made up my mind. If I went after him, he would just wear me out. My only chance was to make him come to me. I filled my lungs as best I could and cried out loud enough to be heard from one end of the arena to the other. "Frigern, is it? No wonder you stand in one spot. No wonder you can't move. But then Goths are so stupid that their cattle make better slaves because of their higher intelligence."

I turned my back on him and walked toward the stands a couple of paces. "Citizens of Rome, did you ever see such a vulgar fat piece of swine flesh in your lives? By all the gods of Rome, I can tell you this from being so close to him: I stand a better chance of dying from the stench he gives off than I do from his sword."

The mob roared with laughter, and Frigern moved. I thought I would have enough warning from the crowd to get out of his way. But it was damned close. The armored bag of suet came on like a bull. It seemed I had touched a tender spot. Barbarians are always easy to aggravate. They all have expanded notions of their own importance. It is one of their failings. But Frigern, suet or not, moved as fast as any I had ever seen, and he damned near took me out. His shield struck me first, with enough force to knock me clear back and off my feet. If he hadn't hit me so hard, he could probably have killed me then and there. As it was, his smash sent me into a complete somersault and I came back up on my feet ten feet away facing him, weapon ready. It must have looked good; the audience was in hysterics of pleasure. And I heard one that knew cry, "Kill the ox, little wolf of Rome. Hunt him as wolves do." Not a bad idea.

And I did, now that I knew his game. I taunted him until he charged. I harried his flanks, keeping him moving constantly until his breath came in choking sobs and his sides heaved with the effort of his breathing.

My teammates in the meantime had done well, and with only the loss of two. The rest had ganged up on the remaining Myrmillones and made short work of them. Normally they would have come to my aid. But Augustus was interested in seeing the contest between me and the Goth, and waved them off. My teammates waited and watched. I kept circling and lunging. Several times I made small scores that left his legs and arms nicked and bleeding. I tried to make use of my longer blade to keep blood flowing on his sword arm, where it would make his grip less sure.

Frigern's eyes had almost disappeared behind his face mask. They were swollen with hate, and sweat fell in fat drops down his hairy chest, leaving clean streaks in the dust that had caked on him. I knew I was just as dirty, and the dust on my own body had served to clot the thin gut wound, though it bled at the corners when I moved too quickly. Frigern finally managed to get me near the wall where my mobility was limited, and we went at it sword against shield, buckler against sica, until sparks rang and bounced off the steel. Head to head we strained. I could smell the garlic on his breath and the odor of his body was almost overpowering, but I held my own in the melee.

And bit by bit I began to force him back into the arena center. His arms were tiring, and his guard was dropping a bit from his exhaustion and the weight of his heavier shield.

He scored a fair cut on my unprotected shoulder, but not enough to slow me up. It just brought another burst of strength from somewhere deep inside me. I think it was my youth that carried the day. I was able to endure for a few seconds more than he, and made my final assault as a whirlwind. Striking high, then low, forcing him to raise his shield high to his head to counter, knowing that each raising of his arm left him a little weaker, and gave him more difficulty in responding. That was what I wanted. I created a pattern. Strike low with my shield, hit high with my sword. This I did enough times to be sure he had spotted what I was doing. Then, in midstroke, I changed. Instead of going for a slice to his head, I made a straight lunge into his stomach. His shield was already covering his head in anticipation of a blow that never came. My sword entered him just above his leather belt and sank a full hand's length into him. He dropped to his knees, sword falling to the ground to lie beside his shield.

On his knees, Frigern held his hands over his wound, blood oozing out on the already well-stained sand to dry and darken almost as fast as it flowed. I removed his helmet and raised it and my sword over my head, and faced the Imperial Box for the signal. Augustus stood and acknowledged the crowd's cry of ''Let the little wolf feed!'' and turned his thumb to his chest.

I bowed my head slightly and turned back to Frigern. He raised his eyes to mine. His face would have been a pleasant one under any other circumstance. He was older than I expected; there were long strands of gray in the hair which had been covered by his helmet. His eyes already had the dullness that says death is not far away.

''Make it clean, young one. Make it clean.''

My sides were still heaving from my efforts and I only barely managed to answer in a dry cracking voice, "It will be. Go to your gods in honor, barbarian," and struck. The blow was good, his head separated properly. I had hit him just between the vertebrae. If I had missed the right spot, it would have probably taken two or more blows to cut through the thick corded muscle of his neck. As it was, the strike was perfect. The crowd roared their appreciation.

The band played the signal to clear the arena, and I marched back to my teammates. In the chambers inside the arena wine and water waited for us.

2

Celer and Crator came to me; I could tell they were more than pleased. They each congratulated me on my win, Crator slipping me a small purse. I opened it and dumped the contents into my hand. I was still weary from the fight and experiencing the after-fight letdown. My thoughts were not coming easy. Ten denarii? What was this for, I wondered? Did Crator have something up his sleeve? He patted my shoulder, seeing the look of awe.

"It's for you, you dolt! And there will be more where that came from. I'm going to make you a rich man. From now on ten percent of everything you win shall be deposited in your account, to be invested for you."

I was touched. He was really a generous old bastard. My own account! I couldn't believe it.

Celer wished me well, saying he must return to his other men and see to their welfare. Crator sat down and helped himself to some of the wine, making a face at its evident acidity.

"I don't want you to go out this night. You are back in my charge now, and I have found you a room of your own." He gave me instructions on how to get there and repeated his order: "Do not leave your room this night!" He didn't say why I shouldn't, only that I must not. I assumed he would probably be stopping by later.

I left the circus, following his directions. They led to an apartment building of three floors. Noticing that the streets were empty, I remembered that the games would continue until after dark and that practically everyone was there.

I knocked on the door and was admitted inside by a man that I assumed was the landlord. He was a thin man, with a hungry look about him, wearing a stained tunic. He told me he'd been expecting me and motioned for me to follow him up the narrow flight of stairs to the third floor. Opening the door, he slipped inside and with a wide sweep of his arms displayed my new dwelling. I entered. The room was about twelve feet square, containing a single bed and a table on which sat an oil lamp, a basin of water and two towels. I spotted a small chamber pot under the bed. The landlord bade me welcome and went back down the stairs.

It wasn't much maybe, according to some, but for me it was great. I'd never before had this much space all to myself. I cleansed myself as best I could from the small basin. After toweling off I lay down on the bed. It was not a rich bed, but it was clean and felt good. I fell asleep almost instantly. The tension and excitement of the day had left me drained and exhausted.

A creaking sound caused me to open my eyes. It was dark and I was disoriented, and unaccustomed to the room. It could be a thief! I reached beneath the bed and grasped the handle of the chamber pot. Other than the lamp, it was the only weapon in the room.

A small voice whispered then. "I am not here to hurt you, young one." The voice laughed, a deep amused sound that was definitely female. I found my voice and croaked out, "Who are you?"

"A gift from your friends, Celer and Crator. They decided that it was time for you to be initiated." She giggled again, lying down beside me.

It was strange. I never once saw the woman's face that night. I knew she was older than I, from the sound of her voice. But her body was trim and as sweet as that of a fourteen-year-old. It was as she'd said, I was to be initiated, and by the gods, I was. I was awkward and unsure, as I suppose all young men are with their first woman, and almost before we could start, I ended. Much to my immediate embarrassment, I might add. She only laughed a little, and huskily told me to lie back and leave things to her. I did, and she certainly took things into her own hands.

By the time I fell asleep I was convinced that I had convinced her that I was the nearest thing to a god that she would ever experience. Crator and Celer had been right in their selection of a teacher. To this day I still have dreams about the woman. Who was she? What did she look like? Was she fair of skin, or dark? I do recall that she was warm, her body perfumed and soft to the touch, and she had made a boy feel like a man that night. I think I was in love.

I questioned Crator about her later, but he would tell me nothing. For a long time I fantasized that she was the daughter of a noble house who had fallen in love with me after seeing me fight in the arena, and had come to me that night after asking Crator and Celer how to find me. These, and another dozen childish imaginings, occupied my dreams of day and night for some time after.

But perhaps Crator was right in not telling me anything about her, or of her whereabouts. That way, she was always a mystery to me, and mysteries never grow old or wrinkled.

There was only one bad thing about that first night: when I awakened I was ready for an encore. I can tell you that the ten denarii Crator had given me did not last more than two days. Normally I could have lived on that sum for two weeks. But once a dagger has been taken from its scabbard, it must be used or it will grow rusty. I assure you, from that night on my dagger was never given a chance to rust. I was enslaved!

I was popular with the women in the audience, I found. They seemed fascinated by one so young who killed like a man while still a babe. I didn't mind. Whatever their reason, it served our purposes, both mine and Crator's.

Crator began granting me more liberty and I took full advantage of it, coming and going pretty much as I pleased. As long as I paid attention to my training, and didn't miss my matches, he left me relatively alone.

When I was not entered in the contests myself, I seldom missed the opportunity to watch them from the stands. Not that I enjoyed seeing men die, but one day I might be facing one of the fighters below. It pays to be aware of the talents of those who may one day try to kill you.

Niger Graecus was said to be the most handsome man in Rome, and the most feared arena fighter in all the Empire. He fought mainly as a secutor. He always chose his own costume and was the idol of thousands. His name was written on walls all over the city. Graecus only fought two or three times each year, and always against other champions, never newcomers. It was said that his fee was over ten thousand denarii a match. Crator told me that he also received a percentage of the concessions and vendors, which could possibly add up to a like sum.

Our goal was to equal this. With that amount of money, I would only have to fight a couple of times each year to earn a small fortune. Crator felt, and I knew, that one day we would have it. I would be as great, if not greater, than Niger the Greek.

However, at that time I had other goals as well. It was hard for Crator to keep me out of the fleshpots. I begged him for money to buy women, as a drunk begs money to drink on. Crator was always understanding, though not always indulgent.

Celer had left Rome at the end of the games, returning to the School of Messalla. He had been rough on me, but he had been fair, and in my own way I missed him. I did see him once or twice in the next couple of years, when I went to fight in the provinces for the school, to honor Crator's debt for my training.

My kill ratio was beginning to add up and, as it did, I moved up in the ratings. At the age of nineteen, I was listed in the top ten of Empire's gladiators. I began to practice more with the shortsword, learning the techniques that the weapon demanded, and exercising with heavy armor. I would soon move up to the ranks of the secutors. The sword play was not so much different from that of the thraces, and the training I'd received from Pyrantis and Celer was easily adaptable to that of the smaller shortsword. It was the rectangular shield of the secutors that was giving me problems. But I was learning fast. I hadn't yet fought as a secutor, but I was anxious to try. Crator, saying I was not ready, hired masters of the shortsword to teach me different techniques, which I quickly adopted. The damned bulky shield, though—it still proved difficult for me. It was too large.

The months passed. My matches were good, but not good enough. I was not exciting the crowds sufficiently for them to cry aloud for the rudis to be given to me. For that, I needed some really great matches and tough opponents, but Crator would not give them to me. I didn't know the reason he was holding me back, but he always said he had one. I did as he ordered, but I was restless. I wanted a chance for the glory that could only come in truly great contests.

I was unable to persuade Crator to allow me that satisfaction, but at least I could satisfy my other hunger.

Women! I'd become a confirmed addict. I'm certain that I would have spent every coin I earned on warm female flesh, had Crator not taken most of it from me. I tried them all, whores from the taverns by the Tiber and the rich ladies of the court with jeweled fingers.

I believe that the women were even lustier than myself, especially after a fight. They seemed to go mad at the sight and the feel of blood on my body. Most of them preferred to be taken before I could cleanse myself of the blood after a fight. Several times Crator had interrupted me in the change room, introducing wealthy young matrons who'd bribed him to bring them to me. They would strip themselves naked after he left and cry for me to take them on the spot, to hurt them and to be their master. I was, of course, too well mannered to refuse any of them, unless they were absolutely too ugly or too poor. I was fast learning to waste my juices on rich women; it was more profitable in the long run.

All things considered, I was doing well, but one thing was bothering me. Crator had made me throw a couple of no-death bouts due to the fact he had placed large bets against me. He laid the wagers through another to remain undetected. He needed the money, I suppose, but it irked me no end. Certainly, the man I was fighting knew what was taking place and was also aware that if he killed me when I fell Crator would see to it that he himself would not live much longer either. Though the money was good, and Crator was happy and grateful to me, I didn't like the feeling of lying on the sands looking up at the blade or trident of a man I knew I could easily have beaten.

After I was forced to throw a match, I usually went on an extended drunk, having many women, trying to drown the embarrassment of the loss. Crator, after I'd sobered up, would try to pacify me, telling me that it was only the ways of business, and that I was much too sensitive. It didn't help much, though he was right. I was too damned sensitive. But I liked winning.

Things went on pretty much in this manner until the eve of my next to last fight in Rome.

3

The night was warm, and the light breeze added a touch of coolness that was pleasing. I was feeling satisfied with myself over my performance that day in the Amphitheater of Flavian.

The kill had not been too difficult, but the man, a Dacian, had had spirit, and the contest had appeared to be a closer match than it actually had been. The mob, or the crowd in attendance I should say, were generous, and I had received a purse from the Games Master as a bonus.

This night I was out on the town. Several well-born ladies had sent me invitations, but I had put them off with word that I had suffered a severe muscle strain in the games.

I usually accepted such invitations, even if the ladies were a bit long in the tooth or as homely as the rear end of Ares, for they sometimes had influential friends or husbands who could make life miserable for those who took their invitations, amorous or otherwise, too lightly. Yes, miserable and oft-times dangerous.

But this night I was feeling good and taking my leisure. Darkness found me wandering through the streets, stopping first at one place and then another, having a drink here and sampling a pastry there. In one I was recognized by several fans, who hailed me over to their table and bought a couple of rounds. Even a few who'd been foolish enough to wager on my opponent came over and wished me well, saying that I had been lucky that day. Naturally, and good-heartedly, I agreed with them. It's unwise to allow them to think one wins too easily.

I finally had had my fill of wine and good fellowship and decided upon returning to my room near the circus. I was taking the Clivus Capitolinus, which passed close to the circus, and was near the Capitoline Gate when I heard the sounds of laughter from somewhere nearby. I could tell by the pitch of the voices that it was a group of young men, more than likely nobles returning to their palaces after a night on the town. I kept to myself in the shadows, deciding to wait until they had passed before leaving the darkness where I stood. I was a little drunk, but not so stupefied as not to know that young nobles who are also drunk can mean a lot of trouble for a slave, even if he is a respected gladiator. The wisest thing for me to do, I decided, was to be silent and hope they would ignore me if they saw me.

My eyes had adjusted to the darkness and I could make them out somewhat. One of those approaching, by the oddness of his gait, seemed familiar. It was still too dark to see their faces, but this one had a limp and I was certain I knew him, or of him as it were. There were three of them in all. Young men, wearing Greek-style tunics. Two of them, I could see, wore small swords at their belts, not much more than long thin daggers actually, but they could do the job if a man knew how to use them properly.

Then I was able to get a good look at the third man, the one who limped. I'd been correct in thinking that I'd seen him before. He had been in the stands near the Imperial Box during the games, and on several other occasions he'd come to the fighter's training areas to watch. It was Claudius, the stuttering and spastic brother of Germanicus, the adopted son of Tiberius.

I recall now thinking that they were foolish to be out alone this late at night, without slaves to carry torches to light their way and bodyguards. Even here, inside the walls, it was not uncommon for the unwary to be set upon by thieves and murderers.

It was about this time that I noticed a movement in the shadows near the south side of the Temple of Saturn, which I had just passed. As a slave I was not permitted to carry a weapon unless ordered to do so by my owner, but the men in the shadows were obviously armed, for I saw a glint of bare metal in their hands as they moved. I counted four of them in all as they hurled themselves on the three partygoers. I was certain that the assailants had not spotted me.

They had one of the young men down before he could even draw his toy blade. The other did manage to get his out and was making a fine effort, though it would be a futile one I knew. Claudius was trying to flee but was stumbling over his own feet as one of the street bullies reached for him.

I knew it would be wiser to mind my own business, but I have disliked bullies and their kind ever since the children of the streets would gang up on me. So, not listening to my better sense, I rushed out from the shadows and grabbed the nearest fellow by his tunic, striking him with my fist at the base of his neck. He went down; I had his weapon in my hand before he touched the stones of the street.

With his fish knife in my grasp I struck the one who had Claudius pinned to the ground in the small of the back, using the practiced cut that enters near the spine and severs the liver and kidneys in the same movement. He tried to scream but he could not. That particular cut also has the peculiar effect of paralyzing one instantly.

The other two assailants were having their problems with the young noble and his toothpick. I paired up with him, removing some of the pressure. About that time Claudius found his voice and began to yell for help at the top of his lungs, crying "Thieves! Murderers! Help!"

His shouting, combined with my presence on the scene, gave the two thieves all the reason they needed to break off the fight and run back into the shadows, heading for whatever holes they lived in.

When the rascals took flight, I turned to see if anything could be done for the young noble they had downed. Unfortunately, a straight thrust had taken out his windpipe. He lay face down and still, a mere boy.

The man at whose side I had fought so briefly grasped my shoulder and pulled me to my feet.

"Your name, man?" he demanded in the tone of one who was used to power and command. He had my attention immediately; it was Germanicus. I bowed, lowered my knife, and responded without hesitating, as a good slave should.

"I am Lucanus, Dominus."

"Lucanus? Is that all? Is there no more to your name than that?" His words were a bit slurred and I knew he was more than a little drunk. More than likely that was the reason he hadn't been able to finish the two thieves off alone. It was well known that Germanicus was a fine swordsman. He eyed me; we were about the same height.

"No, Lord. That is the only name I have."

He shook his head as if to clear it of the wine fumes, then smiled and nodded knowingly. "I know you. You're the gladiator. I have won more than a few denarii on you in my time. Lucanus the gladiator, eh?"

I acknowledged that it was so, and we both turned at a movement at our side. Claudius had found enough courage to get to his feet and look about him. Realizing now that he was unhurt and that his brother Germanicus was all right, he threw his arms around my neck and, while stuttering words of affection and gratitude, he kissed me wetly on both cheeks, much to my embarrassment. But, as I found out later, Claudius was known to be a sentimental type.

Having heard Claudius' cries for help, the Vigeles came upon us about then. They were a full squad of the Praetorians who took turns patrolling the streets of the city. Two of them carried torches that offered some light to the area. They were under the command of a Decurion who, when recognizing Germanicus in the light, saluted the young noble as if he were in the presence of Caesar himself.

The Decurion sent four of his men in search of the thieves who had dared attack one of the best-loved men of Rome. He assigned two others to escort Claudius to his home, and then turned his attention to me, eying the knife in my hand.

Germanicus, seeing the suspicion in the commander's eye, told him of my assistance, turning the Decurion's frown to a smile of admiration. The smile, I'm sure, was more for the benefit of Germanicus than me. He, the Decurion, chose to escort Germanicus to his home personally.

Before they left the scene, both Claudius and Germanicus promised me that I would hear from them. As they walked away, I overheard the Decurion bragging to Germanicus that he had served with the young man's father, Drusus, on the Rhine. He added that he'd been one of the few honored enough to escort Drusus' body part of the way back to Rome after his death. Truth or boast, I was not to know.

Only I and the corpse remained on the street. The fellow I had thumped on the back of the neck was on his way to the Mamertine prison, hands bound behind him, prodded in the ass by the sharp-pointed spear of a Praetorian.

Well, I thought then, waste not want not. As long as the others were out of sight, why not? I bent and searched the dead man, coming up with two silver denarii and three sesterces. All in all, not bad wages for a few moments' work. I had certainly done more for less in my time.

Who knew what would come of tonight's events? It was surely good fortune that had brought me to that particular place at that particular time tonight. Germanicus was well loved throughout all Rome, and his brother, Claudius, though he had no real power, did have the ear of many influential men, including Senators, Ediles and Praetors. Yes, it was a good feeling I had when I finally dropped off into a soft dreamless slumber. I looked forward to what the morrow might bring.

4

When I arose the following morning and finished my ablutions, I ate a handful of olives and bread soaked in olive oil for my breakfast. I didn't like to eat a lot before training. The morning held a bit of a chill as the mist came in off the Tiber, and I could smell the cooking fires of the outer city. It was going to be a good day. I wrapped my cloak about my shoulders, leaving only the sword arm free, more as a matter of habit than in expectation of danger, and walked the three short blocks to the circus.

As I walked, I was joined by several others who, like me, were permitted to live off the premises. Together we entered the gates just as the first rays of the sun started to burn off the mist, talking of who was to fight whom and when.

I left them to go their own ways and went straight in to the arena, now set up for today's arduous training session.

I didn't see Crator anywhere. That, in itself, was not unusual, but he hadn't been looking well lately, and I was a little concerned about him. He had a too great fondness for the fruit of the vine, and of late his color had worsened and his breathing had become more labored. I wished he would ease off the grape and had said as much, but he refused to listen to me—or anyone else he didn't have to, for that matter.

I began my day as usual, with a few exercises to stretch and limber the muscles, then commenced my run around the arena enjoying the feel of my body, of my legs reaching out for the ground and pushing it behind me. In running, I could let all my worries go, losing myself in the motion. Though the day was cool, I could feel the sweat starting to collect on my face and brow, and then on my chest. It tickled a bit when running down my chest and started cooling from the breeze created by my speed. I concentrated on breathing through my nose, controlling the amount of air I took in. I avoided breathing through the mouth; that always burns one up faster.

When I had completed enough laps to equal five miles I slowed to a walk and paced the arena for another two laps, letting my body and breathing settle back to normal. After all, they walked horses after a hard race and if it worked for them the technique should work for the human animal as well. It seemed to soothe me in thought as well.

Later, I sparred with some secutors, using weighted dulled swords and shields. We feinted and struck out, not really trying to hit each other but moving fast enough to develop our reflexes. None of us made any new or really tricky moves during practice. It is unwise to expose one's combat secrets to a sparring partner who may one day be an opponent in the arena.

I was sparring with a retiarius from Pannonia when I saw that Crator had finally arrived, and was just ducking out of sight. I blocked a thrust to the face from the retiarius's trident with my shield and signaled that I wished to stop the exercise. We saluted each other as a matter of courtesy, and I left the arena to find old Crator. On the way out, I was temporarily distracted by some fancy moves during the sparring of two retiarii directly off to my right. One of them was Aemillius of Pannonia, an acquaintance. As I watched, unnoticed, I realized that he was fast becoming good at his trade. I wondered how the two of us would fare if matched together. I knew somehow that the same thought must have occurred to him. I was higher rated than he, and if he should enjoy victory over me it would greatly enhance his standing. In fact, he was fast becoming too good. Aemillius was a naive enough young man now, but could prove to be dangerous to me in time if not stopped soon. I was confident that I could take him now, but if he had a few more fights and gained a little more practical knowledge he would be hard to deal with. He was, as I said, too good. Best to finish him off soon.

I decided to speak to Crator about it. Perhaps we could arrange it for the next munera. Aemillius was an auctoratius and actually didn't have to fight, but I thought he could be induced if I sparred with him a few more times and continued to leave small but not too obvious openings in my guard. The weaknesses I "revealed" should give him the incentive to agree to a contest.

Cammilus had said to me time and time again that more fights are won with the brain than the sword.

Crator was sitting behind his desk going over the accounts and cursing to himself, crying out for the gods to hear. How, he asked, was he expected to gather enough animals, maintain them, feed the slaves, and still have enough left to pay for troupes of gladiators from private schools to come here and fight? Inflation was eating up all his profits. He spoke of the profits from the arena as if they were his own. Actually, he just received a salary (and sometimes a bonus) for running the Flavian for the state. Of course he always received a little under the table from those who ran the concessions, but that was normal and expected.

Finally, he raised his florid face to look at me and reaching under his desk took out a towel, tossing it to me and saying, "Wipe down, you fool, I don't want you to catch a chill."

I did as he bade me and, when he so indicated, I took a seat across from him.

"How are you feeling today, Master?"

He squinted at me through puffy lids and rasped out, "How I feel is none of your affair. You take care of yourself, and I will do the same for me."

Properly chastened, I changed the subject. "I have been working out recently with Aemillius. He is coming along very well. When do you think he will be ready for a main event?"

Crator put his stylus down and looked at me. I could nearly see the wheels grinding in his brain trying to figure out what I was up to. He touched his fingertips together beneath his chin and looked directly at me through red-rimmed eyes. He must have been experiencing a hell of a hangover.

"What concern is it of yours?"

I waved the notion away. "No concern. I was merely making conversation. You are aware, though, that it has been quite a while since I had a match against a really good net man, and I think he deserves a chance to come up in the ratings."

Crator laughed. "Give him a chance? You're no fool. The only chance you'll give him is a chance for a spike in the brain, if you don't kill him first. Now, tell me the truth, why do you want to fight him?"

I grinned and wiped a bit more sweat from my face and bare arms.

"I think we can make a few coins if we do this right."

Crator gave me his full attention. "What do you mean by, if we do this right?"

I rose and looked outside his door to be sure that no one was close enough to hear our conversation. "As I said, he is good. Very good. But not good enough to take me right now. If I continue to spar with him, show him weak spots and openings, he will believe that he can get to me. And if he spots the weaknesses, so will others. We should be able to make a few bets in our favor that could turn us a good profit. Of course we both know that the odds will be on my winning, but we should be able to bring the points down a bit. Yes, I can take him now, but in a year I wouldn't be too sure. I would rather finish him off now than wait until there's a possibility it may be reversed. And, if I have to do it, why not make a profit?''

Crator chuckled from deep inside, his body quivering like a great jellyfish. He laughed, wiping tears from his eyes.

''I knew from the first time I laid eyes on you that in time you would bring this old heart both joy and profit. Yes, go ahead and play with him for the next few days. I'll see about arranging a fight. I think it best if I make sure his agent is present while you two are sparring. If he sees a couple of your mistakes, it's more than likely that he himself will propose a bout between the two of you. That would be best, if the offer came from him. That way there would be no suspicions about being set up. I love it! Go now, and prepare our piglet for the sacrifice.''

I bowed and left Crator to his accounts and schemings. I really was fond of the old thief. We had always understood each other.

When I returned to the training grounds, I saw that Aemillius was watching my approach. I gave a friendly wave and ignored him, going to the chopping post instead. I'd retrieved my sword and shield from the arms master on the way and commenced swinging practice.

I could feel Aemillius' eyes boring into my back and I really got into it, chopping with good solid blows that rattled my arm to the bone. To give him a little more confidence, I went into a series of strikes and counters with my shield. Several times, when I made a lung swing, I would drop my shield a bit, exposing my throat. After I had repeated the error a few times in my practice attacks, I saw him nod to himself. I knew he'd spotted it. The bait had been sniffed; now to see if he would take it.

He returned to his own exercises then, and I worked hard and earnestly until noon, when the heat became heavy and it was time to quit. Overtraining can make the muscles stiff and the reflexes slow.

I asked Crator for permission to go to the baths for massage and oiling, which he granted. He was in an expansive mood. The thought of a profit always brightened his day for him, and I was glad that I was able to bring him a little cheer.

I passed through the streets near the previous night's attack, then took the Via Flaminia past the Capitoline hill on my left and the Forum of Julius. I enjoyed the brisk walk in the sun. I passed several noble ladies and politicians being carried in litters; a couple of the ladies gave me a smile behind their veils.

I passed through the gate leading to the Campus Martius, where the Baths of Agrippa were located, next to the Pantheon. These had been constructed to honor the glorious dead of Rome. I enjoyed these baths more than some of the others, for slaves stoked furnaces of coal beneath the buildings. These furnaces heated the water that ran through pipes to the baths, so one could sit in comfort and let the steam cleanse his pores as well as his thoughts.

The baths were not normally open to slaves, but several categories were given special permission: actors, poets, musicians, philosophers, and gladiators. I assumed that they allowed us inside so that the noble guests would have something to talk about and amuse themselves with. But they kept the price high enough to keep out the riff-raff.

I entered through the marble portico between the tall columns of colored marble, adorned with carvings of the glory of Rome and Agrippa. Inside were many rooms, with waters of varying temperatures. Some barely escaped the boiling point and could turn one's hide into a red broiled-looking mass in a matter of moments. These I avoided, as I did the last room: the cold-water bath. I never could get used to jumping from a hot soak to a cold one, especially in winter. But I have heard many who swore to the beneficial effects it has on the system. For myself, I've never enjoyed anything cold.

The baths were not very crowded at this time of day, which was why I generally chose to come here at this hour. There were not more than a couple hundred people present. The baths could accomodate a thousand but that was a little close for me.

I saw several faces that I knew, a couple of Senators and a crowd of rich young men who spent their hours lying to each other, each pretending the others believed every word about his exploits. In one corner a group of men clustered about a philosopher, listening to things that only philosophers discuss and understand, with great intensity and many loud, meaningless words.

I passed one whose face I knew from the arena, but had never seen up close. The face was unscarred and handsome in a dark way, showing his mixed blood from his homeland. It was said that he was from Hippo Regia in Africa, sired by a Syrian father with Greek blood and an Arabian mother. His hair was cut short, curly and heavily oiled. His eyes were dark limpid pools, heavy-lidded as if he were always sleepy or tired. But the body that carried the sleepy-looking handsome head wasn't tired at all. He had strong wide shoulders, and a chest and waist with no trace of flab on them. Clean lines separated the muscles in his abdomen and chest. His arms looked strong enough to break the neck of one of the white sacrificial oxen of the Priests of Jupiter.

Niger Graecus! The premier gladiator of Rome!

He had a few scars on his handsome figure, just enough to set the hearts of women fluttering. If I had been a woman I think I would have opened my legs to him that day, right there on the spot. He carried himself like Mars Ultor, the Avenger. He was the most absolutely beautiful man I'd ever seen.

He nodded to me in recognition as I passed, smiling gently, easily. The confidence in his face gave my legs the feeling they had turned to water. He walked away then, with slow easy strides.

I wanted him! Not as a lover, but as an opponent. Then we would dance our dance of love and death. But I knew the time was not now. I was no more ready for him right now than Aemilius was ready for me. But the time would come. Finally I had a goal. An ultimate goal.

I wanted Niger the Greek!

A voice stuttering out my name brought me back to reality. It was Claudius, touching my arm.

"L . . . L . . . L . . . Lucanus!" He finally got it out of his mouth and tugged me away with him. "I tried to reach you at the Flavian, but your master said you had come here, s . . . s . . . so I came to find you and thank you again for the service you rendered me and my brother last night. Is there anything we may do for you in return?"

I was tempted to ask for money but decided that the best way to take advantage of my good fortune was to be modest and ask for nothing. That way I might, in the long run, receive more benefits than by making a specific request. I answered him humbly.

"No, thank you, Dominus, you owe me nothing. I consider it my duty and a pleasure that I was able to come to your aid last evening."

I followed Claudius as he limped into the baths. We handed our clothing over to a slave and he gave us a brass token with a number on it in exchange. Claudius was wearing a toga, which only citizens held the right to wear, and told the slave to put my thin blue tunic with his garment.

As we entered, Claudius at my arm, mutters and whispers rose among the other bathers. I heard my name several times, along with those of Claudius and Germanicus and assumed that the story of our adventure the previous evening was making the rounds.

Several prominent men came to me and thanked me, loudly bemoaning the fact that the streets of the city were no longer safe from common thieves and ruffians. Claudius was polite, and I was properly modest. When we were finally able to extract ourselves from them, Claudius led me into the steam room. We located an empty corner on the benches of fine pink-streaked marble and lolled there, taking deep breaths of the aromatic vapors. The hot moisture seemed to relax him somewhat, and his stuttering eased a bit. He took his time, thinking before speaking, forming his mouth before talking.

"Lucanus, my brother and I must do something for you. Tell me, do you think that your master, Crator, would sell you to us?"

I was a little shocked by his question. "I seriously doubt it. Why would you wish to purchase a gladiator?"

Claudius smiled and wiped his slightly drooling mouth of sweat and spittle. "Why, to set you free of course."

That statement really set me back. *Free?* To be a freedman? I was sure that Crator meant to give me my freedom sometime in the future; when we had talked of it, he'd always told me that I was yet too inexperienced to go out into the world on my own, and that I was better off with him having the responsibility over me. I think he believed at least part of what he said, but I'm sure the other side of the coin was that I made a lot of money for him. I must also add that he was setting aside part of the money I earned in contests and was depositing it in the banking houses under my own name, to be given to me on the day I received my papers of manumission or won the rudis, whichever came first.

More than anything else, Crator wanted for me to win

my freedom in the arena. He took a great deal of pride in me and felt responsible for my accomplishments, almost as much as would a father. For my part, I held as much affection for the old sot as I could have for anyone, and even though I was a slave he never gave me reason to feel like one. He allowed me many special privileges, even to having my own room; he trusted me, and that meant a lot.

Even if I were free, I doubted that my existence would be altered much. I was still a fighter, and the arena was the only way I knew of making a living. True, I could always find employment as a personal bodyguard, but there was no chance at any real money doing that, and when I got old there would be nothing for me to live on. Rome is only kind to her poor if they are citizens. They at least receive the daily dole of grain and the donations granted by the Senate in order to buy their votes. For slaves, and for non-citizens, there is only the prospect of hard labor from dawn to dusk for barely enough food to keep the life force inside one's fleshy shell.

With all this in mind I answered Claudius: "Dominus, I doubt if Crator would sell me, though it's true that he has a love of gold that is second to none."

Claudius grasped my hand, squeezing it, not effeminately but as a friend would do. He whispered to me in the manner of a conspirator. "There are ways to force your owner to sell, Lucanus. He holds his present position as Games Master as an appointment and favor of s . . . s . . . state, and Germanicus and I, as nephews of Augustus, have the ear of state. If we wish it, he will sell you to us I'm sure. What say you?"

I was silent for a time, breathing deep of the steam, then made my decision. "Thank you, Dominus, for your consideration, but I have an agreement with Crator and besides I happen to like the old man. But if the time should come when I am ready to be a freedman, may I then call on you for assistance?'' I watched his eyes then, and he nodded in earnest.

''Of course,'' he said. ''We do not forget those who do us service so easily. We are in your debt, and I feel that my family will someday have need of your strong arm. Until the time that you yourself make the decision we shall remain in your debt and call you our friend, though I cannot understand why anyone should choose to stay a s . . . s . . . slave, I must confess. Call on me whenever you wish. Though I am not a rich man, between Germanicus and myself we can usually arrange things to our liking.''

With that, our conversation drifted to other matters, particularly things dealing with the arena. Claudius, I found to my satisfaction, was a true fan of the arena and knew most of the great fighters by name and could call off their victories without pause. To my great surprise, he also knew of my record of wins. He smiled at my astonishment and said: ''Between the two of us, after last night's incident I went to the trouble of looking up your record in the c . . . c . . . circus files. I believe you have the makings of a champion as soon as you get your full strength and size.''

I knew what he meant by that. Though I was nearly twenty, it would be yet a few more years before my body thickened and matured to its maximum; to the best balance of strength and mobility. I had already decided that in two more years I would be ready to take on Niger the Greek, and told Claudius of my decision. He clapped his hands and laughed with delighted pleasure.

''Oh! That is a fight I must certainly see. Do you really think you will be able to take him? Oh, my word, wait until Germanicus hears of this news. I must tell you, Lucanus, he knew your name and reputation before I did, not that your name was actually unfamiliar to me, but Germanicus is a fine swordsman himself and had spotted your talent and potential much earlier. You know he is quite taken with you, don't you? He would have come to see you today, but his duties prevented him. He asked that I pass on his gratitude and regards. The offer I made you previously comes from both of us, I assure you."

I was, of course, very pleased and honored to have members of Augustus' own household take an active kindly interest in me.

Claudius changed the subject back to the projected fight with the Greek. "You know, of course, that a fight between you and the Greek could be a good thing for you in more ways than one?" He looked at me slyly, half-closing one eyelid. He most likely thought it made him look sinister. "You're aware, I'm sure, that if you should kill the Greek Niger you could just possibly win the rudis, right?"

Up to now I had not thought that far ahead. He was right. If the fight were good and I'd achieved enough of a reputation by then, it was most certainly a possibility, especially if the fight received the proper promotion beforehand and I was considered the underdog.

We left the steam room and went to the massage area. It was pleasant lying there on the table, the strong hands of specially trained slaves kneading and twisting my muscles and joints until they felt as if they would drop off. As always, it was quite painful at first, then, as the tendons and muscles began to loosen and relax, the pain would subtly change to a feeling of almost sensuous pleasure.

A good massage always took the better part of an hour and, after we were finished with that, we returned quickly to the baths for a soak and an oiling; afterwards slave attendants scraped our bodies with copper blades, removing the dirt that had been forced from the pores by the steam and oil.

By this time my body tingled deliciously from head to toe, and I was more than pleased with the day, especially when Claudius insisted on paying for everything. I'd intended on paying for myself with the silver denarius that I'd removed from the thief I'd killed the previous evening. Now that Claudius had paid, I decided to spend it on a good clean girl instead. I'd had my eye on one who lived over the market near the Tiber, outside the wall of Tullius.

Outside the baths, I bade farewell to Claudius. He shook my hand warmly, wishing me well, and told me that I would hear from him again soon.

Ahhhhh! Yes! I was definitely in an expansive mood. Then, as I turned to go, I saw Niger Graecus, surrounded by a flock of admiring ladies. He caught my eye and smiled. I could have sworn he knew exactly what was on my mind; he knew of the ruse I had planned for Aemillius and was considering using it on me. That thought took a bit of the pleasure out of the rest of my afternoon, but not enough to prevent me from spending my denarius on the pleasures of Venus that evening. The girl proved more than satisfactory and herself seemed sated when I left her at dawn.

5

When I arrived at the circus the next morning, Crator was already there. One of the other fighters told me he had shown up before dawn and, after checking my rooms, had demanded to know where I was, cursing my name as though he was fit to be tied.

When he saw me, I thought he was going to try and club my brains out, but he only shouted and frothed at the mouth a bit. "Why did you not tell me about rescuing Germanicus and his brother? Where in Hades have you been? Do you know that I have been checking that miserable hovel of yours all night, worried about you, thinking that friends of those ruffians had killed you and thrown your worthless body in the Tiber? Have you no consideration for me at all?"

He was so mad that he was stammering worse than Claudius. I tried to interject an explanation, but was quickly told to keep my stupid mouth closed unless I had something of value to say, and, he added, he seriously doubted that. He finally burned out his madness and settled down enough for me to give him the entire story, including what had happened at the baths the day before. I didn't mention Claudius' offer to purchase me, but I told him everything else, even up to seeing Niger the Greek.

Crator trembled with excitement, his eyes hot in his head as he called for wine. He gulped down two entire bowls without adding his usual water to weaken it.

"This is fantasic. Don't you understand what you've done you, young fool? You've made yourself a name the easy way. The price for you will double now, possibly even triple. You already have a good start in the ratings, but this is the best publicity that we could have hoped for. Both Germanicus and Claudius, the nephews of Augustus Caesar himself! They will personally see that you are placed in the most important events and at the best possible money. The mob will also be watching you, boy. Please, please do not waste this opportunity. Hold your head and we are made men, set for life. I may even be able to give up this pigsty job that is only fit for a butcher of swine and buy myself a proper farm and live like a man of quality."

He raised hell with me for a few more minutes, questioning me on everything that was said in the baths. Afterwards he told me to take my lazy ass out of his sight and get to training. There was no time to spare, he added.

I did as ordered. When I arrived at the training area I noticed that Aemillius had company. A prosperous-looking man of middle age, with a paunch and thinning hair. He wore expensive clothes and was accompanied by a body servant. He was, I assumed, the agent of Aemillius.

I went quickly into my routine, committing the same

error as before, leaving an occasional opening in my guard. I did it twice in one set, then no more. I didn't want them to think me so stupid as to commit the mistake all the time; that would have been too obvious. Just often enough to gain their interest.

Later, the agent approached Crator to talk. The two of them had the same look of greed in their eyes. I could always tell when Crator thought he had sucked someone in. And now, as they usually did when he made the coup, his eyes nearly disappeared into their folds of puffy tissue as he rose and took the man's hand. He motioned me over to join them and introduced me.

"Lucanus, this is Cornelius Gaius, the agent of Aemillius the retiarius. He wishes to arrange a contest between yourself and his man."

I said nothing in reply, merely bowed my head in acceptance of the order. Crator warned me to stay off the streets that night and stay in for rest, and dismissed me.

Actually, it had been my intention to stay in anyway. The young wench of the night before had been more energetic than I had anticipated. With that, and the strain of this day's training, I was more than ready for a good night's sleep.

On the way to my room, I came across some men from the market area. They informed me that the surviving attacker of Germanicus and Claudius had been questioned by the interrogators of Augustus himself. What he had divulged to them my informants did not know, but they did say there was hardly enough of his body left for the executioner to work with. Even now, they said, his body was on display at the Stairs of Mourning. After being publicly displayed there, on the stone steps leading from the Tiber up to the streets, the body had been dragged down to the Tiber and thrown in.

I wondered, as did my informants, what the interrogators had learned from the man before he'd been killed.

That he had talked there was no doubt; the inquisition team of Augustus had techniques that gave my own tough gut the shakes just to consider them.

I said goodbye to my newsbringers and went on to my rooms. The day was drawing short; I lit the lamp, lying down to watch the shadows flickering on my walls, half awake, half dreaming.

A gentle tapping at my door brought me out of my half slumber.

I asked who was there.

"It is I, Germanicus!" came the answer.

Quickly I unbarred the door and showed him inside, somewhat embarrassed at his presence in my poor surroundings. He was wearing the full toga this time; the purple border showing his rank seemed terribly out of place in my humble and squalid room. He pretended not to notice my pathetic quarters, and politely asked for permission to speak to me. I was stunned. The noble Germanicus asked for permission to speak to me? I could only answer in stuttering fashion, sounding much like Claudius I supposed.

"W . . . Wh . . . Why, yes, of course, Dominus. Anything you wish."

Germanicus motioned for me to sit on the bed. I did so as he moved the terra cotta lamp over on my table and, placing one hip on the edge of the table, rested himself in that position. I prayed silently to Jupiter that it would not break under his weight. I had no chair for him.

Germanicus was as nobly handsome a man as I had ever seen. But his bearing was that of true nobility and he wore his richness as one would a cloak of wool. He was a truly gracious and unassuming man, not out of necessity but out of his nature.

"I have come to see you," he began, "to offer my thanks personally, and to give you a warning." His voice was pleasant, and his pronunciation made me ashamed of my street accent.

"A warning, Dominus?" I was confused at this.

He nodded. "Yes, a warning. The man who survived two nights ago was not merely a thief of the streets. He and his friends were hired to assassinate my brother and myself. They really wanted only me dead. Claudius and Aeneus Caelia were their secondary targets and were to die only if they prevented my death or called too loudly for aid."

I stared wonderingly at him, wanting to ask him who could possibly want the son of Nero Drusus dead, but I held my tongue, waiting for him to continue.

"The man didn't know those who'd hired him, though I have my suspicions. But you, Lucanus, have interfered with their plans, possibly placing yourself as a target now. I merely wanted to warn you of the possibility so that you could be on the alert. Those who wish me dead are no concern of yours, and the less you know of them the better off you shall be. But keep your eyes open."

This was my first intimation of the deadly intrigues of the court, and I didn't like it. Killing in the arena as an honorable fighter was one thing, but a knife in the back or a poisoned cup . . . .

Even under these circumstances, Germanicus had the ability to make me feel at ease with him. He was only a few years older than myself, but he moved and spoke with such confidence and authority that he seemed years my senior. He was a born leader of men, I thought as we talked, and I knew that must be the reason so many were devoted to him.

We talked of many things that evening. I learned more about the real world in those few hours then I had absorbed in my first twenty years. He seemed to have a sincere interest in making me aware of the ways of his world, for what purpose I was to find out much later. I knew that Germanicus had a reason for everything he did;

not that he could be considered selfish, because he had a reputation for loyalty and devotion to his friends and the common man.

When Germanicus left me, I had the distinct feeling that drastic changes were to take place in my life soon. Why else would all these sudden and unexplained events be coming together?

It was late when sleep finally claimed me, but even then it was a restless slumber, with strange dreams. Eagles were flying; one of them, the strongest and proudest, flew high above the rest. It swooped downward suddenly to drink from the cupped hands of a man whose face I could not see. He stood proudly, a laurel wreath resting on his brow, allowing the mighty bird to sate itself. Then, all of a sudden, the eagle flew off again to climb high into the air, resuming its place above the others. Then its wings began to flutter desperately, as if they were broken. With a sad cry it plummeted heavily to the earth, to lie dead at the foot of the man wearing the wreath.

I awoke in a cold damp sweat. The dream bothered me, though I knew not its meaning.

With some relief I found that my life settled back into familiar patterns in the next days. But it wasn't long until Crator came to me, saying that the fight with Aemillius would take place during the next festival celebrating the rites of Saturn, the god of harvests. This was good. During the Saturnalia the mob was always in a generous humor. At this festival merriment rules all Rome. Even slaves are allowed unusual liberties. They can even make sport of their masters without fear of reprisal, or at least they are supposed to be able to. It is the rule also that in the span of Saturnalia, wars cannot be declared nor can criminals be executed. Schools are closed, presents are exchanged, and the whole of Rome goes on a wild and drunken spree of gaiety and fun.

It would be a good time to meet Aemillius on the sands.

It would also give Crator time to leak the word that Aemillius had found a chink, so to speak, in my armor. Before the fight we should be able to get the odds of my winning lowered a good deal, perhaps even to one-to-one instead of the two- or three-to-one we would have initially expected to give.

For the next two months, Crator entered me only in contests which were not to the death. He didn't wish to chance my being injured before the Saturnalia. I continued to train as always, watching Aemillius and making sure that he observed the ever-present weakness in my defense. I went to the trouble of dropping my shield during one of my no-kill contests, for I knew that he or his agent would be watching. One had to be careful not to spook his quarry.

Germanicus came to visit me twice in this period, and Crator nearly fell over himself at the honor being shown me. Claudius, too, came around more often. We went to the baths several times together and once to the theater, which I did not enjoy very much. The play was a Greek thing, written a thousand years ago, and made no sense to me at all. The actors, at least to my mind, were stiff and dull. They carried masks in their hands, mounted on sticks, and in mid-sentence would raise one or another to the face to show the changing of emotions and feelings during the acts. I was bored, but Claudius and the rest of the audience gave them an enthusiastic ovation. Claudius even had tears in his eyes. I assumed that the theater was something one had to develop a taste for.

One evening at dinner, at the home of Claudius, when the two of us were alone, I decided to let him in on the ruse I'd pulled on Aemillius and his agent. He laughed until I thought he would have a seizure or stroke. He loved a good joke and besides, it would give him a chance to make a lot of money if he wagered on me. Showing a friend how to make a profit was always profitable in return, it seemed to me, and would strengthen the ties between us. He gave me a good slap on the shoulder after dessert, saying that he would make enough from this fight alone to last him through the upcoming year. I wasn't worried about his losing and being angry with me afterwards; after all, if I lost I would not be around. This was to be a fight to the death.

Aemillius was fairly popular with the crowds and my death would give his career a strong boost, should it come about. I was certain he would go for a death blow before the mob even had a chance to give the sign of life or death; I would do the same in his position. I thanked Claudius for the meal, he thanked me for the tip, and we said goodnight.

The next weeks passed swiftly as the preparations for the munera got underway. There would not be many combats during this celebration, for all entertainment was supposed to remain light in Saturnalia. Most of the acts would be jugglers, or clowns and animal shows. Lotteries would be held with prizes that ranged from free food and slave girls to handsome villas that could even be won by the lowest members of Roman society, if Fortuna smiled upon them.

The most popular event, next to the combats, would probably be, as it had in the past, the bull dancers brought over from Crete. Their act reached far back in time to the half-man, half-bull monster called Minotaur. These young men and women, specially chosen for their beauty, would place themselves in the ring with wild and fierce bulls, darting and teasing while they eluded the ferocious charges. The nimblest dancer would stand in position until the final approach of the bull, or even sometimes run to meet him, and when the bull lowered his head to gore, the dancer would grab the horns, allowing the upward movement of the head to toss him high into the air and over his back, landing acrobatically on his feet behind the bull, teasing him again into a new charge. A few of them had even mastered the art of landing upright on his back and riding him around the ring before jumping off. Only once had I seen one go down. A young girl of perhaps fourteen, with golden hair and barely budding breasts, had lost her footing on a piece of intestine that the ring attendants had overlooked and the bull had gored her straight through the chest, raising her high in the air and prancing around the ring with her body limp and intact on his horns. The crowd had naturally loved it.

I was becoming quite disappointed with the tastes of the crowd. Crator had told me that since his time the crowds was degenerating, and no longer seemed to appreciate athletic fitness and agility. Talent no longer was applauded; they only desired blood. I'm sorry to say that he was correct. But there were still some who could appreciate style and technique in the arena.

On the morning the festival began, the entire population of Rome seemed to wait on the streets for the procession of the gods from the Temple of Saturn.

I was there when the Priests of Saturn came out onto the steps of their temple. They commenced the rites by sacrificing an oxen from their own herd, removing its liver to examine it for omens. Several acolytes waved branches of oak and olive around them and swung braziers of smoking incense. The omens were pronounced favorable, and the procession began. Twenty Priests of Saturn led another, pure white ox by a rope of flowers around its neck, followed by statues of the gods and a larger-than-life-sized statue of Augustus in full armor, wearing the decorations and awards from his many battles.

Augustus' statue was placed directly behind the one of Saturn in the procession, befitting his position not only as Emperor but as Pontifex Maximus and the father of his nation. Augustus personally made a brief appearance to welcome the rites of Saturn and, from his balcony window, warned the young people to conduct themselves with dignity and decorum during the coming days.

The parade, gathering more followers at every corner, reaching finally the Via Sacra and the Temple of the Vestals.

I was never a particularly religious man; I preferred to depend on my own personal strength to survive. I did pay homage occasionally to Fortuna and Mars when I thought my luck needed a little changing. After all, what could it hurt? But, like the majority of the populace, I had a respect for the Vestal virgins that went far beyond mere admiration for their religious devotion. They were the essence of all that was good in Rome. Their history reached back into the dim mists of antiquity, to the very founding of the city itself. The mother of Romulus and Remus was a Vestal, and Aeneus the Trojan hero personally had selected the first girls to be admitted to the cult.

The life of a Vestal is not an easy one. The candidates are selected when they are between the ages of six and ten years. Their training requires a period of ten years; another ten years is spent in observing their performance of the designated duties: tending the eternal flame at the altar of Vesta, bringing water from the fountain of Egeria, and acting as the guardians of wills and other important documents entrusted to their care by members of the nobility. They are also entrusted with the care of the sacred Palladium, a magnificent statue of the goddess Athena in the Temple of Vesta. They are then required to spend a third decade in the teaching of novices. After thirty years, they are free to leave the order if they so wish, even to marry, but during their service they must remain celibate and avoid the attentions of men.

At all public events, they are given special places of honor. In court it is not necessary that they swear to tell the truth before testifying; their word is sufficient. The penalty for offending a Vestal is to be stoned to death on the spot. If a Vestal should ever break her vows, she is stripped of her sacred robes and placed in a tomb with a bed, wine, water, and oil; then the tomb was sealed forever. It is said that in the more than seven hundred years of their order only eight virgins have been convicted of breaking the vows. They are truly a remarkable group of women. One other point of interest: should a criminal on his way to his execution meet a Vestal, she can pardon him on the spot. It is said that Vestals have arranged to meet several condemned men in this manner when they've disagreed with the court's decision as to his guilt, or even the Emperor's condemnation. Their pardons for the condemned are never questioned.

When the Saturnalian procession arrived at their temple, the Vestals came out to join them, wearing their usual robes of pure white. They bestowed blessings on those present, took their position, and walked in stately steps behind the statues of the gods, all the time chanting sweetly the blessings of their goddess upon the crowd.

The procession circled the grove of Vesta while attractive young girls tossed flowers from their baskets into their path. Musicians played on their flutes, lyres, and cymbals, providing music for another group of beautiful young female dancers. They passed the Basilica of Sempronius, finally reaching the Field of Mars, where a public feast was to be held, the food and drink plentiful and paid for by the Senate.

I left them there and returned to my room. This day there would be no combat events. These would occur two days later, after the crowd had become bored with the antics of clowns, acrobats and actors and needed something stronger to excite them. Then Aemillius and I would do our part.

This is not to say that I missed the pleasures of the festival the first days. Certainly I took advantage of the passionate feelings that several ladies, both slave and well-born, desired to show me. For during this time all were permitted, as I previously stated, to do things that would normally have been considered unrespectable. I took my pleasure with a choice few of them, but I avoided the wine. I did not want my senses and reflexes dulled.

I differed with Crator on the subject of women. He was adamant that a fighter should not have intercourse for at least ten days prior to a fight. He thought that it sapped a man's vital juices. Ten days? If I passed ten days without a woman, my back would surely break out in sores and rashes. Besides, women helped me tremendously to relax, if I didn't overdo things. However, I did leave most of the exercise during copulation up to the ladies, while I lay back and enjoyed their tender attentions.

Then it was the day of the combats.

6

Today there would be twenty pairs of fighters. Most of them were veterans, brought in specifically for the occasion. I was pleased; this would be a series of contests for those who appreciated talent and good technique. I noticed that four pugilists, from Thrace and Syria, would fight today, wearing the standard lead-weighted gloves, wrapped in strips of leather and set with small brass spikes at the knuckles. This was one event that I was glad I had not been trained for. Few pugilists survived many years in the arena with all their brains intact. If not killed by a smashing blow to their temple, most ended up as vegetable-like simpletons who had difficulty finding their way to the arena.

As was my custom, I took no food, other than a bowl of boiled barley, dressed and left for the Flavian. I was hailed several times on my route by spectators coming to line up for their seats, waiting for the ivory tokens that would designate their places. The numbers on the tokens were also good for prizes to be drawn during the intermissions. They shouted as I walked: "Give it to him, little wolf! I'll give you a percentage of my winnings!"

I'd heard that before, and they were not promises I would hold my breath on. Others of the crowd, those in favor of Aemillius, would cry that I should cede the match before it started, that I was overmatched, that I was dog meat. Why, they would ask, did I not just simply lie down and die and save their hero the trouble of killing me?

I took their jibes good-naturedly enough, but affected a worried expression, hoping that word of my apprehension would get around and drive up the odds in favor of Aemillius. I knew that Crator had not laid too many bets as of yet, only enough to reduce suspicion. He'd wait as long as he could before laying the real money out through intermediaries.

The crowd was thick by the time I reached the participants' entrance, going temporarily blind as I entered the darker interior of the Flavian. Unseeingly, I bumped into someone, muttering, "Excuse me!"

The one I'd bumped laughed easily, the voice vaguely familiar. "That's all right, little wolf. If that's the hardest you shall ever hit me, it's no matter of concern."

My eyes adjusted and I turned. It was Niger Graecus. Damn! His manners were as pretty as his face. Always courteous and gentle in manner to all, at least until he faced you on the sands. There he would cut your throat with the same easy style.

He spoke again, his words pleasant and full of concern. *Concern my ass!* "Lucanus, it is good to see you again. I was pleased to hear of your good fortune in gaining the friendship of Germanicus and Claudius. One does need friends in this life. By the way, good fortune today, but let me warn you," he winked knowingly. "You should watch that bad habit you've lately developed of allowing your shield to drop. It could get you into serious trouble should it occur at the wrong time."

He smiled the same sweet and even white-toothed grin that dripped with sincerity and walked off, speaking back over his shoulder. "You know, we must have lunch together sometime soon."

When he hit the streets outside, I could hear the cheers of the mob. He was well loved by the crowd. But right now, I was more concerned with his statement about me dropping my shield. He'd been watching me while I used my ploy on Aemillius. *Had he told Aemillius about it?* If he had, then I was in trouble, for Aemillius could easily turn the knowledge of my ruse against me.

I was still brooding about this turn of events when I entered the change room to get ready. Graecus was as smart as he was handsome. I wasn't sure whether my feelings toward him were those of hatred or jealousy.

I was fitting the arm straps that held the mesh of steel rings from the shoulder to the wrist of my sword arm as Crator entered. A slave was helping me; if they were too tight, they could cut off the circulation, leaving the sword arm numb and lifeless.

Crator was perspiring profusely, probably from the walk across the city to the Arena of Flavius. He set a good-sized package on the table. Grunting loudly, he sat himself down on the only stool in the room and wiped his forehead with his already wet and stained handkerchief. I dismissed the slave, certain that he wanted privacy.

"Lucanus," he wheezed, "this could be a great day for us both. The word has spread far and wide that Aemillius has found a weakness in your style and will more than likely upset you. The odds have just passed from our favor to his, and we are now getting three to five on Aemillius' victory. With any luck at all, we should be able to earn us over three hundred gold aurei—sufficient to buy a fine house, staff it with servants and live well for at least a year, in complete luxury, mind you.'' He was more than elated and I could easily see why.

This day's fight could bring me not only the one hundred denarii that I received for fighting, but also one-third of the bets we would collect afterwards. I would earn at least one hundred aurei more—two thousand five hundred denarii—for a few minutes' work. If all went well for me.

Crator picked up the package he'd brought along and opened it. He gently removed a set of silver-embossed leg greaves to wear over my boots and handed them to me. He then took out a matching stomach belt of black leather, set with the same designs as the greaves: silver gladiators. I was surprised at this unexpected generosity, but not for long. He informed me that he had borrowed them and must return them after the fight, and I was to be sure not to mess them up in any way, shape, form or fashion. One thing about Crator, he never changed. He was always cheap. At least I could depend on him to remain consistent.

Other fighters entered to prepare themselves for the events. Several of them I knew, and we wished each other good fortune. I'm sure that some of you find it difficult to understand how men who may have to kill each other one day, can be amiable companions and talk thus casually. To us, it is simple enough. Inside the arena we all have a job to do, and personalities seldom enter into it. We only do what is necessary to get the job accomplished. Outside the arena? Let it suffice to say that we leave our work inside, on the sands, and when not working we cherish no thought of maiming or killing each other.

The room was becoming crowded as others entered, including a couple of the pugilists slated for the events. They were to go on early. As I left the room, two lanistas were giving their personal fighters last-minute instructions.

I walked slowly down to the gates that would allow me

to enter the arena. I could hear the crowd above me. There was always a strange and eerie feeling to the mob as they settled into their seats. Forty thousand avid and anxious voices, each with their own private needs of the day, like us in competition with each other.

I flexed my arms, trying to get the feel of the shoulder guards, ascertaining that they were in proper place and would not bind up on me later. It was for this purpose that I usually dressed earlier than the rest. It was better to find out if one's attire fit correctly before entering the arena. It could go hard on you if it proved wrong later.

7

I was standing at the gate watching the crowds, contemplating the upcoming fight with Aemillius and the worrisome warning of Graecus, when Crator came up to me. His face was now even sweatier than it had been earlier. His voice was anxious.

"Have you seen the line on the billing?"

I had, of course, checked it, and I was aware that we were to go on last as the main event. Due to my recent notoriety in the Germanicus affair, I had not been surprised. He mopped his face again with the same wet handkerchief, eyes bulging out; he appeared to be having chest pains.

"No, you dolt! I mean the *new* lineup!" He seemed angry. I asked him what he meant.

"Graecus is going to fight today, fool. You've been pushed back to second from last. Now you are no more than a warm-up exhibition for the Greek."

Gods, how that enraged me! The smooth-talking, illegitimate offspring of a Syrian whore had upstaged me! This was to be my event and mine only. No wonder that he'd been so polite to me earlier. I complained about the unfairness of it to Crator. He agreed with me, but said angrily that there was absolutely nothing we could do about it. I supposed he was right. He'd learned that Graecus had arrived early and told the Games Master that he wished to fight and would do it for half his normal fee. He had obtained a contract with a worthy opponent, the Greek champion of the thraces, Myrio Claitor. How could the Games Master have passed up such an offer, Crator asked me. Graecus only fought once or twice a year and was a big draw. The master had agreed willingly and greedily, and now I had second billing to the Greek bastard.

I was in such a rage that I'd failed to hear the trumpets sound the first event, and I was suddenly nudged aside by the first group of fighters on their way out to the sands. I was still standing and grumbling when the event was over and the fighters left the arena. Two of them were wounded badly; one was dead, being dragged from the arena by slaves wielding meat hooks; and one stood, bleeding, bathing in the applause and cheers of the mob.

The next group on the lineup were the pugilists from Greece and Syria. I had calmed down by then; it wouldn't do to enter a fight while in a rage. It was a fatal mistake to let emotions rule your mind in combat. I took in a deep breath, holding it for a moment, then released it slowly, easing the shaking in my arms and legs. I felt better, more relaxed.

I looked out to center arena, my face half in the sun and half shadowed, concentrating on the pugilists and their clumsy pounding at each other. One pair had no technique at all, merely attempting to bash each other's brains out of the skull, which, as I watched, one did to the other. The Syrian had caught the Greek with a full swing of his spiked and weighted glove square on the temple. I was approximately fifty meters away from them, but still heard clearly the sound of the Greek's skull cracking like an eggshell. When they carried his body from the sands, I saw that the force of the Syrian's blow had been so great that the entire left side of the loser's head was a grey, gelatinous pulp. I wished silently that it had been Graecus that they carried.

The two remaining pugilists had more style. They were sparring now, cautiously feeling each other out, throwing blows now and then but without any real intent behind them. Their caution made sense to me, but the mob started giving catcalls, wanting them to get on with the action, crying out for them to model themselves after the first two. The stupidity of the mob's demands assured me that I'd been correct: the crowds knew nothing about talent and technique and only desired to see blood. These two were much better than the others and would have turned them into birdfood if they'd been so matched. But the audience desired blood and thought that the more blood let, the better the fighter. *Stupid swine!*

Soon the two pugilists, in spite of knowing that their style was correct, were forced to step up their pace before they were ready, and their calculated attacks and defenses were soon deteriorating into no more than the same slugfest that had preceded them.

Their gloves were soon red and sticky with blood, their naked bodies streaked with sweat and blood mingling as they flowed. Each had severe marks on his ribcage. The ribs of the Syrian were sunken deeply in on his right side, under the lungs, where a heavy blow had crushed several. He retaliated now by taking off the Greek's left ear with his spikes. I admired them both, for their endurance and fortitude. They stood toe to toe at the last, both exhausted, bleeding from a dozen or more crippling wounds, still taking turns at braining each other. One would swing and then the other. They were so tired that they could barely raise their arms now. They leaned on each other, resting. Suddenly the Syrian dropped backwards, allowing the Greek's own weight to pull him forward and off-balance. As he fell, he was met by a full arm swing that I'm certain carried the Syrian's last reserves of strength. The blow came up directly beneath the Greek's chin. The bone collapsed in on itself. Teeth and splinters of bone adhered to the Syrian's spiked gloves as he dropped his arms heavily to his sides. The Greek dropped to the bloody sands as if he'd been poleaxed.

The Syrian was hailed as the victor; the Greek was carried from the arena, his face a ruined mess. He would never fight again. As the Syrian stood accepting the cheers of the crowd, there was no sense of elation on his face, only a sad look of regret and loss. I learned why later. They had been lovers for some time.

After the pugilists' bouts I went back inside. I wanted to get some rest before I was called. I told Crator again that I wanted Niger Graecus, and I wanted him damned soon. He knew it was my temper and not my good sense talking, and he merely shook his head, saying firmly that a fight with the Greek right now was out of the question; he would eat me alive. Perhaps, he said, in a year or so, I would be ready for him. He was right, I knew, but still my ego had been severely damaged. I figured that Graecus had done this deed only to rile me into challenging him too early, before I was ready. The same thing I was doing to Aemillius, setting me up. If he could get me to fight him now his victory was assured, but if I waited, it would be anyone's guess as to who would win. He was deliberately provoking me, and now that I realized it, I would settle down. I'd wait until the time was right for me. I might be able to push the calendar up a bit if I trained hard and used the time wisely. I told Crator to leave me, I needed to be alone for awhile. He left me without question.

By the time the slave arrived to fetch me for my event, I was completely relaxed, except for the usual butterflies in the stomach, and these I always experienced prior to going on.

8

As I went to procure my weapon and shield, I could tell by the muted screams beyond the hall doors that the wounded were now being tended by the arena physicians. I cringed a bit for them. It seemed to me that in this modern age they could find a better method of treating a wound than merely placing a red-hot iron on it, or pouring burning pitch on the stump of a hand to seal it. It was too painful to contemplate.

I spotted Aemillius in the hall. He was ready, trident in hand and short knife in his belt. He wore a round, steel, skullcap-style helmet. All of his gear was new and shiny, a gift from his agent most likely, to make him look better for the event. I wondered where Graecus was. Probably eating grapes from the hands of one of his lovers, bored with the idea of another contest.

I pushed him from my mind, taking my sword from the Arms Master, hefting it twice to gain its feel. I changed things a bit by opting for a lighter shield, one of the small round ones with the steel boss in the center. It was about twice the size of a discus. Aemillius looked at me a little strangely when I took the smaller shield in hand, so I made a wincing movement as I placed my hand through the holding strap, as if I had a minor strain in my shoulder.

The Games Master announced our event then, and the trumpets sounded loud. Side by side, unspeaking, we walked out into the bright glare. In step, we marched to the center of the arena.

The Emperor was not present today, so we were not required to face his box and make the salute. Instead, we took up our positions in the center of the arena, turning slowly in circles, saluting the crowds with upraised weapons and bowing low. I tried subtly once to move into position and place the sun to my back, but Aemillius would have none of that and countered my move so that we both had our sides facing its brilliantly blinding glare. Well, he couldn't blame me for trying. We waited until the Games Master signaled, saluted the audience once more, then took a step to the rear, now facing each other. He signaled again, the trumpets gave their final blare, and the fight was on.

Aemillius looked good. He moved easily, his trident held just below the waist, his net hand trailing, feet spread apart but not too wide.

Like him, I started with the basic moves. I was glad now that I had been a retiarius at one time; it made it a lot easier for me to forecast his moves. We both began slowly, each trying for a more advantageous position. I made the first advance, halfheartedly, just to get things moving. He countered my sword thrust with an easy block of his trident head. He tried then to hook my blade between his prongs, to pull it from my grasp, but I was expecting it. It didn't work for him, but it had looked good and excited the crowd somewhat.

It was midafternoon now, and the heat of the sun seemed to grow with my exertions. Aemillius made a sudden half-toss with his net; this move supposedly would make me step back, off balance, while he advanced. He would then set me up for an earnest net throw while keeping me on the move with his trident. I'd learned all this before he had and had also memorized the countermoves. Instead of doing the expected, I stepped aside, too close for him to use his net or trident, and made a swift slice at his gut. I touched him just enough to cause the blood to flow. The mob needed something now and then to keep them entertained, and Aemillius also needed something to sharpen him up a bit so as to make me look good. From then on he was all business; I'd gotten his attention. We fought hot and heavy. He pricked my shield arm up by the shoulder once; it was nothing serious, but it bled. We were face to face when I butted him in the chest with my shield. He almost fell, but was able to recover and roll out of it with a smooth practiced move. I was somewhat careless as he recovered, and he almost knocked my legs from under me with the butt end of his trident as he gained his footing.

The mob laughed at my discomfort and surprise, and it ticked me off a little. I'd been taken in too easily with his move, too damned sure of my superiority.

We positioned ourselves again and he lunged in with a forward step, straight at my face, his trident in slashing motion. As I moved to cover, his left hand whipped the weighted tips of the net toward my face. One of them caught me just above the eye, laying it open in a gash about an inch long. It stung a bit but I could tell it wasn't a disabling wound. It would bleed a lot, though, and that was dangerous in itself, should it get into my eyes and blind me for an instant. That would be enough time for me to miss a move on his part. As the blood flowed I kept it from my eyes by tossing my head to the side, while yet keeping an eye on him.

The fight had been in progress for about ten minutes, and I could feel the mob getting restless. I decided to step up the pace. I still hadn't given Aemillius the opening that I had so blatantly displayed in my training, the one I knew he was surely waiting for.

I moved in low, ducking beneath a well-placed net swing, slicing at his belly. He moved back nimbly as I kept the pressure on him, never providing a chance for him to recover properly. I could tell he was becoming a little more than worried. He had wagered his life, and more than likely his meager fortune, on the one opening in my guard that was yet to come. He was sweating freely, not just from strain now, but from fear. I could see it in his eyes.

I kept after him, hacking small gouges out of his trident haft, forcing him to move constantly to protect himself from my onslaught, leaving him no room and no range to use his net. I laid open his net arm then, with a long slice of my sword. It opened wide, gaping from his shoulder to his elbow. He struck back in panic; the prongs of his trident barely missed gutting me, and left a slight wound near my navel.

It was time. I went into the crouch position that I had used in practice while he watched. I could see his face light up. This was what he'd been watching and waiting for; the opening was nigh.

I took a deep breath, raising my sword arm high as if preparing to strike for the head, and moved, dropping my shield a bit. He fell for it, committing himself to an extended rapid thrust to my exposed throat and chest. As he did, I dropped my body and moved in close to him. The reason for my choosing the smaller shield must have then become frighteningly apparent to him. With it, I was able to drop low, almost to knee level. I came up inside his guard, thrusting under his shield, my blade entering his gut flat side up, slicing through the muscles of his abdomen. It was always a strange feeling when you hit the gut —a stiffness as the blade entered the tightness of the muscles and they contracted around the cold metal.

He went down. As I withdrew the blade from his stomach, it made that peculiar ''stukla'' sucking sound that I'd never quite gotten used to hearing.

Aemillius was done for. The death glaze was already settling over his eyes as I turned from him and raised my sword to the crowd in victory. They gave me a fine ovation. I was pleased at how well everything had gone. The fight had looked much tougher than it had been. Poor

Aemillius had never really stood a chance, but that was the way of the arena.

I stood there, playing out my role as a noble and honorable fighter; then, instead of allowing the ring attendants drag the body off with hooks, I picked him gently up and carried him nobly from the place of his death, as one warrior honoring another. The crowd loved the gesture of humility, and I knew that it had done much for my reputation. Once inside the hall, out of the mob's sight, I dumped him on the stone floor and went to wipe down.

As I walked down to the washroom, Graecus came out for his event. He was magnificent, that I had to concede. He wore nothing but the best, his armor and sword custom-made by the finest smiths of Spain. The armor was gilded and his leg greaves traced with silver and gold designs in the Greek fashion, as was his high plumed helmet. He looked, I imagined, as the god Alexander must have in his time. He winked at me in passing, and spoke softly.

"Nice gesture, Lucanus. You have a style, or maybe just showmanship. But I sense you have a mean streak in you."

What I started to respond I now forget, but he stopped me anyway by continuing: "I really did mean it when I said we should get together some time. Now, if you will excuse me, I have some work to finish."

With that, he left me standing there, gape-mouthed and furious again. My short-lived glory of the day was lost with just a few well-placed words from his elegant tongue. The man possessed the ability to put me in a rage with casual remarks, without raising his voice or using vulgarities. By the immortal gods, he was an infuriating person.

I was so irritated that I never even watched his fight, as I knew I should to study his style and technique. Instead, I left the arena in a huff, not even going to wipe down. I used my cloak to cover my wounds from the gaping eyes of passersby. The blood was still flowing freely from the wound above my eye, but I didn't care. Someday I would have Niger Graecus where I wanted him, and I would see fear in that smug, confident face when he knew that I held his life in my hands.

Several hours later Crator arrived at my room, asking, no, demanding where in Hades I had gone off to. I had had several invitations to attend parties that night at the homes of prominent men and women. I was not interested, and told him so. He said amiably that if that was the way I wanted it, then so be it, and tossed a sack of denarii on my couch. The rest of the winnings, he said, would go to the bankers for safekeeping. He added that there was enough in the sack for me to have a good time for some weeks and perhaps to buy some new clothes.

I put the sack under my pallet and turned my back to him. He did not have to tell me of Graecus' victory and how much the crowd had loved it. He always won. In forty-two death fights, he'd never received a serious injury. My score, at this time, was only eleven kills, a far cry from his, but as I said before, I now had a goal . . . .

9

After the fight with Aemillius I went on a drunk that lasted three days. When Crator finally found me, I had been laid up with three whores trying to screw my brains out, or so they said. At least they were tearful when I left them, so I naturally assumed that I had performed well enough.

But I was as sick as a diseased dog. Crator didn't help matters much, yelling in my ear, telling me all about my depraved self, all of my bad and degenerate habits, and how in Hades could I do him this way. I caught a fairly good look at him out of my left eye, which was yet partially open and sore. He was livid; the pale spots were back on his cheeks as he screamed at me.

"You little swine, who do you think you are? Caesar?

You are not a free man yet! You belong to me! You are still my property! If I had any sense at all I'd have you beaten and sell you to the Navy for a galley slave."

He continued in this vein for some time, slowing down only when we reached the Flavian, then hauling me into his office for a more definitive cursing. I was properly remorseful when he'd finished. I didn't mind the dressing down so much, I only wanted him to lower his voice a bit, so the pounding of Vulcan's hammer in my brain would not hurt as much. That and a good drink of water would set me straight. I think I could have drained the Tiber right then. Gods, what a thirst I felt!

Crator finally settled down a bit and brought out a pot of wine. He even offered me some, but the very smell of it made my stomach try to turn itself inside out, and I was forced to run outside before I made a mess of his office. When I returned he was all business, my dressing down over with now.

"How bad do you want a match with Graecus?" he asked.

Even with my dry mouth and aching head I was still more than able to answer that question. "I want him so much that hardly anything else matters. I want him on the sands, just the two of us."

Crator sipped his bowl, nodding his head at me. "Good! Then you will understand what I'm about to say. First, you know that I have a certain feeling for you, and, so your mind is clear on the matter, I have already signed the necessary documents of your manumission so that if I should die you will go free. But do not get overly anxious and hurry me along."

We both laughed, knowing that I would never raise a hand to him.

He leaned back in his chair, running his fingers through his few remaining strands of well-oiled hair. He continued:

"Things have gone pretty well for us in the last couple of years, Lucanus. You have established a bit of a reputation for yourself and have a decent following in the stands. The incident with Claudius and Germanicus did not hurt us at all either. You are known in the entire city and in many of the provinces now, but there are many names in Rome and you are but one. We can get better money for your handiwork if you go on the road. You need to bring your kill ratio up, and the best way for you to accomplish that is to fight in exhibition matches. Therefore, I am going to place you in the troupe of Pollio Ruffila. He has a good reputation and has seen you fight. He wants you. You will go with him for one year, maybe more. When you return, if you're successful out there, we will be ready for Graecus."

I started to speak but he waved his hand for me to be silent, that he was not yet finished. "I will make sure that your victories, while on tour, are well advertised. Mind you now, just don't go and get yourself crippled or killed out there, if you truly want the Greek, that is. Now, go and clean yourself, get rid of that hangover, say farewell to your friends. Not your girlfriends, though; we don't have that much time. You will be leaving Rome within the week. Pollio is in the city gathering acts and, when he leaves, you will accompany his troupe."

He waved his finger at me in warning, continuing again. "I tell you this, now. You won't get away with doing the same vile tricks to Pollio that you do to me, so watch your behavior. Pollio will turn you into a castrato in a minute should you forget your place. He will not tolerate foolishness nor disrespect. Now go!"

I did as instructed. I was, I can assure you, a little more than merely excited. This would be my first time to cross the seas. I was determined to make good. I'd thought previously that I would need at least two years to be ready for a face to face with Graecus but, if I had enough bouts and trained hard, I might just be ready in a year. I swore then to Fortuna that until I returned to Rome I would not touch wine again. I started to include women in my oath but thought that might be taking things a bit too far. The wine alone would suffice.

Gods, I was excited! I'd miss old Crator, but I was more than ready to go.

10

I did as Crator advised and made my farewells to the few that I called friends. Actually, there were not many that I would miss. They were mostly veterans and, as such, we all knew better than to build strong friendships with each other. Friendly and courteous backslapping acquaintances, sharing a night on the town now and then together, yes. But more than that could prove dangerous to either of us on the sands one day.

I did go to the homes of Claudius and Germanicus. I missed Claudius; he was out on state errands, so his slaves told me. Germanicus was also out, but his wife made me welcome and showed me a great deal of courtesy, thanking me for saving the life of her husband. I knew that she was being gracious even to receive one such as I, for slaves do not normally pay visits to the greats of the Empire, especially through the front door. But Agrippina, the woman of Germanicus and daughter of Agrippa, once the closest friend of Augustus, made me feel somehow more than welcome in her home.

Agrippina was an attractive woman. She had a good figure, and rich auburn hair done in the style, piled on her head in ringlets. Her manner was gentle, but somehow she gave me the impression that she had a great deal of strength and character.

She showed me into a small, but tastefully decorated,

garden. It was set around a small pond, clear and cool, in which fat silver fish swam lazily. We talked here for a few minutes and waited for Germanicus to make an appearance. It was a bit awkward for me, this conversation. I felt uncomfortable being in this great house, speaking with a lady in whose veins ran the blood of one of the noblest houses in all Rome, or the Empire for that matter. But she soon put me at my ease, and had me laughing as she talked of her children and the mischief they got involved in. There was not much difference, as far as I could tell, between the offspring of the rich and powerful and those of the streets, where mischief was concerned. Funny how I'd always thought that there would be. The only major difference, I now supposed, was that the childhood of the poor ended much sooner than that of their counterparts.

I related a couple of my less daring childish adventures to her. I did not think that she would be amused by stories of one who had spent his early years administering death blows to wounded men.

Germanicus came in upon us during one of our laughing spells and looked pleased. He touched his wife's hair gently and greeted me warmly, a trace of a smile in the back of his voice.

"Well Lucanus, have you been terrorizing my wife with tales of the arena?"

I responded haltingly. "No, Lord! We were just . . . ."

He laughed loudly, slapping me on the shoulder. "I was only teasing you. By the way, congratulations on your win over Aemillius. He had a very promising career, I thought, until you put an untimely end to it, that is. Claudius told me you were magnificent. I do wish I could have been there to see it, but matters of state, you know . . . ."

I didn't know; why would he assume that I should? I nodded dumbly.

"To what do I owe the pleasure of your visit to my home?"

I told him that I had come to pay my respects and to bid him farewell, as I'd previously told his wife, and that I would soon be leaving the country and going on tour.

Agrippina excused herself and went inside the house. Germanicus sat beside the pond, picked up a few pebbles and tossed them into the water, watching the rings as they spread in ever-widening circles, then disappeared completely.

"Lucanus, I wish you would quit the arena and take my offer of service. I feel there is more to you, and that with me you could find more in life."

I was touched by his concern, for I knew it was real. He was actually interested in me, and not just because I'd saved his life. I was careful to put my words in order before responding.

"Lord, you have a great name and house, and you have destiny before you. I have nothing more than the clothes on my back and a good strong arm. You have been raised in a world that is strange and foreign to me. I have my own world, though the reasons I wish to continue in it may not make much sense to you. Every man must have a goal in his life, something to achieve, and I have mine. If you still wish for me to enter your service, I can only do so after I have proved something to myself."

Germanicus nodded his head in understanding. "Very well, my friend, do what you must. But do keep me in mind. When you return from this journey and have accomplished that which you desire, come to me. I feel somehow that there are times before me when we shall serve each other well."

He took a small scroll from beneath his tunic and handed it to me. "This is my offer to buy you. If ever you are in difficulty, do not hesitate to use this. Take it to the Commander of the Roman garrison at whatever place you may be and it shall be honored. You will be purchased in my name and sent to me immediately. This is your way out should you ever need it. I have friends, many of them, in many places. They will see that my wishes are done."

It took a second for his action to register. He had prepared the letter in advance; therefore, he must have been aware that I was leaving.

He caught my thoughts and smiled in that gentle manner of his. "Yes, I have kept myself informed of what is happening to you, Lucanus. I hope you don't mind?"

He rose and shook my hand.

"Take care of yourself, little wolf, and come back to us safely. Vale! And may Fortuna be watching over you, young wolf."

He returned to his duties then, his major-domo showing me to the door.

I was still in a mild state of shock at his generous proposal, but it felt good to know that I was being watched over by friends in high places. That was a new feeling for me. But now I was sure that Claudius and Germanicus were both actually fond of me.

I settled a few small debts here and there, and purchased some new pieces of gear that I would need. When I finished, and returned to the Flavian, a slave was waiting for me with a neatly wrapped bundle. He handed it over and left. I unwrapped the fine covering of expensive silk, the first I'd ever touched. There was a letter enclosed. It stated that the gift was from Claudius and Germanicus, and that they both hoped I would accept this token of their affection in the same spirit that it was given, as friends to a friend.

I was stunned as I pulled the blade from its scabbard. The scabbard itself was of beaten bronze, embossed with images of Romulus and Remus suckling at the teats of the she-bitch of Rome. I removed the blade slowly from its holder, noticing first its grip, constructed of a black hardwood from Africa and wrapped with sharkskin. The sharkskin, I knew, would keep the handle firmly in my grasp though it might be covered with blood and sweat.

The sword was a beauty. Made of true tempered steel in the Damascus style, its final works had been bathed in acid, and the Syrian smith's signature etched in the design on the blade. It was absolutely the most beautiful thing I'd seen in my life.

Such blades were very rare. The secret of their making was closely guarded by the guild of smiths in Damascus. I'd hear a little about the manner in which they were forged, how accurate the information I knew not, for I had not the gifts of Vulcan or those of Haepsuttus. But, as I heard, the basic technique was to hammer out the length of the blade, fold it back in on itself, and repeat the process time and again. In some strange manner, this gave the blade a strength that could not be found in other weapons. When the blade was complete in the raw stage, it was bathed in acid. The whirls and patterns left on the steel by the wash gave it a distinctive look that was beautiful to the eye. Its steel, instead of being silver and shining, was a light grey with whorls and patterns and ridges etched. It was resistant to rust and, when honed, held an edge that was second to none.

I am not ashamed to say, that for the first time in memory, I cried. I held the priceless sword closely to my chest and sobbed like a child.

I was not to meet Pollio until the day before sailing, when he came to get me at the Flavian. I was ready and anxious to be on my way. My kit was assembled in several bundles, including my armor, of which I had two sets. At times it was difficult to have repairs made on the road, or so I'd heard from those fighters who had been on tour.

Inside my money pouch, attached to my belt, I kept the scroll from Germanicus, and the letter I'd received with the gift. I was not very experienced with the ways of the world outside of the arena, but I knew that these two documents might prove to be very important if I ever found myself in difficulties. I had not told Crator of them, but I had showed him the sword and told who had sent it. He whistled through his teeth at the sight of it and asked permission to touch the blade. That was the only time he had ever asked my permission to do anything. Even though he had no use for such a weapon, I knew that it was with great reluctance that he finally handed it back to me. I would have the same problem more than once if I was not careful who I showed it to. The sword of Damascus was an item that many would not hesitate to kill for. I kept it wrapped in its original silken cover and out of sight from that moment on. It would not be used except for special events.

Pollio was as I'd expected from Crator's description. A short, powerful man with a bull neck and heavy sloping shoulders, from which suspended overly long and massive arms. His face was intelligent, though, with quick brown eyes and a slight touch of cruelty at the corners of his mouth. A few scars were visible here and there also.

At his instruction, I hauled myself and my gear into the wagon that was waiting just outside the entrance to the Flavian. Two other fighters were already seated inside, along with the attendant who was to care for our wounds. Hopefully, I would have no need of his assistance, but I made it a point to pass a few friendly words with him. It always paid to be pleasant to one who may some day have the opportunity to amputate one's arm or leg.

We pulled out, on our way to the port city of Ostia. This was to be my first visit to the seaport, considered by many to be the life blood of Rome, but it was not to be my last by any means.

The others in the wagon had little to say, and, like them, I kept my words to a minimum, catching sleep when I could. Between the rocking and swaying of the wagon, the body-shaking jolts when we hit a stone or pot-hole in the road, and the loud cursing of the driver to the animals, sleep was kept to a minimum.

By the time we arrived at Ostia, it was near dusk, and Pollio aimed the driver straight to the wharves. He hadn't said a word to me during the trip, but had eyed me up and down when Crator had handed my papers over to him. I assumed that he was a man of few words, a determined one, however.

There was no fanfare when we boarded the ship that was to be our home for the next months. It was clean and, at least to my landsman's eye, very large, though I was to find out later that, by comparison to other ships, it was only fit for coastal waters and fair weather. But it was sound, and as I said, clean.

The captain was a wiry Corsican whose arms looked as thin and strong as the lines of his ship. His face was a mass of thick, weathered and sunburned wrinkles that fell in on themselves, to the point that you could never get a good look at his eyes. His crew consisted of a half-dozen sailors from various parts of the Empire. There were no oarsmen aboard. I found out the reason for this the following morning, when we caught the tide. Pollio had loudly ordered us out of our blankets and put us to the oars. He was not one to pay for oarsmen when he had a built-in crew of strongarms along. The ship had places for twenty oarsmen and mounted only one square sail.

We sailed with the tide and it didn't take us long to pick up the beat of the hortator. I got my first good look at the rest of the troupe then, seeing only a few faces that I recognized. The rest were strangers, but from the looks of them I could see that Pollio had put together a fine crew with good talent all for his tour. None of the fighters showed any signs of disabling wounds or excessive age. They were mostly about my own age, only a few slightly older. Only one of them, I found out, had a record that approached mine. He was a quiet taciturn man, an auctoratius, who hired himself out occasionally under private contract. I wondered if we would be matched together as teammates. I hoped so, for I liked the steady look of him and the way he kept his own counsel. He was a few years older than me and showed enough scars to prove credibility. He was thinner than I and fought as either a thraces or a retiarius, whichever was called for. I spotted the marks on his wrists that all Retiarii possess, a calloused scar that would never disappear, caused by the leather strap that held the net to the wrist. He recognized me, and nodded as we took our places on the galley benches and picked up the oars.

Now there was the open sea and the good smell of salt air in my lungs as I bent to the task of learning how to use the long oar, not getting it fouled as we swept out of the port and past dozens of other ships at anchor. I saw a massive quadririme, a four-banked galley, and realized then just how small our ship really was. Compared to it, ours was a weak and tiny vessel. In fact, it was about sixty feet in length, affording us barely enough room to sleep all at one time. We had no bunks and had to make pallets for ourselves below the deck, along with the cargo and our weapons, which we'd been ordered to turn over to Pollio for storage. I'd turned over my old sword to him, but I had kept the Damascus close to me. There was no way it would leave my sight or the reach of my hand in sleep, not even if it meant a lashing.

There were a couple of wrestlers and pugilists among us, but swordsmen and retiarii formed the majority. Altogether we totaled exactly enough men to man the oars, twenty in all. I wondered then how many of us would survive to make the return trip. It really didn't matter, though; I was certain that I would be one of them. It was not age that told me this, nor a feeling of false security. A deep sense of destiny lay securely within me, saying there were bigger and better things in store and I would survive to see them through.

The only one in our crew that was not a fighter was the

attendant. He was an Egyptian with shaved head and thin arms. He could have been thirty or fifty; it was hard to tell. He had very delicate hands and carried himself with great dignity. He was the twenty-first man and was not put on the oars. I wondered about this, finding out later that he was a free man and his contract with Pollio left him free to do as he liked, when not needed in fighter attendance.

When we made the open sea, the sail was raised, we shipped oars, and sacrifices were made by the captain and his crew. A lamb went to Neptune to assure us fair weather and smooth waters. I noticed that the Egyptian was making his own sacrifice at the bow of the ship. He opened a small cage and leg a pigeon fly free.

On the bow of the ship were painted large blue eyes that were supposed to help us see our way in the darkness, fog, or heavy storms.

A special place was set aside on the open deck where our meals were prepared. There would be one hot meal each day, the other one cold. Only in this spot, where the boards of the deck were covered with a bed of sand and stones, was a fire permitted. As soon as the meal was prepared, the fire was extinguished. Fire, I soon learned, was the thing most feared by seamen, and they were absolute fanatics about it. In a split second, one oil lamp, overturned, could convert a solid ship into a blazing pyre. With no dry land to escape to, I could readily comprehend their anxiety.

During the next days of our voyage, I would get a better understanding of my new master and lanista. Not all of it was to prove pleasant.

11

The ship turned south to ride the winds as we hit open water. When I say open water, I do not mean to imply that we sailed straight out to sea. The captain tried to keep land in sight as much as possible, which I thought was a good idea. I could swim a bit but by no means was I a fish, nor did I desire to personally feed a big one in the event of trouble. Yes, we stayed to shore whenever feasible. There were always a number of other vessels in sight, both traders and commercial fishing boats, going out for the day and returning before dark. These also provided all of us with an additional sense of security. We were not alone out here.

I was still flush with the excitement of a new adventure. I was determined to make my mark on all the provinces we would visit and, when I returned to Rome, I would have Graecus. It served to keep me in good spirits, this goal.

There was not much idle time on board. Pollio kept us at the oars even when the winds were fair. My body developed aches in regions. I never even knew had muscles. Especially my butt! The long hours on the benches, pulling on the oars, were stretching a mass of painful muscles. Muscles, my aching ass! Tender, newly capped calluses. But I never complained, for I understood Pollio's reasons. If we remained on board ship without exercise we would not be worth much when it came time to fight. The hours of handling the sweeps gave me a new strength in my back, as well as in my arms and wrists. After some days I was looking forward to the rhythm of the rowing. It was easy to lose oneself in the endless repetition, letting one's mind become a distant thing, away from you on a far journey of its own.

The sun soon burned me a dark brown, and I felt better than I had in a long time. The food was plentiful; Pollio did not skimp on that. He knew exactly how much was needed for his fighters to maintain them in top physical condition. Those who were too heavy got less, and naturally the thin ones received more. Pollio handled all arguments himself. There was no one, not even the pugilists, who cared to face him. He had more strength in one of his arms than most men did in their legs, and did not hesitate to use his strength when called for. He had a mean streak in him, for sure, but he did not let it interfere with business. If he felt that a man's head needed knocking to straighten him out, he was always careful not to break the skull. No use permanently damaging a good earning fighter.

Ramsep, the Egyptian, had been forced to leave his own country, for reasons unknown, but his manner and tone of voice were those of a man with a good education. He spoke not only his own tongue, but Latin and Greek fluently, and was well versed in the history of the world. Often, in the evening, I would find him looking out over the waters or studying the stars. I even took to doing the same myself. I found that it afforded one a sense of serenity. It was quiet, with only the slapping of the sails and the rushing, slushing sounds of the sea bed beneath our bow.

We stopped at a couple of Italian cities on the way and staged a few fights and shows. No death matches, however. I performed well enough, I suppose, losing only one match to the retiarius I mentioned previously. He was quicker than I'd thought he would be and caught me in a good trick, one I'd never seen used before. He threw his net in my face, and, when I'd moved to dodge the net, he threw his trident, butt first, between my legs. I went down in a tangle and he was on me before I even knew what was happening. It was well done and I complimented him on the move, while at the same time cataloging it in the back of my mind. It would never work on me again.

Ramsep had few injured to work on after the fights, and these he handled with a deft and careful skill that immediately gave him a favored position among the fighters. They knew now that their lives and well being were in good hands. His only action that confused me was his refusal to bleed a man who'd been cut badly. I asked him about it one evening while we sat at the bow of the ship, looking out over the dark waters. He took his time in answering my question. When he finally did, it was with a trace of amusement.

"Think about it, young warrior. How many times have you seen a man spill blood and grow weak, though his wound was not deep?"

I had seen this often, it was true. I hadn't known what to think of it at the time and I told him so. He shook his brown, sun-baked head, as if sad at the depth of my ignorance.

"Young one, you should make an effort to develop the muscles in your head as well as those of your body. If a man grows weak at the loss of blood, does it not stand to reason that taking more blood from him will make him even weaker, possibly leading to his death?"

That made sense to me. I'd seen several old men die from wounds that had not seemed that severe, but they had lost a great deal of blood, their bodies turning pale and finally stopping altogether. I was learning much on this trip, things that would serve me well later. I have always had the ability to recall nearly everything I've ever heard or seen. Not meaning I'm smart you see, for there is a vast difference between knowing something and having the ability to use it. But yet to this day I have tried to use what I have learned, though I fear that my head has never been as strong as my back.

As we cruised down the western coast of Italia, stopping in various cities for matches, we lost one Thracian to an infected wound. Ramsep was very upset about the man's death and blamed it on the man's use of home remedies. He, the Thracian, had placed hot steaming horse dung on the open wound instead of allowing Ramsep to treat it properly. By the time Ramsep had seen it, it was overly ripe and a fever had set in. He was unable to break the fever, and the man had died. Pollio gave us all a cursing that we will long remember, making it clear that we were all to be treated by Ramsep, no matter how minor the wound. A failure to report an injury would result in fine and punishment, including meeting Pollio head to head with bare hands. This was incentive enough for us to pester Ramsep with every minor scratch we received from then on out.

Pollio told us that the real fights would begin once we reached Sicily. There, and from there on, the action would be heavier.

After we left the coast of Italia and crossed the straits of Messina, across from Reggie, it was hot and heavy. From that time on we did not fight each other any longer. Opponents were arranged for us in every city—local greats.

Pollio told me that he was going to honor his agreement with Crator by putting me in death matches constantly. In these, I always bet everything I had on my winning, no matter what the odds were. If I won, there was profit. If I lost, it would not matter to me financially anyway. I sent back part of my winnings to Crator, along with his entitled share of each bout's profits, for him to use as he saw fit to promote my name in Rome during my absence. He was to hire good people for my promotion and to purchase space in the *Acta Diurna*, where my exploits and record of winnings were to be recounted in great detail. In some cases the tales were filled with so much flattery and exaggeration that I would not recognize the bout I was supposed to have won. Show business is show business, I was to learn.

We made the entire circuit of the islands, with fights at

Augusta, Siracussa, and Avola, then around the Pachynus Promontory and on to Licata and Agrento, Seiaca and Marsala. In Marsala, we staged fights for two days, in honor of some politician's birth. Marsala still has many ruins left over from the Carthaginians. The fort there withstood an eight-year siege of the Romans before falling in defeat.

I used my sword of grey steel in every contest. It became a trademark, and word of my victories preceded me to the next site until, by the time we reached Syracuse, I was the best-known fighter ever to have visited this rocky, scrub-brush filled place called a city.

Our last contest was at Panormus, where I killed three men in one battle. All of them possessed good reputations and were well known in the region. Pollio made it clear to all lanistas and promoters that they were not to send any of their fighters against me that were not prepared for a battle to the death. The audience had grown to expect it when I was on the billing. I was aware that should I ever fall there would be no getting up for me, even if the crowd wished it and gave the sign of mercy.

I was building a reputation and those I fought, knew it. The only man that had been saved from my death blow was one who'd been lucky enough to receive the thumbs-up signal very quickly. Most died before the signal could be given. I was even receiving strange looks from my teammates, and they began to show a preference for company other than mine. That was fine with me. I wasn't too fond of any of them anyway, except possibly for Ramsep. He was what he was. He treated our injuries and afterwards stayed mostly to himself, like myself. I don't think Ramsep liked the way we fighters made our living at all. But no one had made him take the job he had; so we had no sympathy for him. He was a good physician though, and we'd suffered few casualties to infected wounds after his constant treatment. We did lose two fighters at Sicily, and were shorthanded for a while until replacements came in from Italia. Pollio had bought their contracts from their lanistas. We'd fought against them in Panormus, and now they were our teammates.

From Sicily, we crossed over to Africa under fair skies and favorable winds, heading for the ancient city of Carthage.

We didn't fight until we'd been on land for a week. During this off period, we exercised constantly. Pollio stressed the running times. Our work on the galley oars had been good for the back and arms, but it had a tendency to build the legs wrong. Now we needed to stretch them out. At dawn each morning, we would all leave the inn where we'd taken up residence, and run along the beach. I ran naked, using my tanned and well-muscled body as a tool to build interest in us. By the third day of our exercise ritual, we had a good-sized audience on the beach awaiting our arrival. Each time we hit the beach I could hear my name being cried out as we passed.

I was not the personal property of Pollio, and Crator had given him instructions to allow me ample freedom. I had time to taste some of the pleasures of this former capital of Carthage. I found women of the desert, some who'd seen my nakedness on the beach as we ran, who had a savage passion running in their nomadic veins. I had to contain my own passions so as not to overexert myself in trying to keep up with their avid demands. I kept my oath of abstinence on the wine.

After one confrontation with Pollio over the grey sword and my retaining it instead of giving it to the arms master, he no longer bothered me about it. He threatened me with punishment, which he claimed as his right, but I chose that time to show him the letter from Claudius and Germanicus. When he read the names of the donors of the gift and found that they were two members of the Royal family, he relented, even though it was with reluctance.

I exercised even harder than Pollio ordered. Every moment of every period I pushed myself, making good use of the gymnasiums of any city we visited, lifting weights and wrestling with good sized opponents, exposing myself and my body shamelessly to the women in doing so. I knew they would be the ones most responsible for spreading my name, and with each of them recounting their story my reputation would grow even larger. I was receiving a price in the arena now that no fighter before me had ever received in Africa, and I was yet to reach my twentieth birthday.

I was relatively unscarred. My hair had grown long and reached to my shoulders, washed with gold streaks from the long hours under the sun. The people, especially the women, seemed fascinated with me. Part of this I knew was due to the efforts of Crator. He sent copies of the *Acta Diurna* in advance to every place I was to fight. The articles talked of my birth in the Flavian and how I had entered the arena when still a small child. These, and other stories, some fabricated, seemed to prime the audience with morbid fascination. The women, whose bellies I spilled my seed into along our route, would often cry out for me to hurt them, calling me their sweet child killer, taking me into them, groaning loudly. I knew that most of their passions were only in their minds, but that was all right with me. The time I spent with the ladies had aided to enhance my name and, by the time of Munersa, which was to be a good fight to celebrate the victory of Rome over Carthage, my name was written on the walls of the city, and was on the tongues of the people. This fight was one that I truly needed. Champions had been brought in, not only from Rome, but from as far as Egypt. There were to be two hundred gladiators, fighting in teams that would be eliminated to twenty in all. However, I was not to fight in any of the team action. All mine were to be single contests, man to man and to the death in the closing event of each day. I was not to lose the audience's attention by being part of a group. I was to stand always alone and in the limelight of the crowd's eye.

On the first day of the scheduled three-day event, I decided I would do something different. I fought six times in the eliminations and, each time, chose a different style of fighting. I'd been trained in most of the schools of the arts and for the first contest chose to fight as a retiarius. I eliminated a thraces from Smryna and a Greek hoplomachi who fought with the long lance. After that I went through one style after another, as a thraces and a myrmillone though I was not heavy enough in weight and had to make it on speed alone during the myrmillone style.

I discovered that I had an additional advantage. My reputation was helping me to win. I could see dread and real fear in the eyes of my opponents. When I saw this, I knew they were dead men before the first blow was struck. I was now beginning to understand the winnings of Graecus; he'd had this advantage for a long time. His reputation was his greatest weapon. By the end of the contest, my last two opponents had to be urged onto the sands with the aid of red-hot pokers. One of them nearly took my head off with a wild blow that was truly not in the books. It left me with a scar on my shoulder that gives me a twinge to this day.

This was the first time I'd experienced the blind adoration of the mobs, and when I struck the death blow their cheers were like a strong wine to me, making me drunk with my own pride. Women offered themselves to me from the stands and bribed their way into the changing rooms after the contest just to be near me. Several ladies of noble birth managed to get inside before I could wash myself and stood watching my nakedness, touching the blood, both my own and that of the men I'd slain, as it dripped from my body. The feel of the blood would cause their eyes to glaze over and their bodies to arch backwards, their breasts to stick out and their nipples to harden. I think many of them actually reached an orgasm in this manner. I took several of them right there on the benches, and a few in the bath. Something about combat made my blood run hot; in the act of taking them I gained a release from the passions of the arena.

When the contests were over, I was awarded the wreath of honor and paraded through the streets of the city in an open chariot, wearing my still bloodstained armor, to the delightful cheering of the mobs.

I knew now that mine and Crator's plan was working. I lived for the time that I could return to Rome. There would be no way that Graecus could refuse me in contest now and, even better, I was ready for him.

I gained additional popularity by being generous with my purse. The fights in Carthage alone had brought me over two thousand denarii, and when I went to the poor regions of the city, I threw coins in large number to the needy children. I bought bread and gave it to them. I did it all with a great degree of humility and modesty, knowing all the while it would add to my mystique. There was an eerie fascination among the people about me and my actions. My youth and fair looks, combined with my unhesitating dealing out of the death blow and my generosity to the poor, seemed to awe them all. The combination of these traits served me well with both rich and poor. I paid for sacrifices in the name of the citizens of Carthage at the Temple of Demeter, a goddess who watched over their children and their fields.

I spent nearly all the money I'd earned during my stay in Carthage, but it was well done. I knew that my next contest would bring me more than I had won here because of the publicity I'd gained in the city.

By the time we left Carthage, my teammates would hardly speak to me. They watched me with wondering eyes. I knew they all feared that one day they would have to go up against me, and their dread suited me fine. It made no real difference to me whom I fought; I owed them nothing. They were merely steps up the ladder to Graecus as far as I was concerned, and besides, they would have killed me in like manner if they had had the chance.

Pollio was now able to afford a better ship, one that provided more room for us and the crew. I still insisted on taking my turn on the oars. I knew it was good for me. From my own pocket, I purchased a small cabin on the ship, solely for myself, thus isolating myself even more from the team, but this was the way it had to be. If I was to be successful I must set myself apart, not only from the mobs, but from those around me. Even if they hated me or envied me, they would talk about it; as they talked, my name would grow.

Agents and promoters had come to Pollio with many offers to fight. Only the best of them did he accept. We fought along the entire coast of Africa, going nearly to Egypt, with shows at Leptis Magama and Berenice. We returned via the same route, passing Carthage again on our way to Mauretania, with spectacles at Hippo Regia and Caesarea. We finally left the African coast at Tingis. By this time, even the robed desert dwellers had heard of my name and, when we fought, they came out of their mountainous and sandy domains, riding camels and asses and paying their precious coins to see the great troupe of Pollio Ruffila and the young killer, Lucanus.

Across the straits from Tigis, I could see the fabled Pillars of Hercules. The coast of Hispania waited on the other side. From there, we would make our way back, along the coast until reaching Messilla in Gaul, where our final contest was to be staged before returning to Rome. I would not fight again after Messilla; it was too close to Rome.

When word of our ship's approach reached the people of Messilla, they turned out in mass to greet me. I was a wealthy man by this time, at least by my standards, and with what I'd sent Crator I still had over a thousand denarii in various banking houses along the coast. These funds I would transfer to Rome, once I'd arrived. Crator had arranged all this by letters during my absence, and in every city we fought in there was a moneylender waiting to deposit my earnings for safekeeping.

I knew somehow, before even leaving the ship in Ostia, that my days as a slave were coming to an end.

BOOK THREE

FREEDMAN

1

The trip from Messilla to Ostia in Rome had been a short one and without incident. It was high noon when I saw, for the second time, the port city on the coast of Italia. It was a welcome sight. This time, as the sail was dropped, I took no turn at the oars. I stood at the bow as we sailed slowly into the port and tied up beside a fat trader ship from Egypt.

I felt good; I was returning with all that I had set out for. My kills were now at thirty-one; when I'd left they had been eleven. Only Graecus surpassed me now in kills among all living gladiators. He would have to fight me now; his age and pride would demand it. And, I was ready for him. The last months had put more than muscles on my body and scars on my skin. They had put confidence in my heart. I knew that old Crator would be proud of me and could hardly wait to leave Ostia and get to Rome. I wanted to see his old face again and plot with him our next move.

After we'd offloaded and I'd gained the necessary papers from Pollio for my release back to Crator's care, I rented a horse and rode on to Rome, not wanting to wait for the bone-jarring wagon I knew Pollio would lease for the trip. By this time I was doing pretty much as I wished, and there was nothing Pollio could do about it. He hadn't hesitated when I'd asked for the papers, merely saying that he would check with Crator when he arrived to ascertain that I'd reported in to him. All I took with me of my possessions was the grey sword, wrapped in its silk cloth, and my winnings of course. I wanted to see that old familiar look of greed on Crator's face when he counted the amount I'd brought back with me. It would more than delight his thieving old heart.

As soon as I entered the gates of Rome I felt at home. This was my city, and I had missed the sights and smells of it. I went directly to the Flavian, pushing by the slaves and arena workers to enter Crator's office. He was not there. I called loudly for him, my voice echoing through the labyrinth of halls and chambers. No one answered me. I called again, and an old familiar face came out of the shadows. It was Bosra, the old beast man. I hailed him, hugging him gladly about his thin black shoulders.

"It's good to see you, old one. When did you return to the employ of old Crator? When you quit, if I remember correctly, you said you were going home to live the quiet life." Without giving him a chance to reply, I continued. "By the way, Old Bosra, where is the fat wretch of a bandit hiding? He is not in his office. Has he gone home so early today?"

Bosra shook his head sadly.

I felt a catch in my chest. "What is it, Bosra? Crator? Crator's dead?"

Again he nodded his head, slowly . . . sadly.

When I left the Flavian to locate lodging, I was in a daze. I felt a strange sense of loss. Crator had finally been taken by the wine he so dearly loved. Not directly. While in a stupor, he had made the mistake of lying on the soft straw inside one of the animal cages to sleep off his drunk. The beastkeeper, unaware that he was inside, let in two leopards he'd just received from Africa. When he'd returned to feed the cats there was nothing left of Crator but a few scraps of hair, a few tattered shreds of clothing, and his wine bowl. I would have given odds that the cats had a severe hangover after feeding on the tough old sot.

Before I left the arena, the new Games Master had handed me a scroll with my name on it. He'd found it in Crator's desk. I opened it now. Crator had lived up to his bargain. It was a letter of manumission. I was a freedman, with no master other than myself. The Games Master told me that he'd already taken a copy of it to the magistrates to be witnessed and entered into the records. I'd been free now for a period of five days and hadn't even known it. I promised myself that I would make an offering at the Temple of Bacchus in Crator's memory. He would have liked that. He and Bacchus had been great friends for many years.

Free! It was a strange feeling. Not that Crator had abused me, nor made me feel inferior, but all my life I'd known the feeling of being owned, of having a master. Now . . . there was none. I felt terribly alone.

I took quarters in a good clean inn near the Tiber, much better lodgings then I'd had before. I had three rooms on the third floor, with a separate bedroom and a balcony. It may have been considered a luxury, but why not? I could afford it. I made a mental note to see Crator's banker on the morrow.

I didn't rest well that night. Confused and troubled images attacked my sleep and drove rest from my bed. I was more tired when I arose at dawn than when I'd retired.

Without eating, I left my rooms and walked the short distance to the banks of the Tiber, seating myself on the fog-wet stones, watching the mist rise from the river. I sat head in hands, pondering the best way to put my life in order now that Crator was gone and I was free.

Up to now he'd taken care of everything for me; all I'd had to do was fight and train. Now I was forced into the position of making my own decisions, and there'd be many. I knew from his letters that we must have a great deal of money in our joint account, and I was even more aware that I did not have the experience to handle such sums. I could make money, that was true, but keeping it or making it work for me was another thing. I would have to have help on that end of it for sure. And who could I trust?

I knew of several other fighters who had earned vast amounts of money in their time and could have lived out the rest of their lives in comfort if bad managers and investors had not taken all they'd earned, leaving them paupers in their old age. This, I swore, would not happen to me. If I didn't have the brains to handle such matters of finance, and I knew I had not, then I would find someone that did.

I still had no appetite by the time the sun was full and the mist had burned off. I headed for the house of the bankers, taking with me the letter of manumission. I had never before been inside their doors, though I'd waited outside for Crator several times while he attended to business.

I stopped by the baths on the way, to wash away the stains of travel and have my hair oiled and the stubble shaved from my face. My clothes were good enough, made of fine wool from the Tin Isles, with a wide belt of red leather at the waist. I wore matching silver bracelets at my wrists and a purse full of silver at my waist. I would not look like a beggar at the bank. Crator had told me many times that your appearance was important when you talked to men about money, even if it was yours. Especially when one wanted to borrow it.

I'd left my sword at the inn in the care of the tavernkeeper. He'd placed it in a locked box. I warned him that if anything happened to it during my absence I would return and feed him his own balls. He was a large stout man with a heavy belly and the look of a bully about him.

He'd at first started to give me some smart talk at my orders, but upon learning my name he'd turned quickly into a servile sniveler. It proved to me that Crator had done his work well. My name was known and feared.

I regained my horse and rode as a freedman to the house of the banker. It was a large establishment, occupying three entire floors and surrounded by high walls that were being guarded by armed slaves. At the door I was admitted by a tough-looking man of middle height. I'd seen him before and his name came back to me. It was Galucus, once considered one of the finest postulati in all Rome. I hailed him as such. He looked at me queerly for a moment before recognition came to him.

"Lucanus! I did not know you. You have changed much since you left our city."

He was right. I was much broader in shoulder and heavier and stronger in build, but I think the biggest change was in my manner and air. I told him that I wished to see the master of the house. He showed me to a waiting room where I took my ease on a large padded curule chair. He disappeared through a pair of heavy doors and closed them behind him. I could hear muffled sounds of talking behind them, not clear enough to make out any of the words. He finally returned and told me that it would yet be a few minutes. I declined his offer of wine or refreshment while I waited. He returned to his post by the entrance. I noticed a bulge beneath his white tunic, a dagger I presumed.

After nearly an hour, the doors opened and a man came forth. He had a very dignified air, silvery hair and a broad smile. Once he had been built well, it was easy to tell. But now the years of rich foods and easy living showed in the slackness of his jowls and in the belly that protruded over his belt. His fingers were fat and covered gaudily with rings of various designs. His smile and manner of greeting were too much for me, and I knew I did not like him.

He showed me into his office, seating me in a hard chair and himself behind the desk. There was a stack of documents atop it which he immediately began shuffling through. His voice dripped with honey and false concern.

"Well, we finally meet. I'm terribly sorry that your master died so unfortunately, but the gods' wills be done I suppose. Now, what is it you came to see me about?"

"Our money, of course!" I wanted to get this done with.

He shook his head, confused innocence written all over him. "Money? What money?"

At his words I rose from my chair. "Why, mine and Crator's, of course."

He started to say something else, but I quickly tossed my letter of manumission on his desk, which contained the orders from Crator as to the disposition of our funds. All money that was held in the houses of C. Tullio Targuin in the name of Crator, was now mine.

He shook his head sadly as he read my document.

"Young sir, I regret to inform you that there is no money."

He stopped my protest by raising one of his account ledgers for me to look at.

"This," he said, "is the ledger of Crator." He pointed to an entry. "As you can see, in the last months he withdrew large sums of money. Withdrawing, I'm afraid, until there was nothing left. He closed all accounts with us, including yours, only a week before his death."

I could read, though not well, and I had seen Crator's signature enough to tell that this looked like his, but I could still not believe it. Why would he withdraw over forty thousand denarii, all that I had worked for, over five years? It was gone, all gone, save for that I'd brought back with me.

Targuin was all compassion. "I truly do not know why he needed such vast amounts of money sir. That is no business of ours. When a client demands it, we must turn it over to him, all that which is his. You can understand that, can you not?''

I agreed with him. There was nothing else I could do.

He hustled me from his office with the offer to open an account in my name any time I so wished and that he would be honored to render me the same good services that he had given Crator. I thanked him for his time, saying that I'd be in touch, and wandered back into the streets in a daze.

This time I didn't mount my horse. I took the reins instead into my hand and led the animal down the rough stone streets, even now filling with people going about their daily business.

I was still in a state of shock when a familiar voice jarred me from my thoughts.

''L . . . L . . . Lucanus?''

At the sound of my name, I turned around just in time to be hugged and kissed wetly on both cheeks.

Claudius was looking well, his eyes sparkling at the sight of me. He asked a thousand questions at once, not waiting for me to answer before stuttering into another. He stopped suddenly, his face concerned.

''What is it, Lucanus? Why the long face? You s . . . s . . . should be happy, all Rome waits for your return, you are a very famous man now.''

I recounted the events that had taken place since my return. The death of Crator, the letter of manumission, and the banker's bad news. Claudius frowned, asking again the name of the banker. His face took on a sharp look.

''Targuin, eh? I'll look into it. Don't you worry about that right now. There are things to do. Germanicus will be arriving from Germania soon and we must have a reunion, the three of us. Eh?''

He asked me of my plans for Graecus and if I thought I was ready for him. I told him I really hadn't thought about

Graecus since the business of Crator's death, but that I still wanted the Greek. It would probably be some time before a fight between us could be arranged. Claudius tried his best to cheer me up and invited me to go with him that night to the home of a very influential friend. He promised that it would be worth my while and that I would have the opportunity to meet some people who could perhaps do me some good. I asked their name, but he would only shake his head, saying that I would see. There was no way I could refuse his invitation, and besides, the sight of his friendly and concerned face had made me feel better.

He left me at the gates to the outer city. I had to go and see Pollio. I knew that he and the rest of the troupe had arrived by now and were more than likely billeted in the barracks near the walls, established for troupes such as Pollio's when not on the road. On the way I stopped off at a wine shop and purchased a flagon of Falernian. I took my first drink since I'd left Rome, but before doing so, I spilled a small libation out on the floor of the shop, to the shade of Crator, wherever he was.

The wine went straight to my head, and though drinking only the one flagon, I was half drunk by the time I'd left the shop. I decided to ride the rest of the way and cantered into the barracks, where I found Pollio cursing the baggage man for dropping a bundle.

We went into Pollio's room, and I told him of Crator's ill fortune and of all that had transpired since my arrival. I needed someone with experience to advise me, I told him. Although we had had our differences, I still respected Pollio's judgment. He was too much of a businessman not to take advantage of what I was offering him. I made him my personal manager and told him to start getting things set up for me. I wanted Graecus and would fight no other until I had taken him first.

I knew he would put the word out on the streets fast,

and before long Graecus would be forced to respond to my challenge. I made Pollio the standard package deal of most managers and gave him a hundred denarii out of my purse to start things rolling. I had my personal effects taken to my rooms and followed them, after first buying one more taste of the grape along the route.

At the inn, I turned the horse over to one of the attendants with instructions to return it to its owners and redeem my deposit on the animal. I warned him that should he fail to return within the hour I would go looking for him and my money.

He left and I went on inside. I took my meal in the room, not tasting the food or even paying any attention to the girl who delivered it, though she tried to gain my interest by bumping one rounded hip against my arm and smiling coyly when I looked up at her. I probably hurt her feelings by my indifference, but I was definitely in no mood for pleasure at the time.

I lay back on my cot, trying to fight the whirling feeling that was gradually gaining strength in my head. The wine was getting to me. I would have to watch that. It would be easy to begin to rely on its soothing effect on the brain. I must have reclined there for a couple of hours, not sleeping, just thinking random thoughts with no real substance to them. Still tired, I rose and changed. It was time to go to Claudius' house and accompany him I knew not where.

When I arrived he was ready to go. To my surprise, he had two slave-borne litters prepared and waiting, one for me and the other for himself. Four armed slaves carried torches to light our way while others struggled under our weight. I felt somewhat regal, yet guilty, too.

When I asked the purpose of the armed slaves, he laughed, saying that he always remembered a hard-earned lesson, and especially a bad one.

We came finally to a residential area of the rich and powerful on the Via Flaminia, where we left the litters at the bottom of the stairs and walked up through a grove of poplars. Up ahead of us I could hear the sounds of a lively party, clear and loud. Claudius chuckled, saying that I had a big surprise waiting ahead. I asked what he meant, but he would say no more. He looked vastly amused at his secret, although he was having some difficulty navigating the steps with his bad leg and leaned on my arm at times.

When we reached the top of the stairs we were at the garden entrance to a house, the likes of which I'd only seen from a distance. Tall columns surrounded the garden that was decorated with statues and shrubs. The sound of music and laughter came from it. We didn't enter the house but instead went straight into the garden, and were immediately announced by the major-domo, a sophisticated slave of about fifty, who acted as if he owned the place. He called out our names for the guests to hear. When he spoke the name of Claudius it was with servile tones, but in announcing mine, "the well-known gladiator, Lucanus," he used a snide voice of superiority. I was tempted to braid his legs there on the spot, but thought better of it.

A stockily built figure, wearing a plain white toga with a broad purple stripe around the hem, came to us from out of the shadows. He hailed Claudius and extended his arms to be embraced.

"Welcome, nephew."

I nearly swallowed my tongue. It was Augustus, the uncle of Germanicus and Claudius and Emperor of Rome! I outdid Claudius at the moment in stuttering, trying my best to find the proper words of greeting such a noble leader. He took my arm, leading me dumbfounded out of the garden.

He spoke plainly to me, not as the exalted leader of an Empire, but as man to man. "I finally get the opportunity to thank you personally for the services you rendered my nephews a good time ago. I am very fond of them both, you know."

Claudius was following us, but having trouble keeping up with our pace. When Augustus noticed his difficulty, he slowed somewhat. I noticed he had the walk of a soldier. He continued when Claudius caught up. "Claudius tells me you are a freedman. Congratulations. I am truly sorry that Germanicus is not here to welcome you home. He will be returning to Rome soon, however, and I'm certain he will wish to see you. He has told me much about you, all of it complimentary I may add. Now, please come and let me introduce you to some of my other guests." He whispered in my ear then. "Please be at ease. We are only mortals here, and you are among friends."

His words went to my head faster than the wine had done. Here I stood, on the arm of the ruler of the world, and he was speaking to me as one man to another. I found my voice and squeaked out an embarrassed response.

He laughed again and reassured me. "Relax! All this is new to you now, but it will pass when you have the chance to see our faults up close."

He introduced me to several Senators and Consuls. They were all polite, it seemed, though somewhat distant. The women were more friendly with me, a few of them daring to touch the bulge of my arm and making cooing sounds at the hardness of the muscles.

Wine was served, and I was left in the care of Claudius while the Emperor went to greet other guests arriving late. I was relating some of my adventures to my friend when a soft voice spoke at my shoulder. I felt a chill and turned to face the speaker. Graecus was smiling at me, his face lit by the torches. He hadn't changed a bit. Still as smooth as ever. He reached for my hand and shook it warmly.

"I'm delighted to see you again, Lucanus. I've heard much about your exploits, even from as far as Africa. You certainly look fit, I must say. I like your hair that way. Shoulder length does compliment you, young one."

Claudius was smirking. I was now unsure whether the surprise he'd promised me was meeting Augustus or seeing Graecus again. Graecus stayed with us a moment longer, discussing subjects on which I knew nothing. I hated myself for my limited knowledge of all except the arena. He was talking of poets and artists, of sculptors and their finest works, and asking me if I'd seen this or that famous work in my travels. Just as he was called off to meet some admirers, he said, "We must really get together sometime, Lucanus."

I had gained some confidence by now and I replied: "That, Graecus, we will most surely do, and soon I hope."

He nodded his curled head gracefully in agreement and left us. I was no longer infuriated by him, only determined.

I saw the Emperor only once more that night. He'd stopped by to excuse his absence on urgent matters of state, I think he said. Claudius stayed with me throughout the feast. I have never seen such delicacies as I saw that night, most of which I personally did not care for very much. There was venison and partridge, fresh trout from streams in the hills, and one dish I refused to even try, tiny dormice baked in a shell of honey.

There were over two hundred guests that night and they ate everything there, eagerly, many of them gorging themselves until they had to go to the vomitorium, where they tickled the backs of their throats with a feather to make themselves vomit, then returned with empty stomachs to gorge again. I was confused by this action and asked Claudius about it. He explained that the idea was not to just eat until you were sated of appetite, but to allow the taste buds to experience everything possible. It may have made sense to an epicurean, but it seemed very wasteful to me.

Couches were brought out as the night wore on, and we all reclined, listening to the singers and musicians who were playing softly. Slaves stood at our beck and call, waiting to serve our every need. All were young and attractive, both men and girls, but the party did not become rowdy, which surprised me. I learned that Augustus Caesar was somewhat old fashioned and did not allow licentious behavior in his home. This did not hinder several well-born ladies, whose bodies were perfumed with rare-scents and their faces neatly powdered, from becoming overly friendly with me. More than one soft breast found its way near my face or rubbed accidentally against me as we talked. The ladies wanted to hear of my fights and told me how they had waited for my return, how much they'd heard about me, and what a thrill it was to meet me.

One of them did take my attention. She was Antonia, a niece of one of the Senators. She had hair of silk, the color of new honey and the face of an angel of the gods. From the north she said she was, of Tonisa Caprea. She was well formed in body; the outline of her breasts showed clearly through her stola. Her breath was sweet as she spoke to me.

I made arrangements to meet Antonia within a few days, when she had a chance to get away from the watchful eyes of her family. We were near the same age. Only by a matter of months was I her elder. The thing about her that attracted me most was that she didn't have that death-fascinated look in her eyes. I felt she liked me as a person, instead of merely as a gladiator.

When I took leave of the party, Claudius told me to go straight to bed, and alone. For on the morrow we would have work to do. The two of us. I caught one last look at Antonia before leaving. She was on the arm of a knight, from the family of the gens Neronian. She gave me a slight nod of her head and that was all I needed. I would find out how to reach her through Claudius. He was a romantic at heart, and I was sure he'd be delighted to arrange a tryst between the rough gladiator and the dark-haired lovely from a noble house.

So I went to my bed alone that night, though I spent many hours with some very warm and wet dreams. By the time Claudius arrived the following morning, I'd made up my mind that I was in love. I tried to tell Claudius, but he cut me off short, saying my glands could wait until we took care of more pressing matters.

2

We returned to the house of the banker, Targuin.

Limping and stuttering constantly, Claudius told me to keep quiet when we were inside and to let him do all the talking. The way his mouth was presently going, I doubted there would be an opportunity for me to speak anyway.

I didn't know what he thought he might accomplish, but he was from a different world than my own and probably understood things I could not.

Once Claudius had identified himself, we were admitted to the banker's presence with dispatch. Targuin had a concerned expression on his smooth oily face when we entered. Even with his infirmities, Claudius was still a member of the Imperial household.

I must say, it was a pleasure to watch Claudius at work. I gained a new respect for the keen mind beneath the role of a fool he played so well. He nailed Targuin's hide to the wall that day, staying calm, sly, never intimating that Targuin had done anything illegal, but asking to see copies of all transactions made by Crator prior to his death.

Targuin produced them and Claudius, pursing his lips and making irritating smacking sounds, pored over each one thoroughly, shaking his head now and then, letting the banker sweat.

He took his time, almost four hours. When he'd finished with the final document, he looked at Targuin and shook his head in pity.

"You're in a lot of trouble, s . . . s . . . sir!" Claudius clucked his tongue in reproof. The banker started to protest, but Claudius waved one of the documents in his hand.

"Mr. Targuin, s . . . s . . . someone in your employ is a thief. This is an obvious and blatant forgery of Crator's signature. I wonder, if the magistrates were called in to inspect, how many more they would find like this one?"

Targuin blanched at the suggestion. I knew then that Claudius had him.

My limping stutterer continued, his voice dripping with sympathy for the trouble that lay before the banker. He made soft mention of the punishment for forgery, including the confiscation of all the guilty party's assets, banishment, and even death if the clients that had been duped were influential enough to sway the court.

By the time Claudius had finished, Targuin agreed to make full restitution of all funds and to pay an additional five percent interest on the total, retroactive to the date of Crator's death, meanwhile playing the innocent to the hilt. He vowed that he would find out who had dishonored his good name and that of his banking house, promising Claudius that everything would be taken care of with haste.

Claudius stood, shaking the banker's hand. "I certainly hope so. Now, if you will have the proper letters and the amounts drawn up for my friend's signature, we will take our leave and wish you good day."

When the transfer of my newfound wealth was made to a new banking house, Claudius informed me that the amount in my name totaled over one hundred and fifty thousand denarii. I was a rich man, at least by most standards, but Claudius didn't give me time to spend even one denarius before telling me that I needed someone to watch over my accounts, and he knew just where to go.

A friend of his, a junior Senator of the Plebes, was in financial difficulty due to a bad run of luck at the races. We went straight to his home, where Claudius was closeted with him for some time. When he came back out, he held a document for my signature in the amount of two thousand denarii. I started to read it after signing, but Claudius jerked it from my hand, saying he didn't have the time to stand around watching my lips move as I read.

He went back inside and quickly returned, followed by another man. I learned that I was now the proud owner of my first slave. Claudius introduced me to Albinus the Greek, saying this was the man who would take charge of all my financial affairs, adding that if his friend the Senator had listened to his advice in the first place, he would not be in trouble today.

Albinus was a handsome young man with a delicate build and beautiful manners. It seemed to me that, with his education and refinement, he should have been my owner, rather than the other way around. (I'm sure you'll agree with that, won't you, Albinus?)

Claudius instructed Albinus, as well as myself, in his new duties, as the three of us returned to the inner city. Claudius was firm with him as we walked, handing him the copies of all the accounts and receipts from my new banker.

"Albinus, you will take proper care of your new master's accounts and investments. I wish that you would also try to teach him s . . . s . . . some things of value. A little culture won't hurt him. Lucanus," he turned to me now, not stuttering at all, "you will need a home. I know of several estates that are presently up for sale, and the price is right. There is one that I especially like in Herculaneum. It has a grove of trees that goes with the house. Yes! I think that is the one you should buy. There is no need for you to stay in Rome all the time. In fact, now that I think about it, it would be better if you were not seen here too frequently. There are too many things that can cause you trouble here, and you just don't know how to play the game. Yes! You will buy the house in Herculaneum."

By the gods! Was I to have no say at all? I'd gone a simple gladiator to a slave owner and now to an owner of house and land. And without one word from me? But

Claudius was right, and I knew it.

I asked Claudius why a slave should handle my affairs rather than an investment house. He shook his head, looking for all the world as if I were totally retarded.

"You just went through that s . . . s . . . situation once, Lucanus. Any time a great sum of money is involved, people are going to try to have some of it stick to their fingers. If you own your personal broker, and if he tries to steal from you, you can kill him legally, and he knows it. That, my stupid friend, will keep him honest and trustworthy."

I couldn't argue with that.

Before another week had passed, I owned the house in Herculaneum, with a grove of trees, as well as an irritable slave. A smart, quick, well-read and highly educated slave, but yet a grumpy one. He was everything that Claudius said he was.

Before leaving for Herculaneum, I gave Pollio instructions to do as he thought Crator would have in my behalf. He was to hire men who would spread my name throughout the city, always with the same question attached: *Why does Graecus refuse to fight the Wolf?* No direct challenge had been issued as of yet, but the general populace would not know that. The question would spread fast; they would write my name on the walls in every public place where there was room among the rest of the grafitti.

I received one offer to perform in the Flavian that week. The new manager himself made the bid. But I turned it down, saying that when next I fought I would fight the best. He knew what I meant. I would not fight again in Rome until it was Graecus I faced.

Claudius too went along with the scheme. Among the nobility he spread the rumor that he'd heard Graecus was afraid of me. I knew that it would all get back to Niger soon, and I wanted to be out of town when it did, avoiding a direct confrontation in public. Things like that were better left to an agent to arrange.

So, I went on to my new and majestic domus in Herculaneum, to wait for Graecus' challenge, and for something else. Claudius had been pleased to play Cupid for me and had arranged for Antonia to visit my home. She had told her family that she was going to stay with some friends nearby. There was no suspicion on their part, for they knew the people well. They'd told her to have a good time and enjoy herself. That we did!

She stayed with me for a week, and it was the most enjoyable week of my life, to that point anyway. We spent hours getting to know the secret things about each other, searching and exploring different places of pleasure. When she finally was forced to leave, not by me but by speeding time, I passed some days in a very depressed state. I wanted no one else. The sluts of the houses of haetarii were all crones to my eyes, with their painted eyes and powdered faces. I'm afraid that Albinus suffered of my anger, spent on him for minor infractions I would normally have overlooked. (Eh, Albinus?) But, as I said, I was out of sorts, touchy and dissatisfied with any other than Antonia. I don't know how long I would have remained in that miserable state had word not arrived from Pollio that he had made a deal with Graecus' agent. We would fight!

The event was to take place in two months. I had Albinus bring in workmen to convert my garden, beautiful though it was, into a gymnasium. The last time I had fought in Rome was as a thraces, but the years had added mass to my frame until I now weighed nearly two hundred pounds. Constant exercise and training had kept most of it hard muscle, but I'd developed a tendency to put a little fat around the midriff if I laid up for any time. This was no time to lie around getting fat and sloppy. Pollio arranged for sparring partners to visit me, especially those who had fought with Niger and had lived, either from thumbs-up or from non-death battles.

Watching a man fight from the stands of the arena was one thing, but to go against those who could show me his style was another. I learned much about his manner of movement and his finesse from these men. The whole process was expensive, but it mattered even less than when I'd bet all on myself during the tour in Africa.

Pollio had also booked some of his troupe for the games on the same day I was to fight. They were billeted just outside the walls of Rome. A week before the scheduled combat, I joined them. I stayed there in seclusion, sparring with his men, working out ten to twelve hours a day, honing my instincts and reflexes to a razor's edge. Word travels fast though, and I received two invitations from Graecus to dine with him or attend the theater. I refused, naturally.

Two days before the games, Pollio came to me, suggesting that it would be advisable for me to visit the Temple of Fortuna. He'd been stopped on the streets by one of her priests and told that I should come to them for a message. I knew, as did Pollio, that the priests of Fortuna usually had the inside track on most of the sporting events. Fortuna was the patroness of gamblers, fighters, and horse-racers. If a priest suggested you visit them, it generally meant that they had information to sell. Certainly they would not come right out and ask for a donation, but, if the amount of your offering pleased them, they would see to it that your augury contained good information that could mean a victory for you, if you understood it. They all spoke in parables only. I personally was never any good at puzzles, but I didn't think it wise to take any chances.

I went into the city the following morning, going directly to the temple. It was a fair-sized structure, with tall white pillars, situated atop a rise. The priest who greeted me knew me by sight and welcomed me into the cool interior. He led me to the altar where a flame was kept burning beneath the goddess' symbol, a large silver wheel that represented the game of chance, very popular at the festivals.

He had a shrewd look to him, the old priest. While his robes were of homespun, his ring was pure gold, set with a huge sapphire the color and size of a robin's egg.

I knelt before the altar and set a sack of silver on the marble dais. The priest hefted the sack and clucked his tongue, turning away from me and facing the silver wheel.

I knew immediately what he wanted. I dug another purse from beneath my waistband. This time the clink of the coins had a richer tone to it. Gold usually does. He turned back around and hefted the sack between two fingers, smiling. Before I could catch the movement, both purses had disappeared beneath his robes.

He then went into his routine. Leaning over the flames, he cast in some powder, which gave off a pungent odor. He breathed heavily of the fumes and began to mumble in some unknown tongue, his eyes closed, his head back. I've never known exactly why they do that ritual, instead of just getting on with the message. Perhaps it makes them feel better. After a few moments of gibberish he suddenly stopped and looked at me, his eyes glassy. He spoke:

"Your future lies in the clouded eye!"

That was it? That was what I'd paid for? While I was thinking over his words of wisdom he turned and left, disappearing through some curtains behind the altar.

Well, I had received my oracle. Now to try and figure it out. I spent the remainder of the day wandering about the city, looking up at the sky to see if the clouds would translate the message for me. Naturally, they did not. I tried every combination I could think of, but the parable made no sense. Finally I wrote it off as costly nonsense and gave up.

Before I left the city to return to the barracks and the rest of Pollio's troupe, I stopped by to see old Bosra. There was something I wanted to do for him. I found him in a corner of the lower chambers, feeding goat's milk to a lion cub with his finger. He smiled at me and bobbed his woolly grey head in greeting.

We talked awhile about the old days, and he wished me good fortune on my upcoming fight with Graecus. I asked him if he still wanted to return home to Africa. He nodded dreamily, saying it was ever his desire. I gave him my last purse, containing fifty gold aurei. He started to refuse, but I told him that after the fight I would have a hundred times that amount to throw away and, if I should lose, what difference would this purse do me?

He put the cub back in its pen and rose to his feet. Bosra looked tired. He held my hand warmly in his own and gently asked if I minded him not attending the fights. I knew he didn't wish to see me hurt. I told him I cared not.

"No, Bosra! Get your belongings together and leave Rome now. Go home, old man, go back to Africa and find peace."

There was nothing more to be said between us. I knew that before nightfall he would be looking for a ship to take him away.

I wished him well. He had been a good man, and a good friend to a child.

3

The troupe of Pollio left before me the next morning, but I would have no difficulty in catching up to them. This time, instead of marching in with the rest of the fighters, I would ride in my own chariot.

This day I was entered in the main event. I only wished that old Crator was alive to see me returning as champion.

I passed the rest of the troupe at the Appian Gate, my favorite entrance to the city of Rome. I waved at them and lashed my horses onward, showing off a bit. Just to be safe, even though I had already made an offering at the Temple of Fortuna, I thought it might be a good idea to be seen at the Shrine of Mars Ultor, where his aspect was that of the Avenger.

I enjoyed the ride over; the wind whipping at my face was refreshing. The day certainly looked as if it was going to be a good one. Already, I could see, the crowds were turning out and heading for the arena. Most of them were carrying lunches—bread, cheese and olive oil—for the long entertaining day at the fights. They waved at me as I rode by. It was a good feeling to be recognized by well-wishing fans. Pretentious, yes, but a good feeling just the same. I took it as a good omen, a fair sign for victory. If I could only figure out what was meant by the clouded eye. It bothered me.

I left my chariot and animals in the care of two street urchins, giving them each a coin, and entered the Temple of Mars.

Inside, I paid for two goats to be sacrificed at the Altar of Mars. His statue was bronze, twice the size of a man, depicting him in full armor with sword upraised as in the salute of the gladiators.

After the priest read the goat entrails for omens, and my donation of silver had been accepted, they gave me a fair forecast. I would be victorious, but only if I heeded the *clouded eye*. It was all I could get out of them. Priests must stay up nights trying to figure out ways to confuse people with their riddles. I left somewhat worried, still puzzled completely.

By the time I entered the performers' gate to the circus the games were well under way, as could be told from the cries of the crowd. The warm-up events were over, and now there were two sets of andabatae on the sands trying to find each other, which wasn't easy, since they were all blind. Attendants helped them along with touches from their hot irons whenever they strayed too far away from each other. This action was pulling a lot of laughter from the mob. I never enjoyed contests like these, where blinded slaves with knives groped for each other. When they were finally able to strike, it was clumsy and awkward-looking. It was no way for a sporting event to be conducted, at least to my way of thinking. But the crowd liked it, and they were condemned men anyway. Perhaps it was better for them. Their only options were crucifixion or never-ending toil on one of the slave galleys plying the seas from Asia to Africa.

I turned my chariot over to a slave, and Pollio yelled from the gate.

"Well met, Lucanus! Are you ready for this day? It could be the big one. Win today and we will treble our money on the next."

I told him I was ready and asked if there'd been any changes made in the day's events. He said that things were pretty much the same and I was to go on as scheduled. Good! That would give me a couple of hours to try and figure out the oracles.

I went into the quarters of the veterans. Reserved today were two rooms only—one for me and one for Graecus. On my way to my rooms I passed a team of Germanic barbarians. Pollio had told me they were mostly Marcomanii, an obscure tribe from the region of the Elbe. The only thing I knew personally about them was the fact that they'd given Julius Caesar a few problems in his day. But then, so had all the German tribes.

The barbarians that I'd met in the arena all had two things in common. Besides being big and hairy, they were completely without fear and fought with great pleasure and pride. Courage, yes. But not much style.

Pollio returned after checking the schedule again. He told me we were to go on after the Nubians finished off a batch of trained war elephants. I didn't relish that news.

Elephants were a damned hard act to follow.

I suppose by now you are familiar with my routine preparations before going into battle. This day was no different from the others. I relaxed for a few minutes after I'd checked my gear, and waited. Pollio would signal me in plenty of time. Even after the blacks had killed the great grey beasts, a team of butchers would have to be summoned to carve the carcasses into chunks small enough to be dragged from the sands. That would require an hour in itself. Plenty of time.

4

Of one thing I was certain; Graecus would not outshine me in costume this day. I had spent over five hundred gold pieces for my new gear and, if I had to say so myself, I had never in all my years seen such a costume.

Germanicus had sent me to his personal arms maker. It had taken the man over a month to finish the order. What I wore, in terms of general design, was a version of the regular costume. My helmet was similar in style to that of the Praetorian guards, sporting an ornamental visor, inlaid with pure gold tracings set in silver. The helmet itself was of steel, but had a plate of pure silver welded to it. The crest was of gold and held a horsehair plume, dyed a bright blue, reaching to the nape of my neck. The neck guard was slightly longer than the regulation helmet and afforded me more protection.

My shoulder guard was made of the same steel-and-silver combination, traced with gold designs of Mars the Avenger. I wore no chest armor, only a broad strap of blue leather, set with silver badges, that ran from my right shoulder, secured to the arm guard, and down to the gold buckles on my wide leather belt.

Below the waist I wore a loincloth of blue cotton, tucked neatly up and into the belt. My leg greaves matched the rest of the costume.

The shield was made in the manner of my shoulder guards. It was a little smaller than the regulation size, therefore also a bit lighter in weight. I'd selected it because I didn't wish to chance my arms tiring and lowering my guard. I planned on the fight with Graecus lasting for a while, and small things could make the difference in who was to be dragged from the sands by meathooks.

Pollio came to me as I stood at the gate, his bald head sweating. "Well, you finally have what you wanted, a shot at Graecus. Just remember, take it easy, don't wear yourself out. Watch out for the advantage he holds in reach. It's deceptive. He will try to measure you for distance. Don't let him! If he reaches out, you must either move in quickly or step back. If you possibly can, try to work close to him, get inside where his reach doesn't offer him advantage. You're stronger than he is, and younger. Use it to your own good. Use your shield also; pound at him at every chance. Work on his body. He's enjoyed too many years of easy living and is more than likely soft inside."

I listened to him, though we'd gone over this same subject a hundred times. He handed me the flask of posca to rinse my mouth with. I swirled the sour liquid around my teeth and gums and spat it out.

When the horns sounded that the arena was clear and had been freshly sanded and raked, it would be time for us to go on. I expected a good response from the mob. In my will I'd left them my share of the loser's purse, if it was I who lost. It was not a gesture of love for the bloodthirsty lot, but a deterrent to my being poisoned before the fight by Pollio. Normally, the agent or the lanista would receive the purse if his fighter lost and died. This way, Pollio could only see profit if I won, and would see to my welfare before the fight. I also made sure that he'd wagered all he owned on my winning, so as to prevent him from side-betting and making a profit on my death. Actually, he had a great deal to lose if I fell.

The horns blaring brought me out of these thoughts. I took a deep breath, donned my helmet and thrust my left arm through the straps of my rectangular shield. I nodded my head, and Pollio opened the gate to let me through. I watched for the gate at the opposite end of the arena to open. I was not going to let Graecus upstage me by making his entrance first.

We set foot in the sunlight at the same time. The distance across the arena was about a hundred yards and even from where I stood, at that distance, I could see that he was glowing like the sun god Apollo.

As we neared each other, I could see that the Apollo image was the one he was trying to give the crowd. Where I was silver, he was gold. Everything about him glistened as the sunlight reflected off his shield and armor. His helmet was higher than mine, with a red horsehair plume. Where mine was neck length, his reached nearly to the small of his back. His visor was raised to show his face; he was the perfect image of the Greek warrior. His shield was round, with a deep-set inlay of gold on black, depicting Ajax at the battle of Troy. His sword was slightly longer than my own. He wore a Greek skirt of black and gold pleats that reached almost to the knees. His leg greaves were similar to my own, except in color.

None of this bothered me in the least. What did bother me was the confidence he displayed. I had hoped that my growing reputation would cause him some concern, but, if it did, I couldn't tell it.

We met in the center of the arena, neither of us speaking. He smiled at me as if we were about to sit down to a pleasant dinner together, instead of a battle to the death. We turned on and faced the Imperial box. As one, we raised our swords, everything about us a bright contrast of gold and silver. His sword was of shining steel and mine the grey metal of Syria. We sounded off in unison.

"Ave, Caesar! Te Morituri Salutamus!"

I could see that, along with Germanicus and Claudius, Tiberius was also seated in the box to the right of Caesar. Claudius waved to me discreetly.

We turned and faced off about five feet from each other, both waiting for the signal to begin. The crowd broke into loud cheers. For the first time in my career, my name was louder on the tongues of the mob than was Niger's. The strongest shouts for me were coming from the seats of the city's poor. I was their darling, now that I had willed them my wealth. Certainly they would like to see me die this day so as to gain a few sesterces each. But I think that most of them sincerely thought me a noble and good-hearted fellow and wished me good fortune in the match.

At the signal from the Games Master, we began!

We started by circling each other, nothing rushed in our movements. I felt good! This was what I'd wanted and worked for patiently for years. We wove in and out, from side to side, cautiously, looking for an opening in the other's guard, throwing light thrusts that meant nothing, using them only to feel out the other's rhythm of motion and response.

Our movements must have looked somewhat like a ritual dance, although a dance that could only end in a bloody finale. Normally, the audience would have become impatient and rowdy with fighters as cautious as we, taking so much time before making any serious moves. But this was not a normal event and the crowd knew it. The stands remained silent as we parried. If they'd been roused it would have made no difference to Niger or myself anyway. Our total concentration was on each other; the audience was of no importance at all. Neither of us could see them now.

Graecus' sword was a spatha, the thin, long blade used by cavalrymen. He kept flicking it at my face, a silver serpent's tongue, darting at my face and eyes. I was aware that with his longer reach and sword, he held a dangerous advantage over me. Too, the smoothness of the spatha could allow it to go over the tip of an opponent's blade and glide in easily to the exposed face or throat.

My counter was to try and keep him always at an angle, moving to his side, setting up a definite pattern that I would break only when the time was right.

From the ring, nothing was audible to the crowd except the clash of our swords. As we maneuvered, Graecus spoke to me: "It's good to see you again, little wolf. I have been waiting for you a long time now."

He spoke as one who said endearing things to his lover, not one who was trying to kill him. He flicked his point again near my eyes. I blinked and quickly stepped back. He smiled, almost a sad leer. "Now, at last, you have come to me. I would have preferred it another way, but perhaps this is best. Come to me, little wolf. Let me touch you!"

He reached out again with his longer blade. This time I countered, point to point. Twisting my wrist in a quick circular motion, I threw his point up and slid inside with a long leading step that put us close, shield to shield. We locked in that position, swords hooked at the hilt.

I looked into his face as we strained against each other. It was then that I spotted what the priest of Fortuna had meant by the clouded eye. A milky white shadow completely covered the lens of his left eye. This was it!

I twisted my body to the left and, at the same time, lowered my blade to point at the ground. His sword was still locked at the hilt with my own. My twisting movement had the effect of turning him half around, breaking his balance. I made a quick short smash with my shield while he was in this position, putting my shoulder behind the blow, using my superior strength as Pollio had advised. He nearly stumbled, but before I could break contact with his sword and go for his head and face, he regained his balance and came back at me. The tempo was beginning to pick up now. He got in a long jab and nicked me on the shoulder, just enough to start a trickle of blood.

Graecus smiled at me again, the same gentle unrushed expression.

"Your last move was well executed, Lucanus. What do you say, shall we give our spectators something to remember? They should get their money's worth, don't you agree?"

I responded through my teeth. "As you will, Graecus!"

This was now to be the beginning or the end. The fore-play was done with. Our speed and intensity picked up by degrees. We steadily increased our efforts, lunging, parry-ing, striking with both sword and shield, each action and reaction countered and countered again. It was as if we each knew the action that the other would take, antici-pating the act before it took place. We swerved and moved against each other, both responding in unison. I could almost feel the breathing of the forty thousand spectators above us increasing with our every move. They knew now they were observing something unique. We were like lovers, each knowing the other completely. There were no pauses in the action now, but ever-increasing motion that built to a crescendo of ringing sword strikes, steel thuds of shields and powerful lunges.

Sweat ran freely down our faces as we searched for the opening, but it was not to be found. We worked our way to the wall of the arena. I dropped low, almost to my knees and under his sword, then came up with my shield to catch the bottom edge of his, thrusting upwards with my legs, using the power of my thighs to raise his shield arm and expose his stomach. I made a sudden slice to the side that opened a thin streak of red across the muscles of his belly. If it had been anyone but Graecus, this movement would have laid his gut open two inches deep. But Niger had pivoted away from me, countering, and now I found my own back up against the wall and trying to beat off his counterattack.

He laid my cheek open with a slice before I was able to turn him again. I had started to work on his left side, where the eye was fogged, for his response wasn't as quick, or as accurate, when I attacked from the left. If I could place a cut over his right eye, or possibly stab it out, I was sure he'd be nearly blind. That was what I'd started going for.

We stood eye to eye, our helmets touching at the head guard, breathing through our mouths. I could smell the sweat of his body. I moved my head back quickly, allowing his to move forward. As it did, I moved my own back in quickly to meet his face. The visor of my helmet caught him sharply, just above the right eye and exactly where I'd intended. The skin broke open and blood began to flow down into his eye. He pushed me back in order to gain room to use his longer reach. He was shaking his head, trying to clear the blood from his right eye.

I went at him again, the point of my blade reaching for the identical spot my helmet had opened. He countered a bit awkwardly. I could see his face turning pale and knew that it was caused by rising anger. Nothing he'd tried had worked for him. But then, not many of my own techniques had accomplished much either, at least up to this point. He managed to wipe the blood away with the back of his sword hand, then charged me suddenly like a whirlwind, beating me backwards. I'd never seen a blade move with such speed. I countered, but barely, and he'd managed to hack great gouges out of my shield while forcing me back over the entire length of the arena.

I didn't try to stand up to his attack or go on the offense. I was content just to keep him off me while he tired himself. I wanted him to sweat, so the blood would keep flowing over the eye.

When he'd backed me again to the wall of the arena, I decided it was about time to alter the situation a bit. I closed with him, and sneered as I said: "Are you still glad I'm here, Graecus?"

He didn't answer. I hammered at him with my shield and could feel his guard arm weakening with each blow—not a lot, but enough to tell. His legs were tiring now too. He smiled again, but this time his lips were tight and pale.

I threw my sword arm up and over the top of his shield, not attempting to strike with my blade, for we were too close for that; instead, I caught him with my elbow to strike and widen the cut over his eye again. The thin skin gave even further, and blood spurted out to cover his face. He shook his head furiously, spraying me with blood and sweat. He attempted to wipe the flow from his eyes, but I never gave him a chance. I came at him even heavier than before, striking low and to his left side, knowing that with his right eye bloody he would lack the necessary depth perception. My sword struck his leg, entering the large muscle of the thigh to a depth of about three inches. When I removed the blade, I did so with a downward sweep that ripped his leg open to the knee. The cut was a good one; the leg was badly hurt. He put it behind him to protect it from further damage.

In a distant corner of my mind I knew that the crowd was screaming, but it seemed far away, detached from the present happenings.

I moved in again as Graecus took up a position by the wall to the south. This was it. He had made up his mind to go no farther. He would take his stand here, to live or die. He was still dangerous, maybe even more so now, and proved it by opening my rib cage to the bone and striking me across the bridge of my nose with his shield. I felt and heard the bone breaking, the cartilage collapsing, and my eyes filled suddenly with salty tears. He could have taken me out then, when I'd fallen back, stunned with the blow, but his wounded leg slowed him down.

Now I was angry. The pain of my broken nose had one advantageous effect, and that was to clear my head and allow me to use the anger and frustration inside me to muster new strength and direction.

I came back at him. I raised my shield until it was on a level plane, like that of a discus, and swung it over the top of his own. At the same time, I moved my sword down to block any countermove to my stomach by his blade.

My shield slid over the top of his left side, smashing down to lay his face open. I could hear the bone of his jaw crack, fractured by the smashing blow from my shield, and watched as he spat out a mouthful of blood, teeth and bone splinters.

By continuing to work his left side, I was able to administer several more cuts. His armor was covered now with blood and sweat. He was weakening, fast, and he knew that I knew it. He reached out for me with a gliding thrust, but he overestimated the distance. The crossbar of my sword smashed his fingers, breaking his grip on his weapon. It fell to the sand. He grabbed my sword wrist and pulled me to him. We pounded at each other with our shields, toe to toe, head to head, both of us bleeding freely, gasping and sobbing for air. The heat of the day swirled heavily about us. I was losing some of my own vision from the sweat running down my face in quantities that even the cloth wrappings inside my helmet could not absorb.

He tripped me with a back-leg throw and we went down. He was on top and still holding onto my wrist as we rolled in the sand. I let loose of my shield strap and clawed at his face, trying to gouge out an eye. He smashed me across the face with his elbow, then also released his shield in order to get a grip on my throat, his thumb digging deep, trying to crush the cartilage. I caught his thumb in my mouth as I raised my head, and bit down hard. When I released it, the thumb hung loosely by a strand of tendon, and small strings of bloody meat.

We rolled in the sand, our bodies covered with grit that was gathering in clots with the blood, clinging like maggots to us.

I couldn't get him to release my wrist, though I was still holding my sword. Holding to each other, we managed to struggle back to our feet.

Graecus was trembling. The loss of blood was taking its toll. It was just a matter of time now, and he knew it.

I twisted the blade of my sword around, trying to reach his neck, but he restrained me by holding tight to my wrist. He forced my arm down to waist level. If my sword had been three inches longer, it would have been inside his belly.

It was then that Graecus took my victory away from me. He smiled through his broken face, bubbles of blood forming with each gasping breath.

"It's time to end this, little wolf."

His grip tightened on my wrist as he seemed to gather strength from some hidden reserve inside him. He forced my sword arm a bit higher, and his right arm tightened around my back where he was holding me to him.

I was giving my all, yet he would not release his grip at my wrist. The point of my sword touched the skin above his solar plexus. I could see his heart pounding barely inches away.

He put his head against mine, whispering: "Now! Now, little wolf! Come to me!"

He jerked his left hand, still holding my sword wrist, and drove the point of my Damascus into his chest.

I froze! It wasn't fair!

He opened his mouth in agony, blood pouring from his loose gaping lips. Yet, even through the blood and pain, his eyes had a look in them that bordered on utter ecstasy. He raised his head, pulling at me again, this time throwing his body next to mine, his face against me. I could see his bloody lips quivering as the sword reached his heart. His body trembled and he gave one deep and final shudder as the great pounding muscle was severed inside his chest.

He still clung to me, his arms locked about my shoulders. Then, as his legs went limp, his lips left a bloody streak on my face and neck as he slid slowly down the length of my body. He lay in the sand, eyes open but unseeing, his once handsome face now a ruined wreck.

My sword had been pulled from his chest by the downward movement of his body and I stood, looking down at him, my weapon limp in my hand. He was doubled up in the fetal position on the arena floor, as if praying.

It was then that the roar of the crowd reached through the bloody fog surrounding my mind. "Lucanus! Lucanus!"

I understood something then, something that had only scratched my mind's surface before. *Graecus had been in love with me!*

I raised my sword above my head, acknowledging their ovation. Wreaths of flowers flew down at me from ten thousand hands, raining on the floor of the arena, a carpet of flowers covering his blood.

I walked slowly across the sand and faced the Imperial box.

The crowd was calling my name, screaming loudly, insanely.

"The rudis! The rudis!"

It was like thunder. Forty thousand voices in one mindless frenzy, yelling to the Emperor to give me the wooden sword. It was too late to give me my freedom; still, it meant recognition which gave me equal standing with any fighter in the world. I only regretted that old Celer wasn't here to see it. Even if the rudis didn't mean freedom for me, it did mean the Emperor would have to give me his purse if he acceded to the demands of the mob.

A woman threw herself from the stands to the sands, ripping open her stola, exposing her breasts, crying out my name. An eerie feeling came over me as I looked at her. Her eyes held the same glazed look of ecstasy that Graecus' eyes had held on the moment he'd killed himself.

I ignored her and saluted Augustus. Again I raised my sword to him. He signaled for the trumpets to sound, silencing the mob. When all were still, he rose to stand at the edge of his box, looking down on me.

"Lucanus! You have given the people of Rome something extraordinary this day. Let your example be one that all will follow. The people of Rome wish to honor you, and, as their servant, I can do no less than obey their wishes. At the same time, I would add my own praises for your valor."

He raised his hand, showing the rudis to the stands, holding it there for all to see. Then he tossed it to me, following it with the heavy purse that hung at his waist. It seemed to me that he was more reluctant to part with his gold than with the wooden sword, for custom had it that the purse of the emperor must be full . . . and Caesar was known to be a frugal man.

I caught the rudis with my free hand and the purse of Augustus on the point of my bloody sword. As I held them both in one final salute to Caesar, I caught a glimpse through sweat-fogged eyes of Claudius. He was crying . . . .

I started back to the gate, letting the new cries of the audience escort me. As I neared the exit I saw the cleanup crew coming out with their meathooks to remove the body of Graecus. I stopped them, and gave them my weapons and prizes to carry, knowing that not a coin would be missing when I reclaimed them. Then, as I'd done with the body of Aemillius some years before, I walked over to where he lay and picked Niger's limp body up into my arms.

I held him there for a moment then, to the roar of the crowd, carried him from the arena and into the cool chambers beneath the Flavian.

This time I did not dump the body on the floor, as I had Aemillius' lifeless shell. Instead, I placed it gently on a bed of straw. Pollio came running in then, ecstatic, raving over my great glory and victory. He had my blue cloak in his hand. I jerked it free and spread it over the bloody corpse of the noblest opponent I'd ever fought.

"*Shut up, Pollio!*" I screamed the order out and did not care. I was drained of everything but dullness. I was weak and exhausted. I looked down at my cloak covering Graecus and felt a strange sense of loss. He was gone! It didn't seem possible.

I left after giving Pollio instructions for the funeral. I would pay for all. I wanted the finest funeral that could be bought, as if he were a member of the finest and noblest house of Rome. I wanted burners and sacrifices made every hour on the hour in every temple in the city.

I could do no less. After all, Graecus had loved me . . .

5

Well, my distant reader, are you still there? I hope that I have not bored you with my tale up to this point. I have sincerely tried to be as honest as possible. Even my faults have been laid bare. A man is known not only by his good qualities, but also by those he would normally prefer to keep locked up, away from the condemning eyes of others. Myself, I do not care, for by the time you read this I shall have been long in my grave, so it matters not. Perhaps you think me a bit brutal, but these are not gentle times and death is always a cheap commodity. After all, the word of a single man can send tens of thousands to their death, merely for his amusement.

Some of you might ask why I did not resist my present fate more strenuously? Might I could have, but when one is not born to riches or power, and lacks the ability to purchase loyalty from those who could help him, there is little to be done. Or perhaps it is merely that I am weary of my own existence. Death is certainly no stranger to me, so why should I fear it? It must come to all. And in death I shall perhaps find the peace of heart and mind, and even soul if there is one, that has been denied me in my worldly life. Perhaps so, perhaps no! Either way it really doesn't matter, we all die just the same.

Now, where was I? Ahhhh . . . Yes! I was still in Rome. Stop your bitching, Albinus, lest I take a staff to your back! Stop grumbling and write as I tell you!

6

Niger was dead now, and I stood in his place: the premier swordsman of the Empire. I recall wondering then how long it would be before someone said the same thing about me. Not that it mattered . . .

After my victory over Graecus, Germanicus invited me to enter his service and leave the arena behind. Though I spent much time in his company, and truly enjoyed it, I wasn't ready for such a move, and told him so. He and I, along with Claudius, had the run of the city, and they seldom attended the social gatherings of the rich and powerful without me. I met Augustus twice more at such gatherings, and at a reception honoring Germanicus' return from a triumphant campaign, I met the Augusta for the first time socially. The woman had the coldest look in her eyes that I have ever seen to this day. I knew right off that she didn't like me. Perhaps my low birth or the manner in which I earned my living was offensive to her. But somehow I had the feeling she didn't really like anyone very much. Not even her son, Tiberius, who had recently adopted Germanicus at the request of Augustus. I'd seen them together a time or two and she gave me the impression that she was the decision maker of the two. Augustus had a good reputation as a soldier and a general; why was it I had the feeling she'd built that reputation? I was to find out in time. Yes! Livia had an aura of controlled energy and purpose about her.

I remember trying to imagine her as a young bride. I could tell that she had been beautiful at one time, but she had turned to the use of cosmetics to cover the ravages of time that had slowly gained on her. Yes, she was still a proud-looking woman, with sharp, angular features and a thin aquiline nose. But it was her eyes that fascinated me. There was nothing behind them but cold and impersonal intelligence. I can tell you frankly, the woman frightened me more than any man I'd ever faced on the sands.

I went on tour shortly thereafter for two years in Egypt and Syria. During my absence, Augustus died and Tiberius, his adopted son, assumed the seat of power, wearing the wreath of the Caesars. Yes! Tiberius was Caesar all right, but I knew who was giving the orders. It was his mother, Livia Drusilla Augusta!

I regretted the death of Augustus, as did most of the Empire, and when I received word of his death and deification, I made sacrifice at a temple in Thebes to honor him. I didn't know if it was possible for a man to become a god or not, but I didn't think it could hurt for me to pay my respects. After all, he had been the greatest of the Caesars, and Rome had prospered under his leadership.

I had an eerie feeling about Tiberius taking over. Though he'd been acclaimed as a great soldier, it was known that he possessed a mean streak. That, combined with the ambitions of his mother, Livia, could prove ill for any who gained their disfavor. Now that Livia's husband was dead I seriously doubted that she would be as tolerant of criticism of her son.

I must confess, however, that at the time I was not overly concerned with politics and Ceasars. I was tremendously enjoying the attention and the wealth I'd earned. My slave, Albinus, was doing well with his investments for me, and I had to be, according to all standards, considered a very rich man. I owned apartment houses and farms as far as a hundred miles from Rome. I also had shares in two merchant ships that were prospering well. Claudius had been correct. Albinus had proved to be exactly what I needed to manage my business affairs.

When I at last returned to Rome, I spent a few wild nights with Germanicus and Claudius, attending parties in my honor as well as their own. When I finally sobered up and noticed that things had tightened up a bit under the reign of Tiberius, the city began to bore me, as well as frighten me. I left for my home in Herculaneum.

During the long lazy months there, Albinus tried his best to instill some culture into my thick and empty head, much to his frustration. He had succeeded in teaching me a few basics in proper manners, and spent many hours in effortfully improving my reading abilities. He even attempted to teach me Greek, which he claimed was the tongue of all civilized men. I failed miserably, but Albinus was patient with me, probably because I allowed him complete freedom to do as he wished with my money. I figured that his incentive to do well with my investments was based on the fact that I would be forced to sell him if I went broke, and his next owner would not be as dumb and lenient as the young wolf.

I was truly fond of my home in Herculaneum. It sat at the edge of the city. In the mornings I would take my breakfast in the garden, where I had a clear view of Mount Vesuvius. I was never able, however, to spend as much time there as I wanted. Pollio and Claudius were constantly calling me away to Rome for one reason or another. On the last trip to Rome, at Claudius' summons, I'd learned that Germanicus was in danger, at least to Claudius' point of view. There were rumors around the city, Claudius said, that something dreadful was planned for Germanicus, that his future lay in the hands controlling the throne. Livia's! I returned to Herculaneum, but the words of Claudius kept nagging at the back of my feeble (according to Albinus) mind. Besides, I was getting tired of Albinus' efforts at playing my professor, and a little bored with my lazy existence.

I had Albinus write Germanicus, offering him my services if he still wished them. I'd learned that he was to be assigned to Gaul, along the Rhine. I felt that perhaps this might be the time to experience warfare in a more formal fashion than the conflicts I was accustomed to. Besides, the change would do me good . . . and I could keep an eye on Germanicus' back. And I'd often heard that the women of the barbarians were beautiful, with red and golden hair, which we seldom saw in Italia.

The answer from Germanicus came quickly: I was to pack my gear and get to Rome on the double.

I'd been back in Rome and in the employ of Germanicus for about two weeks when I met Sejanus for the first time at a party for Claudius. Sejanus was the Commander of the Praetorians and the Roman garrison and, as such, was responsible for city security and the chief magistrate over all criminal matters. Next to Tiberius himself, Sejanus was the most powerful man in the Empire.

He was a handsome man, dark-haired, with a good tight build, but he had a hard set to his eyes and mouth that showed no humor. Several times, that night and at other social affairs, I saw him head to head with Livia. Something always bothered me about them together. It was like watching two snakes trying to decide which bird was to be eaten next.

Then came a memorable dinner at the palace of Tiberius. I would have normally stood by, not participating in the dinner, simply keeping an eye on Germanicus, but Tiberius called me to him, telling Sejanus to get up and give me his seat on the couch to the Emperor's right. I took my place beside him, noting the vengeful look in Sejanus' eye as I did.

The Emperor was most gracious, and knew a great deal about me, I found. He asked me a thousand questions about my life and my journeys, and my feelings toward his adopted son, Germanicus. He told me that if I served Rome well during my travels with his son, it was altogether possible that I would be awarded full citizenship upon our return. I was elated! It was something I'd dreamed of, to be a citizen of Rome. Tiberius told me of the great responsibilities of his office and how difficult it was to find men he could depend on. He said he much preferred an honest fighter, like myself, over the court toadies, who only sucked up to him to gain his favor. I nodded, merely agreeing. I promised him that I would be true to my oath of loyalty to Germanicus and serve Rome to the best of my abilities. He frowned a bit at that.

"Loyalty to oath and service to Rome? Lucanus, my boy, the two are not always one and the same. Just remember, loyalty to Rome should always come first, before all else. Do this, and you will go far in my favor."

Sejanus approached me later, talking to me as an equal, praising my victories. He even went so far as to offer me a position in the Praetorians when I returned.

The honors being heaped on me that night were even headier than the fine wines we drank. When we finished dinner I was in a glowing mood, until Claudius asked me to take a walk with him in the cool evening air. To clear our heads a bit, he said.

Claudius led the way, limping and sputtering as was his habit, through the palace gardens. At last we sat on benches of fine pink-streaked marble, watching the water fowl and the tame deer.

I began boasting about how well I had handled myself before the master of Rome. To my surprise, Claudius gave me a fairly good thump on the side of my head.

"Duh . . . duh . . . dummy!" His face was red, and there were white splotches on his cheeks. He stared at me. "Don't you know that Livia and Tiberius are merely setting you up for purposes of their own? Do you really have the audacity to think the Emperor of Rome would s . . . s . . . socialize with a common gladiator?"

The last comment hurt my feelings a bit, and I started to protest that I was no common gladiator. Claudius cut me off in mid-sentence with another thump.

"S . . . s . . . silence! It seems that I s . . . s . . . shall have to give you a history lesson. Now, don't interrupt me again until I've finished, then I will answer your questions, if you can force one out of that solid piece of gristle that you call your head!" He held up one finger. "First we begin with the Augusta and Augustus. You must believe me when I tell you that Livia is the most dangerous person in all of Rome, man or woman! It is s . . . s . . . she who directs Tiberius, though of late, I must admit he seems to be doing more things his way. But you must never trust her. It cannot be proved of course, but I believe she poisoned Augustus, her husband, in order for Tiberius to s . . . s . . . succeed him. After Tiberius took over, Postumus, the other adopted son of Augustus, was killed. Tiberius claimed that his death had been ordered by Augustus and he'd merely carried out the Emperor's final orders. I must admit that I didn't mind that very much. Postumus was a callous brute, and would probably have been worse than Tiberius, had he taken the throne. But

I'm getting ahead of myself. Before Livia had Postumus killed, on the island of Planasia—" He looked at me again as my brows shot up in question. "Yes, it was Livia's orders! I told you not to interrupt me! Postumus was in exile there, again at her connivance. She had managed to eliminate all other contenders before Augustus' death, namely Gaius and Lucius Caesar, whom Augustus had adopted into the Imperial family as a s . . . s . . . sign of favor to his old friend and comrade in arms, Marcus, their natural father." Claudius paused to catch his breath.

It was odd. When he lectured me as he was doing now, his stutter almost completely disappeared. He wiped his mouth before continuing.

"After Tiberius assumed the purple robes, he looked to do pretty well for a time. But, in the last year, he has begun to see enemies in every shadow, and dulls his senses with wine while he s . . . s . . . sinks ever deeper into a pit of self-gratification and corruption. He uses not only slave girls and the wives of Senators for his perverse amusements, but even small boys. And he delights in the most sickening of degeneracies with his ever-present 'toadies,' as he calls them. But, don't let this fool you. He is dangerous in the manner of a jungle beast. He still has a s . . . s . . . shrewdness to him and an instinct that warns him of those who plot against him, but Livia, my aunt, plants a lot of false enemies in his head. She is the most dangerous of all. She selects her victims well in advance, and doesn't wait until they obtain prominence or great popularity, so that they might present a real threat. No! The sweet old lady sniffs them out long before they can get an opportunity to harm her. Most of her schemes are handled through Sejanus. I saw you talking to him tonight. Watch him! He has eyes everywhere. Even now, he has an arrangement with Livia that he shall marry into the Imperial family as a reward for his services."

I interrupted him. My head hadn't cleared much, and I

was getting a little tired of his sermon. "You say Tiberius sees enemies everywhere? How about yourself, Claudius? You've already counted more than you say Livia has had killed." I shook my head, laughing, disbelieving in my drunkeness. This was all too much for me to comprehend, and I was getting sleepy.

Claudius screamed, "S . . . s . . . silence, you great hunk of mindless flesh! You may be a killer in the arena, but in this circus you are like an andabata, totally blind! Do you hear me?" He lowered his voice and looked furtively around us, making certain we were alone. "Lucanus, you must learn who and what you are dealing with, so listen to me. I really don't know why I even trouble myself with you, but I will. Keep your mouth shut and learn something that may save your life. Livia and Tiberius, as well as Sejanus, are merely cultivating you because of your relationship with Germanicus."

"So what?"

He thumped me again. I was happy that his arm wasn't any stronger. "So what? You ask me, so what? You dolt! Germanicus is the last strong claimant to the throne. All others have been eliminated. Everyone with blood claim to the Emperor's seat has been killed. Germanicus has become too popular in Rome, and he is in danger. Even in Gaul, away from the city, he will be in danger. You must watch his back. Trust no one, do you hear me? Germanicus is the sole heir to the purple and they will try to do him in. Livia and Sejanus will not rest until they poison the ears of Tiberius with threats of Germanicus stealing his power."

My head was beginning to clear, and I thought I had him there. I asked: "How about yourself, Claudius? You're related by blood to both the Augusta and Tiberius. Huh? How about that?"

He shook in a minor spasm, he was becoming upset with me. "That is true, Lucanus! But they consider me no threat. It's unthinkable that one like me, a s . . . s . . . spastic, could one day ascend to the throne."

I couldn't argue with that. The people would never accept an Emperor with the infirmities that Claudius possessed. He got a little testy when I agreed with his last statement, but at least he hadn't thumped me again. He warned me of one more thing before we entered the palace again to find Germanicus and say our farewells.

"Remember this, you muscle-headed savage: The first law of power is survival, even if it means the liquidation of one's own children, or immediate members of the fam ily."

It was a hard thought. The exercise of power was as alien to me as my own occupation would be to a farmer. I had done a lot of bad things in my lifetime, but nothing to compare with the devious deeds of those who ruled. I would not easily forget Claudius' lecture.

The next afternoon, an Imperial messenger knocked at my door, handing me a package. It contained a hundred gold pieces and a message from Tiberius that asked me to remember the conversation we'd had the night before. Beware of Emperors bearing gifts! I worried about the gift and considered returning it, but there was no way to do so without offending the Emperor.

When we'd left Rome and were aboard ship for Messalla, I told Germanicus about the gift from Tiberius. He smiled and told me he was aware of it, and that he was pleased I had told him of it myself.

Our crossing was a bit rough. I suffered a minor bout with seasickness, which left me weak and wobbly up until we disembarked. It took two days on land for my legs to steady themselves.

I rode with Germanicus through the fields and forests of Gaul. The country was fair to see, and the women walked straight and proud, with good figures. I regretted our haste. I would have sampled a few of them if Germanicus had not been in such a hurry. But he was to take command of the Frontier Legions at Vetera, and he would waste no time in getting there.

By the time we arrived at their encampment my butt was a solid mass of blisters. Germanicus had set a fast and painful gait, saying not to worry about my backside, that in a few more weeks it would be as tough as leather.

He spoke the truth, but to this day I still possess a true dislike for riding horseback. I'd much prefer to eat one of the bastards than to ride him.

It didn't take him long after our arrival to whip the men in shape and put things in proper order for the coming campaign.

Finally, he gave the order to break camp. With us went Flavius, brother of the Cheruscan chieftain Arminius, whom Germanicus was to pacify. Flavius himself had taken service with Rome.

It promised to be an interesting campaign.

BOOK FOUR

WAR BEYOND THE RHINE

1

We had reached the Weser. On the other side stood the forces of Arminius and his chieftains. Arminius had sent his messenger, bearing the branch of truce, to ask if he might see his brother, Flavius. Germanicus had granted permission.

I hadn't accompanied him for the meeting, though I would have liked to have seen Arminius first hand, but Germanicus had had other duties for me. I found out later that when Arminius had asked Flavius about the wound that had cost him an eye and of what rewards he'd received for his service to Rome, Flavius had named his higher wages, decorations, and the wreath of honor given him by Tiberius. Arminius responded to his brother, "The wages of slavery are low."

Flavius had tried to convince Arminius to end the war and surrender. But Arminius would have none of it. He had recounted the misdeeds of Rome and called on the ancient and terrible gods of the forests to recognize the justice of his cause. He had attempted to persuade Flavius to leave the service of Rome and return to his own people. Neither could convince the other, and the meeting had ended in name calling and threats, some of which were in Latin, for as you know Arminius had once commanded an auxiliary force of Cheruscans for the Roman armies.

Now Arminius had drawn up his forces on his side of the

Weser and was waiting for our crossing. Obviously he hoped to catch our main force in midstream, where his archers and spearmen could do deadly work with little risk to themselves. But Germanicus told me he would not fall into such an obvious blunder. He had sent out scouts, many dressed in the furs of the barbarians, and they had already returned with the locations of a number of fording sites.

Germanicus gave orders for the cavalry to cross at the fords. The horsemen were under the command of Lucius Stertinius and one of Germanicus' staff officers, a pompous man but a good fighter. The cavalry were to advance and split the Cherusci and their allies. But Arminius was not to be caught so easily either. The Germans pretended to fall back, leaving an opening on their side of the river. With their chieftain, Chariovalda, leading the way, our Batavian auxiliaries forged immediately across the strongest part of the river's current. Once the Batavians were across and on land, still exhausted from the efforts of crossing, the Cherusci counterattacked, surrounding them in a clearing, doing most of their damages to the Batavians by hurling a hail of missiles into their tight-packed masses. Javelins and stones from slingers found many targets. When the battle closed in to the point of man to man, Chariovalda tried to fight his way through and was killed when a flight of javelins turned his body into a pincushion.The remainder of the force would more than likely have been wiped out if the cavalry had not come to their aid.

This action gave Germanicus the time to get his main force of infantry across the river unscathed and set up a defensive camp in the Roman manner, complete with earthworks and latrines. One thing I still believe about the Legionnaire is that he is half mole, for surely none in the world can dig as fast or throw up as much dirt as the common Roman soldier.

Germanicus was everywhere, and I stayed with him, especially when we went around the camp of the auxiliaries. One could never tell when a tribesman might try to become a legend in his own time by killing the Roman Commander.

Shortly before dark, a deserter crossed over to us, claiming the amnesty that Germanicus had offered to all. He informed Germanicus that Arminius had chosen his battle ground and that reinforcements were arriving steadily, gathering in a grove sacred to their war god, Tyr, and that they were planning a night attack on the Roman positions. This information was confirmed by a reconnaissance party that returned to report that the tribes were indeed massing and were working themselves into a frenzy with much loud boasting and beating of drums.

Germanicus told me that he was somewhat worried about the morale of his men, even though the Centurions and Tribunes seemed cheerful enough. But Germanicus always preferred to know firsthand and, as usual, he dragged me along with him while making his rounds. Not that I really minded, but it was mess time and I hadn't eaten for hours.

He took off his rich armor, replacing it with some animal skins for disguise. I just threw a hooded cloak over my plain gladiator's armor and moved my shield to my back, and we left the rear of his tent to walk the perimeter and listen to what the common soldiers were saying.

There was no doubt about his popularity. Not once did we hear a single bad thing said about him, nor about the coming fight. Never have I seen a man so universally liked by those that served him. Perhaps the great Julius enjoyed such unswerving devotion from his men, but then I could not say for certain.

At any rate, the short tour around the cooking fires assured him that the men would do their part and were confident in him as their leader. I was glad when we got back so I could fill my gut with the boiled barley and cheese that served as our evening meal. Germanicus ate the same; he believed in sharing the fare of the common soldier. It could have made his men a little more fond of him I suppose, but it did little for my tastebuds.

"Lucanus?" As he spoke, Germanicus moved his chair around, facing me as I shoved the barley in my mouth with a wooden spoon.

"Aye, Dominus, what is it?"

"Stay close to me and wear your gladiator's armor when the fight begins."

I asked why. He told me it would aid his men in knowing his location if the struggle became confused. That made good sense, because my arena costume would certainly stand out in the crowd. The bad part was that it would also make me a good mark for the javelin throwers and stone slingers. But it was not mine to reason why.

Before dark, an enemy warrior who could speak our tongue came riding up to the stockade. Staying a little out of bow range, he called out in Arminius' name, offering a wife, a hundred sesterces a day, and land to every Roman soldier who would desert. This offer was answered by shouts from the common soldiery: There was no need for the Germans to make such an offer, for by tomorrow they would have the women and the land and wealth of the Germans anyway.

The rider spat on the ground, turned his horse back into the treeline and rode out of sight. The men considered this offer a good omen, showing that the tribesmen feared us. Germanicus laughed with great pleasure when he heard of the Legions' response to the offer. He slapped me on the shoulder.

"Good! Good! That's the best thing I could have heard. Now I have no doubts that we will win."

Germanicus slept for a while as I stood guard over him. Covered only with his cloak, he tossed and mumbled in his sleep, and I knew dreams were with him.

When he woke, he smiled at me. "Lucanus, I have had a sign." He sat up erect on his cot, all sleep gone from his eyes. "I dreamed that I was making a sacrifice to Jupiter. The victim was one of the great wild oxen of the German forest, the Aurochs. When my blade struck, its blood spattered all over my robe, staining it bright red. Then," he paused to take a drink of water, "then the Augusta gave me a new and more costly robe to replace the bloody one."

I personally never took much stock in dreams, but if he did, and thought it augured well, then it was good enough for me.

The Germans made a try at the stockade that night around midnight, but they were not very well organized and were beaten off with only a slight loss to ourselves. The real battle would come on the morrow, but still Germanicus kept one man out of every three on the wall.

At the hour of first light, the army was called into ranks, except for those on duty atop the walls, and Germanicus strode from his tent. He was a young Mars the Avenger, his plumed helmet under his arm, red cloak billowing behind him, everything about him, in fact, fairly glowing. From his burnished armor to his face, just the sight of him gave an additional rise to the already high spirits of his soldiers. The commanders called their men to attention and Germanicus addressed them.

"Soldiers and friends of Rome, this is the day! Remember that open ground is not the only terrain suitable for battle to a Roman. Forests and wooded hills shall suit our purpose if we use our brains. The barbarians' great shields and huge spears are not as manageable among the trees and brush as are our shorter Roman swords and javelins. Once you begin, strike often. Never stop. Aim for their faces, for they are vain creatures. Most of them wear no armor or even helmets, and their shields are not of iron, but are mostly poor things of wicker or painted boards. What good spears they do have will be in the front ranks only; the rest will be armed with clubs or axes. The savages are fearsome in appearance, but they are only good for a short fight. If you hurt them, they will run. They have no discipline. If they win, I warn you, they respect no laws of God or man.

"Are you tired of marching and sailing? This fight will end those things. We are nearer the Elbe River than the Rhine. Give me a victory where my father and uncle have fought before me, and the fighting will be over."

The army raised a cheer in the damp morning air, and I'm certain it reached the ears of the tribesmen. We learned later from captives that at about this time Arminius was giving a prebattle speech to his warriors and chieftains. According to the captives, he had told them that the soldiers of Rome who faced them now were Varus' deserters, and had run away before. They were men who had mutinied to avoid battle, and most of them had wounds on their backs; the rest had been crippled by storms at sea. The gods of Rome had deserted them. This was, he'd told them, the land of the Cherusci and Subeii, of the Chatti and Semnones. Now, the Romans faced a remorseless enemy, and when they came under attack they would try to escape on their ships. But, he'd loudly professed to his men, once the battle began neither the wind nor their oars would save them. He reminded them of how greedy Rome was and how arrogant. This day, he promised, there could only be freedom or death.

After his speech, the barbarians swore to deliver our heads to Arminius' feet. They moved out then to an area they called the Idistaviso, a level piece of ground between the Weser and the hills. At one point, it was narrowed by some bluffs and high ground; at the other end it was widened by a bend in the river. To the rear was the forest, great tall trees with very little brush among them.

The barbarians positioned themselves on the flats and in the treeline, the tribesmen of the Cherusci waiting on the high ground so they could charge down when the battle began.

While the Germans were doing this, Germanicus had ordered up his forces, leaving behind only one cohort to guard the camp and baggage train. We advanced to meet them.

To the best of my recollection, the auxiliaries, both Gauls and Germans, were in the first ranks. They were followed by unmounted bowmen and slingers, then by four Legions. Germanicus and I were next, staying with the four cohorts of Praetorians sent him by Tiberius as a sign of his favor, then four more Legions reinforced by mounted archers and light infantry, then the rest of the native units. All told, our forces numbered about forty-three thousand men, and they were all ready for battle.

I was caught up in the excitement of the moment. It was different from entering a fight at the arena, where, even when you went out on the sands as part of a team, you were still alone. Here there was a strange excitement at being a part of a massive machine that moved with one mind, in one direction.

I kept my shield on my back, protecting it from any stray arrow shots as we rode. I know I must have made a strange sight in gladiator's rig, with my sword-arm guard of meshed iron rings, and my broad-brimmed helmet, on which I kept the face shield lowered to see better. My armor, a gift from Germanicus, was of fine steel. It gave me a bit more protection then the regular issue of armor, as it covered more of the gut and chest area. It must have cost him a sesterce or two for a fact. It was richly embossed with tracings of gold and silver in many designs. My cloak I had tied to the back of my saddle; it would only have served to get in my way once the fighting got hot.

Germanicus was in his element. The plumes of his

helmet waved bravely, and even his horse was putting on a good show, prancing and throwing its head about in good spirits.

Then some of the Cherusci, unable to contain themselves, made a premature attack. Barbarians seldom have any patience. It is one of their great failings and has brought Rome many victories over them. More than once their impatience aided me in contests and muneras.

When Germanicus saw the Cherusci assault, he ordered some of his best cavalry to hit them on the flanks while the Equites, under the command of Lucius Stertinius, came around to hit them from the rear. Germanicus himself brought up the rest of his men in person. About that time I saw some specks in the sky. To me they looked like vultures, but Germanicus cried so that all could hear. "Eagles! Eagles! Eight of them. Forward! Follow the Eagles of Rome. The gods have sent them to protect us."

At this, the cavalry hit the enemy from the flanks and rear as our infantry assaulted them from the front. The Cherusci were now split. Some were breaking to run into the trees; others headed for the open ground where their brothers were still in position.

Arminius gave the word for the rest of his force to attack. He personally led the battle, nearly wiping out our bowmen and almost breaking through to our rear. He would have, if the auxiliary hadn't held him back.

Germanicus was in the thick of it, and naturally I was with him. Once I was thrown from my horse when it stumbled over a pile of bodies. Before I could rise, a tribesman, his body painted blue and his face covered with charcoal, tried to brain me with his club as I struggled to rise. Germanicus laid the back of his neck open and called for me to quit lying down on the job, adding that I was supposed to be watching him, not the other way around. Then he was off, leaving me on foot to try and catch up.

I knew the barbarians had broken, but the fight was

swirling about me. I cut and slashed my way through a knot of Cherusci warriors, aided by two Praetorians who had also lost their mounts. Together, we formed a small wedge and hacked our way back to our unit. There was no art to this kind of fighting, just hack and strike . . . .

Many of the savages had great courage, but they had no technique, and their spirit was already broken. When the Cherusci were split and put on the run, it took the heart out of the rest of them. I believe, to this day, that they were mainly fighting just to get away, which a number of them did, including Arminius. He was a slippery devil.

The battle quickly changed into a slaughter. The barbarians had no leaders, and in moments changed from bloodthirsty, screaming killers into a panic-stricken mob. Some tried to swim the Weser, only to be swept under by the current or speared in midstream by the javelins of our troops, who thought it great sport and were making bets with each other on how many they could hit. We were forced to shoot some of the barbarian warriors out of the trees, as if they were squirrels.

It took until noon before the killing was done with. For ten miles the ground was covered with bodies and weapons. I came across a pile of chains. I presume that Arminius had meant the shackles for us.

Our losses were light, and the troops were elated with the easy victory. At Germanicus' direction, they hailed Tiberius as victor, for Germanicus had fought in his name. He had a mound erected; upon it we set the standards, along with the weapons of the tribesmen we'd defeated.

It is difficult to understand the mind of the savage. We had just beaten a well-organized force (for them, that is) but somehow, the setting up of that mound brought every German tribesman for miles around back to fight, even those who hadn't planned on getting into the act. They threw themselves on us, a mob of howling revenge-crazed animals. And howl they did, like wolves. There were old greybeards among them, and boys whose faces had never seen the whisper of a beard. They almost broke through again to our rear. It was only the discipline of the Legions that held them. In parade field style, the Legions formed ranks of living flesh inside a wall of iron that repelled the savages, dropping them in their tracks. Their bodies piled up and formed knee-high walls of flesh that the Legionnaires could stand behind.

This kind of fighting was not to my liking at all. There was too much chance of being killed by accident. At least in the arena you usually had only one or two men to deal with. Here, they swarmed about us like gnats, picking and gouging, trying to find chinks in our armor. These barbarians were insane. If you cut off one's hand he would stick the spouting stump in your face, trying to blind you while his comrades attempted to separate your head from its trunk. It was too much for me to comprehend. Two short hours earlier, they had been beaten, frightened curs running with their tails between their legs. Now, for some reason known only to their equally insane gods, they were absolutely fearless beasts.

The battle surged back and forth like a bloody tide. At last the barbarians threw up some earthworks to fight from, and Germanicus and the infantry stormed the mound, pushing them back. I was cut on the left shoulder, but not seriously. Germanicus had not a scratch on him. He personally led the Praetorians into the trees at charge and I, after finally catching up with him, caught a spear with my shield that was meant for him. He laughed and said, "What's the matter, gladiator? Don't you like a good fight?"

I said nothing, for this was not my way of battle but his, and he did it well enough. It was hand-to-hand combat in the trees and we did good work, leaving nearly a thousand dead behind. The end came when the Germans were finally bottled up with a marsh behind them; we were holding the high ground on either side. The Germans fought fanatically, but their large numbers and their poor weapons beat them. There were too many of them to be able to fight properly. Those in front were pushed into our spears by their comrades from the rear, anxious to get through to us. It was butcher's work.

Germanicus removed his helmet so all could recognize him and called for the Legions to hear, "*Kill! Kill! Kill!* None were to be spared. He would put an end to them once and for all.

The Legions formed ranks in four lines, one behind the other. Shields held close, they advanced a step at a time, their shortswords striking at the unprotected faces of the tribesmen, then slashing low for the gut. Those in the rear used their spears to form a wall of deadly bristles that kept the savages from any chance of breaking through. Each rank would fight for about ten minutes; then, at a signal from the trumpets, the next rank would take their places in the front line while the first retired to the rear to catch its breath. This mode provided fresh fighting men in the first rank at all times.

Step by methodical step, the Legions and our allies advanced until there were no Germans left, save for the dead and the dying. We searched for the body of Arminius, but once again he had slipped through our fingers. The man had the luck of the mad.

When the body count was made, it came to over sixty thousand. Our own losses were less than six hundred dead.

You could smell the blood in the air, thick and heavy. The wounded were being put out of their misery by the auxiliaries. That task alone took them hours. Germanicus wiped his blade on the furry robe of a Subeii chieftain and grinned at me: "I think that this just may do it. Arminius is beaten once and for all. He'll never be able to muster another force after this."

I didn't argue the point, but I had a feeling that

Arminius was not to be done away with that easily. Somehow I knew we'd hear from him again.

For the second time, a victory mound was erected with the arms and trophies of the defeated. Germanicus ordered an inscription be made to stand over the sight: DEDICATED TO MARS AND DIVINE AUGUSTUS BY THE ARMY OF TIBERIUS CAESAR AFTER ITS CONQUEST OF THE NATIONS BETWEEN THE RHINE AND THE ELBE.

Germanicus said nothing of himself. He knew that Tiberius was jealous of him, and he wanted to avoid any friction with the Emperor. He gave all credit to the man who wasn't there.

2

The night had fallen, and with it came a steady drizzling rain of the kind so common in these wild dark forests and endless plains.

I stood at the doorway of Germanicus' tent. He had removed his armor and had turned it over to his slave to be cleansed of the blood and gore that covered its rich embossments. Behind me, he was sitting quietly at his field table, head between his hands, fingers grasping his skull as if he were trying to force out the deeds of the last hours. His hair was damp with perspiration and clung to his head in tight curls.

For my part, I was too tired to sit and was standing at the open flap of the tent watching the drizzle.

My only wound, the slice on my left shoulder, was giving me a little trouble and I hoped that the night air would not cause a fever to set in.

It was at this time that a lone figure made its way out of the dark and approached our tent, only to be hailed by one of the sentries on duty. I said nothing, watching as the small shape approached the Legionnaire. The form was concealed in a long, dark, hooded robe, but from the way it moved I could tell now that the figure was a woman. I wondered why she was here. Surely she was aware of the fate that the tribeswomen were to have at the hands of the Legions. As she reached the sentry, she called out, "Germanicus?"

That was enough for me. I stepped out into the darkness to see what had brought this woman of our enemy to the tent of her people's conqueror.

The sentry was attempting to remove her hood so he could view her face. I interrupted him, forcefully removing his hand from her person. I recall now that he had some reluctance to give her up to me, but my reputation was well known and he was wise enough not to contest the matter. I was in a bit of ill humor, and I suppose he could tell.

I took the woman by the shoulder, moving her a few paces away from the sentry, keeping a careful eye on her. It was always possible that she was an assassin sent to avenge the deaths of her people.

"What do you wish here, woman? Are you mad to come to this place so brazenly?"

She turned to face me, her face lit for an instant by the flickering of the lamps inside Germanicus' tent. By Hera! That first glimpse of her face beneath its shadowed hood still haunts me. It was one of those rare moments in life. Sometimes one sees something so startling, or so beautiful, that the heart stops beating for a moment and catches in one's chest as if a hand has grabbed it for a second.

She looked at me. Her eyes were of crystal mountain ice, and tendrils of golden hair protruded from beneath the protection of her hood. Her voice showed no signs of fear or defeat.

"You're the killer, aren't you? The one called Lucanus, the wolf? Bodyguard to Germanicus?"

I nodded and asked, "What is it you wish here, woman?

Have you come to fill your belly with the seeds of Rome?''

The look she gave me could have shriveled the brass testicles on the statue of Mars the Avenger. Her voice held the same ice that was so apparent in her eyes.

''Butcher! You will speak to me with respect. I am Britta, sister to Arminius. I have come as a messenger to speak with Germanicus, and I claim the rights of courtesy and protection that are due all messengers from heads of state.''

Well, I had to admit, she had me there. All such messengers *are* due courtesy. But I did insist that she be searched before showing her into the tent. Let it suffice to say that I took my leisure in the frisking, enjoying it thoroughly. She accepted my attentions stoically, ignoring me as if I were not even there. Her indifference bothered me not in the least; the feel of those ripe mounds concealed beneath the coarseness of her robe made the ache in my shoulder leave and move downward to the nether regions of my body.

I escorted her to Germanicus' tent and called to him from the entrance. Germanicus rose from his seat at the field table, shaking his head as if to clear his mind. I saw that he was very tired.

''Dominus,'' I said, ''This is the sister of Arminius. She has ventured as his emissary to parlay.''

Germanicus greeted her graciously. ''Come, sit near the brazier. It will take some of the chill from you that the dampness of the night is sure to have brought.'' He bowed and took her hand, escorting her to his field chair as if she were one of the great ladies of Rome. Indeed, at least to my mind, she carried herself as if she were one of them. Even though it was apparent that she had endured much and weariness sat heavy on her, she still had the look of one who knows herself and expects nothing less from the enemy.

I positioned myself behind her, within arm's reach, still

not trusting her completely. It was entirely possible that, even after my careful search, she might still have a small blade concealed somewhere on her person.

Germanicus poured her a generous cup of wine and waited patiently for her to begin. When she did not, he spoke. "What brings the sister of Arminius to my quarters this night?"

Britta pulled back her hood before speaking, and at that moment I was lost. I had seen more beautiful women in my time, in silks and with painted lips and toes, but never had I seen one with her force of personality. Her face glowed with health and strength, not with the paint of the courtesans of Rome or Parthia. She was truly a vibrant and most complete woman, fit to be the mate of a warrior king anywhere in the entire world. Her hair was as summer wheat, with strands of gold running through it in waves. I fell in love at that very moment. Deeply, hopelessly in love with this messenger of the enemy.

I could see that even Germanicus was impressed by her self-possession in the enemy camp and her evident command of the present situation.

"I am Britta, sister to Arminius, Chief of the Cherusci. My brother," she said proudly, "would have parlay with the Roman Commander this night." Her voice was strong, with no trace of tremor, or hesitation. She spoke as one equal to another, not as a member of a near-vanquished people.

Germanicus pursed his lips for a moment before speaking. "Under what circumstances would Arminius have us meet?"

"My brother respects your word and your honor. If you guarantee safe conduct, he will come to this place to meet with you. Do you give and guarantee such safe conduct?"

Germanicus looked at me for a moment. I shrugged my shoulders; this was a matter in which I could offer him no advice. He turned to her again.

"Does he come to surrender and ask for the mercy of Rome?"

Britta's shoulders surged backwards, her spine arched.

"That, Roman, is a matter you shall have to discuss with him. I have given you the full content of his message. What is your reply?"

Germanicus rubbed his hands together over the charcoal brazier trying to work some heat into them. He turned then, his face weary and his eyes sunken with exhaustion.

"Lucanus, gather a detachment to give the lady Britta a safe passage. Follow her instructions and protect the person of Arminius until he comes to me. With your life if necessary! Do you understand me?"

"I hear and understand, Dominus." I would have gladly slaughtered half a legion myself if they tried to harm one hair on the lady Britta's head. This Cherusci princess I would protect with more than my life. As for her brother, I would do as I was ordered, though perhaps not with the same enthusiasm I would show for his sister.

At that, I went out into the camp and rounded up a squad of Legionnaires from Germanicus' personal body-guard, men that could be trusted, had them form into two files, and announced to Germanicus that all was ready.

Britta walked out of the tent without another word to Germanicus. I guided her to the center of the two files, where she would be protected on both sides, and took up my position directly in front of her with sword drawn. I would take no chances; this night the fever of killing and rape still ran hot in the blood of the soldiers of Rome.

As we marched, she called out the directions we were to take. We were harrassed by some wild troops, and twice I was forced to use the flat of my blade to keep them away. We soon entered the trees and were surrounded by complete darkness. The sounds of the camp grew dull and distant. The rain gathered strength, and flowed in small rivers down my face and back, irritating my eyes. It was difficult enough to see without this added irritation. I was feeling damned uncomfortable out there with only a squad of ten men. There could be literally hundreds of barbarians lurking in the shadows and brush, waiting for an unwary Roman. But orders were orders.

We marched perhaps a mile into the dark forest before Britta finally called a halt. She ordered me to wait there with my men and hurried off into the night. It seemed a damned long time that we stood there alone in the dark, each man with his own thoughts, every rustle of wind against bush giving rise to images of barbarians swarming out to slaughter us and take our heads to nail against the trunks of trees as they had done to the Legionnaires of Varus.

A whistle brought my attention back from my dark thoughts, and Britta's voice came out of the night.

"Butcher! We are here."

She and one other, larger form approached us from the gloom. That it was Arminius, I had no doubt. Though he was cloaked, he had the same proud stride and squared shoulders as his sister. Even in the dark you could feel his presence and personal power. Without further word, they took their place in our midst and we returned to camp. Britta again directed us as we marched.

The sentries permitted us to pass on, making our way over the soaked earth and damp leaves to Germanicus' tent. I stationed the escort around the tent on all sides, with warning that I would personally castrate any man who failed in his duty this night. My tone of voice left them no doubt that I meant every word I said.

Germanicus welcomed Arminius with the same grace he had afforded his sister. The two leaders sized each other up a moment. I could tell that there was great respect between the two.

I kept watch that night while the two leaders talked. Mostly, though, I kept my eyes on Britta. I was unable to get my fill of looking at her, it seemed. I had given her a dry cloak to replace her soggy one, and she'd taken a seat near the brazier, nodding now and then as her brother and his conqueror talked of things that men such as they have in common interest. I am no politician, but I knew that they would never reach a decision which would satisfy both.

Arminius wanted Germanicus to set aside an autonomous area of the frontier where the tribes would have no interference from Rome. The tribes across the Rhine, Germanicus said, had for too many long seasons been creating uprisings among the tribes that had previously accepted the Pax Romana. Germanicus informed Arminius that even if the Senate and Tiberius agreed to such a proposition, he himself never could. The tribes of Germania were not united enough to obey a stable leadership.

Germanicus, as I have said, was weary. The events preceding this meeting had taken their toll on his strength. His words were heavy and laden with sorrow. "No, Arminius! There can be no settlement, except the destruction of the tribes that oppose Rome. Even if we agreed to your proposal and you led your people well and honored our treaty, what would happen after your death? There is no one else that can demand and receive the loyalty of the Cherusci, the Subeii, the Marcomanni and all the rest; only yourself. No, with your death it would start all over again, with each tribe going its own way, deciding which points of the treaty to honor and which ones to break."

Arminius said nothing. I could see that Britta was biting her tongue, wishing to speak, but Germanicus continued. "As you, Arminius, have your reasons to see Rome beaten and driven from your borders, so Rome has its reasons for requiring dominion and security on its frontiers. When this campaign's bloody business is done with, there should be peace on the Rhine for many years. That will give us time to bring those in our provinces to the point where they can defend themselves when your tribesmen again move against us. And they will—you know that better than I do. There is something wild in the breasts of your people that drives them to dangerous adventures. Who knows? Perhaps one day they may even succeed. But not now. Not as long as Rome stands in their way."

Arminius nodded his head, his face resigned somehow. "Yes, it is true. There is something in our hearts that we will not let Rome take from us. I had hoped that we could come to an arrangement. I had hoped for time to bring the tribes together and form a great nation."

Germanicus smiled thinly. "That would not suit Rome's purpose. She would much rather have the tribes splintered in their loyalties. If they ever do come together to form one nation, they could cause the death of the civilized world as we know it. No, Arminius. I cannot let that happen in my time."

Arminius rose from his seat, put his cloak about his shoulders and raised his hood to cover his face. "We each have our own destiny to follow, and now I must go to follow mine. Bid my brother Flavius well for me. Though we are opposed in this war, I know he does what he believes to be the best for our people. Tell him I hold no bitterness, only disappointment. Now, Roman, with your leave I will go; unless you will break the laws of truce and try to keep me here?"

Germanicus shook his head. "No, you are free to return. For the great losses you have suffered, it will be difficult for you to rally the tribes again. If you were dead, or my prisoner, another might take your place and be successful at it. As long as you are free, you will aid us by creating dissension among your people. Lucanus!" he added. "Escort Arminius and his sister back to their lines." He rose. "Farewell, Arminius. I wish that it could be otherwise."

Arminius made no comment. The two men stood looking into each other's eyes for a moment before Arminius smiled and turned. He spoke with his back to Germanicus, as if on second thought.

"Germanicus, I leave you with this: if you should ever claim the throne of Rome and need the tribes of Germania, I think we might be able to strike a bargain. At least with you I know the words aren't split from their meanings." His voice gained in intensity, and he turned to face Germanicus. "As long as Tiberius lives, there can never be peace on the Rhine. For I shall come at Rome again and again, until we are given the living space we require.

"You think that the losses I received in this battle will weaken me for years? You are mistaken! They can be replaced in days. To the east are tribes you know not, with warriors that number as grains of sand on the coast of Gaul. And one day they will rally under one banner, if not mine, then another, and Rome will weep and she will die, never to rise again. For even now there is a rot setting into the soul of Rome that only a great cutting can remove. Germanicus, take what is rightfully yours and save Rome from the fate that is certain, though it may be centuries away. Take my offer and I will bring tens of thousands to your aid. Give me the lands of Gaul and I will make no further demands on you. All the rest shall be Rome's. Give your word that you will take the throne, and I will hold back until you give the signal. We can be friends, for you are the only voice of Rome that I trust. Give me your word and we can save both our peoples from years of senseless slaughter."

Arminius shook with emotion, and I knew that Rome's troubles with the barbarians were not over. Not by a long shot. Arminius would come again, or if he did not, then it would be another.

Germanicus grasped the wrist of his guest in the Roman

handshake. There was worry on his haggard face. "As you have said, Arminius, I keep my word. I have sworn fealty to my stepfather Tiberius, and will not break it. For if I betrayed him, then how could you ever be certain that I would not do the same to you?"

Arminius thought for a second before responding. "You would not do it to me, because I would have you for a friend. Tiberius sees you as a threat and will see you dead if you do not move first, and fast. There is no loyalty returned to you from Tiberius. Therefore your pledge to him is not binding."

If a mere rumor of what had been said here ever reached the ear of Tiberius, he would go hard on all of us. In the world of treason, guilt came often as not by mere association. I coughed a bit loudly to attract their attention. It evidently worked, for both of them started.

Germanicus spoke to Arminius. "If time proves you right about Tiberius' feelings toward me, perhaps on that day we will have more to talk of." He released the wrist of Arminius and turned to me.

"Lucanus, you hulk, escort our guests, and when they are safe return straight to me. There is work to be done this night."

I acknowledged his order and opened the flap of the tent for Britta and Arminius to depart. As I did so, there came a great clap of thunder that threatened to blast down trees by its sheer force.

Arminius grinned at Germanicus. "That is Thor, issuing you warning."

Germanicus smiled in return. "Perhaps it is Jove the Thunderer instead of Thor. Remember Rome rules here this day."

Arminius smiled. "So you do, but there is always tomorrow. Farewell, son of Rome."

"And to thee, Arminius of the Forests."

With the men we left the camp. I took the lead, with

Arminius pointing the way. The Praetorians were in a foul mood at having to go back out again in such dreadful weather; they were a little spoiled from their soft duty in Rome. I could sympathize with them somewhat as I was not a woodsman by nature myself. I liked not these great dank forests where death could be lurking in every shadow. The trees dripped fat drops of water intermittently; the rain had slackened and the thunder of Jove, or Thor, had moved on to other regions.

A single sound saved us. It was the snick of a blade being removed from its scabbard. I may not have been a woodsman, but my instinct for survival was second to none. I whirled about to stop the thrust of the sword with my shield, which I used to cover Britta at the same time. Her brother, I thought, could take care of himself. The squad leader of the Praetorians was probably a good enough soldier, but he had not the experience of hundreds of individual combats in the arena. It took no great effort on my part to deflect his blow and, at the same time, cause his own forward motion and momentum to make him lose his footing. My sword slid across his throat as he stumbled past me. Without hesitation, I took out another escort before he even had his javelin in thrusting position. It was so close among the trees and brush that the long spear itself had hampered his movements. He would have had a better chance if he had drawn his sword, as had his leader.

By the time I had dispatched his shade, Arminius' long sword had pricked the throat of the only remaining Praetorian. I say remaining, because that fine wench of a woman, Britta, had already thrown herself straight at one wretch's face and had driven her knifeblade into his left eye all the way up to the hilt. By all the gods of all regions, she was a fine girl!

While Arminius was beheading the dead, I figured out that he and Germanicus had possibly been overheard, and this was the result. The Praetorians were the personal instruments of Sejanus and Tiberius. It stood to reason that they had taken matters into their own hands.

As I was thinking this, shadows detached themselves from the trees and around forty of the largest tribesmen I had ever seen stepped forth. Arminius stopped them from adding my head to the ones on the ground.

Arminius had arrived at the same conclusions as I had. We now reached another conclusion. It was most likely that other members of the guard would make an attempt on the life of Germanicus.

I started to take my leave of them, but Arminius made it clear that I would not survive the trip back alone. There were still large numbers of his warriors wandering about, looking for a chance to kill another Roman or two. It was then that he spoke to his sister in their barbarous tongue. I remember her arguing fiercely, but he stopped her protests with a firm slap that must have left her ears ringing for days. I didn't interfere. Family arguments are to be avoided unless one wants to catch it from both sides. Arminius then told me: "Britta is to return with you, fighter. She will be your safe escort back to your lines. She will stay until Germanicus sends her back to me. She shall act as our link, our messenger as it were. For surely this act of the Praetorians to assassinate me will be just the beginning. Now Germanicus may come to his senses and take advantage of the offer I made him tonight.

"I have also noticed you watching my sister intently. I know there is feeling for her inside you. Therefore she is in your charge. As to whether you can bed her or not, that is a matter the two of you shall have to work out. I warn you, she is headstrong, and used to having her own way. I don't think she dislikes you as much as she would have you think."

He turned to her. "Britta, you are the gladiator's until Germanicus sends you back to me. If you pretend to be his captive and slave, no other will bother you and none will question your reasons for being with the Romans. Act the part! Now,'' he pointed at me, ''take him and go!''

Arminius and his warriors faded into the dark, leaving Britta and me alone.

I wasn't sure if I should be pleased. I was getting into things best left to others, for I had not the quickness of wit to deal with the subterfuges of power-seekers and kings.

The woman certainly was sulky and unfriendly on the way back to our encampment. She said not a word to me. I still wasn't quite sure what had taken place, but I had the feeling that the next few weeks were not going to be dull.

A flash of lightning lit up her form as she bent under a branch. Yes indeed, I thought, from the brief glance I'd just had of the well-rounded curves beneath her wet tunic, the time that lay ahead would be anything but dull.

When we returned from the forest to Germanicus' tent, I didn't wait for him to ask before launching into my explanation as to why Britta was still with me. When I got to the part about the Praetorians' attempt to kill us, he looked extremely worried, saying: ''I fear this matter is not over with. Those in your escort were only underlings, it's true, but the real threat is still with us in the person of Aquila the Tribune, commander of the Praetorians that Tiberius assigned to me. By this time, I'm sure they've sent a message to Sejanus. I have done nothing that smacks of treason, but the fact of your brother,'' he nodded to Britta, ''even proposing an alliance could prove disastrous. Sejanus will find some way to use it against me. As for you, Lady Britta, I think that your brother is right. Make it appear to all eyes that you are no more than a captive slave belonging to Lucanus.''

Britta lowered her eyes. Germanicus then pointed his finger at me. ''Now, you listen to me, you great hulking ape. This is a lady of noble birth, and you will not subject her to unwelcome advances. She must share your tent, but that does not mean that she must share your bed. Now, leave me. There is much to do tomorrow. Lucanus, try to become friendly with Aquila. He fancies himself a marvel at swordplay. It shouldn't be too difficult for you to gain his confidence. You have my permission to make a few uncomplimentary statements about me. I think he may rise to the bait and try to turn you into an informer for him. Now, go!"

3

The next two weeks were spent primarily in mopping-up operations. The Angavarii, cousins to the Cherusci, were starting to act up and Germanicus sent Stertinius with two full Legions to put them in their proper place. He gave them no choice: it was unconditional surrender or be wiped out as a people. The survivors, if any, would be shipped to Rome as slaves.

The Angavarii accepted the terms and Germanicus took a page from the book of great Julius, granting an unqualified pardon. Hereby, he showed the mercy of Rome and her willingness to be allies to those who would submit to her rule.

As Germanicus had ordered, I spent a great deal of my time cultivating Aquila. I flattered him shamelessly, praising his skill as a fighter in the actions against the Germans. I showed him a few minor techniques of my own and, by the end of the week, had him believing that he would have made a first-rate secutor.

During this period I took pains to let slip an occasional comment concerning Germanicus and my weariness at being treated like a common house slave. I told him that it was Lucanus, go and get this, or Lucanus, bring me my supper, and so on. Such things, I told him, should be left for slaves, not fighters such as him and me.

Cultivating the arrogant swine was not difficult at all.

He believed all that I told him of his strength and prowess with the sword. Why shouldn't he? I was only confirming what he already thought of himself.

We were edgy, waiting for word from Rome on the subject of the alliance between Germanicus and Arminius. We didn't know whether Sejanus had informed Tiberius of the conversation between the two or not. The not knowing was almost as bad as receiving a summons to appear before the Senate on a charge of treason.

To add to my frustrations, Britta was rejecting all my advances and attentions. It was not easy for me to obey Germanicus on the subject of this woman. Knowing, at night, that she was within arm's reach, several times seeing her in the nude while she was washing herself, was driving me mad. Gods! The set of her breasts and strong thighs still gives me hot flashes to this day, and I was a much younger man then. You can easily see how hard it was for me.

But I knew that Germanicus had meant what he'd said. If I took her against her will, he would have me crucified. He was a little old-fashioned about such things anyway. If I had won her as a true spoil of war it would not have mattered, but I had not, and I must live with it. Damn!

Finally, he gave the order to break camp. All that could be done here was done; it was time to move on. Part of the army was sent on foot back to the winter quarters in Gaul; the rest were sent up and down river to requisition every boat they could get their hands on, from two-man skin coracles to log canoes and small trade ships. To these vessels were added a few from the Roman fleet which had come up river to serve as our escort on the way back out of Germany. Once we reached the mouth of the river, ships would be waiting to transport those who had journeyed on the smaller craft.

I'd arranged for Britta and me to be on the same shallow-draft trader that would be carrying Aquila. You could never tell when a man might lose his footing on a slippery deck and fall overboard. It happened often enough. Germanicus had given me no orders to arrange such an event, but what he didn't know couldn't hurt him, and besides, I didn't like the man very much. Aquila had offered me three pieces of silver if I would let him lie with my slave Britta. I put him off by describing the sores she had beneath her shift, but the offer had still rankled me.

The morning was cool, and I was glad when we finally slipped the mooring lines and anchors. The current would do most of the work for us. The oarsmen would only have to work hard enough to keep us in the channel. Occasionally I spotted furtive figures in the woods beyond the banks, but they never gave us any problems. They were probably glad to see us go. That suited me; I'd seen enough of dank forests and rain. It was high time we returned to the warm suns of Italia.

I found a spot for Britta and myself in the covered section at the bow. She still resented having to play the part of a slave in public, and I suppose I wasn't helping matters by making her wait on me hand and foot. I could see the muscles working in her jaws, fighting back the near urge to kill when she was forced to pour wine for my "good friend" Aquila. She probably would have killed him if the trip had taken too long. For her people regarded the tribes of Germanii as being little better than animals, fit only for slaves, and then only if they'd been castrated.

Britta had done her hair in long braids and wrapped them about her head. To me, it looked as if she wore a crown of gold. I wanted to hold her and touch her, and whisper the feelings I had for her, but I held my peace. She was having none of it, and her denials were making my trip miserable.

It took only three days to reach the mouth of the sea. We lay at anchor there for one day, then headed out for open waters. Once, on the river, I'd had a chance to dump

Aquila over the side, but a couple of his men came on deck to relieve themselves just at the crucial moment. I remained patient, for the way to Rome was long, and there would be other opportunities. The only thing better than throwing him overboard would be the chance to give him a real lesson in the use of the sword, and emasculate the hero before gutting him like a fish. Gods! I would enjoy that.

Germanicus planned for us to sail between Brittania and Lugdunensis until we reached a fair port in Aquitania. From there, we would cross overland to Messilla and take ship again for Rome. Going by sea would save us about two hundred miles of land travel and, while the ships were not luxury vessels, they were still far better than five hundred miles of pounding against a saddle.

There were nearly a thousand ships and boats in our convoy, vessels of all sizes. Most of the lesser sizes were to accompany us only as far as the first Roman garrison on the Gaulish coast facing Brittania.

The weather was fine, with no warning of what was to come. However, several of the old sailors made signs to ward off bad luck and foul weather, sacrificing chickens to the water gods. Did they know something we didn't, and weren't telling us?

It was near noon on the next day when the first dark lines of the squall came racing over the waves. The waters changed before our eyes from sky blue to the color of ink. With the squall line came the winds and rain, whipping the waves into a foaming broth. Landward, we could see white swirls of boiling foam, where the growing waves broke over the hidden reefs and bars.

The ships of our convoy were fast becoming separated, each tending to its own problems. Our crew was securing the ship, rearranging the sails, setting out what they called a sea anchor, and trying to keep our head into the wind. In less than two hours after the storm had set in, we could make out only four ships on the immediate horizon.

Germanicus' war galley was not one of them. The two sides of my stomach picked that inopportune moment to attack each other. It was most likely the fresh squid I'd had for breakfast that caused it. That, and the warm strong goat's milk I'd washed it down with.

The waves grew even higher. Our stumpy trader would slide down one watery mountain, then quickly be raised to the peak of another. Each time she dropped, I was certain that the ship's own weight would drive her under and we would sink to the deeps, leaving no signs that we'd ever been. But the old girl was stronger and stouter than I'd thought. Her captain cursed like a demon and held tightly to the steering oar. He later tied himself to the oar so as not to be swept off. I thought it was an admirable gesture on his part, for we would surely be lost if we lost him.

I dragged Britta to a more secure place amidships and tied us together with a length of line. Her hair was wet and streaming in the raging wind, but her eyes were bright with excitement, and the way her robes clung to her wet body almost made me forget the monsters that lay beneath the roiling, surging seas.

Aquila was busy trying to secure his horses, but he cut the lines and let them go when the frightened animals kicked the brains out of two of the men who had been helping him.

He came within a couple of inches of my reach once. Had the ropes binding Britta and me together allowed me some slack, I could have kicked him over the side. But I missed the chance.

The storm worsened with nightfall. The wind howled like insane women, grieving over the bodies of their dead. The lines that held the tattered remnants of our sails were humming like the strings of a lyre. I could see that Britta was growing weak, and with a little urging from me she finally relaxed against my shoulder. I used my arms and body to protect her as best I could from the winds and rain that whirled about us. Huge driving drops were pounding down upon us like the lead pellets used by the Balarian slingers of the islands. They stung the eyes and could have closed them if they'd hit dead on. I pulled my cloak over her head to provide more shelter as she clung tightly to me in the darkness, her face against my chest.

Several times in the night it appeared that the ship would surely capsize, but the ballast in the hold was sufficient to keep us upright. I'd never before felt such danger riding with us as I did that night. The old vessel's timbers creaked, trying to tear loose from her hull, and she kept leaning to the side until the mast was almost parallel with the waters. If she'd leaned an inch more, she would have gone over. As it was, we were half drowned each time she'd tip, and gasping madly for breath when she righted herself, spitting salt water, and turning to see who had survived. Most of the crew had been lost the first time we nearly went over.

One of the Praetorians was miraculously rejected by Father Neptune for some reason, which was a sight to see. After he'd been washed from the deck by one swooping wave, he was picked up by another, thrown high into the wind, flying like a bird, and tossed back up onto the deck, landing safely in a stack of bundles and stores that hadn't yet been lost to the ravages of the storm.

I thought the heavens themselves had broken open and were pouring forth the wrath of the gods. Thunder claps threatened our hearing; Jupiter's bolts lit up the night, terrifying us even more by showing us the monstrous waves falling so mercilessly upon our fragile decks.

It was near the hour of dawn when the ship began to scream in earnest. She was tearing apart, trying desperately to warn us with her sounds of final agony. The captain was gone now, vanished into the deep some time in the last hours of darkness. The deck was moving and twisting beneath my feet, and the mast was beginning to bend and whip, like a supple twig in a child's hands. I knew our time was near; to remain tied as we were would be to die. My fingers were so swollen by this time, from retaining my hold on both Britta and the lines, that I could barely untie the knots that bound us. I finally used my dagger to slice the lines. The quick release caught me by surprise and allowed the waves to toss us like dolls to the deck.

I held tightly to Britta. We both rolled over and against the railing at the edge; I managed to wrap one leg and one arm tightly around a stanchion, and kept us from going over. The position was tough on Britta I knew, but at least she was still on board and she was not complaining.

One final scream from the old ship, and she came apart at the seams. The sounds of her disintegration quickly silenced the screams of what few were still aboard. I found myself in the heaving waters, still clinging tightly to Britta, her soggy tresses wrapped tightly in my left fist. She was unconscious. A timber from the ship floated by; I grabbed at it frantically with my free hand, finally hauling it in.

I had the lines that we'd previously used tucked beneath my belt. I pulled them loose and once again tied us both to the beam. I was not much of a swimmer and besides, swimming would sap what little strength I had remaining. We rested on the beam.

Time stood still; minutes were eternities. Finally, I noticed a slight ease in the intensity of the storm and, after a few more minutes, as suddenly as it had arrived, it was gone. The sea turned a strange grey and the waves, though still quite large and ominous, no longer came at us like hammers and soon settled down into huge easy rolling swells.

My cargo of one unwilling slave had survived the ordeal. She woke, and immediately vomited a large amount of salt water, then fell unconscious once more. I raised her a little higher out of the water and looked about us. There was no sign of the ship now, or any of the others, and I wondered if they'd all gone down.

After we'd floated for another endless time, Britta finally came to herself. The sun was up and providing us with much-needed warmth and light. Gulls were circling overhead, giving off shrill cries as if they were extremely surprised that we'd survived.

As our beam crested a small wave, a different sound came to my ears. I scanned the area; not far away a man was clinging tightly to what appeared to be the door to the captain's quarters of our ship. He was waving frantically, crying for help. With my one free arm, I paddled towards him. Nearing him, I could see that it was Aquila. He was probably thanking his gods for this stroke of luck. Too bad! A few moments more and we lay alongside of him. Britta had fallen back into a faint, or sleep, I didn't know which.

"Lucanus," he called faintly, "I need help! Please! My leg is broken! Help!"

Well, I thought. How about that?

"Leave your door and cross over to us. Our beam will hold the three of us; we'll have a much better chance of surviving if we stick together.

He cried out, "I cannot swim."

I paddled closer. "Reach for my hand so I can pull you over to us."

He reluctantly let loose of his half-submerged door and lurched out to my hand, catching hold. I didn't pull him in, and fear burst into his eyes. Suddenly he understood.

"Help me, Lucanus! Help me!"

"That I will, Tribune," I responded. "I will help you to meet the gods of the deep."

I freed my other hand from the beam just long enough to strike him hard between the eyes. My blow caused him to release the hold on my other hand, and I used it to gain a new grasp on Britta.

He had the most embarrassed expression on his face

when he went down. I think he must have known then that I'd been playing him the fool, instead of the other way around.

A few air bubbles marked his position in the vast expanse, then abruptly ended. I knew I would not see him again. So much the better for all. Especially Germanicus!

4

The hours I spent in the ocean were, at least up to that point, the worst I'd ever passed in my life. I continued having visions of dagger-toothed sharks, or even more horrible creatures of the deep, coming up beneath me, to grab my legs and pull me down to their black domain, where they would tear my body to pieces hungrily.

Britta had taken it much better than I. Even soaked and ill, she was the most vibrant and attractive woman I'd ever seen.

After several hours we finally spied a dark line on the far horizon of the heaving waters. I thought at first it was just another dark cloud, full of wind and rain, coming to ravage us again. But Britta screamed for me to start kicking my legs. It was an island! She straddled the beam, using her arms to paddle. I was directly behind her, hanging on and kicking wildly. My efforts were aided by the view of her firm, well-muscled, heart-shaped rear, wiggling about a foot in front of my face.

At last we reached the surf that was rushing into the beach of the island. My feet struck the bottom and we were able to catch a wave, riding its crest onto the stony beach.

We lay there on the rocky strand for a time, trying to catch our breath, still unbelieving the luck that had come to us. We were shivering from the chill of the North Sea; it seemed colder out of the water than it had been in it. There was still a brisk breeze blowing.

I started to rub her legs down, massaging the calves to keep the chill from giving her cramps. She quickly told me to keep my hands to myself.

"Lucanus, you animal, if you have strength enough to try that, then you also have enough to get up and find us something to eat."

She was a bossy bitch, but I loved her for it. The knife at my belt had survived our journey, and we set out to look for food and shelter.

It took less than a half hour for us to walk completely around the small island. After five minutes, we came across the body of a sailor. He was half-covered with seaweed and sick-looking strands of kelp. I checked the body thoroughly, but there was nothing useful to us except the rags on his back, which we took.

The island rose to a rocky center of large boulders, with patches of tall yellowing grass in clumps here and there among the huge stones. Time had smoothed out shallow basins in some of the boulders, and we found water enough to sate our thirst. It had a salty taste, but it was still drinkable. We located some other smaller basins that contained better water, left over from the rainstorms. At least we would not die from thirst, not immediately anyway. The water would soon be fouled by the salt spray, or evaporate. Maybe there would be rain again. One could always hope.

Britta was of more use than I. She'd been raised in hard lands like this, lands where every child had to learn to survive by his wits, or die! She took to giving the orders necessary to our own survival, though I think she would have taken over even if she'd known nothing. It was her nature.

Searching further, we found a patch of dried gourds, out of which she constructed containers for our water. She was very proud of her find and laughed delightedly over the gourds, as if they were golden cups, filled with rare wine. Perhaps they would prove to be as valuable.

She left me again, going in search of something to eat. My stomach was growling like the bears in her forests, and right then I could have eaten the north end of a south-bound jackal. Before leaving, she told me to pile rocks into a shelter from the elements. I used the beam we'd floated in on to support a makeshift roof of seaweed and kelp. It was not completely waterproof, but it would serve our purpose. I had placed the beam between two large boulders; now I started piling rocks between them until our rough hut was formed.

Britta returned from her quest with a fair-sized fish in her hands. It had washed up on the beach during the storm. She'd also pried several mussels from the rocks by the shore. She was beaming about her find, but the first thing she did was start complaining about the hut.

I had expected it and fired back at her: "If you wanted a palace, you should have been shipwrecked with an engineer, not a fighter."

She turned around and laid into me again, hotter than before. By the Golden Titties of Venus, this woman was beautiful when she was mad, which was a fair part of the time. Her eyes flashed, the blue of them turning as dark as the depths of the night sea, and her long golden hair blowing wildly about her face.

"Fighter?" she yelled, "Give me any more of your insults and I'll really teach you how to fight. Don't forget your position. We are not on ship now, or in camp with your vulgar soldiers, where I was forced to play your slave and drudge. You are a common, lowborn swine. I am the sister of Arminius and daughter of a race of kings. Until aid comes to us, you will obey me and keep your opinions to yourself. If you fail to do as I say, when we are rescued, whether by Rome or by Arminius, I will see that you are punished. And when they are through with you, you will not call yourself a fighter any longer. But you may be able to sing in a much higher voice.''

Gods! How I loved her! I almost knocked her down and spread her legs right then, but I hesitated to do so; I respected her too much. (A shame, now that I think of it.)

I took her bit of temper, giving her the proper lower-class response to a superior. I bowed my head, saying in my best slave-like voice, ''Yes, Domina! Anything you like, Domina! I apologize for my rudeness, Domina!''

This seemed to mollify her for the moment and I asked her about the fish. It looked a trifle scummy about the gills. I don't mind a piece of meat that's been aged a little, but this one, to my taste anyway, was a little past aged.

''Are we going to eat that thing?''

''Give me the knife.'' I did; she commenced gutting the rancid beast, slicing it in pieces and saving the guts. At last she said, ''No, you fool!''

That was all, just no? Well, it had been courteously uttered at least. So much for trying to get on her good side.

''Then what are we going to do with it, if not eat it?''

She finished with the fish and started on the mussels, cracking open the shells but leaving the flesh inside. ''I'm going to use this to get us something proper to eat. Do you think you could possibly build a fire, or is that beyond your capabilities? Fighter!'' She'd mocked me again!

I responded a bit nastily. ''And just what do you suggest I use to start it with, noble lady?'' Ha, let her answer that one, smart-tongued wench!

She looked at me as if I were a stupid moron. ''Go up on the rise and bring me one of the pieces of flint rock. They are plentiful there. We can use your knife to strike the flint and set a fire with the dry grass.''

Now, why hadn't I thought of that? I suppose I did seem ignorant to her country savvy.

''I am a city boy. What does flint look like?''

She threw me my knife, blade first. ''Forget it, I'll get it myself. Meanwhile, finish the mussels."

After she'd gone, I opened the rest, sampling a couple. My stomach gurgled happily and cried for more. When she returned she frowned at the empty shells but said nothing. Hell, she'd tried a few herself, hadn't she?

She took a piece of the clothing that we'd removed from the drowned sailor, and tore it into strips, making a rough net. Inside this, she placed morsels of the fish and mussels, saving one long strand of the cloth as a rope. She then went to one of the tide pools, located a good spot on the rocks, and lowered the contraption into the water. In only a few moments, she hauled it back up to a position just below water level. Clinging to the homemade net were several large fresh crabs, trying frantically to get at the meat inside. She reached down with her free hand and picked them off the net. One escaped, but we had two of the crustaceans for certain. She repeated the process, moving from one spot to another, successful each time.

While she caught our meal, I'd managed to get a small fire started using the flint she'd found. Once it caught, there was no problem in adding bits of driftwood until I had a strong flame.

We had no pot to cook the crabs in, but once again the ingenuity of woman took over. She dug a small hole at the base of our fire, placed the crabs inside it and covered it with stones. In just minutes I could smell the sweet meat cooking. We dined royally that day on the sugary flesh of the sea crabs.

During the second and third days, it was Britta who found most of our sustenance, but I was learning a few things myself. I used my knife to whittle a fair-looking fish hook out of a piece of driftwood; it even met with her approval. With her net and my hook we were able to catch enough meat from the deep to sustain us well.

I did my utmost to gain Britta's appreciation, though it seemed that everything I could do she could do better. She was an annoying woman for certain. By the fourth day, I'd just about made up my mind that we were doomed to spend the rest of our lives marooned there, and I was not going to take much more of her sarcasm. I was about ready to toss her in the air and take what I wanted of her when she came down. It was then that I spotted a dark spot on the ocean.

I ran to a nearby mound for a better look. It was a boat! Not one of our ships, that was clear from the size of it. I could make out two figures inside it. I whistled softly for Britta to join me. The boat was now just yards from the breakers.

"Britta, we have to get them to land. But how?"

"You know little about anything, including women, and even including men. Stay still."

She quickly removed her tattered rags. The sight of her exposed breasts, jutting out like the prow of a galley, nearly drove me to taking her then and there, but, before I could grab her, she was off and running across the rocks to the beach. She stood there, thigh deep, pretending she hadn't yet seen them, basking in the ocean spray.

The men on the boat saw her, however. One pointed and yelled. They broke out two boards for makeshift oars, let down their rag of a sail and started rowing madly for shore. The closer they came, the more speed they picked up. I couldn't blame them, she looked for all the world like a sea nymph standing there in the salt spray. Wet golden strands of hair hung down about her shoulders and to her waist; her full breasts sparkled from the wet spray of the ocean's mist.

When the boatmen reached the surf, starting to ride the waves in, she began to step back, acting frightened at their approach. She turned and started toward me, ignoring their entreaties for her to wait for them.

She ran haltingly back onto dry land, glancing at them over her shoulder as the boat came to rest on the beach.

They leaped out of their small craft and started after her. She flicked her pretty rump in the air, let out a frightened squeal and headed straight for me. I lowered myself further down into the high grass.

When she reached a spot near where I lay concealed, she halted and kneeled down, as if she were giving in to their pursuit. They reached her; they were both seedy-looking individuals. One of the men grabbed her by the hair and threw her to her back, trying to spread her legs. The other untied the lacings that held his pants up.

I rose, charging them from their rear. I caught the one that was lowering his trousers directly in the small of his back, my fish knife going deep. He went down without a word.

The man holding Britta started to rise, releasing Britta's arms in doing so. She took that opportunity to stick a long sharp thumbnail full into his eye. Before he could complete his screaming, I had him laid out, his ugly gaping throat open to the winds.

She rose and, much to my regret, walked over and donned her rags again.

We stripped them of their clothing and took their knives. Neither possessed a sword, to my dismay, but there were two fish spears, a cooking pot, and one or two other useful items in the boat.

I raised the skin sail the following dawn, according to Britta's instructions, and pushed us off. We were away, heading back out into the open waters.

That afternoon another storm overtook us, pushing us along. It was not nearly as severe as the one that had destroyed our ship, but we were forced to let the wind and the waves take us where they would. We rode them for two more days. The boat rode high and easy, as long as we took turns bailing now and then.

The storm passed, leaving us wet and soggy, with wrinkled skin. But we were lost, with no land in sight.

5

Neither of us had any idea how far the storm had carried us, and now a heavy fog covered us and the horizon like a wet blanket, not allowing us to see what lay ahead or to our sides.

I was sleeping when Britta's voice woke me. "I heard surf breaking. We must be close to land."

We dropped the ragged skin sail and listened. It was hard to determine directions in the mist, but we finally agreed and set the two oars, pulling heavily.

We caught a series of waves and were able to ride them to shore. Its appearance was not too different from the island we'd left and, for a time, we were certain that's what we'd landed on, another damned island, or perhaps the very one we'd been on previously. Maybe we'd drifted in circles? I hoped not, but it was possible for two as ignorant of the sea as were we.

We spent the night in the shelter of the boat, which I upturned to protect us from the chill. We both slept through until the morning. The best thing I'd derived from the night was that Britta had lain with her back against me and my arm around her. Once, in the night, my hand had found her breast. She had not taken my hand away. I knew she was awake, because her breathing quickened and the nipple hardened. Though she hadn't spoken, I was smart enough to leave well enough alone. It was enough for me to know that she was at least considering our relationship.

We crawled from beneath the boat at dawn. The mist was gone, and it was a fine crisp morning. I noticed that when Britta told me to get our things together and get ready to leave, she wasn't quite as sarcastic as she normally was. A good sign!

I was wearing the homespun robe and the furs of one of the men we'd killed on the island. With these, and the fact that I hadn't shaved while on the island, I knew I must look the part of a barbarian, at least enough to fool the local tribesmen, if I kept my mouth shut and let her do the talking. She would, anyway.

We moved inland. The pack on my back contained our few pitiful belongings. My knife was at my belt and the spear was in my right hand, at the ready. Britta carried the other spear and the fishknife of one of our victims at her waist. Together, we must have made a fearsome-looking couple.

As we went, we realized that we were not on an island, much to our relief. She was in her element now. Being aware of what roots were edible, and knowing how to set snares for hares and birds, she again took complete charge. It was due to her efforts that we hadn't starved on the island, and that we didn't starve now.

We went on for weeks without finding any sign of human habitation. She started needling me again, mocking my ignorance of the wild, challenging my ability as a man. I got a little perturbed and told her to stop it. That night I tried to hold her, and she pushed me away sharply. I was beginning to wish that she'd make up her mind. How could she expect me to keep my hands from her? She would bathe naked before my eyes, in the cold running streams, her nipples tightening as she climbed out and dried herself. The golden flax between her legs was driving me mad, and she knew it.

When we'd been wandering about in the dark overgrown forests for about a month, I was getting edgy as hell. I was about ready to slap her silly if I heard one more complaint or insult. Then I would take her as I wished. Arminius and Germanicus could do with me as they pleased. A man could only take so much, even if he was a disciplined fighter. These were my thoughts as we were making our way through a small ravine. A heavy rustling from a high thicket of brush to our front ended my thoughts.

Perhaps it was a deer; the idea of venison made my mouth water. I eased my pack down from my shoulder and laid it on the ground. Keeping my spear, I motioned for Britta to be quiet, then moved closer to the bushes and the sound.

My visions of fresh venison suddenly turned into the reality of a huge reddish-black bear with blood in his eyes. As he broke from the bushes, I nearly wet myself. He spotted me and stopped dead in his tracks. The fur on his neck and back rose, standing in a ridge. He hissed loudly, snake-like, and started tearing up the ground in front of him, his claws ripping large gashes in the earth.

Britta moved up to my side, holding her spear level before her. I'd had enough out of the smart bitch. This was my kill. With one hand I knocked her back out of the way. By the gods, if I couldn't have venison, then bear would do just as well. He rushed forward, rocking back and forth from foot to foot, still making the piggish squealing sounds. I had seen bears in the arena before and had learned something about them from Bosra. I knew, because this wily one had not yet charged me, that he was merely warning me to get out of his territory. I also knew that the most vital point to hit was on their underside, where you could get a shot at their heart. I had to get him to rise on his hind legs. Something Bosra had told me came back, and suddenly I knew what to do.

I dropped to all fours and faced him, beginning to howl wolf-like myself. Britta must have thought I'd gone completely mad. The bear stopped his shuffling, staring at me through his pig eyes for a moment, as if he too were confused. I bounced up and down on my hands and knees a few times, imitating the bears I'd seen in the arena. He started to imitate me, and together we bounced up and down, hissing at each other. Suddenly I stopped and stood up, raising my arms, holding the spear in my right hand.

The bear stood also, raising his front legs, and before he could return to all fours I hurled the spear straight into his massive chest. He stood there for a moment, frozen in position, looking with disbelief at the shaft protruding from his chest. He began howling like a woman, then rolled over in the brush, tearing at the spear.

I knew then that I had missed the heart. I drew my sword and looked for an opening as the animal screamed, but he rolled farther back into the brush, making horrible sounds of pain and anger. I didn't follow him into the dense thicket, knowing that there I would have little chance to spear him.

The brush stopped shaking after a while. I thought perhaps I had hit a vital spot after all; perhaps it had taken some time for the huge thing to die. I moved closer to the brush, slowly, cautiously, listening for the slightest sound. My face was dead level with the nearest bush when I nearly lost my nose.

A black paw broke from the brush, followed by the rest of the bear. The spear had broken off, the jagged edge of the shaft still protruding about a foot out of his chest, lodged between the ribs. I backed away frantically, making a wild swing with my knife. It caught the beast across the face, laying it open to the bone. It hadn't done any real damage, but it slowed him down until I was able to gain my balance.

He swarmed me then, rushing in low this time, not rising to his feet until he was full upon me. On his hind quarters, he stood a full head taller than I and probably weighed three times as much. The force of his attack bowled me over and I went down. His bleeding muzzle was trying to bite my face off in retaliation for the wound I'd given him.

Everything was confused and disjointed for the next few

moments and I don't recall a lot of it. I do remember that I tried desperately to hold him to my chest, keeping him close so that he could not use his claws to rip my stomach out. His feet were clawing at my back, and I was more than thankful for the thickness of the rough furs I wore. Even with that, he was still able to cut through. I could feel my skin opening, the steel of his claws piercing the muscles of my back. There was not a lot of pain, only a strange distant numbness, wet and hot. My knife had been knocked from my hand and lay some distance away. The jagged piece of the shaft in his chest was jabbing me in the gut. I grabbed it, pushing it in further and twisting it with all my strength.

I heard a scream, and thought at first that it had come from my own lips. Then, over the beast's shoulder, I spotted Britta. Her face was pale, her hair flying wildly, as she stabbed at the bear's back with her own spear, screaming wildly for the animal to get off of me. I was heartily agreeing with her, but the beast was paying no attention at all. His total concentration was on tearing me to shreds.

He whipped me around on the ground, trying to get at my face. I wrapped my legs around him as best I could and hung on tightly, still twisting the spear and hoping to hit a vital spot before he could finish me off.

The spear finally came loose and pulled out into my hand. I wasted no time. With my one free hand I shoved the point upwards and into the neck, searching for the great vein. I found it! I struck deep and hard, pulling it out quickly and striking again. The bear squealed as hot blood spurted from the wound. He managed to sink his fangs into my left shoulder and then raised me like a doll, shaking me as a dog shakes his kill.

From somewhere inside I found the strength to strike again. I don't know how many times I sank the iron tip of the spear into the beast's throat, but I would not quit. A madness was rushing over me. I wanted him. My kill would not be denied me.

From a corner of my eye I saw Britta's face. Tears were streaming down her face as she struck the animal in the back with her spear, again and again. Her furs were covered with the blood of the bear, or of my body. I didn't know which.

At last he began to weaken. He released my shoulder and rolled over onto his side. I crawled out from under him and managed with some effort to stand.

Britta rushed to me then, throwing her arms about me, sobbing. I recall looking at her as if everything was all right, and trying to say something clever just before I passed out.

It was dark when I regained consciousness. Britta had made a lean-to for us, and we were sheltered. My body was on fire. I tried to sit up, but was unable to raise more than my head. I fell back with a groan and lay still.

Britta came over to me. My eyes were a bit fogged, but I was able to make out a glow behind her. She had built a fire. I tred to speak, but she shushed me, spooning warm broth into my lips. She answered the question I could not ask. "Yes! It's your bear that you are eating. Now, be quiet and rest. You are badly hurt."

"How long?" I managed to croak.

"Three days. Now go to sleep as soon as you eat. There is nothing to worry about, I am here."

She spooned some more broth into my mouth. I had to follow her orders again, though not without silent protest . . . . I slept. It was a fevered time, for I would sleep and wake again, ranting and raving that my wounds were on fire, then fall asleep again. She made poultices of herbs and leaves to draw the poison from my wounds, but I was still unable to rise or feed myself. There were moments when I was lucid enough to speak sensibly to her, but they were short. A strong fever set in. For three days I had chest-racking chills and cold sweats that drained my body of its moisture until my skin looked loose on my bones.

At last the chills ended, and the fever lessened. I became aware that Britta was lying next to me, keeping the chills from my body with her own warmth. I whispered groggily into her ear: "I love you!"

I didn't know if she'd heard me or not, but I did feel her move a little closer and I slept again, this time more peacefully.

When I woke, my head was crystal clear. I was weak, but I felt strangely fit and I was hungry enough to eat a . . . bear! I found my voice and called for Britta. She came to me. Gods! She looked worse than I did. Her eyes were red from lack of sleep, her hands scratched and raw. I could tell that she'd done little for herself while I'd been ill. She gave me a swallow of water and brought meat, her eyes missing nothing as I ate for the first time since my fight with the bear. I finished, and I asked, "How long?"

She moved a long strand of hair out of her eyes. "Ten days, maybe more. I lost track."

"Where is the bear?"

She moved aside and pointed to a rack outside the lean-to where strips of meat hung on a cross pole, over a small smoking fire. She forced a smile.

"There's your bear. He has saved the two of us. His flesh has given you your strength back."

The word flesh made my mouth water. I asked her for more meat; I needed some to fill the empty void in my gut. She brought me a piece that she'd been boiling in water. My mouth wanted it, but my jaws were still too weak to chew it up. She cut it into small pieces, putting them in her own mouth and chewing until the meat was soft enough for me.

We stayed there one more week, until I'd recovered sufficiently to walk under my own power. Still, I had to use a staff, and I knew I would be stiff for several weeks to come. Three ribs had been broken by the gentle hugging of the bear, and the wounds on my shoulder were slow to heal.

The night before we were to leave, I'd been cleaning our gear and was sharpening my knife with a piece of stone, sitting by the fire, when I heard a noise behind me. I turned quickly, thinking it might be another bear. What I saw then startled me more than the sight of a bear would have.

Britta stood there in the red glow of the fire, her hair hanging loose at the shoulders, soft golden strands hiding the nipples of her breasts. There were wildflowers in her hair and, even with the strong odor of the fire, I could smell the clean fragrance of her. She had washed her body and had rubbed it down with sweet herbs of the forest.

I was speechless. Never had I seen such a sight in my life, nor have I since. She stood there as pure as the waters of a crystal spring. The fire glowed from her skin, shadows moving around the curve of her belly and thighs. I nearly swallowed my tongue.

Awkwardly, I stood up, looking at her in wonder. Gone now was the evil temper and sharp tongue. In front of me was a gentle maid, all woman, and warm. I felt like a young boy when I reached to take her hand.

She turned and led me away from the fire and into the darkness of the forest. Neither of us spoke a word. Suddenly she stopped. There, on the bed of the forest, she had prepared a place for us beneath the boughs of an ancient oak.

I knew then that this was to be our wedding bed, made of wildflowers and soft moss. The oak tree was sacred to her tribes, and this was the reason for our being here. She was not giving me her body only; she was offering her life and her love.

There are some things that are too personal and private to write down. I can only say that I've never experienced such a night of gentle love and fulfillment. It was passion and tenderness wrapped in one. I had never known what the bards and poets meant when they spoke of love until that night with Britta. One would think that the simple act of man joining with woman would always be the same, no matter what partner, but the act changes when you are joined in love and the love you feel is returned. It makes the one experience feel as if it were your first time. There is a new and different texture to everything, the senses change, and when you are joined it is as if you both are one in being, as if you feel what she feels and both know without speaking how to give the other pleasure and share in the giving.

We spent the night in our bed of flowers, lying in each other's arms and, even in sleep, we were one beneath the giant oak.

I swear that to this moment there has never been another one to compare with that night's pleasures. Gods! How I loved her . . . .

BOOK FIVE

THE CHATTI

1

We had survived in these inhospitable lands for two months when Britta said, for the first time, that she recognized some landmarks. The shapes of the mountains to the east were familiar, she said. It was a relief to think that she might have some idea where we could find tribes friendly to Arminius. The great cold was coming; we could feel crispness in the air as we stopped at a spring to drink. Tall pines mingled with the oaks, whose leaves had already fallen to lie in soft carpets on the earth. I leaned over the spring. It amazed and startled me to see a hairy-faced barbarian, dressed in the skins of animals, staring back at me from the pool below. I certainly looked the part of a Germanic warrior. Maybe that was why Britta had stopped insulting me lately. After all, she had been brought up with men that looked like this. Anyway, I thought I made a rather fierce-looking animal and wasn't that displeased with the change.

We spent the night by the spring. I made a rough shelter of branches and pine needles, and draped a skin over the front part of the lean-to to keep out the wind. We lay down our robes to cover the earth, first spreading a thick layer of damp leaves to cushion us a bit from the stones and twigs that always seemed to find a tender part of the body and tediously poke it during our sleep.

We snuggled in. Our breath was misting in the crisp air as dark closed in and the shadows grew long and dark. I was tired and was wishing that I could have had a rubdown and a hot steam bath rather than trying to sleep in vermin-infested skins. But I made do; I had to, I had no other choice. At least when the snow came, as Britta said it would tonight, the lice on the outside of the skins would go to sleep. Then only the ones next to us would give us trouble.

Britta lay next to me, her back to my stomach. I covered us with a thick robe, putting my arm around her waist, my nose in her hair. One sniff and I was out.

When I awoke, there was no light coming into our shelter at all. Then a drip fell on my nose. I realized snow had fallen silently to cover our lean-to.

I moved out from under the furs. Britta's hand searched for me with little patting motions, then stopped as she gave a delicate lady-like snore. I stuck my head around the flap at the front of our shelter.

The world had changed overnight, from dark forest to a land of white and softly wondrous magic. The snow blanketed everything to a depth of a foot or more, and the branches of the trees hung down, seeming sadly burdened with the weight of the white.

It was beautiful, but I knew it spelled hard times for us. We still had over two hundred miles to go by Britta's calculations, and if we didn't find mounts soon it would be hard going. Very, very hard.

There was a squirming behind me, and Britta stuck her pretty head out beside mine. "The ice giants came in the night," she said sleepily.

I didn't know who the ice giants were, but I agreed anyway. We pulled back inside.

"How far to the nearest tribe that is friendly to Arminius?" I asked.

She thought it over, then replied, "Perhaps three days'

march in this weather. Ten if it snows again, which it probably will.''

Three days on foot across this cold earth didn't excite me much. But there was no choice as I saw it. We had only enough food left for one, maybe two days and in this cold the body needed more than usual to keep it going.

We broke camp. I took the lead, breaking a path through the drifts for her to follow in. We trudged all that day, taking time out only for a short breather or to chew on a piece of dried smoked fish. For water, the streams were still running and clear and we had our fill. But the clouds were gathering, dark and angry, and the tops of the trees were beginning to sway back and forth, dropping the loads of snow from their branches. With the winds came a chill that numbed the face. A freeze was near. We started to look for shelter for the night. This was going to be no night for a lean-to in the open.

We came to a great plain, and I decided against trying to cross it before the storm came. Already the snow, which had been soft earlier, was beginning to form a crisp crust on its surface which cracked with every step. We could not tell how long it would be before night fell. The grey of the gathering storm was complete; not even a shadow was to be seen.

Sweat from my exertions gathered in my beard and turned to ice. Britta was clearly feeling the strain. Her breathing was becoming rapid and labored. I could tell that the cold was hurting her lungs. I half carried her, despite her protests.

To the left was a thick grove of pines, with a little open space in the center. I hoped the trees would break the growling wind. We went there.

I scraped away the snow from the open ground; it hadn't frozen yet. I took my knife and began to dig. Britta sat, still wrapped in her furs. I'd warned her to keep out of my way; I could work faster by myself. It wasn't true, but I wanted her to rest. She had not been feeling well for the past few days, throwing up and having the cramp. It was no doubt the strain of our journey; I was worried about her.

The snow began to fall again. This time it was like razors riding the wind. The treetops weren't swaying gently any more, they were whipping the sky. I had to hurry; it was coming. At last I had a hole that resembled a wide grave, about a foot and a half deep. I lined the bottom with one fur robe and motioned for Britta to lie down inside. When she looked fairly comfortable, I wedged myself in beside her and pulled the rest of the furs and robes over us, covering even our heads. Then the storm was on us.

I don't know just how long we lay there, holding each other, as the wind howled through the branches and the snow fell even heavier with the winds.

We slept, not knowing if we would wake again, holding each other like children, arms encircling, face to face. If we did not wake, then this was the best way I could think of to die. Here in the arms of the woman I loved. I had heard that when the cold takes you, it feels like going to sleep. Therefore, if death came, it would be gentle. That was what I wanted for her, to go to sleep with no suffering, no pain, just the long deep sleep of eternity.

I woke first. My arm, beneath her head, had gone numb in the night and was tingling. In fact, my whole body felt numb and heavy. I discovered why when I tried to sit up. At least three feet of snow had drifted about us during the night and now lay like a heavy blanket atop our bodies, shielding us from not only the cold above but also, I assumed, from the light of day. I was cold and numb, but I was elated. We were actually alive.

After digging out, I left her alone in our makeshift pit and ventured out in search of fuel for a fire. I finally found some small dry twigs and with my knife removed some powdery pulpish wood from the core of a dead tree. This was what we would need to save us this day.

Near the pit, I scraped away snow until I had made a hollow in dry ground—not actually dry, but frozen. From the trees above us I broke off small branches; having frozen in the night, they cracked loudly in the silence. I broke the branches into pieces no longer than my hand and set them aside for later.

Bending down over what I hoped would soon be our fire pit, I carefully placed the pulp wood and dry twigs into a small pile and removed the flint and iron from Britta's pack.

After several futile attempts, a spark caught in the pulpish wood and glowed. I blew on it carefully. Soon a tiny flame grew out of the pulp. I placed a few of the dry twigs on the tiny flame; soon, the twigs themselves caught fire, and I was able to add a few pieces of the small branches I had broken up, setting them nearby to dry and finally to burn.

The process had taken time, but in a few minutes more I had a fire big enough to dry some larger branches, and to warm the body. I called to Britta; instead, I had to leave the comfort of the fire and help her from the pit. She was stiff. The cold was severe enough that we could hear the trees cracking as their sap expanded and their limbs burst.

Now that the fire was fueled, it was time to do the same for our stomachs. She wanted to help but I told her to stay by the fire and keep it alive. From her pack I withdrew our small copper pot, taken from the men on the island, and added to it some of our smoked fish, and two strips of our scarce meat, and a scoop of snow. I set it on branches over the flame. I added more snow to the pot, and soon it was half full and starting to boil.

I served Britta the steaming broth and tried some myself. It tasted horrible, but it was hot, and we needed that. I fished out the pieces of limp meat, giving her one and taking the other for myself. An hour later, Britta threw up again and emptied her stomach. I had to be truthful with myself: perhaps she had contacted the wasting disease that left the body nothing but a wrinkled, withered husk without strength to support life. But Britta gave me a weak smile, and told me that she was all right.

I hated to do it, but we had to move on now, while the weather was clear. It was one of those bright eye-blinding winter days of crystal-clear skies and searing white.

I tied more wrappings around my feet, and around Britta's. I discarded everything from our packs that was not essential to our immediate survival. I kept the pot, for we were sure to need something warm in our stomachs again before reaching safety. I arranged our packs so I could carry them tied to my chest. Britta tried to rise, but was too weak. Using some strips cut from our robes, I formed a harness and raised Britta to my back, found a suitable branch to use for a staff, and started out.

I don't know how long I went on, crunching through the ice crust, my legs sometimes sinking in up to the thigh. My mind settled into a numbness that made the aching of my lungs a distant memory. One step after another, I plodded on. Several times I fell, and each time I found it more difficult to rise. Gods! How my legs throbbed and my back muscles burned.

Finally I fell face down in the snow, and was too exhausted to raise my face from it. I lay there breathing heavily, melting the snow below my mouth. My head was thick, and it was difficult to think or try to talk. I felt a weight leave my back, but still my legs and arms refused to raise me up. I passed out then, and an easy relief flooded my entire being.

When I came to my senses, Britta had a fire going and was holding my face to her bare breast beneath her robes, trying to warm me. I must confess that even then the feel of her breasts gave me more cause to want to live than anything the gods could have provided. I kissed one tight, chilled nipple to let her know that I was all right. She thumped me on the head with a finger snap and yelled, in a pretense of anger, "You animal, don't you ever think of anything else? Even when we're freezing?"

From somewhere I found a laugh inside me. Weak, but still a laugh. She pushed me away from her breast, and I warmed myself at the flames. After a bit, we talked seriously.

"Britta, do you have any idea where we might be?"

She shook her head. "If you didn't walk in circles while I was on your back, we should be near a wide river. When we come to it, we won't be far from the village of the Chatti, the tribe friendly to Arminius." She looked carefully at the position of the sun. "We should go that way." She pointed to the right.

We ate then and repacked our equipment. This time she refused to let me carry her, saying: "What am I going to do if you die from exhaustion, you animal? Shall our child have another man to raise him?"

It took a moment or two for her words to register. Then I bellowed out, "Our child? You mean we . . . I . . . that is . . . you and I?"

She laughed, her lovely eyes sparkling impishly. "Yes," she mocked me. "I mean we . . . you . . . us . . . . That's the reason for my sickness each day, you fool! Do you know nothing of women?"

I grinned back at her a little sheepishly through my ice-encrusted beard. "I know something about women, yes, but I have never been a father before. If we have a son I shall ask Germanicus if we can give him his name."

She slapped me playfully. "Remember, you dog, I have a little to say about that. Arminius is just as good a man as your Roman."

I begged truce, offering a compromise that she agreed to. If it was a boy we would name him Lucanus Arminius Germanicus. This satisfied her and we set off on the next leg of our journey, hoping to find the river she'd talked of.

The goddess of fortune had surely been with us on this dreadful journey. Not only had I chosen the right direction in my stuporous plodding, but I had also covered a lot of ground. We were less than a mile from the river, and reached it with a couple of hours left before nightfall. I had covered more ground than either of us had thought possible.

She pointed the way this time, northwest, following the bank of the river. Should we miss the Chatti village, she said, there would always be another one, as long as we were heading toward the coast.

We had trudged a few more miles on numb and aching feet when suddenly she stopped and raised her face to the wind, nose up and straight ahead.

"What is it, Britta?"

"Smoke," she said. "I smell smoke on the wind."

2

I left her in the shelter of a grove of tall pines and went on ahead to have a look, taking my spear and sword. I tried hard to avoid making noise, but I could not prevent the crunching of my boots through the half-frozen snow.

After a half hour I came to a line of trees that bordered a clearing, and what looked like a stockade.

I had no way of telling who the people might be, but Britta had been right so far, and it was most likely as she'd said. This was probably the Chatti village.

I returned to her. Helping her to her feet, I shouldered my pack again and gave her my arm for support. The tracks I'd left while going and coming back made it a little easier this time.

At the treeline we stopped again. I unslung my gear, keeping my spear in my right hand, and waited. We could hear voices coming from the stockade now, but they were indistinct, and Britta was unable to make out the words. We decided to take our chances. We could either go in or stay out here and freeze.

She called out, loud and clear, her voice carrying crisp on the winter air. She yelled again, and the voices in the stockade fell silent. Once more she hailed them. I could not understand her words, but caught her name and that of Arminius.

Suddenly the gate opened. A half-dozen men came out, all carrying weapons, but displaying no hostility. However, they did look wary. It is a well-known fact that when the tribes beyond the Rhine are not waging war on Rome, their favorite pastime is raiding and slaughtering each other. I intended to practice a little wariness of my own.

We left the treeline and faced the tribesmen across the clearing. I laid my spear in the snow beside me and raised my empty hands. Britta moved to my side and showed them her face. That was enough. There was muttering among the men, and one of them stepped forward. He was an old man, his face wrinkled with age, but his back was strong and erect. He came closer, leaving the rest of the men behind him, unmoving. His pale blue eyes lit up suddenly, as if in recognition, and he began to half run, laughing, crying out Britta's name.

The two of them hugged each other, the old one near tears as he pulled her to his chest. I wanted to stop him from such forceful displays of affection, afraid that he might hurt her, or the baby she carried, but I did not move. She pried herself loose from him and turned to me.

"This is Arduus! When Arminius and I were children he was our guard and tutor. He was as close to us as our father. Our father left us more in Arduus' care than in his own."

The old man was crying freely now, tears running down into his crusty grey beard, but he made an effort to control himself and spoke to me in Latin: "Young man, you will never know the pleasure you have brought me this day. We had word that Britta had died in a great storm and that her body was not to be found. This day I will surely make sacrifice to the gods of fortune and luck for returning her to us."

The men behind him seemed a little confused at this turn of events. One of them called out to Arduus. He answered in his tongue, Britta translating for me, that all was well and we were who we'd claimed to be.

Once this was all cleared up, we were invited into the compound as their very welcome guests. The palisade of stripped tall trees, sunk into the ground to form a primitive wall, protected a rough collection of log cabins. There were a few places on top of the walls for spearmen but I learned later that the walls had been planned more to keep out bears and wolves than to protect them from human intruders.

Most of the village women looked wilder than their mates, but they took Britta to them like a lost chick, and like hens they clucked over her, murmuring sympathetically of her ordeal in the forests. They led her off while I was shown into the longhouse where single males were billeted.

The longhouse was about fifty feet in length and ten feet high, with beamed rafters of smoke-stained oak. A poor palace for a king, but infinitely better than the chill north winds outside the gates.

I had surrendered my weapons to the men outside, and now they were brought to the longhouse by a warrior with tattoo marks on his face. The signs were those of some strange angular bird, done in blue lines. The rest of them had no marks that I could see.

A large smoking fire in the center of the longhouse burned high. Its tall column of pungent smelling smoke was escaping through a hole in the roof, though not all of it was making it out, as was evidenced by the heavy haze inside, hanging densely other everything and everyone. Sleeping places were spaced on either side.

It was difficult to see to the other end of the house due to the smoke, but I thought I could make out a figure sitting in a chair there. As we neared, Arduus whispered to me in Latin, telling me to be careful because the chief held no love for Rome. Suddenly it struck me. Arduus' Latin was perfect, no trace of accent at all. He could have just come from the Via Aregeletum. But there was no time for speculation now; we had arrived in front of the chief of this miserable sty. Arduus introduced him proudly: "This is our great and brave chieftain, Inguimer!"

The chief sat silently, brooding. I guessed his age at about fifty years, maybe more. He was well scarred from battle, I could see, and had the look of one who killed for pleasure. His face contained a multitude of broken bluish veins, probably from too many pots of their ale, I thought. He sat in his poor wooden chair, half reclining, as if he was Augustus Caesar himself upon the marble throne of Imperial Rome.

I'd heard Inguimer's name mentioned before, by Arminius and by survivors of the slaughter that had decimated Varus' legions. Inguimer had been a powerful chieftain then, but he'd made a big mistake. Arminius had advised him to let the Romans out of their fortified position, so that they would take positions where Inguimer could better deal with them. Inguimer had gone against Arminius' advice and, with the support of some of the other chieftains, had made a direct assault on the palisade of the Roman camp. This was exactly what the Romans wanted. The Germans had been butchered on the walls by the thousands and the rest put to flight. As a result, Arminius was made war leader of the tribes of the Germanii. Perhaps that was why Inguimer now ruled just this one pathetic group of ragged barbarians. Perhaps, I thought now, it might also mean that he had no love for Arminius or his kin, such as Britta. Barbarians like Inguimer often carried grudges for life, some clans even maintaining blood feuds for so long that no one could remember what had started it all in the first place. If Inguimer did bear ill feeling to Arminius for taking his command, then there might be trouble. I wished then that I had my sword.

The old man had a mean look to him, the set of his mouth filled with bitterness. The eyes were set far back beneath thick, wire-like eyebrows. I couldn't make out the color of his eyes in the smoky gloom, but they were dark and had that glint to them, the glint that I had seen in the eyes of fighters who killed merely for the enjoyment of killing.

Arduus finished speaking. I'd heard Britta's name and my own several times. At the first mention of Britta's name, I could have sworn I saw a spark of interest in the old eyes. He looked at me as if he'd enjoy having me for lunch.

Inguimer stood up. He was as thick as he was tall. reminding me a bit of Celer. He moved over to stand before me. I stood still, noticing that my guards were holding their weapons a little tighter than previously. He stalked around me, not saying a word. I thought it best to keep my big mouth shut.

He made a full circle and returned to stand facing me, his eyes not much lower than my own. I could smell the sourness of his unwashed body and the staleness of his furs. He raised one dirty hand to wipe his mouth and beard. His wrists were as thick as the ankles of a large-boned woman. He was ugly, but he was also damned tough-looking, and I could tell immediately that he didn't like me at all.

He spoke in pidgin Latin: "So, you are the bodyguard of Britta, sister of Arminius, eh? How did she come by one such as you, Roman?"

Arduss started to speak but was stopped by Inguimer's snarl: "I was not speaking to you, old man. Hold you tongue or lose it!" He returned his attention to me. "I asked you, Roman," he grinned, showing strong yellow teeth with a gap in the center, "How did you come to be the guard of Britta?"

I tried not to lock eyes with him. It could only make things worse if he saw too much anger or challenge in them; this was no time to start a fight. I related the story to him that Britta and I had agreed on when we'd first set foot in these lands.

"Lord," I began, "I am the servant of the Lady Britta. I came to her as a gift of her brother. He bought me in Gaul, where I was sold into slavery for debts. I serve the lady because she promised me freedom in five years if I serve her well."

My answer seemed to please him. He chewed on his mustache a bit and moved back to his chair. He laughed a little, a nasty sound, and spoke.

"So, you are a slave? What is your name?"

"My name is Mordius, Lord!" I used the name Britta and I had earlier fabricated, bowing as I spoke.

He thought a moment, his eyes lost beneath his beetle brows.

"You have the look of a fighter about you. I have heard of one such who serves the swine Germanicus. Do you know him, or have you seen him?"

A touch of fear ran through me. "Yes, Lord! I have heard of such a one, but never have I seen him."

He called for a cup of whatever the foul brew was that they concocted here, and swilled it down, yellow drops spilling in his haste to be soaked up in the greying mat of his beard. He leaned forward.

"I have heard also, that the one who watches the back of Germanicus is a gladiator. Have you ever been a gladiator yourself?"

Before I could answer, he threw the horn cup straight at my face. Automatically I moved so that it barely missed me and remained standing in the same spot, hardly able to contain my growing anger, in spite of the armed men about me.

"Yes, Lord! I have fought in the arena before." My words were a little short.

He grinned his yellow-tooth leer again. "I thought so. If you had said otherwise, I would not have believed you. I know your type. Your servile manners are all on the surface. Inside you have no humility. But," he continued in a sneer, 'if you were truly a professional, you should not object to providing me with a little entertainment, eh?"

I did not like the way this was going. It could only lead to trouble. But before I could voice any objection, he stood and pointed to a man behind me.

"Voldan, come here to me!"

At his command, a monster of a man stepped smartly to the front and stood beside me. By the gods! He was gigantic! He stood a full head and a half higher than me and walked more like a beast than a man. The spear in his hand was as thick as my wrist, tipped with an iron head. He held it like a small twig.

Inguimer pointed to me, laughing. "Voldan, I have a Roman mouse for you to play with."

The monster smiled, looking at me like an overgrown child. His face bore no malice. His blond hair hung long and thick, in a mane that reached to his massive shoulders. He would have been a fine looking man if not for the slackness of his features. He had crystal-blue eyes, like most Northlanders, but they held a weird uncomprehending glaze. It hit me then! The man was a simpleton, but none the less dangerous for it. Here was a man that could hurt you and consider it child's play. His arms and shoulders spoke of a strength that he probably didn't even know the limits of. Voldan moved closer to me, removing his furs, leaving his chest and arms bare. He handed his spear to one of his comrades and waited for word from Inguimer to rip my arms from their sockets.

Inguimer turned to me, sneering cat-like.

"Do not worry, Roman. He will not kill you, he will only break you up a little. But, if you are a trained fighter as you say, it may be the opposite. You may have no problem at all defeating an oversized child like little Voldan." He was mocking me now.

I spoke up, asking for a weapon. I wasn't worried about the giant if I could arm myself, but barehanded it would be risky. If he caught hold of me, or hit me with one of those ham-like fists, it could very well be all over for the wolf. But Inguimer refused, saying that this was merely going to be a wrestling event. It would not be polite of me to refuse the challenge, he said.

I had no choice. I removed my own furs, as had Voldan. I did not want anything the giant could get his grip on. The size of my body surprised Inguimer and his men a bit, I think. The furs had made me look smaller than I actually was. I was still well muscled, without a trace of fat on me. The scars on my upper torso said that I was a man to be reckoned with. I wished now that my appearance hadn't given me away to them. If I hadn't looked like a fighter, I wouldn't be having to fight this big bastard now. But it was too late to worry about that now. I felt that Inguimer suspected I was the one who watched Germanicus' back, although he wasn't positive, I knew.

I spoke again. "I have no objections to teaching your pet bear a few things, but in order to make it more interesting, and to give him some slight chance to win, it would be best if you give him something to protect himself with. Something besides his inexperienced hands."

The giant smiled his loose-lipped, contented grin, not understanding what I'd said. I doubt that he had a mean bone in his body. He was merely a huge clumsy child who would do as his ruler told him, without question or thought. But his hands were the most dangerous things I faced, and if I could get Inguimer to put something in his hands, something to keep them busy, I'd have a better chance to take him out. Whatever weapon he used would dictate a certain behavior that I was trained for.

Inguimer laughed, the sour odor of his breath reaching to where I stood. "So you think my little man needs a weapon? What, if I may ask, did you have in mind?"

"It makes no difference; anything will do. A spear or a stave would probably help him a bit."

Inguimer called for staves to be brought in quickly.

Arduus whispered in my ear that I had made a grave mistake, for the giant had already killed several men with staves. His strength was such that few men could block one of his blows. There was no need for him to tell me that. I could tell that the ogre was powerful enough to break me in half. The thick bands of muscled tendons that stood out in his neck and shoulders were evidence.

The staves were brought in, two equal lengths of cured oak, six feet long and treacherous in appearance. One was given to the giant, and looked quite small in his hand. Inguimer smiled, saying that since I'd called for fair play and had offered Voldan a weapon for advantage, I would also be given one. My plan had worked, and I was damned well relieved that it had. The tribesman handed me one, and I hefted it to gain a good grip. The two of us squared off and waited for the command to begin. Inguimer rose, and whispered in the giant's ear, then moved quickly back to his chair. When he was comfortably seated, he yelled, "*Now!*"

Voldan stepped forward, grinning, his staff whistling through the air, striking at my head. But I wasn't there. My greatest advantage was mobility. It had worked in the arena many times for me against men such as this. He struck again. This time I didn't block the blow, only deflected it, letting his stroke slide along my own staff, his weight propelling him forward. As he lunged, I stepped in close to him, pivoting, swinging my stave around to catch him in the face, full on the jawbone. It was a fair blow, and a normal man would have fallen as if he'd been pole-axed, but Voldan blinked his eyes and only looked a little puzzled. He wasn't even noticing, as far as I could tell, that there was blood streaming from his mouth where several teeth had been smashed.

I tried again, this time moving under his forward attack and thrusting straight to the gut with the rounded tip of my staff. The heavy oak stave bounced off his knotted abdomen, leaving only a red mark. I barely missed losing my brains to his club when he returned my thrust with a swing of his own. I chose then to parry for a while, and try to figure out how to put this man away. He was like the Cyclops, gaining strength every time he touched the ground. I was unable to hurt him, or, if I did, he was too stupid to know it. His brain was so dense it would probably take three days for the message to reach him from the broken jawbone.

He smashed and I parried. The contest seemed a rough one to the onlookers, but I knew I was in no real danger unless I grew careless or came in too close to him. He gave me one blow that had broke through my guard and hit my left shoulder. It sent me rolling to the floor to land at Inguimer's feet. He looked down, laughing delightedly: "You're not much of a gladiator, to allow yourself to be tossed about by this overgrown child."

I quickly regained my feet and dodged a blow from Voldan that barely missed breaking my back. His stave rebounded off the wooden floor as I moved from beneath the strike. I was beginning to see that there was no way to tire this giant and wear him down. I remembered something then that one lanista had told me. No man, no matter how large, can stand after a good blow to the kneecap.

I lunged in straight, the tip of my staff aimed at his eyes. Voldan, by defense, moved backwards. As he did, I took one more step forward, lowered my body and whirled around, changing direction. The movement gained momentum as I whirled in the squat position, the full weight of the stave swooping in the direction of his knees. I completed my turn just as the oak staff cracked across the joint at his knee. His legs went out from under him. He fell backwards with a resounding boom. Before he even tried to rise, which I knew would be difficult, even for this bastard, I moved quickly and swung, this time to the temple, a short stroke that nearly crossed his eyes before the lands of the Dari could close over him. He was still only unconscious, not dead, and lay there with the same child-like look of innocence on his face. I looked at Inguimer, grinning myself now.

"Do you have anyone else, Lord Inguimer?"

He fumed and called for his men to drag Voldan out of his sight. With a half shrug, he acknowledged my victory and told me that I was the charge of Arduus. With that, he left us, going out of the longhouse by the back door.

I went to aid the men who were struggling to raise the giant from the floor. It was amazing! The blow to the temple should have killed him. Yet I doubted if he'd suffer more than a mild headache after awakening. Damn! As we got him to his feet, he was already awake! He grinned, speaking shyly through thick lips, looking as if his feelings had been hurt. Arduus translated.

"He wants to know why you tried to hurt him. He says that he was only playing with you."

I couldn't believe it. I instructed Arduus to tell Voldan that I wasn't mad at him and had only wanted to show him that he was playing too rough, like a bad boy. This seemed to register. After all, Voldan was a child in a man's body. Arduus told me that Voldan said he would not play rough any more if I would promise to be his friend. I quickly agreed. Who would want one such as he for an enemy? And there was a nice quality to the giant youngster. I clasped him about the shoulders, standing on my tiptoes to do so, and patted him on the back. He laughed and spoke some gibberish to me. I asked Arduus to translate again. He'd asked if I would play with him again soon. I was somewhat leery about what he meant by play, but I told Arduus to tell him that now we were friends we would play together often.

We left Voldan scratching his head and smiling, his eyes full of harmless good nature, seemingly pleased to have found a new friend. Myself, I was wondering if the day might not arrive when I would need his tremendous strength. It might definitely come in handy, and besides, I was becoming attached to the monster.

Long cold days passed. Britta and I were forced to live apart. I stayed in the longhouse with the bachelor men, and Britta with the single girls and old crones who had lost their men in battle, or plainly had outlived them.

It was a frustrating time for me. I wanted her badly and every time I saw her hips swaying across the village my back would break out. Inguimers promised to send runners to find Arminius as soon as the weather broke, and tell him that his sister was alive and well. But the bad weather hung on and, when the days did clear a little, the drifts were so deep that it was impossible to travel.

When I did get the opportunity to see Britta, it was very evident that she was putting on more weight, her breasts becoming a bit fuller and her hips rich and wide. She was not yet showing at the belly, but that would not be long in coming. The weight, and her growing beauty, made me want her the more. We would have to do something soon. I wanted to marry her and she knew it, but marriage was not permitted without the permission of her brother, as head of the clan. The best we were able to accomplish was a brief touching of the hands, a few words, and parting looks that held a promise of the future.

I avoided Inguimer when possible and, except for a dirty look now and then, he ignored me also. The only one of the tribe that was civil to me, other than Arduus, was the simple giant, Voldan. He followed me around like a puppy. I think he liked to be near me, not only because I had beaten him, but because I refused to take part in the village sport of teasing and badgering him. His mind seemed to work better at times than it did at others, but I could see plainly the confused pain in his eyes at their badgering. Then it would disappear and he'd smile and nod his head agreeably, whatever they were doing to him at the time.

My weapons were not returned to me. Inguimer had plainly put me in my place when I'd asked for them.

"Roman," he'd said, "You have no need for weapons here. While you may be Britta's bodyguard, during your stay she is my responsibility. You shall have your things when you leave, not before."

I did manage to steal a skinning knife, and kept it hidden in a crack in the logs by my sleeping place. My bed was no more than rough boards covered with straw and rags.

I was not permitted to join the warriors on their hunting excursions, which was all right by me. They never went far and were always back by dark, but I didn't relish leaving Britta in the village with Inguimer. Several times I'd caught him licking his lips as his eyes took in the curves of her ever-ripening body. I planned on getting us out of there as soon as the snows thinned enough for us to travel. If the bastard kept staring at my woman, we'd leave sooner, or I'd be forced to kill him. I didn't really care which it might be.

I spent some pleasant hours with Arduus, seated by the fire, sipping our ration of thin sour beer. I was interested in how one of his education and knowledge had come to be in a place like this. He had spent time in Rome, he told me, as well as other great cities of the Empire, including Alexandria. But he had been born in these wild lands, and he had revered the father of Arminius. When Arminius grew, Arduus thought he'd seen a future leader of great potential. A leader who might bring all the tribes of the Germanii together and forge a nation. Arduus pictured himself as Aristotle, teaching a new Alexander. But he shook his head sadly now, saying:

"It is not to be. Arminius has many of the capabilities of Alexander, but the times are not the same. Alexander did not have Rome to contend with and he also had a well-disciplined army to follow him. Here, it is not easy to get the young warriors to follow a single will." He sipped again of his thin beer.

"No, I do not think Arminius will succeed. But I do know that he has to try. If he could live another hundred years, he might have a chance, but not now. He will die, certainly, before he succeeds. But perhaps his example will provide inspiration for those who follow after. As for me, I am too old to stay by his side. That is why he sent me back here, to stay until he has need of further counsel."

"But why did Arminius choose to send you as mentor to a village ruled by one who hates him?"

"Inguimer was not the chieftain of this village when I returned. The wife of Inguimer, who was the daughter of the chief and died before the snows came, put him in the position of assuming command upon the death of her father. There were none strong enough to oppose him. Inguimer is not a stupid man, contrary to what you may believe, and he will stop at nothing to get what he wants. But you are correct when you say he hates Arminius. I fear also that he would like nought better than to do harm to his sister, Britta. Or, even more, to take her to his bed. By doing this, he would gain an advantage over Arminius." He sipped again, finishing his beer.

"Be careful, Roman! He hates you too. If the opportunity presents itself, he will see you dead before you can leave this place. When the time comes, I may be able to assist you and the woman in escaping safely. Perhaps I can help you lay hands on weapons and food, and show you the way to the Rhine. He has no intentions of sending runners to Arminius, and none here dare go against his orders. Watch your back, Roman. Sleep lightly if you would wake again.

"Do not make the mistake of thinking him a coward. He is a fierce and wily fighter who has taken many heads of even the noblest Roman officers. And he will attempt to take yours also. I think he is aware that Britta is more to you than the sister of Arminius in your charge. Let me say again, watch your back!"

I kept a closer eye on Inguimer after our talk, and noted the warriors that stayed close to him. Several times I noticed him eyeing me, then turning to whisper to one of his lieutenants. They would then laugh.

Inguimer's cabin was situated close to the stockade. I could often hear the sounds of boisterous drunken laughter inside as he and his men took their pleasure with the women of the village. The thought of his dirty hands touching Britta in the future would drive me into a fiery rage, barely contained.

3

I told Britta what Arduus and I suspected of Inguimer's intentions. She tossed her head haughtily, saying with disdain that the swine wouldn't dare; if he touched her, Arminius would have him skinned alive, his head separated from his body in order that his spirit could not be joined in the afterlife.

She was much too pigheaded to believe my warnings, ignoring my advice as if I'd never given any. I felt like taking her across my knee and turning her lovely rear a bright rosy red, but I couldn't do it. However, I did promise myself that once we were clear of this mess, I would give her the spanking she should have gotten as a child.

Things continued pretty much the same for another two months. The spring thaw melted off most of the snow, and the weather warmed a bit. I chose this time to ask Inguimer if messengers had been sent out as he'd promised. He sneered at me through his blackened teeth.

"Certainly, Roman! I told you they would be, didn't I? But who knows if they'll get through? The snow could come again at any time and catch them out in the open, and too, there are always the bandits and thieves that lurk in these parts. But," he grinned, "I'm sure they'll make it. Do not worry, Roman. Do not worry!"

He was lying through his teeth, and he knew that I knew it. He still grinned at me knowingly as he walked away. One day I would turn his sneer into a permanent scar of the same shape, maybe running in a different direction, though.

He was right about the storms coming again, however. They bore down on us again. I could not take Britta and head back out into the savage winds and ice, not while she carried our child. I would just have to wait until all possibilities of storm had passed. Then would I make my move.

But Inguimers forced the issue. During the third thaw, a man appeared at the gates of the village and was admitted. I was impressed with him, though I did not know his importance at the time. He had a quality about him that seemed to demand deference and respect. He was tall and thin, wearing only a light robe of homespun wool that reached to his ankles, carrying a staff of oak in his wiry hands. His face too was thin and angular, his cheekbones prominent, his black eyes sunk deep in their sockets. He had a small pack at his shoulder and sported a beard that looked as if it had never been cut, reaching below his chest. He was spotlessly clean, though I could not understand how he'd managed it.

At his appearance, all the villagers poured out into the muddy streets, touching his sleeves and presenting their children for him to touch and mumble words over.

Arduus, in a reverent tone of voice, told me that the visitor was a Druid, one of the wise men of the Celts. I asked how he'd managed to get here, for the ground was still frozen and, though it had warmed up a bit, the nights were still cold enough to freeze a man to death. Yet this man looked as if he'd walked only a mile or two on a warm spring day. Arduus said that the Druids were known to possess many strange powers. He'd been seen before, sitting bare from the waist up, during a freezing storm that had lasted the entire night, without fire or robes to protect him. The night had been so cold that deer and other animals were dying throughout the forest, but the Druid had been warm to the touch and unharmed.

The Druids, he said, were holy teachers who held many secrets. They came and went as they pleased; no man dared interfere with them.

Arduus spent much time talking with the Druid, though personally, I could never find anything to say to the man. To me, he was like the scholars and poets of Rome, interested only in things that were untouchable, unseen, or inedible, concerned with their minds more than their bellies, and they interested me not. Nor did the Druid.

Inguimer was more than agitated at the arrival of the Druid, but he made the proper respectful sounds with his mouth, though bitterness was still evident at his lips.

Arduus told me that Inguimer hated the Druids because they had forecast his defeat before the battle of Idistaviso. He'd blamed the loss on them as much as he had blamed Arminius, claiming that their forecast had forced bad luck upon him.

The Druid remained for several days, passing now and then among the villagers, touching the heads of children or stopping to say a few words to the men or women. One day, when approaching Britta, he reached out a thin, blue-veined, hand and gently touched her face, looking down at her stomach, which had barely begun to swell. He said nothing as he did this, merely nodded his head knowingly and walked off, heading, I supposed, for the longhouse and his daily nap.

I returned to my own problems. I was becoming deeply worried. Inguimer had propositioned Britta for her favors more than once, and had not taken well her refusals to his advances.

I feared that she was taking her position as Arminius' sister too confidently. Inguimer didn't seem overly impressed with it. And I was beginning to doubt that I could hold my temper much longer, with him eyeing her and attempting to fondle her at every passing. He was also taking his cups more often now, if that was possible.

There would be trouble if we did not leave soon.

4

The next morning I woke early, as I had been doing since we'd arrived in the village. I wrapped a fur robe about my shoulders, and walked out to the center of the village. It was windy.

I heard a muffled cry, then what sounded like hushed cursing in a man's voice. Instinct told me that what I'd feared was now coming to pass. I moved fast toward the sounds, now increasing in volume, gasps and groans mingled with muted sobs, and the heavy sounds of slaps being administered.

I ran to the rear of the women's longhouse and froze at what I saw. Inguimer, his bare back to the sky, was on top of Britta. She was completely covered by his heaving body.

One of his men was holding her arms behind her head; another was holding her legs apart for his master.

I screamed, throwing myself at them, grabbing Inguimer by the throat from the back and twisting to pull the bastard's head from his shoulders. A blow to my head knocked me to my knees, breaking my hold. His men, including the one with a club who had hit me, grabbed my arms. Inguimer raised himself from Britta, who lay sobbing on the ground, and faced me. He was naked from the waist down, his member shriveling in the cold. He was drunk, as were his men, and he walked over to me. slapping me hard in the mouth. He picked up a spear and placed its point to my chest.

"I'm going to kill you, Roman! Slowly! I'm going to push this blade into your body until you beg for me to take your woman and kill you quickly. But I won't kill you quickly." He laughed drunkenly again. "I will still take your woman. When I tire of her, I will give her to my men for their pleasure. She will satisfy the whole village, the bitch sister of the dog Arminius!"

I shook the fog from my head, trying to move, but the warriors held me back. I felt the blade enter my stomach ever so slightly, just enough to let the blood trickle.

Suddenly, someone pushed the point of the spear from my stomach and stood facing Inguimer. It was Britta, bruised and naked. She screamed vehemently, "You are the one who's going to die, you piece of slime! Arminius will burn your eyes from their sockets and feed that filthy meat between your legs to his dogs."

She cursed him then, calling him every vile name she

knew. "You are a dead man, you dirty stinking brute. But if you let us go I will be silent. Leave him alone and you will live. Touch him again, and I swear by Odin that you will die an awful death."

Inguimer staggered back, shocked by her ferocity. He spoke, his voice low and menacing. "So, you will tell Arminius, slut? Then I shall have to make certain you cannot."

He drove his spear into her. I watched it protrude through her back, the tip dripping with her blood, touching me.

With that, I broke. A red haze rushed over me. I jerked my arm free from the man on my right and twisted him around, grasping his throat. My fingers dug deep into the cartilage, my thumb sinking to its full depth, crushing him until he fell to the ground, dying. Only then did I release him. I grabbed the other and threw him backwards across my knee, relishing the sound of his spine snapping, bone on bone. I raised him from me, holding him by the throat, seized his legs in my other hand, raised his body over my head as I stood. I threw his weight at Inguimer, who was tugging at the spear in Britta's breast. She was not dead yet and was holding tightly to the shaft, keeping it inside her. He placed his foot on top of her, kicking and pulling, twisting until the spear came out with an ugly sucking sound, taking Britta's life with it.

Then I was on him. I ripped the spear from his hands and grabbed him. I wanted no weapon; I wanted the feel of him dying in my hands. My beloved Britta! He was strong, but the rage inside me gave me power I never before knew I possessed. He beat at my face, but I felt no pain. I was beyond physical hurt.

I grabbed his face, my thumb in the corner of his ugly mouth, and ripped upwards, splitting his cheek. He backed away, pulling a knife from inside his fur. I moved in again, tears running wildly down my face, tore the knife from his hand and threw him to the ground. I heard bone crushing as I kicked him in the head. He lay still, bleeding and dazed. In my madness, I laughed, bending to pick up the knife. I knelt and forced his legs apart. He tried to rise but I slashed him cross the face and moved back to his legs. He screamed like a woman, knowing my intentions: *"No! No!"*

The knife was dull, and I was forced to saw back and forth. Finally the limp piece of flesh that he had so recently used came loose in my hand. I held it before his face.

He screamed again, loud agonized screams. I could hear voices around me, but the red haze clouded my eyes; I could see nothing but Inguimer before me. I remember vaguely a hand reaching for me, and I think I hacked at it with the knife. But I was not finished with what I'd started and turned back to Inguimers. I forced his head back, and inserted the knife into his mouth, prying his jaws open wide. I placed his organ into his mouth and jammed it down his throat, using the knife to shove it deeper, and deeper. I pushed until he gagged, gasping for air, life-giving air, and I whispered to him asking him how it felt. Then I said it aloud. I wanted all to know that their filthy chief was choking to death on his own dirty meat. He squirmed on the ground, his hands digging at his throat, desperate to remove what was blocking his windpipe. He couldn't do so, and he knew it. That was what I wanted, I wanted him to know it!

I stood, seeing the fear in the faces around me, scared of the madness in my own. I bent down, lifting Britta's body, and held her close to me. She was limp, the life force gone from her, leaving me only a small hurt shell to hold. And inside her was our child, dead before he'd had a chance to know life.

I heard nothing then, only my own voice howling like a beast, coming from my head held back, wolf-like. I screamed until a club from behind drove me into darkness.

I don't know how long I was unconscious, but when I woke I was cradled in the arms of the child monster, Voldan. He was half-walking, half-staggering, carrying me as he would a baby. I looked back over his shoulder and saw spears hurtling towards his back. Blood was streaming down his face and covering my body. His face was heavily marked by blows, almost unrecognizable, and he was crying.

The thud of the spears drove him to his knees, yet he laid me gently on the ground before collapsing at my side. They charged me again, clubs upraised. Then the old Druid stepped before them, blocking their path to me.

"This man is touched by the gods," he called out. "Evil will surely befall anyone that slays him."

It seemed at the time that all this was happening to someone else. My own consciousness was far away, while my body seemed to be acting of its own volition. I thought perhaps I'd gone mad. My brain seemed to have been split in half, each part watching the other, one of them wanting to kill and hurt until it too was destroyed.

I must have been a fearful sight. I was covered with blood, my mouth frothing and spitting, tears running down my face like small rivers. My whole body was in the grip of a spasm of hate that I could not control.

The Druid had them place a rod behind me, tie my arms securely to it, then cast me out of the village.

5

I was taken from the village and kept somewhere for two days, being given neither food nor drink. I didn't know where I was, and neither did I care. A dark red haze had settled on my mind, blocking out all thoughts and feeling. Branches could whip at my face, laying it wide open, but I felt nothing. I was completely mad. But the other part of my mind, the one that was yet watching, noticed the men of the village making signs when I looked their way, signs to ward off evil.

I knew they wanted to kill me, and I actually wanted them to, but the Druid's warning kept them from doing what they should have.

On the third day, after binding my legs together, they allowed me to shuffle along behind them without being pulled. My arms, though, were still tied to the staff behind me. At a clearing in the forest, they left me, still tied in the same manner, and returned to their village. As their holy man had ordered, they'd done me no harm, and could not be held responsible if I died simply because I couldn't move. My fate would be at the will of the gods. They'd left me alive and unharmed, as the Druid had ordered. If the gods wished me saved, then so be it!

I lay there in madness all that day, not even trying to free my arms and legs from their bindings. Then, when dark had fallen, the rains came. Fat, heavy, drops beat down on my face and cracked lips. Godsent and livesaving rain. It had been three days or more since I'd had water, and without conscious effort my mouth opened to catch the moisture from the heavens.

The rain fell heavier, until it was a full storm. The wind whipped the rain about me, and small streams of water ran over the earth. I gulped madly, licking my cracked parched lips, letting the moisture slowly ease the swelling of my tongue and the ache in my soul.

I managed to turn myself over and face the ground, where I could suck from the streams formed by the storm. I vomited several times, but with each spasm a bit more of the distant part of my mind returned.

I slept then.

When I woke it was dawn; the storm had passed in the night. I felt drained, purged, empty. But I was back to myself. The madness was over. The thing that the Northmen called the berserker rage had passed. Now, all I felt was emptiness and sorrow at the loss of Britta and our unborn child.

I knew then that I would not die, but would continue my existence a time longer. Therefore I must free myself from my bindings. It was not too difficult. The rain had softened the bindings on my arms, and I knocked the rod at my back against a nearby boulder; it came free and one end dropped to the ground, freeing my arms. When the tension eased, the pain came. My circulation had been cut off from being bound; when the blood started to flow again I thought my arms were on fire. It took some minutes before I was able to untie my legs. The fingers didn't want to work correctly. At last, however, I was able to free myself and staggering, regained my feet.

I didn't know where I was, and it took some control for me to settle down to think my situation over. From the sun I could locate a southerly direction. That was where I must head. South, to civilization and Rome. I wanted no more of these dark wild lands.

Somewhere deep inside me I'd found a strong desire to live again, and I set about doing just that. I ate grubs and roots, anything to fill my stomach, though it was true that my gut had shrunken extremely, requiring very little to fill it up.

The next day my nose led me to real food. Cached in some brush I found the leftovers of a kill that some animal had made. It was the hindquarters of a deer, ripe and smelling to the high heavens, but it was meat. I tore off chunks of the ripe flesh with my hands, eating it raw and ignoring the heavy odor of early decay. I lost my meal several times before I was able to keep enough of the flesh down long enough to do me any good.

I was hesitating to leave my newly found food supply, fearful that I would find no more, when the deer's killer returned. A rustling in the nearby brush caused me to turn. Two yellow eyes, set deep over a long fangled muzzle, were watching me intently, with imposing hatred. A large grey-black wolf of the northlands.

I was aware that wolves in these parts had been known to attack man, but I didn't care. He'd left this meat, and now it was mine. I was not going to let him have it back. He paced around me, slowly at first, then advancing to a loping run, giving off low belly growls that I supposed were meant to warn me off. I was not going to leave. I turned as he did, keeping my eye on him, watching for some sign that would tell me he was about to attack. The lesson I'd learned from Bosra, the bestiarius, came back to me. This threat I knew how to handle. It was different from a blind feeling of grief over something I could not change. This was something I could put my hands on.

The wolf was no more dangerous than I. In fact, I probably looked even wilder at the time than he did, my face scratched and bloody from the branches that had beaten and lashed it, my beard a clotted mass, and the rest of my body filthy.

I went into the crouching position over the carcass. Then I snarled back at him, showing my teeth. On all fours now, we watched each other. The tone of the wolf's growl changed subtly. I knew that he was thinking the situation over. Then he came! A grey streak of knotted muscle and gaping teeth shot in, straight at my throat. I caught the full weight of him in mid-air, grasping him to me firmly, then rolling over and throwing him to land on his side in the brush. He came back up immediately on all fours, his head extended, his sides heaving. He stood his ground. That suited me fine. I needed this fight, and I was ready for him.

I threw my head back and howled loudly, the tendons in my neck so taut that I was certain they'd break through the skin from the sheer power of my cry. I wasn't aware that I was going to do it; it just came from somewhere deep inside me. It started low in my gut, working its way slowly up to my mouth and forcing the lips open wide to release the anguish I felt inside.

The wolf answered my call to combat. Two beasts, each with our own needs and hates. His feeling, I suppose, could not be called hate as we know it, but mine was.

He came for me again! This time he hit for the face, then turned to my side, aiming for the back of my neck. I caught a handful of fur and rolled over on him. His fangs laid open my shoulder and part of my face on the left side. I didn't even feel it. I hugged him to me, my arms around his ribcage. I squeezed, each hand locked tightly around the opposite wrist, moving toward my elbows an inch at a time, increasing the pressure on him. The breath from his fanged mouth was fetid and sour as it was forced from his lungs.

I kept my chin low against my shoulder to protect my throat, ignoring the frantic raking slices he was giving my shoulder and the side of my face. I kept the pressure on, building, cutting off his air, pushing the sides of his ribs in on each other. I could feel him weakening, his breath coming now in short painful pants as his nailed paws raked at my stomach and legs. He tried frantically to free himself from my bear hug, but I would not let up. I buried my face in his fur, enjoying the damp rich smell of his pelt. I filled my lungs, called on every ounce of strength remaining in me, and put it all into one great squeeze that ended when I felt, then heard, his spine snap beneath my arms. Several ribs caved in at the same time, puncturing the lungs and giving out an angry whooshing sound.

I let loose of him and rose to my feet. His eyes were glazing over with the gathering of his death, but even then he tried to reach me. I knew he was finished, and I felt exultant. It was as if in fighting this animal on his own level I had regained something that I'd previously lost. I paid homage to his spirit as he spent his final moments, his legs moving without control, his jaws snapping futilely at the earth. He died.

I had survived, and the victory had somehow removed me from the depths of my despair. I honored the wolf for what he was. In many ways we were kindred spirits, for was I not named after him? I asked that the spirit of these dark woods welcome his shade and left him lying there, victim to the creatures of the forest. I had another place to go.

6

I took the remaining portion of the deer carcass with me as I moved south, naked, weaving my way through the valleys and forests, covering my nakedness with leaves and brush at night to keep the damp and chill from me. I fed on the meat until it finally became too rank, then discarded it. From then on, it was anything I could lay my hands on or sink my teeth into. Leaves I chewed frantically and swallowed, the tender part of the pines, anything to satisfy my gut. Once, I caught a few fish. I ate these raw, as I had the deer meat.

I survived in this manner for two weeks or more; I was uncertain as to the passing of time. At any rate, I finally reached the banks of a broad, swift-flowing river. It was near dawn and mist was rising from the waters. I could not see the other side, yet somehow I knew that it was the Rhine. I was near the road home now, and nothing would have stopped me at this point.

I found a log and, straddling it, pushed off into the water, ignoring the chill. Gods! The water was cold.

By the time I reached the other side the sun was well up. I had drifted far downstream from my starting place, but at least I was across, and the feel of the thick mud beneath my bare feet was good. I let the log drift free downriver. For me, I knew I was near my destination.

I shook myself, as a dog throws off water, and entered the woods. I was half running, paying no attention to the vines that were trying to snare my legs, nor to the branches that were whipping my face. There was a sense of urgency about me; I had to run.

All that day I raced through the trees and underbrush, stopping only when exhaustion forced me to. As soon as strength returned to me I was off again. I was still running when I heard the command to halt. It took a moment for me to register that the words had been spoken in Latin. I fell to the ground, my sides heaving and my legs quivering from the strain of my day's pace. I passed out.

Some time later, the prod of a spear butt in my side aroused me. There was a voice again.

"By the holy gods of Olympus, I have seen a lot of barbarians in my time, but this one is the worst."

I raised my head a bit and tried to focus my eyes on the men standing over me. The strained croaks coming from my mouth sounded only barely human, even to me. One of the Legionnaires spoke again.

"Will you listen to him? The beast thinks he can talk."

I was able to force one audible and recognizable word out of my mouth before I passed out again: "*Germanicus!*"

When I came to, I was in a tent. Darkness was full outside, and I remembered it had been daylight when I'd last known awareness. I was lying on a soldier's pallet. I started to raise up; a spear point pushed me back down.

My throat was so swollen that nothing would come forth. I couldn't even focus my eyes properly in the gloom. The soldier guarding me must have sensed my needs, for he opened a skin of water and held it to my lips. A few swallows later my throat loosened up enough for me to speak.

"Where's Germanicus? Has he been found?"

The soldier didn't answer me. He called to someone

outside the tent that I had found my tongue and that I was speaking Latin.

The water had given me strength; I took another drink. The flap of the tent was thrown back, and a Centurion entered. He was wearing the insignia of the tenth Legion. I must have looked more animal than human to him with my filthy knotted beard and my body scabbed with a thousand scratches and cuts. Many of my sores had broken open again and were festering and odorous.

The Centurion turned away from me and walked back outside, ordering the soldier to help me to my feet and bring me out into the open air. If I wasn't already used to my own stink, I would have likely felt the same as he. The Legionnaire must have had a strong stomach, or maybe he'd worked as a butcher before. He didn't even wrinkle his nose at the stench, but grabbed me by my arm and helped me up. Half-supported by his arm I staggered outside into the night. There were a number of campfires in sight, and I could hear the familiar sounds of a Roman encampment.

The Centurion in charge was a young man, with intelligent brown eyes above the kerchief he was holding to his nose against my vile odor. I pulled myself as erect as I could, forcing out the words: "Forgive me if I offend you. If you will show me to the nearest stream I will try to get the worst of my journey off my body."

He coughed under the kerchief. "By Mithra! You do speak our tongue. Where did you learn it, savage?"

It took me a moment to find enough saliva in my throat to speak again. "I am Lucanus, bodyguard to Germanicus."

He lowered his hand from his face, exposing his nose. "*Lucanus?* Lucanus is dead! He was lost at sea, along with everyone else on the ship." He hesitated a moment. "Who are you? What is this trick?"

I shook my head. "Who would say such a thing, were it not true? I know what I must look like, but I am who I say."

He thought it over, and then asked me a few questions about Rome and the arena, questions that only one who had been there could have possibly have answered. He asked about my campaigns with Germanicus, what he looked like, and who served as his staff officers. I gave him all the right answers, finally convincing him. Again I asked about Germanicus. He told me that he'd been found a couple of days after the storm and spent months in Gaul before returning to Rome. By now, he'd been back in the capital for over six months. He asked me what he was to do with me, now that I'd been found.

It was simple, I told him: "Let me bathe, give me some food and clothes, and help me get out of these forests and back to Rome."

He thought it over for a bit and stood, smiling pleasantly. "So be it, Lucanus! I am sure that Lord Germanicus will be very pleased to have you back again. Consider yourself my personal guest until you are able to travel."

He called to his guard to take me to the stream, to provide me with a tunic from his own wardrobe, and to summon the camp barber.

All this was done and, in the space of an hour, I'd been transformed from a wild savage into a beat-up but decent-looking Roman. The Centurion held a bronze mirror before me so I could study my features. The improvement was actually shocking, even to me, but there was something else shocking as well. I looked at least fifty years old. There was a trace of silver in my hair that had not been there when I'd gone mad.

Crovius, the Centurion, proved to be a good host, and soon helped me return to the coast and the port of Messilla along with a detachment of old veterans who were being sent back for retirement. He had provided me with enough denarii so that I could appear a gentleman instead of a poor castoff. He'd been more than generous. Of course, he had no doubt that he'd be repaid several-fold for his kindness, if not by me, then by Germanicus. I found out later that Germanicus had posted a generous reward for my return if I was found alive. No doubt the Centurion knew of this before he'd even found me.

By the time I reached Messilla, Germanicus had received word of my survival, and had provided an armed escort, plenty of money, and a ship to bring me home. I spent only a day in Messilla. I bought suitable attire, visited the thermae and took a decent bath, letting the steam soak deep into my pores, then moving to the masseurs to be kneaded and pummeled. My body twisted till the joints cracked. I groaned in agony that slowly turned to grunts of pleasure under the strong sure hands of the masseur. To top things off, I had a final oiling and scraping, then had my hair cropped short. Now I was ready to face life again.

The memory of Britta I pushed back from me. To think too much on her was the road to madness, and I surely did not want that again. If it should come back to me, I might never return.

Still, I knew she would come to me at times, in my dreams. She would always be smiling and gentle, and she would tell me of our child. In my dreams she would live, and so would our child, a fine manchild, with Britta's golden hair and my dark eyes. The dreams would help me, for I felt that she would not come to me unless things were well with her and with our child.

But the ache for her remained a long time. I wanted no one else. Women offered themselves to me, but it was nearly a year before I allowed myself to submit to their wishes.

But now I am getting ahead of myself, dear readers. Albinus is looking weary, and he grumbles about needing his sleep. Well enough! The night has been long and there is yet more to speak of.

We will continue on the morrow. I still have two days left before I go into the arena again.

BOOK SIX

GERMANICUS

1

Germanicus met me at the port. It did my heart good to see his clean honest face again. Claudius was there, too, all smiles and laughter and spittle. His stutter worsened in his excitement at seeing me again, and he could barely make himself understood. It was a happy reunion for us all.

Germanicus had only arrived in Ostia two days before me, and told me that there were honors to be had for his triumphs over the tribes. He'd put off the date of entry until I returned. Claudius told me this; Germanicus was much too modest to make a show of his feelings. But this honor he'd done me sunk deep in my heart and I loved him the more for it. He treated me as a friend and I was sure that I would never fail him for it, even to the death.

In Rome, I took rooms in the apartments of Claudius, on the Capitoline hill, where the nobility lived. Dear Claudius! He wept like a baby when I told him of Britta and our unborn child. But he brightened when I told him of my dreams, clapping his hands in pleasure, stuttering out: "That's g . . . g . . . good, my friend. That means that s . . . s . . . she and your child are waiting for you beyond the Styx. She has been honored by the gods for her devotion and her love for you. She is at peace. One day you will join her, and the two of you will live forever. Perhaps even now she waits in the garden of dreams."

He wiped tears from his eyes and sighed heavily. "Oh, how I envy you the love of a woman like that. Pure and honest, even beyond the grave. If she were of Roman birth, I'm sure the gods would place a s . . . s . . . star in the heavens to mark her ascent to the ranks of the immortals."

I did not see Germanicus again until the day of his triumph, but the city had been preparing for it for over a week. The streets were gaily decorated and the people were happy, for Germanicus was well loved.

I went outside the walls to the Field of Mars, where the parade would start. Tens of thousands were lined up along the route of the procession, waiting. I was hailed several times by those who knew me. A few women looked at me, sighing deeply, and I assumed that the story of Britta had made the rounds. Claudius loved to tell stories and the romance of my adventure had likely touched the heart of more then one jaded lady of Rome. But, as I said, I was not yet ready for any of them.

At the Field of Mars, the parade was getting into order. I found Germanicus and asked him where I should be. He smiled, saying, "With me, where you belong, naturally!"

We entered the city through the Appian Gate. I was awarded the honor of leading the horses of Germanicus' chariot. In one hand I carried the reins, in the other was the captured standard of the Cherusci chieftain who had died in battle at my hand. The standard, set on a tall staff, was a human skull. The hollow sockets had been set with red glass, which caught the light like fire, and a rack of antlers had been attached to each side, giving it a truly frightening effect.

It was a glorious moment for us. Slavegirls by the hundreds, all young and beautiful, danced naked before us, scattering flowers on the stones in front of our procession.

It was the law of Rome that no Legion could come inside the walls without special permission; only those who had shown exemplary courage were allowed to march in the parade. These brave men numbered over three thousand, and the remainder of the military was represented by a full cohort of the Praetorian guard.

Chariots, wagons and slaves bore the spoils of war for the people of Rome to see—captured weapons and trade goods of all kinds. Slaves carried paintings depicting the battles we'd fought in and the lands of the barbarians, with their high-reaching, snow-capped peaks, wide rivers, and endless forests and plains.

Then the captives. They numbered in the thousands, the warriors separated from their women and children. All of them would be sold at the auctions later. Yes, it was glorious. Musicians played on lyres and flutes; drums kept the measure for the hundreds of trumpeters, whose long horns bounced their piercing sounds off the stately buildings we were passing.

The mob cried with uncontrollable adoration at the sight of Germanicus. Tall, well-formed and handsome, he represented the best of all that was Roman. Brave and noble of carriage and mind, he was the best man I'd ever met, and I was proud that he called me friend. He looked like a young Mars the Avenger, high in his gilded chariot. Riding with him were five children of the streets. He had stopped along the route, offering them the opportunity to share in his glory. The commoners loved it. Germanicus belonged to them. He was theirs.

The procession wound on, passing beneath the marble arch near the Temple of Saturn. It had been constructed in order to celebrate the return of the Eagles, which had been lost in battle by Emperor Varus to the Parthians and returned to Rome by Germanicus.

Not even in the arenas had I seen such passion displayed among the people. In the arena, it was a lust for violence and slaughter, but this was a near-fanatic outpouring of love for the brightest and fairest light of the Empire. Soldiers cleared the way until we came to a halt before the steps of the Senate. There Tiberius and his mother, Livia Drusilla, the Augusta, waited.

I stood at attention as Germanicus stepped down from the chariot. He marched up the steps to be met halfway by the Emperor who, as a sign of honor, descended to meet him. They embraced, and Tiberius, his face fleshier than when I'd last seen him, and his hair thinner, turned to the crowds. He spoke sweet words of affection for his adopted son. He spoke of the honor that Germanicus had brought to the arms of Rome. And, he said, as a gesture of his love for his son, he would today award three hundred sesterces to every man, woman and child of the city.

Tiberius' words were certainly sweet, but I saw behind the honey something that spelled hate and envy. It lay heavy in his voice and manner, and in the eyes beneath the puffy lids. I wondered if Germanicus could see it? Probably! He didn't miss much.

I turned my attention to the Augusta. Her smile was thin-lipped as she stood waiting at the top of the steps. Her eyes never moved from Germanicus; she watched him as a snake does a bird. The look she was giving Germanicus said he was already a dead man.

I don't think Germanicus saw this. He was too noble-minded to notice the warnings of treachery in the woman. I may seem a little simple, but in the school of life I'd learned to recognize danger from man and beast by their motions and the looks in their eyes. She had the right look about her.

Without thinking, my hand went to my sword hilt. The Augusta caught the movement and turned her dark emotionless eyes on me, giving me the same thin-lipped grin. The glory of the day turned to ashes in my mouth at that moment.

Sejanus, Commander of the Praetorians, came out of the Senate to stand beside Livia. She whispered in his ear for a moment, and he looked first at Germanicus, then back at me, smiling. I'd always thought that Sejanus, the Prefect of Rome, had a hungry look to him, and I wished now that I'd paid more attention to the things Claudius had told me about him. I knew that I must convince Germanicus to leave Rome and the jealousy of Tiberius, and the hate of his mother, the Augusta. I knew instinctively that for him to stay in Rome was to die.

2

Tiberius was elected to the consulship for his third time, and Germanicus for his second. It was then that we were sent to Achaia and the city of Nikopolis. I think, personally, that Tiberius merely wanted to get Germanicus out of Rome. He was fast becoming too popular with the people.

We took time to visit Actium, the site where Germanicus' grandfather, Mark Antony, had lost his entire fleet in his war with Rome, and then moved on to Athens. He was royally received there and I, as well as he, enjoyed our visit to the Home of the Gods, to holy Mount Olympus. It was impressive, but there were too many Greeks around us at all times. I was never completely comfortable around Greeks. They thought too much, and seldom acted in a manner that was direct.

Germanicus was joined by his wife and children at Euboea. Agrippina went on with him to Lesbos, where she gave birth to a daughter. Germanicus named her Julia Livilla. She was a beautiful child, with fat, round cheeks and soft hair finer than any silk. He let me hold her for a moment, and she took that opportunity to put me in my proper place by wetting on me.

Germanicus made good use of his office as consul, visiting many places, listening to grievances passing judgments. He replaced incompetent administrators and lowered taxes for all. Germanicus was as fair as anyone in his position could be, and all the people knew it. Never had I seen a man the people could take to their hearts so easily. I could not fully understand how one raised in the court of Rome, where intrigue and deception were an accepted and honored pastime, could have such a sense of morality and fair play. It just wasn't logical, as the Greeks would say.

But he was the way he was, and I, along with the commoners and much of the nobility, loved him for it.

He left Agrippina, the new baby and the rest of his children at Lesbos while we made another tour. We stopped off at the Thracian ports of Perinthus and Byzantium, moving on into the Bosphorus and the Black Sea. When we returned, he wanted to put in at Samothrace, but the strong winds made a landing impossible. We went to Colophon, where we visited the oracle at Calrus. At Calrus there are no priestesses; only men serve the oracle, men chosen from special families and possessed of the gift of prophecy. We descended into a cave, where a scabby-looking creature awaited us. His skin was dirty, and his eyes were strangely dull. Surely, I thought, this cannot be one of the seers? But he was!

He asked who wished to have his fortune told. After Germanicus gave the wretch his name, the seer went into the lower regions of the cave and drank from a spring. He returned soon and sat quietly for a moment on a stone, unspeaking, his eyes staring at nothing. I was becoming a little impatient with his meditation. Germanicus motioned for me to restrain myself and keep my mouth shut. I did!

Shortly, the priest rose to his feet and began to mumble. His eyes glazed over, and his face suddenly took on a different aspect. The pale, dirty wretch of a man we had first met was gone. Now his face glowed with vitality, and even in the dim light his eyes were bright and knowing. His manner and voice gained in strength as he spoke. We were able now to distinguish clearly every word: "Hear me well, noble prince, and pay heed. The boldest eagle must never drink from the hand of power, for he will surely fall from his lofty heights to despair!"

That was all? I grumbled to Germanicus as we left: "We traveled all this way, sat in a cold damp cave and listened to an old man speak two lousy lines about birds!"

Germanicus cut me short. "For once, will you just shut up, Lucanus? The number of verses he gives is not important. What he says matters, and it is up to us to interpret his meaning."

I was properly chastened now. Germanicus returned alone to the priest to talk further. He joined me a half hour later at the cave's entrance and placed a donative in a stone bowl. For the oracle, I supposed. I was still a bit angry and hurt. As far as the oracle was concerned, I could have given him one as good myself. Eagles, indeed!

Just then, my dream of long ago came back to me. I started to tell Germanicus of it, but thought better. He would not believe me anyway. And my dream didn't make any more sense than the ramblings of the old priest. Their similarity puzzled me, though.

We went on to Rhodes, where we were joined again by his family. Also waiting for us were several letters from Claudius, delivered there by a trusted friend. Cnaeus Calpurnius Piso had been given the governorship of Syria, and would be passing through Athens and Rhodes. This was not good! Piso had always hated Germanicus, and I knew that he and Sejanus were close. It was a combination that could only spell trouble.

Piso stopped in Athens on his way to Syria and savagely attacked the Athenians, calling them the common dregs of the world and no longer fit to be called men. He upbraided Germanicus, without actually naming him directly, for giving compliments to a people that no longer deserved them. He recalled the time when the Athenians had allied themselves with Mithradates VI, when they'd fought against Sulla and oppressed the Roman people when they'd had power. He spoke about Mark Antony and his wicked rebellion against the divine Augustus for the sake of the Egyptian whore, Cleopatra.

Piso had reasons for his hatred of the Athenians. I found out later that his close friend Theophilius had been sentenced to death by the court of Athens. It was like Piso to have a forger for a friend, I thought. I did not like him. His eyes were set too close together. I could find other reasons, too.

I don't know why Germanicus refused to take direct action against him, then. I suppose it was his forgiving nature. Had I been Germanicus, I would have castrated the son of a whore on the spot and maggoted the open wound.

As soon as Piso reached Syria, he set out to undermine Germanicus' influence by giving expensive gifts and bribes to officers and officials, and also to the common soldiery. He replaced many commanders known to be loyal to Germanicus with his own men. He let the soldiers do as they wished, without fear of punishment. His wife, Placina, was as bad as he. She even attended Cavalry exercises, unbecoming to a lady of her position, and slandered the names of Germanicus and Agrippina freely. I learned, after we went to Syria, that the reason so many went along with Piso was that he professed to have the support of Tiberius in all his deeds. It was one statement from Piso that I could believe.

When I informed Germanicus what was happening, he said only, "First things first, Lucanus. I have things of major importance to take care of in Armenia." I grumbled —what could be more important than his own head?—but he studiously ignored me.

Armenia occupied a strategic position, sharing a frontier with Rome and Parthia. The people of Armenia, it seemed, had forced their king, Vonones, into exile. Germanicus' reputation for fairness had inspired them to ask him to be their arbitrator in settling the matter of succession.

Germanicus had agreed to their request and he and I went to Armenia. Once there, he went out into the streets, asking the common people their preference. Afterwards he asked the same of the nobles. He found that the man most wanted to rule them was Zeno, the son of Polemo of Pontus. Zeno had the personality of most Armenians and was devoted to hunting and feasting. He had adopted their style of dress and many of their personal customs, and paid homage to their gods.

So Germanicus, in the greatest of Armenian cities, Artaxata, crowned Zeno king, giving him the name of Artaxias III, in honor of the city in which he'd been crowned. By this means, Germanicus had established a staunch ally. Zeno and his people would act as a buffer between Rome and the ambitions of Parthia, should Parthia ever decide to move west again.

Germanicus took care of several other problems. Solutions seemed to come easy to him, and he had the ability to please everyone with his decisions. He converted Cappadocia into a Roman province, and, at the same time, annexed the province of Commagene to Syria, placing it under the leadership of his old friend, Quintus Servaeus. He assumed that this would force Piso to move a little slower, knowing that an army friendly to Germanicus and commanded by his loyal friend was on his flank.

However, Piso showed no sign that he was willing to be reasonable. Germanicus gave him a direct order to move part of his forces into Armenia, affording the new king a degree of security and support from Rome, while allowing him time to consolidate his power. Piso ignored this order, sending not one cohort. He was still as arrogant as if

Tiberius himself were at his back, supporting him.

When we left the wild lands of Armenia, where the people were just as wild as the forests and high mountains, we ventured to Cyrrhus, the winter quarters of Piso, in Syria.

Germanicus might be a friendly and forgiving man, but I and a few other friends how to hate, and we did our utmost to incite Piso's men against him.

When Germanicus summoned Piso to a banquet, Piso rarely showed up, even though protocol demanded his presence as governor. When he did attend, he was always sullen, hardly civil to his host. It was hard for me to restrain my short temper. I wanted to beat his brains out, but Germanicus told me to tend to my own affairs and leave the matter of rule to him. I replied that his welfare was my business, and that if he truly felt I was no more than a fighter, I would gladly make my way home to Herculaneum. He soothed me and I stayed on. But the scent of danger was clear to me, and to Claudius, who wrote to us, giving veiled warnings about Piso and others that we knew. He never named names, though.

There was one last mission ahead of us before we left Asia Minor. A deputation from the Parthian king, Artabanus, came to Germanicus, asking him to renew the pact between Rome and Parthia, a pledge of non-hostility on both parts. The Parthian king would do Germanicus the honor of coming in person to the banks of the Euphrates to meet with him. This we did.

There king requested that Germanicus remove the former king of Armenia, Vonones, from his exile in Syria. His agents were stirring up trouble among the nomadic tribal chieftains who were still loyal to him. These tribes freely crossed the boundaries of Armenia and Parthia, and also those of Syria. Germanicus was delighted with the request, and had Vonones removed to the town of Pompeipolis on the coast of Cilicia.

This move put Piso in his place. He had become fast friends with Vonones, a condition that not even Germanicus could tolerate. It would not do to have an exiled king living so close to the lands he'd lost, or have the friendship of the Roman governor, who might decide to restore his friend to power against the wishes of Germanicus.

No, Germanicus was having none of it. Ha! One up on Piso.

We spent the rest of the summer in various provinces on tours of inspection. I think Piso was tremendously relieved when our forces were finally out of his sight, leaving him and Placina to their plotting.

We returned to Rome for a short period. Ovations were awarded not only to Germanicus but to his cousin, Nero Caesar, as well. He had enjoyed great victories over several Germanic tribes under the standards of Marboduus.

I had never met Nero Caesar before and I liked him on sight. He had a lot of the same qualities as Germanicus, but he was more of a realist, less of a dreamer. Nero carried himself well and with modesty. His coloring was close to his cousin's—fair-complected, with dark eyes. He was tall and strong in body. I suppose that they had acquired some of the same looks and characteristics from their mutual ancestors.

I went to my home in Herculaneum for a time to see how my affairs were being managed under the care of Albinus. My slave and tutor was all smiles as he showed me the records of our investments. He had bought heavily into some orchards near Ravenna, part of a cooperative, where several investors shared in the profits as well as in the maintenance costs of the property. I could see we had done well, and I thanked him for his loyalty and devotion to duty, and gave him two hundred sesterces as a reward to spend as he saw fit. He was especially pleased with my gift of a small carving I'd bought for him. It was a carving of the god Apollo, riding the Chariot of the Sun.

While I was at Herculaneum, Claudius came to visit me for a few days. He was welcome and I let him know it.

We spent some pleasant hours sampling wines and foods, reclining in the open air on warm evenings, talking of many things. He, I noticed, made sure that not even my slave Albinus was present when he spoke of Tiberius or Livia. The mere mention of their names made his stutter even more pronounced, and the twitching of his head would increase to the point where I was certain he would have a fatal stroke. I have never seen anyone who lived in such fear. Their names could send him into uncontrollable spasms. If I'd been in his shoes, forced to be around them every day, I might have developed a few tics myself.

He asked if I was going to fight again, and if so, where and when.

I told him, "Claudius, my noble friend, I have no wish to go back into the business of butchering people, at least not as long as Albinus continues to make his wise investments. Besides, I want to be near at hand if things start to go bad for Germanicus. He will have need of me. I know it. And I received word from Germanicus today that we are leaving again, for Egypt this time."

From Germanicus' letter, I assumed that we were leaving soon, but it was not until early the next year that we were able to depart.

By that time Germanicus was no longer a consul, nor was Tiberius. Both had refused the nomination in order to give other worthy citizens an opportunity to serve the Empire. I think Lucius Balbus, and Marcus Torquatus, filled their vacancies.

3

Germanicus gave as his reason for our trip to Egypt the necessity to inspect the granaries there. But once we'd landed, he headed for the hinterlands, dragging me along with him, away from the comforts of Alexandria, its good food and hot, dark, musky dancing girls. The man was a maniac! He took us by ship to the mouth of that great muddy swamp of a river called the Nile, stopping in Thebes, where we viewed monstrous ruins and temples that put those of Rome and Greece to shame. These were gigantic, built to last through the ages.

At one ancient obelisk, covered with squiggles and forms of birds and other animals, the writings of ancient Egypt, he found an old priest of Amon to translate the writings. I stood by, feeling bored. But the words of the withered, bald old priest, in his white robes and bare feet, made me listen for more, my mouth agape at what I was hearing, understanding how powerful the Egyptians of olden days had been.

The writings dated back to the reign of an Egyptian king called Rameses II. Rameses, it was written, had over 700,000 men of military age in his lands. The nations that paid tribute to Egypt at the time were Libya, Ethiopia, Persia, Scythia, Bactria, Media, and many lesser states. The nations he'd conquered and ruled over directly included Syria, Armenia and Cappadocia. The limits of his Empire reached to the coasts of Bithynia and Lycian, up to the sources of the Nile and as far as a man could go in to the deserts, where no man in his right mind would ever tread anyway.

The tributes paid Rameses—in gold, horses, grain, ivory, spices, weapons—more than equaled all that Rome and Parthia combined received from their subject states.

One other item caught Germanicus' curiosity, as well as mine. There was a statue near the mouth of the Nile, a monstrous thing of stone that we learned was the god, Memnon. The strangest thing about it was that it spoke; strange howls and hollow tones wheezed out of it when the sun rose and the heat of the day drove off the chill of the desert night. Only then did Memnon speak. It was a bit scary. I'd never heard anything like it. If it was truly the god that was speaking, I was beginning to wish that it would learn Latin so that I could know what it was saying. It might have been a proper warning.

Germanicus took me to the Pyramids, those great tombs of the ancient Pharaohs, and even to Elephantine, the last Roman outpost in Egypt, though the Empire technically reached clear to the Red Sea and the great gulf bordering Persia.

When we returned to Alexandria, there were several letters waiting for us. Most of them were from Claudius, who always sent me his kind regards. Vonones had tried to escape, probably through the connivance of Piso. Claudius thought Vonones was more than likely heading for the lands of the Albani and Heniochi, who still paid him fealty. He also had blood relatives among the Scythian tribes who would grant him sanctuary. He'd been hunting with his escort and had used a bribe or ruse to lose them. Claudius added that the torturers would tell them which, later. He'd made for the Ceyhan River, but fast messengers had beat him to it and forced the riverside inhabitants to tear down every bridge, and Vonones was quickly recaptured by a Tribune of the cavalry, named Vibius Fronto. A good man, said Claudius. A few days later he was stabbed to death, in order to keep the plottings of Piso a secret, Claudius thought.

Germanicus also received one letter from Tiberius, reminding him strongly of the ruling set down by Augustus that no Senator or knight could enter Alexandria without the Emperor's permission. Augustus had implemented this ruling in order to prevent any noble with ambitions from gaining control of Egypt's grain, thereby gaining the power to cause famine in Rome. Germanicus crumpled the letter angrily, but he said nothing.

Just before we left Egypt, Germanicus learned that all orders he'd issued to Legion and city commanders had been canceled by Tiberius. He had another meeting with Piso in Syria, which rapidly deteriorated into mutual recriminations. It was one of the few times that I'd seen Germanicus really mad. His wrath scared not only me, but also Piso, who was used to getting away with almost anything he wanted.

Shortly after that confrontation, Piso said that he intended to leave Syria and return to Rome, but Germanicus took suddenly ill and Piso was forced to stay. I was in attendance at their last meeting, a dinner, standing guard behind Germanicus, wearing my gray sword in Legion fashion, hung from a baldrick so the scabbard rested on my right side. Beneath my favorite blue tunic, I wore a light shirt of mail, a gift from Germanicus. I didn't trust Piso, and kept an eye on him throughout their dialogue. The only time they agreed on anything was when Piso made a toast to the Emperor. It was the only thing that Germanicus took during the entire meal. He wouldn't have had that, but there was no way to refuse to drink to his stepfather.

It was after this dinner that he suddenly became ill. His bowels loosened and flowed like water. He was unable to keep anything on his stomach and experienced chills and fever. For several nights he complained of stomach cramps and had to rush to the vomitorium to throw up. The fluid that came from his stomach was a green color, and vile in odor.

As I said previously, Piso had canceled his trip to Rome in false courtesy to Germanicus' illness, sending his phony requests as to Germanicus' progress daily.

I was really quite worried for my noble friend, but after a few more trying days he seemed better and blamed his illness on bad water. I told him that I didn't trust Piso and that he should let me take him out once and for all. We argued over the matter, Germanicus reproving me for having thoughts of murder. I snapped back that it was not murder, but self-defense. I knew that Piso would not rest until he was dead, and I told him so. I added that if he didn't have the stomach for the job, I would see to it personally, and with pleasure. We fought for a couple of days over it, but I could not get his agreement.

A letter from Albinus came, saying that everything I'd worked for was going to be ruined if I did not return home immediately. A great pestilence had hit our orchards and farms. We had already lost most of the harvest, which we'd previously sold to speculators, and there was no way to return their money; it had already been spent in acquiring more land. I had to return or lose it all. He could keep our debtors at bay only a few weeks more, unless I returned to Herculaneum.

Germanicus was improving so I chose this time to go. I think he was somewhat relieved. He wouldn't have to hear my warnings for a while. He would never listen to me, anyway. Still, I hated to leave him, for the words of the old priest came back to me.

4

I left on the next available ship, one of the swift Ligurian types that could make three times the speed of the standard Roman vessel. In ten days we would arrive, hopefully in time to protect my life's work and security.

Germanicus ordered the captain of the Ligurian ship to make all haste and avoid all ports until we made Ostia. He told the captain that I was the bearer of important messages for the Emperor.

He had not lied. I did have messages for the Emperor, from Germanicus. As soon as I sat foot on solid ground in Ostia, I hired messengers to go to Herculaneum with the order for Albinus to meet me in Rome. I then rented a horse and rode as fast as I could to the Emperor's palace, near the Palatine, left the scrolls, and headed off again to the Flavian arena.

I was in luck! There was to be a celebration for the rites of spring, and I was in time to get my name on the lists of auctorati who would fight. The Games Master was more than pleased that I wished to participate and said that he would have no difficulty in finding a proper opponent for me. He asked me to act as the team captain of the fight between secutors and thraces, but I would have none of that. I wanted a single combat, where I couldn't fall to a lucky blow from some amateur full of gusto.

He agreed, and the following morning, in the *Acta Diurna*, my name led the events. I wondered if the man whose name I'd knocked out of top billing was as angry at me as I had been at Graecus when he'd done the same to me.

My opponent, another secutor, had a good reputation. I had seen him fight in Africa, and I knew he would put on a good show. My biggest concern was whether I was in good enough shape for a tough fight. I'd exercised all along, but all the traveling with Germanicus had made it difficult for me to keep up a proper schedule. But I had no choice; it was the only way I could possibly save my investments. Perhaps I could have borrowed the money from Claudius, but I didn't want to. I'd gotten myself into this mess and it was up to me to get myself out of it. This was all I knew.

I'd sent word to Claudius of my return. Now he came to visit, and we had a chance to talk a bit. He told me of the plot against Germanicus by Sejanus and Livia. Tiberius, he said, kept himself apart from any direct involvement, but knew of his mother's designs and did nothing to hinder her.

We went to the baths, which we both enjoyed, and when we came out the streets were in a festival mood. The letters I'd brought gave news of Germanicus' recovery and the people of Rome and, as I learned later, throughout the Empire were giving thanks to the gods. He was truly loved.

When the mob filled the Flavian two days later, Sejanus was seated next to the Imperial box with several of his officers of the Praetorian.

The secutor matched against me was seven or eight years younger than I, and he gave me a proper workout. I was finally able to put him down with a combination leg trip and shield smash, knocking him off his feet to lie helpless under my sword. We both had some minor cuts, enough to make us appear bloodier than we actually were, and it satisfied the mob. The man had fought well, and the people were in great spirits, so they gave the thumbs-up sign for me to spare his life. I was glad of it; I didn't really want to kill him. He had the makings of a champion if he lived. I suppose the mob, in thanks for Germanicus' recovery, wanted to show mercy in the only way they could.

Sejanus, his face flushed with what looked like both excitement and disappointment that I had not been killed, left the stands as soon as my man had hit the ground, not waiting for the crowd's verdict of either life or death for my victim. The only death he was interested in was mine.

Albinus had showed up the day before the fight and had been meeting with bankers and investors ever since. I'd seen him enter the stands in the last part of the contests, accompanied by three fat, well-dressed men with the look of greed about them.

After I'd cleansed myself, I went to the inn where I'd taken rooms. Albinus was already there, the fat men with him. The purse I'd won would give him enough to settle their claims for another year. Their deals were made and they left, one of them thanking me louder than the others. He'd placed a small fortune on my winning, and though the odds were five to one in my favor, it still had provided him a good profit. I was polite, wishing them all good fortune and prosperity.

After they'd left, I cursed Albinus for getting me into such a mess in the first place. Once he explained, though, I felt I'd been unfair to him. No one can predict an onslaught of locusts, or droughts or floods. It was the gamble of a farmer. I apologized, but still instructed him to get out of the farming business as fast as he could and buy us something else. We were still heavy at it, trying to figure our direction of investment, when Claudius entered and pulled me aside, whispering frantically.

"G . . . G . . . Germanicus is worse and not expected to live much longer, Lucanus. The word just arrived. He may be dead even now. You know the time it takes to deliver a message."

I shucked Albinus off with orders to do whatever he thought best, and took off for Ostia. I found passage on a fast light ship of the Imperial navy, bribing the captain to take me on board and let me off at Antioch. It didn't require much persuasion when he found that I was headed to Germanicus' side. He loved him, too.

My trip was uneventful. All the storms were in my mind, not at sea. I felt guilty now for leaving Germanicus in a fit of temper. Perhaps if I'd have stayed there it wouldn't have happened, or maybe I could have done something to help. What, I didn't know.

I slept only a few hours that night. My eyes kept sweeping the watery horizon and searching for land, although I knew that it would be eight more days before we landed. Perhaps it was still not too late? Maybe there would be time? My mind was made up, though. I would kill Piso as soon as I saw to Germanicus. If they crucified me for it, then so be it. For Germanicus was worth a thousand Pisos, or even the same amount of me.

The world did not hold so many good men that it could afford to lose one such as Germanicus.

5

As soon as we landed, without waiting for any of my baggage, I set out for the house of Germanicus. As I went through the streets of Antioch, I could see that the city was already in mourning, prematurely I hoped. Other than the sounds of weeping and wailing, it was quiet, and there was a heavy sullen feeling in the air.

At the steps of his house I was met by Agrippina. She looked as if she had aged twenty years in the last few weeks. She told me that Germanicus had sent Piso away. So, the bastard had finally done something for Germanicus to drive him out of Syria? I wished that he'd left the worthless wretch where I could get my hands around his neck.

She whisked me into Germanicus' sickroom and whispered in my ear that many foul, evil things had been done. They had found, hidden in the bedroom, many signs of black magic. Even in the walls, she told me, they'd come across human remains and the signs of curses and spells. Bloody ashes were found beneath his bed, and tablets of lead, inscribed with curses and his name.

I wasn't sure how potent such things were, but when I saw him lying there, there was no doubt in my mind that evil spells, or poison, or perhaps both, were at work.

He was asleep when I entered, and I made no attempt to wake him, knowing that he would need whatever strength he could derive from his sleep. I called the slaves together and gave them orders that nothing was to pass his lips that they had not tasted first. I drew my sword, wrapped my cloak about my shoulders and stood near his bed. I was furious with the world, and with myself for leaving him. It would not happen again. I would be with him to the end of his life, however long that might be.

I hoped that his natural strength and vitality would pull him through this ordeal.

At dusk, braziers were lit, and healers came in to give him elixirs and potions. One of them wanted to bleed him, but I put a stop to that. I remembered the words of old Ramsep on Pollio's ship, that when a man bleeds too much, he dies. Agrippina arrived and, after listening, agreed with me. The healer left, angry, his white robes dragging the floor. He made signs with his hands when leaving. I wasn't sure if they were for good or evil, but I helped him out the doors with a solid boot in the backside that sent him tumbling in the gutter. I was in no mood to be trifled with.

The following morning, Germanicus opened his eyes and saw me. My heart nearly broke at the sight of his weak, pale smile. He raised a feeble hand, motioning for me to move closer.

"Lucanus, old friend, I am glad to see you, even though this is a dark time for those who love me."

I fought back tears, gulping out the words: "Dominus, forgive me for leaving you," I cried.

He stopped me with an upraised finger. "There was nothing you could have done to stop this day, Lucanus. Neither you nor I have the kind of mind for this evil that others use so freely. Tell my wife to come to me."

He coughed; traces of blood flecked his mouth. I summoned Agrippina to his side, and left them for a moment to speak alone. She was crying when she left his bedside and I returned to my position at the head of the bed. I could not comfort her then; her hurt, like mine, was too deep for soothing. I neither ate nor drank that day; I wasn't going to give them a chance to poison me and take me from my post.

It was late afternoon when Agrippina returned, escorting a few friends of Germanicus, officers of his Legion and good men who had served him well. He motioned for me to join them at the foot of his bed, where he could see us all without straining.

Agrippina propped him up with pillows. Gods! How pale he was! The color was gone entirely from his usually ruddy cheeks, and they'd sunken in. He had dark hollows under his eyes, and his lips were faintly blue. The cast of death was upon him. He smiled gently, then wrenched with pain before speaking.

"Friends,"—I was pleased that I'd been included in that category—"I feel the chill of dark in my bones. I am dying!"

We all started to protest, but he cut us short.

"Don't you think I have witnessed enough death in my time to know when my own is near? Now be silent, and let me speak while I still have the strength to do so. Even if I were dying a natural death I would still be angry with the gods for taking me from those that I love while I am still so young. There is much that I yet wished to do in this life. But it is not the gods who are calling me to the dark river, it is the evil deeds of Piso that have cut the threads of my life. I have asked you all here to honor my last requests. You, Servaeus, will tell my father and brother of the treason that has brought this ugly death of mine to pass."

He paused for a moment, catching his breath and gathering up his strength. The anger he felt at this moment brought a flush to his cheeks, then quickly faded.

"My friends and relatives, who share in my fortune, and even some who were not friends, will lament that I should die in this manner. When I've survived so many terrible battles, I must now go to my grave, victim to a woman's treachery."

I gave him a sip of clear water that Agrippina had taken from the fountain with her own hands. He raised a weak hand.

"You must all protest to the Senate and invoke the law.

The duty of a friend is not to walk behind the corpse wailing pointlessly, but to remember the wishes of the dead and to carry out his desires.''

He looked me straight in the eye.

''There are some who would have prevented this day, had I listened to their warnings and done what they suggested. But that is as it may be.''

I knew that he was talking of my offer to kill Piso, and I vowed then that I would do it, even if it meant my own life.

He coughed a great mass of bloody phlegm from his throat and wiped his mouth with a silk handkerchief, apologizing for it.

''If I have loved you, then you must avenge me. Show my wife, the granddaughter of the divine Augustus, to Rome; cry out the names of my children. You will have the sympathy of all honest men. Accuse Piso, and you will be believed. Now, if you love me, give me your oaths to do as I've asked, no less than I would do for you.''

One by one, his friends knelt at his bedside, swearing to die before they would leave his death unavenged. I waited . . .

Germanicus then called his wife to him, and spoke with tears in his eyes.

''Submit to them, Agrippina. Do not become involved with my revenge. It would not serve you or the children well. Do not attempt to fight those that are much stronger than yourself.''

The rest of the men had moved away during this part of the conversation. Only I had remained close, within earshot, as I knew he wanted me to do. I heard him whisper to her.

''Beware, Agrippina. Beware of Tiberius and the Augusta, for they love us not.''

She agreed to do his bidding. Then he summoned me closer. His strength was fast fading; I could see the fluttering of his heart in the pulse of his throat. It was like watching a wounded bird, its wings beating feebly and futilely. He grasped my hand, squeezing as hard as his strength would allow.

"Piso, Lucanus! Kill Piso for me. If he lives, then there is no safety for my family."

He never heard my oath to do so, for with his last word, dark claimed him, and death took his soul. I threw my head back and howled in grief. The sounds coming from my throat were completely alien to me. I could not control them. I ran wildly from the room, screaming, *"Piso . . . Piso . . . Piso . . . PISO!"*

Some hours later, still full of grief and loss, I collected my senses and returned to aid Agrippina. There was much to do for her before . . . .

His funeral was a poor thing, compared to what it should have been. There were no statues in procession, nor symbols of his deeds. But there were a multitude of eulogies and mourners. Many compared him to the immortal Alexander, for both had died at the hands of treachery, in a foreign land. Both of them had been able and fearless warriors and generals and, lastly, both had died shortly after their thirtieth birthday.

Before the cremation took place, his body was displayed in the main square of Antioch. The keening of the mourners could be heard for miles. The women rent their clothes and cut their faces with their nails; many strong men broke down and wept loudly at the altar, for many had hoped that Germanicus would one day assume power in Rome, bringing enlightenment instead of the tyranny of the Caesars. I stood guard by the body, permitting no one to touch him, protecting him in death as I should have in life.

I would have gone after Piso immediately following the cremation had I known where he was. I was in the process of investigating when Agrippina asked me to accompany her and the children to Rome. She was to bring her husband's ashes back to the capital city. Though we both knew it was dangerous for her to do so, custom demanded it be done. There was nothing I could do but agree to go with her.

For the third time in as many months, I crossed the Mediterranean to the port of Ostia. This trip was the worst of all my journeys, despite the fair warm winds and sunny days. Agrippina stayed to herself, taking her meals in her cabin and seldom coming to the deck. She left the entertaining of little Caligula, the third boy, to me. I didn't mind. The boy was quick and intelligent. We spent hour upon hour sparring with each other and, when he made a touch with his toy sword, he would cry joyfully, "*Iugula!*"

Caligula had always been an appealing youngster and the apple of his father's eye, but I had never truly felt comfortable around him. Perhaps it was because he was overly bright for his age. He could speak Greek and wrote fluently in both Latin and Greek. He smiled and laughed as other children do, but there was something about him that troubled me. At times, when he thought no one was watching, his face would change from that of a happy child to one that held cruelty in the eyes, and they would grow hard and stern. I think that if Germanicus had lived his son would have brought him no pleasure. The boy had a cruel side to his nature, and when he is fully grown, with no one to control him, I feel he will give in to that cruelty. But then, what do I know of children?

6

When we landed at Ostia a tremendous crowd had gathered, anticipating our arrival. We learned that some of them had been sleeping on the docks for days. We were escorted by the throng to the gates of Rome, where

Praetorians came out to accompany us to the house of Germanicus. There, Agrippina gave me leave to go my own way, thanking me with a small kiss on the cheek for being so kind to them. I was somewhat reluctant to leave her and the children to the unexpected, yet I was relieved to be free of the responsibility for a while. There were things I had to find out, and I knew just where to go. Claudius!

I was unable to locate him on the first day back, and spent the night in the inn I'd used on my last visit. That night in my bed, thoughts of Piso and his bitch wife, Placina, ate at my gut. That, and the knowledge that there was nothing I could do until I found him.

I sent a letter to Albinus in Herculaneum, telling him of my return and ordering him to stay there until I came.

It was first light when a knock came at my door. Still groggy from lack of sleep and worry, I rose and answered the pounding. It was Claudius.

"Lu . . . Lu . . . Lucanus," he stuttered, "I'm so glad you have returned. These are evil times, and I do not know what to do."

He sat beside me on the bed. His toga was stained with wine, and his eyes showed that he had enjoyed even less sleep than I had.

"Tell me, Claudius. What is happening? And, where is Piso?"

He leaned close to me. I could smell the sour odor of stale wine on his breath. He touched a finger to his lips for silence, giving me a look of warning.

"You should forget about Piso, Lucanus. He is the friend of Tiberius. I should be telling you nothing." He shook his head in worry.

I swore at him as I rose from the bed. For a moment, he thought I was going to strike him, and I would have, if he had not stopped me.

"There is no need for you to go after Piso, Lucanus. He

will be returning to Rome shortly."

Claudius had an ear for information as no other did, and it belied his slack features and limp lips. People in the court thought him a simpleton and spoke freely in front of him, as if he were no more than an ignorant slave. He, unbeknownst to them, absorbed every word they said. Now he was passing at least some of what he'd heard on to me.

Piso had returned to Syria where, as soon as he'd learned of Germanicus' death, he'd tried to take back the governorship of the province, with the aid of Domitus Celer. Piso had gathered what troops were still loyal to him and had led them into what many had declared a near civil war. Piso had been forced to take refuge in the fortified town of Celenderis. There, with the help of men sent to him by a few Cilicia chieftains he'd bribed in the past, and now promised even richer rewards, he had amassed a force that was fast approaching the strength of a Legion.

Claudius stopped at this point and asked if I would send out for wine and water. I stuck my head out of the window and yelled loudly for the landlord to send up a pot of his best. When it was brought up, I watched as Claudius nervously poured himself a bowl, cutting the wine with only a slight touch of water.

He caught my look of disapproval, saying, a little testily, "I happen to know, Lucanus, that the wine in this inn is already watered to begin with."

After he'd drunk the bowl and poured another, he continued his story once more.

"Cnaeus Sentius, who became governor after the cremation, warned Piso to stay out of Syria. And, he meant what he said. Sentius, as you know, Lucanus, is a man of about fifty, still strong in spirit, and loved Germanicus as much as you and I." He hesitated momentarily, and I urged him on before he got drunker.

"Sentius cornered Piso and his troops in Celenderis and

gave him one chance to surrender. Piso refused, and Sentius ordered an attack on the city."

I had been to Celenderis with Germanicus; it was constructed suitably for defense.

"Piso had a good position, Lucanus, but his men were poor material and disheartened, and, when attacked, they ran away. Piso did make one counterattack, with what few men he had left, mostly deserters from the Legions. He tried to burn the ships that Sentius had used to transport his army, but he was beaten off and forced to return to the city wall, utilizing his favorite trick of trying to buy loyalty. Only one answered Piso's call and that was to his eternal regret and shame. On the next day, Sentius began his assault in earnest. With the trumpets and bugles sounding, his men threw up tall ladders against the walls; they scaled them while machines hurled stones and fire over the top."

Piso finally called a truce, and, according to Claudius, begged Sentius to let him remain at the fortress if he gave up his arms. Piso wanted to remain there until the matter of who was the rightful governor of Syria was settled by the Emperor himself.

Claudius drained the pot of wine, wiping his lips with the hem of his toga, using the purple edge so the stains would not show so readily.

I prodded him for more information, and he shook his head. I raised my fist, telling him I loved him like a brother but would not hesitate to rearrange his face if he didn't tell me more. I could see in his eyes that he knew I was serious.

"I already told you, Lucanus; you do not have to go after Piso. He will come to you. Sentius agreed only to send Piso to Rome with an armed escort. This news came last night. Piso should be arriving in a few days."

That was all he knew. But he still warned me that I should leave Piso alone. He had the ear of Tiberius and his protection.

I told him that since we were on the subject of ears, I might string those of Piso on my belt when I got him.

7

Piso! I wanted him as other men wanted food, or women. I lusted after him. The thought of my being punished for what I was planning was no deterrent. I was beyond being stopped now, and if anyone got in my way, even Tiberius himself, then they would just have to take what came to them.

I'd been watching Piso's house for some days, staying close to the shadows, or mingling with the crowds. Gods! how I hated the worthless wretch.

The honors that had been shown to Germanicus upon the return of his ashes to Rome were no help in pushing the dark thoughts of vengeful murder from my mind. *Murder?* No, not murder! *Justice!*

I cared not that Tiberius had publicly mourned the loss of his adopted son, and had given him every honor that could be bestowed on man. What good did it do Germanicus to have his name entered into the Salian Hymn, or to have chairs crowned with oak leaves placed among the seats of the Brotherhood of Augustus? The knights of Rome gave his name to a block of seats at the theater, and on the fifteenth of July his statue would be paraded through the streets so that no one would ever forget what he looked like, and to give the mob the opportunity to pay homage to the best-loved man in all of Rome. Arches were to be dedicated to his memory, standing above the Rhine and atop Mount Amanus in Syria, with inscriptions recounting his deeds and the giving of his life for his country.

None of these mattered to me. What good were honors

after death, especially death that was yet to be avenged?

Piso had been charged with the death of Germanicus and also for inciting rebellion. His answer was that he had been the rightful governor at the time of the rebellion, and as for the death of Germanicus, he denied any complicity whatever.

Claudius told me that a notorious poisoner, named Martina, had been brought to Rome from Antioch, where she had been at the time of Germanicus' illness and death. He told me also that the woman had visited the houses of Livia and Plancina more than once. However, before she could be called on to testify, she mysteriously died in convulsions. I didn't care about her. Even if she'd been the poisoner, she was only acting as the instrument of Piso and his wife, in partnership with the Emperor's mother, Livia. I wished them all in the darkest pit of the nether world, to lie there and rot for all eternity.

Tiberius himself was asked to take charge of the inquiry into the matter. With him sitting in judgment, I felt certain that Piso would get off lightly. More than likely there would be no punishment at all. But that did not bother me. The punishment he so deserved would be doled out by myself.

Today, at last, Piso was back in Rome! The news had arrived! I'd made my way into Piso's house undetected and was standing in the shadows. I wore soft shoes of leather so that no sound would come from my movements, though I was certain that the beating of my heart was loud enough to be heard by all. I heard voices coming from somewhere down the hall, and I strained to see where they were coming from. Piso's wife was coming out of his bedroom. She walked down the hall, turned the corner and disappeared from my sight. I heard another door close then and assumed she was the one who'd closed it.

I hesitated a moment, then made up my mind. If I was going to do it, it had to be now. I walked softly to his door and tapped firmly, but not loudly enough to be heard at any distance. His voice asked bitterly, ''Who is it?''

I muffled my voice. ''A message from Sejanus, Dominus!'' I knew my calling him ''lord'' would put him off guard. Titles of respect have that effect on the nobility. He grumbled that he was coming and I should wait a moment. I raised my dark cloak so as to conceal not only my body but also my face. In my hand I held a dagger, of Syrian design, with a wide curved blade and a bone grip.

The oak door swung open when he unbolted it.

''Give me your message from . . .''

His words were cut off when I smashed the door open with my shoulder, knocking him back into the room. I lunged inside, grabbing him by the throat, choking off any cry for help that might escape his lips. I kicked the door shut behind me.

I finally had him. My dagger was at his throat as he squirmed beneath my grasp. Hate was full on me as I whispered in his face.

''Now, you swine, you shall get the judgment you deserve.''

His face was starting to turn red and I knew I was cutting off his air supply. I eased up a bit; I wanted to enjoy this moment.

He choked out, ''Who are you?''

With my knife hand, I pulled the hood away from my face. I wanted him to know who was about to kill him.

''Lucanus!'' His eyes panicked for a moment, then, just as quickly, he gained control of himself.

''Yes,'' I hissed, ''Lucanus! I only wish that I had the time to make you suffer the way Germanicus did, but I do not. All that I can give you is a quick death, not the lingering pain of death that he knew.''

With my hand still firmly clamped at his throat, I pulled him erect to look directly into his face. He was aiding me, holding onto my wrists to pull himself up. I was confused for a second. The fear had left him. His eyes were calm, and his voice was steady as he answered me. He showed no trace of fright whatever, as if all was accepted.

"Then get on with it! I am weary of all this, and if I must die, do it and bother me no more."

I knew now what it was. He had lived with this fear for so long that he was glad it had finally arrived. He had accepted it, and when a man does that, fear holds no meaning for him. I'd seen the same look many times on the faces of those that had fallen under my sword in the arena.

I released him, shoving him back on his bed. I knew that he would not call for help; it would be too late when they arrived. No! This was between him and me, and he knew it also.

He fell from his bed to the floor. I laughed quietly. It was good to see him on his knees, even if there was no fear. It was still going to be a pleasure to finish him off, as far as I was concerned.

He came quickly off the floor then, a shortsword at the ready. It must have been hidden beneath the bed for emergencies such as this. It mattered not to me. It merely added more spice to what we both knew had to be done. He stood erect before me, his face puffy, his eyes red from lack of sleep. He wore only a light tunic in the Greek style, that reached to the knees and was belted with a soft rope of blue cord.

I motioned for him to come to me, a sneer on my face. It was to be the shortsword against the dagger. I knew that he'd been a soldier and was trained in the use of the blade, but not as we of the circus had been trained. His movements were slow. He lunged, and I deflected the thrust with an easy gliding motion of my knife blade. He was growing pale and sweaty with the exertion, and I knew that I must end it before someone heard us.

He raised his sword for a downstroke and, instead of

making an effort to move away, I closed with him. Before the stroke could be completed, I was inside his reach. My left hand went to his wrist, and with a wrestler's trick, I heaved him up and around, off balance completely. I tripped him with my right leg while he was tottering and threw him to the floor. I stood above him, looking down. This time the sword was in my hand, its edge to his throat. I put the dagger in my belt and hefted the sword.

Smiling, I spoke to him softly. "It seems a shame to taint the steel of an innocent sword with the blood of the likes of you, Piso. But I shan't tell anyone if you do not."

I reached down and pulled him to his knees. Moving behind him, I held him firmly by the back of his neck. There was no comparison in our strength; he could not move.

I moved my hand then to the hair of his head, placing his blade edge to his throat in front. He reached up in automatic response and grabbed my hand. It mattered not. I slowly ran the cold edge of the blade across his windpipe, then pulled it back again, opening his throat to expose the white cartilage of the esophagus, letting its whiteness blend with the red of arterial blood that was gushing forth in pumping arcs to stain his clean floor.

I held to him, his back against my knees, enjoying the feel of his death at my hand. His final shudder gave me a chill of pleasure. Never had I found such delight in the death of another, but then again, never had I hated such as I hated now. The feeling, I suppose, was a mixture of pride in the keeping of my oath to Germanicus, and the relief in knowing that such slime as Piso had been removed from the world.

I left the body where it lay and placed the handle of the sword in his right hand. I wasn't sure why I did that, it just seemed like a good idea at the time.

Going out, I raised the bar latch to where it was angled slightly to the door's edge and balanced. In the hallway, I gave the door a firm pull and heard the click of the latch as it fell into position, firmly locking the door from the inside. Ha! Let them figure that one out. For a moment I hesitated, thinking I should go down the hall to the bedroom of his wife and give her the same treatment. I decided not to push my luck. I had done what I'd wished. For now I would have to be satisfied with the death of Piso.

I slid back into the shadows and went out the same way I'd entered, out and over the garden wall, letting the dark mask my movements.

8

After finishing off Piso I decided it would be wise to return to Herculaneum. I expected a loud cry for his killer, but was surprised when I heard nothing about it. Some time elapsed before I received word from Rome that the official statement had finally been issued: Piso had committed suicide. How unfortunate for the poor widow, I mused.

I could not believe that they really thought he'd taken his own life by slitting his throat. The cut was much too deep and wide. However, if that was the way they wanted it, it was fine with me.

I stayed to myself for the next few weeks, until my walls were closing in on me. Cabin fever, the old-timers called it. I took a trip to the coast. There I spotted a familiar figure playing with a small child on the beach.

Antonia! She had filled out since I last saw her. Her face was a bit fuller, as was her figure, but the years had been kind to her. She was still beautiful.

The child was a boy of about three years, with large brown eyes and dark curly hair. He was playing in the sand, making castles. The waves would wash his near-completed model away, and he would patiently start all over again.

I was hesitant to break in on them, not knowing how welcome I would be, but was unable to restrain myself. She greeted me warmly, however, as a friend, and we three walked along the beach. I had not received word that she'd married, so I asked her about the child. She avoided the question and went on to other subjects. I didn't push the matter, thinking perhaps she'd lost her man or something else that was equally unpleasant to recall.

I played with the child a while under her watchful eye. I think she was afraid that my rough paw might break him. But he was stout enough and showed no fear as we ran and wrestled on the beach that day. I seriously considered asking her to return with me to Herculaneum, but there was too great a gulf between us now. I left her there on the beach with her son and returned to my house. However, I carried with me a sense of loss I could not understand.

I was glad to be away from Rome. Things were not going well in the city. Tiberius had taken the bit in his teeth and was threatening death to any who were even remotely in opposition to him. No one was safe; already, over five hundred had gone to the executioners. I wondered if my name was on his list, either due to my association with Germanicus, or possibly for the death of Piso, his pet toadie. The answer came the next day.

9

Early in the morning, a Decurion of the Praetorians visited my house, along with his escort. The Decurion looked a bit uneasy; in his hand he fondled a document bearing the Emperor's seal.

He mumbled a few prepared words and handed the document to me. I read it over quickly. It was, as I had suspected, an order for me to return to Rome, in the company of his Praetorians, to face charges of treason.

I offered no resistance, placed Albinus in charge of things, and had my horse brought around.

We made good time on the return ride back to Rome, and passed through the gates of the city at dawn the next day. We went directly to the Mamertine.

I had passed by the infamous prison often enough on my way to the contests. It was a massive stone building with an arched front, ugly in comparison with the fine temples and public buildings that surrounded it. Inside, to my surprise, I was shown to a waiting chamber; I had expected a dungeon cell. At midday a Praetorian came for me, escorting me to the inner office where Sejanus waited. He was pleased with himself, but polite. He called for wine for the two of us, which I refused. Then he got down to business.

"Lucanus, you have caused us a great deal of trouble. I know it was you who killed Piso. It really doesn't matter to me; it's just as well that he is out of my way. The trail stopped with his death and, to my pleasure, before it could reach Tiberius' ear. But be that as it may, you did kill him, and you must be punished."

I said nothing in reply. I knew he understood what I thought of him.

He sipped his wine, looking very scholarly. "We could have you executed for his murder, or just simply have you disappear into this vast building, but I don't want either to happen. If we arrest you, it might give friends of Germanicus cause to make more trouble for us. Though we are taking care of them a few at a time, there are still many." He was talking of the executions of those that Tiberius considered in opposition to him.

He wiped the wine from his lips with the back of one hand before continuing. "No, Lucanus, I have another thought on the matter. As you have interfered with us, the government of the people, I think you should be allowed to repay the people by providing them with a little entertainment. I wish I could take credit for this idea,'' he was nearly purring, ''but it was the inspiration of the Augusta. I want you to go into the arena. This time you will die!''

I grinned at him, more a sneer. ''What makes you think you can force me to commit suicide in this manner, Sejanus? As you said, Germanicus still has many friends, and some of them may decide to use your own methods to end your miserable existence.''

He nodded, unoffended by my insult. ''Exactly, Lucanus! That is why you will enter the arena of your own free will. You saw Antonia the other day. She is looking well, is she not?''

So I had been under surveillance all the while.

He went on, smiling knowingly. ''That's a fine-looking boy she has. You know, Lucanus, he reminds me a lot of you.''

So that was it! The truth of what he said took me by surprise. I knew he was not lying. The boy was my son, my blood.

''Lucanus, if you refuse my offer, I shall have no choice but to execute you for treason. And, as you know, Tiberius believes that when a traitor is condemned, those of his seed should also die. And the boy's mother as well. Really, Lucanus, your options are limited. I will see you dead. You have no other choice. You alone, or you and the woman and your brat. There must still be some honor left in you.''

I wondered how he managed not to choke on the word honor.

''Now, Lucanus. What's it to be? Yourself, or them?''

He had me. We both knew it! True, Antonia was only a part of my past, and I didn't know the child, but he was mine, and I would not have them die because of me. I wanted to reach over and twist the life out of Sejanus' smiling, smirking, face. But it would have gained me nothing, other than the moment's satisfaction.

He must have seen my decision in my face, for he spoke. "Good! I'm glad that you've decided to listen to reason. You shall die in the games to celebrate the sixth year of Tiberius' reign, which are five weeks off. You may return to Herculaneum now. During those weeks it will give me much pleasure, knowing that you will be thinking about your death every waking moment. That is all! You may leave now!"

I was escorted out of the Mamertine and returned to my house.

As I sit here dictating to Albinus, I can see my escort in the courtyard. They are never far away from me, although there is no reason for them to guard me. I will not try to escape. Death comes to all. It is inevitable; only the time, the place, and the manner are uncertain. I am fortunate. I know the answers to all three of the uncertainties. Oddly, it does not bother me in the least. I am reconciled to my fate, even, in some strange manner, looking forward to the day. I wonder who will be the one to kill me?

Albinus will relate the final chapter of my life to you, dear reader; he has sworn to do so. I am tired now, and I will rest.

Two more days and I shall die. Only one regret comes into my head at this moment: it shall be my last time to use the Damascus presented to me by Germanicus and Claudius.

Dear Germanicus . . . Dear Claudius. Friends, both!

BOOK SEVEN

ALBINUS

1

I have returned from Rome. My master is dead! My master is dead? Somehow those words are both pleasing and painful.

I know that at best he was a rather rough animal, with no sense or appreciation of beauty. Yet . . . .

But actually, it is with no regret that I claim this house and all that was his. I have earned it. Through the long years I have endured his abuse and neglect. When I think of the time I wasted trying to instill a small amount of culture into that over-muscled vulgar body!

Yes! I stayed with him because I knew I was in his will, but it wasn't easy. But I shall live up to my end of the bargain. He made me swear that I would recount his final moments; therefore I shall begin.

On the day of his death the Flavian stands were full. The crowd consisted mostly of crude, ill-mannered members of the *populi*, but a lot of my master's ardent fans were in the stands also. I was careful to seat myself with a few friends of a more refined sentiment and nature.

There is no need to go into all that took place before Lucanus made his appearance as the day's main attraction. (He has certainly done that often enough in this disgusting ode to his own immortality, and, upon reading it over, I have noticed that he neglected to stress my contributions.)

I must say, with all honesty, that he did make a striking

entry, striding across the arena as if he were Hercules reincarnate. That was his intent, I'm certain. The sun reflected from his polished armor, sending dazzling spirals of light into the eyes of us all. His helmet was of fine Spanish steel, traced with gold inlay in designs of the Gothic style, as was his shield. The cost of his armor would have paid for a fair-sized farm. Even his leg greaves were made to match.

He was gorgeous. If only he had returned a small portion of the affection I offered him, I might have been able to prevent this day from coming. But no matter now, it is done!

The mob began to chant his name in unison and rhythm. "Lucanus! Lucanus!"

He raised his grey Damascus, of which he was so proud, and marched twice around the arena, acknowledging the ovation of the stands. Many women were overcome by the sight of him, exposing themselves to him, offering their bared breasts. To my disgust, even one of my friends forgot his dignity in the moment, throwing a garland of flowers out to the stands, begging Lucanus for one small embrace, saying that he would gladly die from the sheer ecstasy of having Lucanus' arms about him. So would I have, but not here, not in public. It was absolutely disgusting behavior on my friend's part. I shall certainly not invite him to the celebratory dinner at my new home in Herculaneum.

Lucanus finally ended his grand parade. He halted in front of the Imperial box, where Tiberius and Livia, the Augusta, sat. They were, as usual, escorted by personal guards, handsome barbarians from the frontiers. Of course, the Praetorians were also present, under the ever-watchful eye of Sejanus.

I had a good view of the proceedings. Lucanus removed his helmet, looked directly into the faces of the nobility above him, and gave the mandatory salute. *"Ave, Caesar! Te Moritu Salutus!"* He lowered his voice and said something else that I was unable to distinguish, but I did see Tiberius' face pale, and the Augusta's thin body shook in anger at his words. I presume that he was telling them what he thought of them, as he was going to die.

The only face in the Imperial box that showed any sign of regret was that of the drooling fool, Claudius. I never understood what Lucanus saw in the man. He looked then as if he were going to break into tears at any moment.

Tiberius stood, and, with a twitch of impatience, signaled to the Games Master for the event to begin.

Lucanus bowed. I think even then he was mocking them. He donned his grand helmet and turned to face the center of the arena. The determination on his face did give one the impression that he was not going to die easily.

He was magnificent, I must admit. There is no way to deny that he was now giving the best performance of his career. His final act would be his greatest.

Tiberius whispered in the ear of the Praetorian at his side and the guard went immediately to the Games Master, also whispering through cupped hands. The man bowed his head in the direction of Tiberius and disappeared back into the inner chambers of the arena.

Lucanus had begun pacing back and forth on the sands, asking the crowd what seemed to be the matter. Were there no men left in Rome who would face him, he asked. He tore his helmet from his head and threw it against the wall. He beat his sword against his shield, its clamor echoing throughout the Flavian. His hair was pasted to his head from the heat. Then he was crying loudly that there would be no thumbs-up for any man who faced him this day. "Kill me," he cried, "or I will kill you!" There was a madness about him that was glorious!

His answer came when a team of three secutors came onto the sands. Behind them, I could see the Games Master, a whip in his hand. He was having to beat them to make them face this madman. They wanted no part of the lunatic on the sands who cried out for blood.

But they came on. If they refused to fight they were sure to be killed. Out here they stood a slight chance of surviving. They approached him cautiously, taking small tentative steps, their swords changing hands nervously, their shields held high to protect their throats, even though they still were fifty feet from Lucanus. He laughed when he spotted them, his chuckle reverberating off the walls, almost an insane giggle.

"Come to me," he cried, motioning to them with his sword. "Come to me! Kill me, and the rudis may be yours. Kill Lucanus and earn your freedom! But fail . . . and you shall die. Ha, Ha, Ha, Ha!"

He lunged at them, running, and threw himself on the nearest secutor. The others dodged to the sides and away. It was their first mistake. They should have stayed together. He smashed his man to the ground with his shield and slit his throat before the unfortunate one had a chance to strike even one blow.

The other two had positioned themselves to his front and rear, at a distance of about ten feet. When the one to his front had closed to five feet, Lucanus removed his shield from his left arm and held it loosely by the straps, swinging it back and forth. The one to his rear was confused. The secutor before him was now within sword range. Lucanus swung his shield; its edge sliced out and knocked the helmet from his man's head, barely seconds before Lucanus' sword found an opening beneath the fellow's sword arm. The blade entered at the armpit, deep and deadly, pulling him to the ground to lie writhing in his own gushing blood.

Lucanus turned quickly to the other man.

The last secutor broke and ran, dropping his shield and sword, heading desperately towards the inner chambers, away from the madman on the sands.

By the time he reached the gate, however, Tiberius had

spoken to Sejanus, and the bodyguards of the Emperor hurled their javelins with great accuracy. A half-dozen shafts pinned the man to the gate, protruding from his back like the quills of a porcupine, their points holding him there, quivering in death.

Lucanus watched for a moment, then turned and walked across the arena to the Emperor's box. On his way, he stooped and picked up the sword the secutor had dropped.

He raised both swords in salute to Tiberius, his words sounding out clearly to all in the stands. "Your Praetorians are very good at spearing men in the back from a distance, Lord, but do any Praetorian heroes have the courage to come down and face me?"

Tiberius hesitated; Sejanus turned pale with anger at the affront. Claudius, the dolt, was crying like a baby, tears running down his foolish face.

Sejanus leaned over the railing, looking down at Lucanus below him. "Lucanus, you go too far!"

My master laughed. "Really, Sejanus? How far is too far for one such as I? Send down your heroes, one, two, three of them, it doesn't matter how many. You and I both know that the end will be the same."

The audience thought he was boasting about killing the men, unaware that he was expecting his own death.

Sejanus nodded. "It is time to put an end to this farce, and, to you, Lucanus!" He whipped around, speaking to the leader of his Praetorian guards.

The man nodded and left, taking with him all but two of the escorts to the Emperor.

Six men? Against Lucanus? The mob in the stands fell silent now, then suddenly began to hiss, crying that Lucanus should be given a fair chance.

Lucanus silenced their outcry with his upraised sword, yelling loudly, "Let them come! My whole life has been spent in entertaining you, why stop now? Perhaps you will find what is about to happen even more than amusing."

The Praetorians entered the arena through the gate used by the gladiators, marching out in two ranks of three. They wore full parade armor.

Lucanus positioned himself back against the wall, and waited, grinning.

The guards paused twenty feet from him and formed a single line, shoulder to shoulder, locking their shields in the manner of Legion attack. They moved in then as if they were on a parade-field exercise.

Lucanus allowed them to come a little closer. Then he dodged suddenly to his left, still keeping his back to the wall. He hit the Praetorian on the end of the line, swinging his swords in sequence, one blade striking down for the legs as the other moved up for the face. The guard didn't know which to cover first and, as a consequence, went down when the tip of the sword in Lucanus' left hand reached into his mouth, between his teeth. I could see the blade enter from where I sat. Teeth splintered on the steel of Lucanus' blade, and the man's jaws clenched tightly in the death spasm.

Before the other five could turn their line to face Lucanus, there were only four of them left. He took out another as they turned, laying his throat open with a spinning side-slash movement. He was proving to the world that the pampered Praetorians could not match a man who fought on the sands for his living.

The remaining four huddled together. He would not come at them singly again. They boxed him in, driving him to the wall, using their shields for cover. Step by careful step, they advanced towards him. They were doing much better than before, each covering another, not allowing Lucanus to concentrate on any single one of them. They knew now that their lives depended on them working together.

I think to this day that Lucanus could have broken them

apart any time he'd wanted to, but I believe that he felt it was time for him to take a stand.

I know he must have been exhausted, for his body was glistening with the heat of his labors. Yet he stood proudly, parrying and thrusting, countering every attack from the grouped Praetorians. Finally, the wild flurry of the four swords, thrusting and slicing savagely, was too much for him. No mortal man could protect himself from so many blows, coming at him from four different angles. He was cut repeatedly. One blow took off a finger; another slit his face from his mouth to the ear.

He reached one man by throwing himself over the tops of their locked shields and thrusting down knife-like, as if he were spearing a fish. The Praetorian went down, gurgling and spouting red vomit. Now there were three, but Lucanus had not avoided another wound. He was hurt badly now; a deep cut had laid open his left leg to the bone. Blood was pouring from the wound like rain.

When he dropped from the crippling blow, they thought they had him, but he quickly put his good leg behind him and pushed upwards, closing with the three remaining guards. Swinging his sword to parry again, he went after the man on his left, raising his body high, as if he intended the same movement he'd used to kill the last man. The Praetorian facing him raised his shield in panic to cover his throat. As he did so, Lucanus dropped to his good knee and swung the blade in his right hand with all the force he could muster, severing the man's leg at the knee. The Praetorian dropped, screaming wildly as he rolled away.

Lucanus took another hit from a Praetorian's sword as he lopped the leg off. It was a blow that caved in the left side of his chest. The muscles were bare and exposed, and he could hardly keep the left sword arm up for protection.

Now, two Praetorians remained. They separated, undoubtedly figuring that if they came at him from front and rear they could hack him to pieces at will.

Lucanus acted as if he were about to rise again, then, as the two of them charged, dropped to his belly and rolled under the shield of the man in front. The Praetorian screamed and began to run. The sword from Lucanus' left hand was firmly wedged in the man's gut where the armor joined the skirt. It was angled up about thirty degrees. It had to be buried deep, perhaps into the liver. He ran in circles, screaming, and finally careened blindly into the north wall and crumpled to the ground, shivering, his legs beating a silent drum on the sands. Then he was still.

He was number five. Number six had courage, I'll give him credit for that. I still don't see how he was able to face the fearful apparition before him, waiting to make him his ninth victim of the day.

Lucanus had to be drawing from the last reserves of his life's force. Blood gushed from his wounds with his every movement, horrible pools gathering at his feet whenever he stood still for more than a moment. He shook himself like a dog would throw rain from his coat, a spray of red.

He was moving much slower now, dragging his bad leg behind him, his wounded arm held close to his chest, the fingers of his hand stuck through his harness to keep the useless limb out of the way. His face was fearful to see. I'm not sure, but I think he was smiling. It was hard to tell; the slit at the mouth had now widened until his teeth were readily visible through the torn flesh.

The last Praetorian stood his ground and waited. Lucanus stopped a few feet from him, his sides heaving and his mouth open wide, trying to suck in vital air. He motioned for the man to come to him. He did!

Keeping his wounded leg to the rear, Lucanus countered everything the Praetorian threw at him, the swords clashed until sparks flew from their steel. The audience was going mad. They'd probably been screaming in the same manner for some time, but I'd been so involved with the fight below that I hadn't paid any attention to them.

"The rudis! The rudis! The rudis for Lucanus!" They clearly wanted the fight stopped.

The Praetorian closed with my master, trying to force him off his mark, swinging his shield to hammer at him. He slashed Lucanus across his badly wounded face. It was by this act that he killed himself. The blow evidently filled Lucanus' damaged mouth with more blood, forcing him to expel it or choke to death. He spat out wildly, a great gout of dark blood, straight into the eyes of the Praetorian guard.

The momentary blindness gave Lucanus all the time he needed. He eased his wounded arm from its sling and threw it over the top of the Praetorian's shield, letting his body weight force the man to the ground. Lucanus sliced off the man's hand and rose to rest his knee on his chest. He ran his sword into the guard's throat, ending his frantic struggles.

Oh! Gods! Lucanus was hurt so terribly! I didn't think he would be able to rise from the man's chest. But using his sword point as a lever against the man's armor, he pushed himself erect slowly and stood there, tottering.

He staggered, half-dragging himself, back to the front of the Imperial box, back to Tiberius and Sejanus.

The roar of the crowd was like thunder, echoing over the sands. Nothing could be heard above it as it reverberated from the walls of the arena.

Lucanus raised his good arm once more, pointing the dripping blade at Tiberius, and raised his head. The stands went silent. His chest was heaving; bubbles of blood broke from his mouth and the side of his face with each exhalation. Blood was clotting in pools at his feet, as he slowly dripped his life to the sands. Tiberius and Sejanus, as well as the Augusta, were on their feet.

He spoke, and though he barely had the strength to hold his sword in the air, his voice was loud, although the words were somewhat slurred.

"Ave Caesar! Te Moritu Salutus! *Mortuus sum!* I am dead!"

Sejanus screamed down at him, "And so you are!" He jerked a javelin from one of the two remaining bodyguards.

Lucanus looked straight into the eyes of Sejanus and dropped his arms to his side, sword still in hand. He cried out once more. "Hail, Caesar!"

The javelin flew from the hand of Sejanus. It entered Lucanus' throat with such force that it knocked him backwards and pinned him to the sands. He quivered only once and released the sword from his hand.

Lucanus had died as he'd lived!

I looked for Claudius again, to see if he was weeping, only to find that my own cheeks were wet with tears, and Claudius was nowhere in sight.

The Emperor was being hurriedly rushed out, as the mob was beginning to rumble, rising from their seats, low animal sounds coming from deep inside their bellies.

Sejanus had led the way for Tiberius, with Livia bringing up their rear. They would all have to be careful for many days to come.

But it was all over and done with. Nothing really made any difference any more.

2

There! I have lived up to my agreement, and have set down the final moments of Lucanus, premier gladiator of Rome. But my promise did not include making the story public.

I shall place these writings in an amphora, and bury it beneath my storeroom floor. There it shall remain for eternity, or at least until Vesuvius should decide to destroy Herculaneum.

I am Albinus of Greece, freedman . . . .